Tall, Dark, and Deadly

Tall, Dark, and Deadly

Heather Graham

AN ONYX BOOK

ONYX
Published by New American Library, a division of
Penguin Putnam Inc., 375 Hudson Street,
New York, New York 10014, U.S.A.
Penguin Books Ltd, 27 Wrights Lane,
London W8 5TZ, England
Penguin Books Australia Ltd, Ringwood,
Victoria, Australia
Penguin Books Canada Ltd, 10 Alcorn Avenue,
Toronto, Ontario, Canada M4V 3B2
Penguin Books (N.Z.) Ltd, 182–190 Wairau Road,
Auckland 10, New Zealand

Penguin Books Ltd, Registered Offices:
Harmondsworth, Middlesex, England

First published by Onyx, an imprint of New American Library,
a division of Penguin Putnam Inc.

ISBN 0-7394-0369-9

PUBLISHER'S NOTE
This is a work of fiction. Names, characters, places, and incidents either are the prod-
uct of the author's imagination or are used fictitiously, and any resemblance to actu-
al persons, living or dead, events, or locales is entirely coincidental.

Dedicated with love to the memory of Elda K. Bradbury,
and for her family, Joe, Michael, Beth, Jeff, and Faith,
who are truly beautiful people, inside and out,
and always a part of her.

Tall, Dark, and Deadly

Prologue

The swamp was deadly.

But the swamp could hide a million sins.

He steered his small boat through the water, watching the woman as she lay in the rear of the boat. So fragile and beautiful, smiling at him, eyes glued on him. He smiled in return. It was dark and lonely, and here they were, together in a solitude that was rare to find. He had chosen to come here. And so they had come. His whim, his love, his night.

Because the night, like the swamp, could hide so many sins. He loved the swamp, and he loved her, and she had learned at length that she loved him as well.

"Not long now," he told her. "Not long now."

She never wanted to come here with him. Yet tonight, she had silently agreed. She never wanted to give him the things that he needed. Tonight, he had given her no choice. And he felt the greatest elation, a sense of power and pleasure, for there she lay, beautiful lips curled, smiling at him. It was his night. He had made this decision. She was here, with him, and he was ready to see it through to the end.

The sky was strange. Only a few stars dotted the heavens, sometimes covered by clouds, sometimes crystal clear. The moon, a beautiful, gibbous curve, appeared and disappeared, touched by dusky clouds. One minute it was entrancing, touching the surface of the water, illuminating them both as they moved through the silent wilderness. Then a cloud would cover the moon, and the shadows would descend again. He felt an odd sense of peace and power because he knew the night, and he knew the swamp. Knowledge was survival here. Knowledge that all which was so beautiful could also be so deadly.

It was still, barely a breath of air stirring now and then. The quiet around them was haunting, compelling, and yet he knew . . . they were watched. The denizens of the night, of the darkness, tracked their passage. He knew, because he liked to watch himself, to study those around him. He tried to make each stroke with his oar a powerful one, for the sound of it seemed loud, like a strange drumbeat in the night.

A savage beat, he thought, for a savage place. Even in the dim light he could make out what appeared to be stonelike fixtures in the water. But they weren't stone. Given the right incentive, they would sink the bulk of their bodies beneath the water. With only eyes and nostrils seen at the water's surface, they would glide in silence, zeroing in for the kill . . .

Gators. Wondrous creatures. There were just a few here, though. Farther along the canal, there were more. Just as there were moccasins. Strangely beautiful creatures, so sleek and smooth, elegant in their movement, able to master land and water. There were other dangerous creatures in the swamp as well. Coral snakes, Eastern diamondback rattlers, and the little pygmy rattlers. The rattlers liked the hammocks. The moccasins haunted the waterways. And still, despite the dangerous creatures, there was so much beauty. Orchids that grew wild, birds with colors no artist could ever reproduce. And the sunsets and the nights . . .

Nights like this one.

"Cold?" he asked her. Cold, how strange. The temperatures here could be suffocating, but night brought a cooling; he imagined that she shivered.

"Of course you're cold," he said, then realized he had left his jacket back at the car. "Oh, sweetheart, I'm so sorry . . . I forgot my jacket, and you're in practically nothing at all. I should have thought . . . I'm so sorry. But it won't be long now."

His oar touched the water. They shot along through the night. And there, ahead of him, lay the area he was seeking. There was an air of expectancy to the darkness and the silence of the night. The stillness.

But beneath the stillness . . .

They'd suffered a dry spell this year. Common enough. But this was one area where the water had remained deep, where the foliage had remained heavy. The birds came here, hundreds of them. They came to drink, to build nests, to seek fish, insects.

Small animals came, too. Possums, squirrels, foxes, even an occasional cougar, though hunters had made the fabulous cats all but extinct. And where they came . . .

Life was, after all, just one big food chain.

"My love, look, we're here!" he told her. He set down his oar and moved carefully, coming before her hunkered down, and staring out at the water by her side. "They're fantastic," he breathed with reverence. "Nature created them as such incredible machines, don't you see? They're old as the dinosaurs, millions of years upon the earth." He sighed, enraptured by the scene.

Then he remembered himself, and his purpose.

"Oh, well," he said flatly. The sense of poignancy was over. He looked at her again.

Yes, for once in her life she was smiling at him. He'd made her smile before, but this time he'd taken her lipstick and drawn that damn smile on her haughty features, features that had, too often until recently, expressed the fact that she was too good for him. She was just a tramp, who took her clothes off in front of strange men.

He touched her flesh. He'd been right. She sure was cold.

Stone cold.

Stone-cold dead.

Too bad. There were enough gators here, maybe even enough really hungry gators to have ripped her right to shreds if she'd been alive. What an event that would have been. He smiled, thinking of the way she would have screamed.

But that was all right. He'd played long enough, and he'd waited long enough. And when it came to a point of danger . . .

Well, he'd learned from the gators. Make the kill. Just make the kill, be certain that the victim can't fight back.

She'd been so haughty . . .

Until she had learned to listen. To obey him. It was almost too bad that he'd had to let her go. She'd just been getting good, whimpering all the time. Actually, she'd become far too pathetic. Killing her had been easy.

All that pride, all that arrogance . . .

And she hadn't even fought.

He was smart. He didn't want to get caught. Always, he'd waited, he'd been careful, he'd taken his time. He'd watched the forensics shows on the cable station. Autopsies could point straight to a killer. But a consumed body was damn hard to autopsy.

"Out with you, bitch!" he said impatiently. He'd had enough of the night, and the swamp. He started to laugh. "It was wonderful while it lasted, but it's all over now."

He pushed her overboard.

She didn't start to sink right away. He made her arm waggle in the water.

At first the gators didn't move.

"Come on, you bastards!" he cried.

He swore, soaking his good shirt, as he leaned over, making her body move more vigorously in the water.

He heard a splash . . . one of the creatures slipping into the water. Another splash . . . another gator.

The body was viciously wrenched from his hold.

He smiled.

And he watched.

There was a tremendous frenzy in the water. Giant, powerful tails whipped about. Jaws snapped, huge heads swung back and forth.

Then she was dragged down. Gators were excellent at the work of survival. They dragged their victims down into the water, drowning them, to keep them from fighting back. Not that gators had many vulnerabilities. Their hides were tough, their jaws could exert more pressure than most steel traps. But like all good predators, they dealt with their adversaries' defenses before they could become dangerous.

So . . .

She was gone.

Given time, the creatures would consume her.

What would be left? Pieces of flesh, torn away in a frenzy? Nah, the little fish would see to that. Bone . . . bone that was consumed, then eliminated? Maybe, but would it ever be found? He doubted it. Would there be a snatch of fabric, a tuft of hair? Would even that remain? Maybe. What could it prove? Nothing—except that she was gone.

Simply gone.

Oh, yes.

The swamp was deadly.

And the swamp could hide a million sins.

And there were so many more women out there to pay the wages of sin.

Chapter 1

The house was coming along beautifully. Marnie New-castle breathed a sigh of pleased relief as she opened the door and peeked into the old home she'd been renovating. It was almost done. There were still a few odds and ends to be taken care of—the contractor still had workmen coming in to do touch-up painting and carpentry. But she was thrilled—she finally felt as if she'd come home. It hadn't been easy. She'd been ready to kill the contractor. He'd been ready to kill her. But it had finally all come together.

She stepped into the foyer and absently closed the door behind her, looking around. The floor here was beige marble with accents of amber, the walls were ivory, and the antique chandelier was showcased against the plainer backdrop, making it a true focal point. To her left, she could see the living room and its captivating fireplace, flanked on either side by a goddess, Athena on the right, Hera on the left. To her right was the library, already filled with her books. Before her was a spiral staircase to the rooms above; around it was the hall to a completely renovated kitchen.

No, it hadn't been easy. She knew that all the men working on it, from the contractor to the plumber, had called her names behind her back—while accepting their checks, of course. But now even they could be proud. They had rebuilt a masterpiece.

She stepped into the center of the foyer, whirling around. Yes, she was home now.

The phone started to ring. She automatically reached into her purse for her cellular phone, but it wasn't there. She frowned, wondering where she had left it. Back at the office, in the car? But it wasn't the cell phone ringing anyway, it was the house phone. Where were the lines she had in at the moment? She'd only been sleeping here for a few days now. The phones . . . there was one up in the bedroom and one back in the kitchen . . . yes, that was the closest, a minimum of steps.

She walked through the hallway, still feeling a sense of satisfaction. The kitchen had a center butcher-block work stand and state-of-the-art stainless-steel appliances. She had wanted all this so badly, and she had gotten it. She worked, she'd sacrificed, she'd achieved. Her friends had always called her focused. She paused, biting her lip. Yes, she was what people called "hard." That was because they didn't understand how she had gotten this way.

For a moment she felt some of the old discomfort. Let them grow up with an abusive, alcoholic father and they'd figure it out fast enough.

She allowed herself a smile. She was good. She'd pursued some of the toughest cases out there, defending no-good—but rich—criminals to get where she wanted to be. She was a realist, and realistically, someone was going to take the cases, make the money. The way she saw it, that someone ought to be her. She tried to explain to her friends, that to move forward, you had to get your hands dirty. People said that attorneys were like sharks. Maybe. She had to be, though. She was a woman, and there were other associates in the firm ready to step on her, anxious to make partner first. They were always swimming with their jaws wide open.

The phone kept ringing. How did anyone know she was here? Silly question—she'd told her secretary she was coming here. And, she reminded herself, she lived here now.

She reached the phone, picked up the receiver, said a breathless "Hello?"

"Marnie?"

"Yes?"

She didn't recognize the voice. It was very low and raspy, almost a whisper. Her contractor? No, he always sounded brusque and angry.

"Hi, Marnie."

"Who is this?"

"You like the house?"

Was it her contractor? Must be. Maybe he had a cold. Or a hangover.

"Yes, it looks fabulous. Phil?" Phil Jenkins and Associates were the people working on the place.

Soft laughter followed.

"You didn't answer. Do you like the place?"

"Yes, of course, it's fabulous. Look, Phil, I've had a long day. I don't mean to be rude, but I don't want to spend time—"

"Time, Marnie. Time. Your time is so limited. More precious than you know."

"Yes, my time is precious!" she said impatiently. Hmm. Maybe she'd given Phil a bit too much of her time. He was getting possessive. Men never understood that there were women who lived on a logical plane. Not every relationship in life had to have a deep emotional meaning. "Look, Phil, I want to enjoy my house. Call back when you have something to say, huh?"

She set the phone down, annoyed. For a moment, though, she wondered if it really had been Phil.

She looked around her kitchen again. It led to the family room, which led to her pool and patio. The sun was beginning to set. The sky was the gold that came just as night blanketed day. The water in her pool seemed to be aquamarine. There was a little fountain in it. And beyond the pool was the bay. She could see all the way over to Key Biscayne. Upstairs, her bedroom looked out on that same incredible view. She couldn't wait to sleep here, have her first party here . . . entertain here. She thought about her beautiful bedroom. For a moment she allowed herself to feel wistful. It would be nice to find a special guy. A really special guy.

The phone started ringing, irritating her back to the moment at hand. Phil again, being annoying, or one of her friends? Samantha Miller lived next door and could easily see her car. Maybe it was Sam and she could hop on over and see the house. They were right next door on the beautiful little man-enhanced finger of land reaching into the bay.

She picked up the phone, feeling happy once again. "Hello?"

"Don't hang up on me."

The same voice, grittier. Angry.

"Oh, no? Who the hell do you think you are? I'll hang up on whoever the hell I want to hang up on, asshole!"

She slammed the receiver down, shaking her head. She turned from the kitchen and walked back to the stairway. He was ruining it, whoever he was. Her first trip into her almost absolutely completed, beautiful new home. A place that was everything she had worked for.

She frowned as she walked up the stairs. Didn't that idiot Phil read the papers? They had said that she was beautiful and brilliant—and cold as ice and hard as steel. They could have been just a bit more imaginative, but still, she had liked the billing. And her firm had been inundated with requests after the article. Beautiful and brilliant, hard as steel, cold as ice—she was hardly likely to tolerate irritating phone calls.

Forget it, see the house! she told herself. Her home. Her achievement.

* * *

From her kitchen window next door, Samantha Miller looked over at her friend's house. She turned from the window to her oven. Time to flip the fish. Delicate stuff. Fresh dolphin, brought to her just that afternoon by Ann and Harry Lacata, clients of hers. She'd helped Harry get back in shape after a heart attack, but it was their son, Gregory, with whom she'd formed the most important relationship. She called him the man in her life. At age nine, Gregory was one of the most beautiful children she had ever seen, but he lived in his own world. He didn't come out often. Sometimes Sam could coax him out, and in the coaxing, she'd fallen a little bit in love. She glanced through the open kitchen doorway back to the glassed-in Florida room. Gregory, a lock of his pitch-black hair falling over one eye, was watching *Lion King* on the video. He could watch it for hours. Over and over again. Frequently he didn't respond when his name was called, but he could sit down at a piano and pick out any piece of music he had heard, barely missing a note on his first try.

Back to the matter at hand, she warned herself. Fresh seafood. Cook it just right, it was delicious. They were having dolphin the fish, not the mammal—she thought mechanically, something she always said to Northerners unaccustomed to the fish. Dinner was important tonight, and she wasn't exactly the Galloping Gourmet.

"Laura!" she called to her cousin, who was perched on one of the kitchen counter barstools. "I think Marnie is home. Why don't you give her a call and see if she wants to join us?"

Laura had been in the process of carefully touching just the tip of a raw carrot into a bowl of raspberry vinaigrette dip. She looked up, startled. "Call Marnie—tonight?"

"Sure. We've got plenty of fish."

Laura hesitated. "But—"

"She's just moved in. Call her, please."

Laura sighed. "It's just that . . . well, this is for Aidan."

"Aidan likes Marnie."

"What male doesn't?" Laura murmured.

"He's your son," Sam reminded her.

"Umm, she likes 'em young and innocent."

"Laura . . ."

"It's family night, and we already have Gregory here."

"Aidan is great with Gregory, and Gregory loves to see Aidan."

That was true. On some level, the very nearly adult Aidan and the nine-year-old autistic boy communicated beautifully. Their language was music.

"I adore Gregory, too, you know," Laura said a bit defensively.

"I know. You're trying to find an excuse not to call Marnie."

"All right, all right. I'll call her. We could use some free legal help with Aidan's copyrights and all that stuff. I'll call her. Maybe she can't come anyway!" Laura said cheerfully. Then she sobered as she stared at the carrot and dip.

Sam sighed deeply. "Laura, take a chance. Be daring. The dip isn't from a health food store, it's Marie Callendar's, right out of Publix."

Laura looked up guiltily. "All right, all right!" She popped the carrot stick into her mouth and started to dial, then stopped. "Wow! Great dip!"

"See what happens when you take chances in life?"

"Yeah, well, take a chance sometimes, and you've got a mouthful of jalapeño!" Laura retorted philosophically. "What's Marnie's number?"

Upstairs, Marnie wondered which way to go first . . . ah, the guest suites. There were two of them to the southward side of the house, the rear of which looked out eastward to Key Biscayne. She walked out on the south balcony of the rear suite. From there she could see Sam's place. Cute as a button, but nowhere near as nice as hers. Sam didn't make her kind of money, not to mention the fact that Sam's family had owned the old place. It needed renovation badly; lots of the real estate people watched her house, waiting for it to go on the market so that a contractor could come in, make it brand-new, and sell it for a fortune over cost. Sam's folks had never had any money. Her father had been a schoolteacher, of all things. But his father had just happened to have a chance to buy waterfront property after a hurricane—when it was definitely at its cheapest—and so Sam had one of the nicest little places in the world. This kind of waterfront property was dwindling away now; it was almost nonexistent so close to downtown.

From the guest suites, she walked back down to her own bedroom. She admired the mahogany four-poster bed frame and her matching dressing table and dresser set. They gave the room so much symmetry. All right, she admitted to herself with a smile, so she was an organization freak. It had its benefits. She smiled, walking to the dressing table. A beautifully etched silver tray held her makeup in perfect order. Foundation, blush, liner, shadow, and mascara, all in a line. And to the side of the tray, her lipsticks and nail polishes—reds together, browns, mauves, and so on. She couldn't help it; she liked order. Order gave her more time.

The phone started ringing again. She hesitated, then walked over to the bedside table and answered it with a no-nonsense attitude. "Listen, asshole, leave me alone."

There was a hesitation. "Marnie?"

Marnie exhaled on a long sigh. "Laura?" She recognized the voice right away. Sam's cousin. She made a little face, which, of course, Laura couldn't see. Laura was sometimes too critical, but Sam could be fierce about the people she cared about. She was a love-me-love-my-dog type person, except that it was the people surrounding her that you had to love—or at least tolerate. And Marnie honestly liked Sam. She was, in her strange way, like a rock; even when they'd been in college, she'd refused to bow to peer pressure. She was a true friend—a rarity in this day and age.

"Yeah, it's me," Laura said, annoyed. "Why'd you call me an asshole?"

"I didn't call *you* an asshole, I—I thought you were someone else. Sorry. What's up?"

"I'm over at Sam's, and we thought we saw some life over at your new place."

"Yes, well, obviously, I'm here," she said, her pride and excitement growing. "Want to come and see it?"

"Can't right now—Sam's in the middle of cooking dinner. She's watching Gregory so his folks can get out, and I'm waiting for Aidan to show up—he promised to come over for Sam's fish and chips. Teenagers! I don't get to see much of my own son. Thought you might want to come over for dinner, too. Maybe fill us in on the tall, dark, and handsome character who just bought the new place on the other side of yours."

"How do you know he's tall, dark, and handsome?"

"I saw the back of his head the other day when he was going into the house. He's definitely tall, and dark. I didn't see his face, so I suppose that he could be ugly as sin."

"He's not."

"Have you met him yet?"

"Oh . . . yes, of course I've met him." She made her voice sultry and suggestive.

"And?" Laura responded impatiently.

"Umm. Yes, he's quite tall, dark, and handsome. Wonderful. And guess what? He's actually someone we know—from Gainesville. Well, of course, you—being so much older—weren't really there with Sam and me, but I think you met him as well."

"Okay, so—shoot. Who is he?"

Marnie opened her mouth, then paused. She wasn't telling Laura yet. Laura would naturally tell Sam. Prepare her. Sam was her friend, honestly. But sometimes she couldn't help but feel jealous. Sam could accomplish with a word, the lift of a brow, a simple *look,* something that might take her twenty minutes of flirting to do. Elegance and grace came as naturally to Sam as breathing.

The new neighbor had changed like night and day, hearing that Sam was just a house away. Something would happen there, but Marnie would be damned if she was going to be the one to get it going.

"Oh, sweetie, you'll see him soon enough. Yes, he's tall, dark, handsome—and charming. I can't wait to spend more time with him, get to know him all over again." She hesitated, smiling slightly, determined to tease Laura and get her wondering for the rest of the night. "I'm sorry, can't tell you, not yet, you've got to stew a while. As to tonight, well, I'd love to come to dinner, but I have plans, thanks," Marnie said. Plans. Did she really have plans? Well, yes, if she wanted. And if she chose to back out on the invitation she had accepted, well . . .

She didn't want to do a boring family thing. And Sam had that strange kid over, too. She understood that he was different, of course, but he unnerved her. He looked at her all the time as if he could see any little evil thought in her mind.

"Oh, Laura! Honest, you should see my place now, it's really fantastic. They finished up almost all of the last-minute touches today. Sam needs to come over. I can give her some good ideas for when she decides to redo her place."

"Yeah, she'll come soon enough. Well—"

A beeping on the line cut off Laura's voice. Call waiting. Modern technology was just wonderful.

"Hang on, somebody's on the line, and come to think of it, it may be my date for this evening—someone tall, dark, and handsome," Marnie told Laura. She clicked the button on the phone. "Hello?"

"Hey, Marnie. How do you like the bedroom?"

That damn voice again, a whisper, but deep and husky. This time the raspy sound of it unnerved her. "How do you know I'm in the bedroom?" she asked before thinking.

"Oh, I know where you are, Marnie. I know you. 'Cold as ice, hard as steel.' What they really meant was that you're one hell of a bitch."

"You call again, and I'll call the police."

"Oh, I won't exactly be calling again, Marnie. Don't worry. Because I do know where you are. I know exactly where you are."

This time the caller hung up. "Jerk!" Marnie whispered before clicking back to Laura. "Hey, kid, I guess I gotta—" She broke off, this time hearing a knocking sound downstairs. "The workmen are screwing around," she told Laura. "I've got to go scream at someone."

She started to put the phone down. It beeped again. Automatically, she clicked it.

"Hello?"

"Hello, Marnie." Deep, deep. The voice was chilling, the phone was strange. He sounded close. As if he were in the next room. She was starting to feel scared, and she hated the feeling, so she grew angrier than ever.

"You said you weren't calling again."

A husky laugh seemed to fill the line, and then the air around her. Then the whisper again, rasping. "I know. I lied." Like nails raked down a blackboard, the sound of that voice seemed to rip down her spine.

"I couldn't resist. Really, how do you like the bedroom, Marnie? I had to call; I had to come. I had to see you. Here."

Marnie's fingers tightened on the phone. She spun around. The caller had been near all along. And now he was here. Smiling at her, talking from a cellular phone. Why hadn't she recognized the voice? She knew the caller, all right. Intimately.

"What are you doing, playing phone games, coming up here?" she asked angrily.

"Oh, Marnie. I've come to talk."

"Here? After this ridiculous phone business? Not on your life."

"No, Marnie. Not on your life."

The caller casually dropped the cellular phone on the bed. Her cellular phone, she realized, as he walked toward her. She saw that his hands were gloved. At first all she felt was an irritated curiosity.

Then she saw his eyes.

And then she knew.

No, Marnie, not on your life!

She opened her mouth to scream, suddenly, horribly aware that he hadn't been playing games.

Cold as steel, hard as ice, she was frozen with horror. She could still bleed like a stuck pig. And like a hog going to slaughter, she discovered, she could certainly know fear, smell danger. She wasn't so hard at all, she was . . .

Going to die?

No. It couldn't be. He was threatening her, trying to scare her . . .

Trying? Doing a damned good job of it.

She opened her mouth to scream. Oh, God! It was like a nightmare. She couldn't force sound from her throat.

He reached her. His hands—gloved hands—touched her. He was pleased, so pleased. His eyes mocked her, even as she heard the sound of his laughter again, rasping . . .

She never managed to strike him. As she struggled, he slammed her against her dressing table.

The silver tray went down. Lipsticks, polishes, liners, shadows . . . scattered. "Bitch!" he told her softly. "Now I'm going to have to pick that all up!"

He dragged her away from the table. His hands tightened upon her. Finally, she gurgled out something of a sound. A shooting agony brought it forth. It was almost a scream . . .

"Oh, yeah, sweetheart, you've got a date tonight. A date with me," he told her softly. It was amazing how sensual his voice sounded.

Next door, at Sam's house, Laura waited, tapping her foot impatiently—eating another carrot.

"What's up?" Sam asked, leaning over and opening the oven door. A sweep of honey-brown hair fell forward as she did so, and she quickly caught it and tossed it back over her shoulder—barely saving it from landfall in the oven. She could imagine the flash fire that might have ensued, and the possible morning headlines—FITNESS THERAPIST INCINERATED WHILE COOKING HEALTH-CONSCIOUS MEAL! There could be a new show. *The Burning Gourmet,* or *The Blazing Gourmet.*

It was only dinner, she reminded herself. She didn't usually obsess over food or cooking. But Laura was excited that her son was coming to dinner. He was twenty-one, living at home on paper, almost never there in fact. Lacey, Laura's daughter, was twenty and enrolled at the University of Miami. Sam loved her young second cousins, and she knew how much the evening meant to Laura. Plus, Sam had never had a large family, and especially since she'd lost her father, every member of her small clan had become very important to her.

"Laura, what's up, is she coming?" she asked, pulling the fish out of the oven and glancing at her cousin.

"I don't know!" Laura said impatiently, shaking her head at the phone. "Marnie said wait, then she put me on hold . . . I think the line is open again now, I heard her screaming at someone—it's amazing that she's kept a contractor and workers. I'd have killed her for sure, if I'd been that Phil—but . . . oh, damn it!" Laura stared at the phone and shook it. "Leave it to Marnie. She got distracted and just left me hanging here. I think she must have a hot and heavy date tonight. Maybe he showed up for her."

"And she was screaming at her hot and heavy date?" Sam asked, grinning.

"Hell, who knows, with Marnie!" Laura said.

"Oh, well, give her another minute. And if she doesn't come back on—well, at least we tried to get her over here," Sam said. "She'll know we wanted her."

"Yeah. Sure," Laura said, making a face.

Sam gave her cousin what Laura called "the look." It was meant to chastise; Laura wasn't always particularly patient with Marnie.

Laura shook her head. "Don't go getting mad at me when I say this, but sometimes Marnie is just downright rude. She wanted you to come see the house. I think she just wanted you to see that it was much nicer than yours. She's jealous of you."

"Marnie never really had her own money until now; she grew up dirt-poor."

Laura made a face. "We were all poor."

"We weren't rich, but our folks had jobs. Marnie's mother deserted her, and her father was a bum." She hesitated. "Maybe he even abused her, Laura. We never dealt with anything like that. No matter how tough she seems, I feel sorry for her. She needs to prove things, to others and to herself," Sam said simply. "You and I don't need to do that."

"Right. Well, she has a lot to live down."

"We've all done things we're not proud of."

Laura arched a brow. "Mary Poppins, do get serious

here! Some of us moreso than others. Like Marnie. You do realize she was out to get Joe."

Joe was a personal trainer, a partner with Sam in a gym and physical therapy studio they had purchased together when the original owner had decided to head back up north. Joe was devastatingly good-looking, muscled to the nth degree. He and Sam had been friends, they had gone out, and Laura had thought they almost had a thing going. Then Marnie moved in. Laura just couldn't believe— as Sam insisted—that Sam and Joe had been friends and no more. But then, Laura was her cousin, blindly defensive for her, no matter what. Sam had tried to tell Laura that she had never been really interested, and she'd been glad of Marnie's interest in Joe, because her business partnership had meant more to her.

"Laura, please listen and please believe me. I was relieved that she liked Joe. To work with, he's just fine. I need him. Badly. To keep things running. But to date . . . I could never actually have dated him. Joe's a nice guy, but he can't tear himself away from the mirror." She grinned. "Didn't I tell you about the time when we were just re-opening, and I nearly lost the entire maintenance crew? One girl was in tears—he kept harassing her because she just couldn't get all the streaks off the main mirror in the weight room?"

Laura shrugged in acknowledgement that Joe might be a wee bit on the narcissistic side. "Yes, but Marnie was still right there to scoop him up."

"Ah, but poor Marnie! She realized that his ego outweighed his other assets, and I do admit they are formidable!"

"Do you know what she told me once?" Laura murmured.

"No, what?"

"She said she loves to hang out with you. She assessed you as if she were keeping a scorecard. She said you've got great amber eyes, rich, beautiful hair to match, and a compact five-foot-five body that is both perfectly lean and perfectly shapely. You could be a bit taller, but then, good things do come in small packages. You're quick-witted, and charming, and she loves to meet people through you."

Sam laughed. "She actually said all that?"

"You're not offended?"

"I think she was complimenting me."

"But she admits she uses you to meet people—"

"Laura, she's beautiful and talented and has a great job where she meets a million people—"

"A million crazy criminals! Murderers, rapists, thieves."

"Maybe some of them aren't crazy—or even guilty. Laura, try yelling into the phone. Maybe she got distracted and just forgot you were there."

"All right, all right. It's your call. Just remember that I warned you when your sweet, beautiful friend next door accidentally slips a knife into your back!"

"Laura, be nice."

"Oh, God, I'll try," Laura said, rolling her eyes, her hand over the mouthpiece of the phone. Then she yelled into the handset, "Marnie, dammit! Marnie! Pay attention to me, answer me!"

While trying to reach Marnie, Laura noted that Gregory was standing, staring out into the darkness of the night. Watching the bay? No, he was in front of the glass that faced Marnie's house, just standing there, swaying slightly back and forth. He was a beautiful child with those huge blue eyes and dark hair. His physical therapist had instilled excellent manners in him, and he was precise with his napkin, his fork, his spoon. He was fastidiously clean too, brushed his hair, cared for his teeth. He was quiet and sweet. And in a different world. Laura bit her lip for a moment, suddenly thanking God that her own two children were healthy and well. Her heart went out to Gregory's folks. His parents had often despaired. Everything he had learned had taken tremendous time and patience. Except for his music. His music came from within.

"Gregory, is the video over?" Laura called. Then she thought she heard something on the line. "Marnie! Marnie, answer the damned phone, Marnie, please?"

Marnie didn't respond. Neither did Gregory.

Marnie heard her name. It seemed to come from far, far away, somewhere out of a dark tunnel. It seemed to pull her back.

Back . . . to horrible sensations of pain.

And him! Oh, God, he was still there. Now he was busy by her dresser, picking up all the things that had been knocked over. Her head hurt. She felt a trickle of blood by her eye. She'd slammed against the dresser, he'd nearly throttled her, and then . . .

She must have fallen and struck the bottom of the bedpost, near where she lay now. Maybe he was finished with her . . .

No. He was finished at her dresser. He was looking at her again, gloating, smiling. Why hadn't she known, why hadn't she seen . . . ?

"Marnie!"

She tried to reach the phone.

She twisted, praying she was able to move. Inch by inch. She crawled. She almost made it. She tried to scream again. But now her throat was too raw. On fire. No sound would come at all—nothing, nothing, just breath . . .

The laughter started again. Rasping. Raking down her spine.

"Marnie? Marnie?"

Help, help, help me, oh, God, help me. She wanted to shout the words.

Didn't matter. Not to him.

As if he had read her mind, he spoke to her. "Oh, honey, I'm all the help you're going to get tonight."

He quietly replaced the phone on the receiver.

"Damn her!" Laura said. "Now she's hung up on me!"

"The hot and heavy date must have gotten there," Sam said, taking the fish out of the oven. "You can dial her back."

"For what? She'll just hang up on me again. And I think Aidan's here. I just saw his car out there."

"I didn't hear him drive up."

"Neither did I," Laura said, "but his car is out there."

"Well, it's perfect timing. Dinner is cooked—and I didn't burn it!" Sam said, relieved.

"Smells great, and thank God Aidan made it. Honestly, he's usually late all the time now. Or maybe it's just with me. I'm telling you, Sam, it's a rough road. Kids! You give them your life, and suddenly they're just gone, and they don't understand that after all the years you'd like a little piece of their lives now and then in return. I'm going to go get him."

With an excited smile on her face, Laura hurried on out of the kitchen.

As Sam started to move the fish from the baking dish to a serving platter, she noted that Gregory was staring out the glass enclosure. Did reflections attract his attention? she wondered. The porch was dark, though, except for the light spewing from the *Lion King* tape in the VCR. That must be it—animated creatures playing on the glass.

"Dinner, Gregory." She would probably have to lead him to the table. But he turned to her when she spoke, looking grave. He pointed an arm toward Marnie's house. She was surprised; Marnie sometimes seemed uncomfortable with Gregory, although, to her credit, she was always gentle, affectionate, and patient with the boy.

"She's not coming, Gregory. She's busy," she said, wondering if he had really wanted Marnie, and if he really understood anything she was saying.

But Aidan was here, and dinner was ready.

Marnie hadn't wanted anything to eat anyway. Sam would call her back in the morning herself, go on over, ooh and aah over the house.

She wouldn't call back tonight.

It seemed that Marnie's evening was already all planned out.

Chapter 2

HEATHER GRAHAM

Rowan could feel the heat—a fierce, terrible burst of heat within him that suddenly seemed to saturate his body.

And then the cold.

Icicles dripping through him, wrapping around his limbs, his veins, his insides, his soul.

Because he could still see her face in death. Her flesh, so white, her eyes, wide open, staring. At what? What had she seen as she died? He would never forget seeing her face. . . . Entering the house, calling her name. He'd been angry with her, as usual of late. She'd wanted her own life, but she'd refused to leave him alone. She would tell him that she was hurt, but then she'd go and do things that cut like a knife. Nothing seemed to matter, nothing was sacred to them anymore. What they shared hadn't been a real marriage in a very long time. She'd caused him more than a few nights in the holding cell of the local jail, because she'd lied, and she'd bled him financially over and over again. He'd paid for many of her nights with her lovers, and yes, it had made him mad enough to see red . . .

Mad enough to kill? The cops had asked.

And there she'd been . . .

But now, in memory, in the dreams that taunted his sleep, she was dead, and yet she turned. She turned with

*wide-open eyes, swollen tongue, pasty—once beautiful—
face. "You did this to me!" she shouted at him.*

*He protested. "No. I said you needed help, I said we
needed help."*

"You wanted a divorce," she reminded him.

"You wanted other men."

"You loved another woman."

"Not until—"

*"You did this. You said you loved me once, you loved
me still, but in a different way. And it wasn't enough, you
cared but not enough. You cared about the band, too, but
not enough. Reilly was your friend, and you said that you
would help, but it wasn't enough. The way you cared for
me, it wasn't enough, I wasn't enough, I betrayed you, but
you—you didn't know how to forgive. There was never
enough, you could get so mad . . ."*

*Mad enough to kill? The cop asked again in his dream.
Buddy, if you were, I could see it. Just admit it, you were
mad, you hated her. She drove you over the brink. So
where is the body? You know you hated her, had to hate
her . . .*

*No, he had never hated her. The cops didn't know about
the times she had cried to him, about the times they had
tried over again. He would never forget the day after she
had come back the last time, the way she had looked at
him, huge blue eyes filled with tears. He'd known then
that anything he'd hoped for in his own life would just
have to go on hold. There was nothing else to do; she was
in a dangerous mental state. "Why do I do this, Rowan?
What's the matter with me? Why can't I stop? I don't want
to hurt you, but I start on something, and I can't seem to
stop. I've made you hate me."*

"No, I love you."

*"You can't!" she whispered softly. "You can't any-
more."*

"But I do. Honestly. I'll always love you. Clean slate, we'll start over."

"Don't leave me."

"I won't leave you. We'll get help. Rehab. It's not you, it's the addictions you've acquired. I'll be with you, I will always love you."

Her smile was so sad, the way she touched his hair . . . "I'm just like Jessica Rabbit out of the movies, huh? 'I'm not really bad, I'm just drawn that way!' Oh, Rowan, what have I done to you, to us?"

"Dina, it will be all right. We'll get the best help."

"Don't pity me, don't be kind. You're trying to do the right thing, but you don't love me anymore."

"I do love you." He did, yes, they'd been through a lot together. But she was right; it wasn't the love she wanted. That had been lost somewhere along the way, in a hotel room, in a bottle of pills, a fifth of Gordon's. He couldn't let her see that now.

"You're just saying that because you're worried about me. You think you can save me. I wish I were different. You can't love me enough. You can't make someone love you enough . . ."

"I can help you to stop drinking, I can get you off the pills—"

"And the other men, too, Rowan? Can you stop me from wanting to—"

He awoke with a start. Sweating. Shaking. Damning himself.

It was the weather.

Hot. Yes, hot as hell. It was the middle of the day. May. Not summer yet, but close enough. He'd listened to some of the talk down at Jimbo's the other day. If May was this hot, God help them all! July, August, and September would be hot enough to kill.

Enough to kill . . .

Hot, yes, as the expression went, it was *killer* hot.

No, not so bad when he sat up—there was a slight breeze. He'd fallen asleep right on the deck by the pool. On the bay there was always a breeze.

Standing, Rowan faced the water. He halfway closed his eyes. Water and sky blended in a beautiful blur of aqua and powder-puff blue. The breeze was wafting over his hot flesh, almost like a caress. It was so beautiful here. He loved it already, as if he'd been born to it, this balmy breeze, in front of invitingly warm water. He was an excellent diver, and now he could jump in anytime he liked. He hadn't been born to this life; he'd come from very far away. A different world in thought, style, and heritage. Here the land was flat, he was surrounded by water. Where he'd been born, crags and mountains had risen up everywhere around him, and any water he might have touched had been freezing. His family home was not far from Loch Ness, where even in the height of summer, the water remained just above freezing. He still loved his home in the gray and mauve valley near the loch where his father had made his money—as his father before him—in sheepherding. And he loved his father deeply—despite the tremendous disagreements they'd had over his chosen profession. Naturally, every argument they'd fought had been enhanced by the events that had plagued his career. After Dina's death he had gone home for a while, and it had been a good thing to do. They hadn't talked much, but standing by his mother's grave, he'd felt closer to his father than ever before. He knew that his father had hoped he'd stay home, but he'd become far too Americanized, restless. He longed for warm waters. And Robert had understood. The arguments, the days of his rebellious youth, were gone. They were both adults, they'd both learned their lessons, and between them now there was both peace and love.

Different from what it had been.

His first fight with his father had been at seventeen. His mother had already passed away from the cancer, and Ewan, wise beyond them all in his fragile form, had been gone since Rowan was thirteen. After no effort, no prayer, on his part could change the ravages of disease that stole his brother, Rowan had decided that he didn't believe in God. Hindsight being great, he rued the heartache he had added to his father's life at the time, but bitterness had sent him running. His flight had taken him to the States. Music had been his solace, and he had found himself playing backup for a group that had brought him to the college town of Gainesville, Florida. His father had flown over and suggested that since he'd run to an American college town, he at least go to an American college. He did so and got a bachelor's in fine arts while making a success of his group. Success had bred wild days, and he was surprised that his father had stuck with him. But Robert Dillon was a deeply spiritual man; while Rowan had been denying the existence of a god, his father had steadfastly told him that he was entrusting his son to God's hands and, God help them, they would both survive.

Well, he had survived. Others hadn't. But standing by his mother's and brother's graves in the ancient Scottish valley, he had grudgingly admitted that his father's God might well have been there, granting him that survival, against all odds.

And so he was here now.

He'd fallen in love with this area when he came here to play years ago. South Florida. In the restlessness of his youth he'd often felt like an interloper. But so many here were. In buying the house, he'd had a sense of coming home. He'd felt a sense of peace unlike anything he'd ever experienced.

So . . .

Why?

Dina had been dead more than five years. Why was her ghost haunting him now? Why had he seen her so clearly in his dream?

Maybe because he had inadvertently bought himself right back into the past.

He hadn't expected to find himself suddenly neighbors with old friends.

He looked up at the house next door to his. Marnie's house. He shook his head. Great. The way they'd started out again . . .

Well, it had been fine. Nothing more than some pleasant conversation, a few beers, talk about the old college town. Then a bottle of champagne, celebrate his being back. Yeah, he was back. Then they'd been in the hot tub. And they were both well over twenty-one, both alone, definitely scarred, and both a little wary, a little jaded, and so . . .

He'd felt sorry for her. Marnie confided in him in a way he didn't think she confided in other people. She seemed to know about Dina in a way that other people couldn't. About Dina—and about Billy. Losing Dina had been bad enough. But then there had been Billy. He had talked in a way he hadn't in a long time. Marnie understood addiction.

In turn, after that bottle of champagne, she'd talked about her past to him. A little girl deserted by her mother, abused by her father. She'd envied Rowan his family, and admitted that she was always out there searching, desperately searching. She had always seemed so strong, but really she was so vulnerable.

Then he'd learned that Sam was living next door to her.

And he'd shriveled, inside and out. His soul had gone as cold as his flesh. He felt as if he'd been hit in the chest with a bulldozer.

There were still a few of the original families

around—he'd bought into Old Guard property, although, the way his realtor had explained it, the face of the city had changed so much, there wasn't really much Old Guard left. He'd found the real estate attorney through Jerry Styker, a retired cop who'd decided to befriend him against all odds in the north of the state. Jerry was moving down to the Keys to retire, and he'd used this law firm to find his property. Best people in the world to find what you wanted and close a deal. Rowan hadn't known that Marnie was with the firm until he'd seen her in the office. She had never mentioned Sam's house.

Not until he'd moved in. Not until he'd realized exactly where her property was.

Yep, she had a house here. There were three houses on the farthest spit of land; his, Marnie's, and Sam's.

Had it all been by chance? *How much had she known about him and Sam?* Hell, had it meant anything at all?

The yards—small yards, close to the downtown area of Coconut Grove—were all right on the water. But he couldn't really look straight through Marnie's yard to see Sam's—there were high hedges separating all three yards. Coconut Grove was known for its foliage. But looking up, he could see the top of Sam's house. One of the original homes here on this limestone peninsula, built in the early twenties. The realtor had mentioned those facts. He hadn't mentioned the family name of the property owners.

What if the realtor had mentioned it? Would he have looked elsewhere? People changed in five years. She might be married now, with the statistical two-point-three kids. She might have forgotten his face. No.

Ego? Male pride? Why not?

How could she forget a man who was accused of killing his own wife?

He turned back to the water, suddenly feeling as rigid and defensive as he had at the time. All you had to do was come from money, and you were a spoiled rich kid. Couple that with being a rock musician and you were surely on drugs, the spawn of Satan, capable of any evil. The devil incarnate.

Not that some of his past didn't deserve serious scrutiny. There had been some wild days. When he'd come to the States and joined the music scene, he'd had friends. And he'd had girls. More adulation than he could handle. The new world in which he lived had been intoxicating; success at something he loved so much ignited a wild streak in him, and he became a demon.

He met Dina in those days. And she was a wildfire. She flamed so brightly and so desperately that she burned herself out. He loved, and he lost, and he paid the price. And learned to live with his demons.

But now . . .

What about Sam? She might hate him, but she hadn't forgotten him. Of that he was certain.

He turned and walked toward the house. Fuck it. What the hell else could he do? Sell the house? Politely disappear?

He'd come here for peace. For stability. For a new beginning. He'd come to bury the past. He was going to live his life the way he wanted. With or without past friends.

Or lovers.

Sam nibbled the end of her pencil, staring over at Marnie's house.

She wasn't surprised that Marnie had turned down fish and chips, though the evening had been really nice. Aidan was all excited about the way his career was going, and he actually thanked his mom for being so supportive and helpful. He played a new tune for Gregory on the guitar, and Gregory picked it right up on Sam's old grand piano. Laura was walking on clouds. If

Marnie had shown up it might not have been such an intimate evening.

Marnie was the type who would break a date with friends if a new guy walked into her life—she would never in a million years blow off a date to spend an evening with friends. Insulting, of course, but something that she did with all honesty, expecting other women to understand.

But now Sam was getting worried. Marnie was just so thrilled with the house, so proud, that she would want every little nook and cranny appreciated. Her crown moldings, her Spanish tile, her granite countertops, and so on.

Sam glanced at her watch. Three-thirty.

Maybe the guy had been the answer to Marnie's prayers—and she had stayed out with him all night. Yet something wasn't right.

Marnie wouldn't have slept with a guy on a first date—if it had been a first date—but she would have made him come to her house. She was blunt about men. She liked them; she needed them in her life. She was the perfect huntress. Sex was a simple human instinct, she said. Those who wouldn't admit it were repressed fools. But she liked men on her terms, and Sam couldn't begin to imagine that there was an Adonis in existence who could have made Marnie forget her new house. She had talked about bringing men to the house, how cool it would be to seduce a lover in the huge marble whirlpool tub that was the centerpiece of the master bath. She had adored her queen-size bed, facing the eastern windows so she could see the sun rise in the morning. She had purchased black satin sheets in anticipation of quickly finding a lover to go with her new furnishings and lifestyle.

Sam rose from the desk in her bedroom and walked

around the room for a minute, stretched, came back and
sat down.

She picked up the phone and dialed Marnie's house.
The answering machine clicked on. She left another
message.

She stared at the phone again. Maybe something
had come up. Maybe Marnie had come home and gone
to work.

She dialed Marnie's private number at the law firm.
Marnie's voice came on—leave a message. Sam did. On a
whim, she called the main number. To her surprise, a
woman answered.

"Hi. I was looking for Marnie Newcastle."

"Miss Newcastle isn't due in this weekend. If it's an
emergency—"

"No, this is just a friend. No emergency."

"Have you tried her at home?"

"Yes. She isn't there."

"Well, perhaps she's out with other friends."

There was an undertone in the woman's voice. Or was
Sam imagining things?

"Well, if she comes in, please make sure to tell her that
Sam has been trying to reach her."

"My pleasure. I'll be sure to give her the message."

"Thanks."

Sam hung up, more worried than ever. So Marnie hadn't
come home and gone on into work. But maybe she had still
come and gone while Sam was out at work that morning
herself. Mrs. Cassie Jefferson had recently undergone a hip
replacement, and her doctor had sent her to Sam's place,
which was, of course, great—postsurgical therapy was her
specialty.

So Sam had been out early, and back early, and she was
becoming more and more certain that Marnie hadn't
come and gone in that time.

The phone rang so suddenly that Sam nearly bit her

pencil in half. She leaned across the desk to grab the receiver, hoping it might be Marnie, feeling like a fool for being so worried about a grown woman with—in all honesty—the morals of an alley cat.

"Marnie?"

Silence. Then a hurt tone. "No, it's Laura, your cousin, your flesh and blood. Remember me?"

Sam smiled. "Sorry. I'm just worried."

"Why?"

"I haven't seen Marnie."

"Is it cocktail hour yet? If she thinks it's too early for a drink, then she's probably still sleeping."

"Laura, you're being cruel."

"You're being naive. She'd walk all over you in a second. She would. Only if it was necessary, of course—she does really like you. And don't you argue with me. Uh-uh! You see, I may be in another place, but in my mind's eye, I can see you now, throwing up your arms and saying patiently, 'Laura! Don't always think the worst. People can only hurt you if you let them!' "

Sam stared at the receiver. It was exactly what she'd been about to say.

"Well, it's true," she said defensively.

"No, it's not true," Laura said with a strangely bitter note to her voice. "Ask Teddy."

That was Laura's husband, a cop, in homicide. Ex-husband now, Sam reminded herself, for almost two years. Laura and Teddy had met at Sam's house, introduced by her father. Sam and Teddy's younger sister, Posie, had been childhood friends, and Teddy had taken them out fishing in the Everglades dozens of times. Teddy had since taken Laura and their kids out fishing dozens of times. Their marriage had been a familiar story. Years of marriage, raising kids, struggling, finally getting it together—then boredom. On Teddy's part. There had been another woman. Laura had been devastated, then furious, vengeful

. . . then morose. In all those years she'd become a couch potato, giving up on herself. She'd gained too much weight, she'd gotten gray . . . and Teddy had fallen for some younger woman. Laura had never found out just who it was that caused her divorce, and to give Teddy credit, he'd been willing to try to make up. He loved his kids. But Laura had been too hurt.

Sam felt closer than ever to her cousin now. She'd done her best to take Laura in hand, get her moving, back into life—and improve her self-esteem. The gray in Laura's auburn hair was gone now, and thanks to the regimen she practiced at the gym, she was in exceptional shape. She'd spent years being a wife and mom and little more, taking little interest in herself. Now she spent time with a masseuse, thrilled by her bimonthly manicures and pedicures, and took pride in her trim new appearance.

Of course, it had all backfired a bit on Sam, too. At least as far as Teddy went. She liked Teddy. He had been to see her a few times, asking her to intervene. Which she had tried to do. But Teddy didn't waste time while trying to make it up with his wife. He acquired a new blond girlfriend. "Just a casual acquaintance," he assured Sam. But Laura didn't see anything casual in it, and she'd been hurt all over again. She wanted Teddy to pay, and with her lean figure and sophisticated new look, she managed to make him do just that.

In their divorce settlement, Laura had received the house they'd bought at the start of their marriage. Teddy's great pride in the house had been his enclosed back porch with its spectacular whirlpool and sauna. Laura had seduced a young man at the gym and brought him home— to Teddy's whirlpool. Strange, what sets people off. She knew exactly where to strike to get Teddy. If she had taken half a dozen older lovers, he might have thought it was little more than a fair trade, but bringing a young hunk into his whirlpool sent him into a fury.

Free will, Teddy, Sam thought dryly. *You might have talked it over with your wife, kept your fly zipped.*

"Now as to Marnie . . ." Laura said.

"Yes?"

"Admit that Marnie is selfish and self-centered, and tell me you won't spend hours worrying about her. Although . . ."

"Although what?" Sam asked.

"Nothing."

"Don't 'nothing' me after that kind of a lead."

Curiously, Laura still hesitated. "Nothing . . . really. Except that . . ."

"Laura!" Sam implored.

"Well, it's just curious, that's all."

"What's curious?" she demanded, shaking her head as she realized she was almost shouting. Sometimes she just had to sympathize with Teddy.

"Well, Teddy had told me this, you realize."

"Told you what?"

"Well, Teddy knows about some things that have happened at Marnie's law firm."

"Like what?"

"Well, one of their young secretaries disappeared without a trace about a year ago. Marnie said she must have gone off with the Colombian she was seeing, but her parents came down and filed a missing-person report on her."

"And what happened? Did they find her?"

"Not a trace."

"Maybe she really did run off with a Latin American and is living happily in Cozumel."

"Maybe. The case is still open; the cops are still looking. But there's so much swampland down here, so much ocean, so many islands . . . sometimes when a person just disappears, there's nothing that can ever be done. The disappearance stays a mystery forever."

"How terrible for the poor girl's family!"

"Then one of their clients at the law firm disappeared as well. Don't you remember? This one was in the papers because of shady dealings. Mrs. Chloe Lowenstein, the hotshot society belle? Well, she had a reputation straight from the gutter, of course, but it seems that's allowed if you raise money for every charity known to man. Except that there was some scandal about her keeping money that was raised. The firm was representing her; in fact, she was Marnie's client. Then . . ."

"Then?"

"She just up and disappeared one day. Can you imagine?"

"Yes, I can. I do remember that story. I was talking to one of Marnie's associates soon after it happened—Kevin Madigan. He thought she had money stashed all over the world. And the IRS was after her. If she was very, very rich—and on the take and in trouble—she could easily be living in Argentina, Bolivia, Switzerland, or so on."

"Umm. Maybe, maybe not. It's just awful curious, don't you agree?"

Damn curious, Sam agreed. "So, if people disappear, maybe I *should* be worried about Marnie."

Laura snorted. "Maybe she's already sleeping with the new neighbor. From what I understand, he's been a client for a while, too."

"The new neighbor?"

"Your new neighbor, remember? The other side of Marnie's house. The one she seems so possessive about—and so smugly secretive, to boot!"

"The new neighbor is one of Marnie's clients?" Sam asked.

"No . . . silly. He's a client with the firm. He was looking for property for a while, from a distance, I guess, so he was with Eddie Harlin, the real estate attorney over there. That's how he and Marnie crossed paths again." Laura let out a sigh of impatience. "Sam, we talked to her not a full twenty-four hours ago. She's a grown woman. No, I take that back. She's a grown barracuda!"

"You're being mean. Your claws are showing."

"I'm old. I've got a right to be nasty. Didn't anyone ever explain to you why really old people are so crotchety? Life made them that way. Every year you get a little older and meaner."

"You're not old."

"In my forties, kid. And you haven't even hit the mini-big three-oh. Give yourself time. Soon. Then you too can grow to be a raving bitch."

"Laura, honest, I think I should hang up now. Really, I'm not so sure there's anything I can say that will make you happy at the moment," Sam said. Laura was definitely in one of her moods.

"Yes, you can. You can tell me that you want to go shopping."

"Shopping? For what?"

"Something that will make me look younger. Aidan's group is playing the Hot Patootie tonight on the beach. You're coming with me."

"I am?"

"Didn't I tell you last night?"

"No, you didn't tell me." Sam said, wincing. She wasn't sure she was in the mood. She was glad Aidan's group was getting some good-paying gigs, but the Hot Patootie was small and poorly air-conditioned—and it was usually peopled by a pickup crowd.

"You have to come with me. Please. I need you."

"What about Teddy? I'm sure he's going to go—clap his little heart out and support his son and the like."

Laura hesitated. "Yeah, amazing, isn't it? All those

years I emotionally supported the kids. I went to every Little League game and dance class, every doctor's appointment and school meeting. Teddy was always busy. Now we're divorced and superdad is everywhere."

"Well, now I guess he has to prove he loves his kids. That's kind of a good thing, Laura, to be forced to be supportive himself, and not depend on you."

"Yeah, well, Teddy said something about maybe having a date. Which I don't have. I just have you."

"Ah. Thanks."

"I don't mean that the way it sounds. I'm lucky to have you, you're great—you're just not a guy. But I do need you. Moral support. Please. Don't let me down."

"All right, all right."

"Shopping?"

Sam hesitated, glancing at her watch. "Laura, it's already after three. I need to shower, and if you want to get there tonight—"

"Oh, don't worry. Aidan doesn't even go on until eleven. He's all excited about that. They're the closing band. Apparently, the later, the better. I'll get you about seven, the malls are open until nine, we'll come back to your house, dress, and go. How about it?"

"I guess—"

"Think that's enough time for me to find something great to wear? Something that's wonderfully sexy but doesn't say 'older-woman-trying-to-look-young-and-coming-off-ridiculous-instead'?"

"Actually, come to think of it, I know where you can find something terrific. I know exactly where to go and what would look great on you. I saw it on a mannequin in a window yesterday. At Cocowalk. Come get me at six. I can be ready by then. All ready. That way we can just buy you a terrific outfit, you can dress right there in the Grove, and we can head on out to the beach."

"You probably could be ready earlier—"

"Six. Okay? Bye, then. I've got some stuff to do before you get here."

"Sam—"

Sam hung up quickly, pretending she hadn't heard the last. She looked over at Marnie's house, wondering what on earth could make her feel so uneasy about her friend. Laura's information about a disappearing client and secretary didn't help much, although, come to think of it, she remembered the year-old scandal about Chloe Lowenstein. She was certain that Chloe—a bright woman, even if she proved to be a crook—was living somewhere in Europe or South America, surrounded by maids, men, and money.

As to the young secretary . . . Young women did just run off. The world was full of runaways.

She shrugged, then realized that she'd been feeling a growing restlessness. Okay, so Marnie hadn't been gone that long. Didn't matter. Sam decided to go over and see if her friend was there. She had the key to the house. Marnie definitely had her quirks, but in her way she could be very generous as well. She had told Laura to use the house anytime, borrow anything at all from the fridge or the wine cellar, take linens, anything.

Determined, Sam picked up Marnie's house key from her desk and hurried downstairs to the front door. She didn't bother to lock her house. She never locked it when she was just in the neighborhood.

As she crossed the lawn to Marnie's, she reflected on her friend. In many ways Marnie was still like a little kid. She wanted things, dozens and dozens of things. She needed to be envied, but once envied, she was happy as a lark to share, to give things away. Marnie's lifestyle said a lot of things about her.

Psychology 101! Sam taunted herself, reaching the huge carved double doors at Marnie's entry. Maybe her own lifestyle said things about her as well.

Did it? Like what? She lived alone. She worked. She did well with her clients, especially the older men and women in therapy. As to her general-fitness members . . .

She did fine. She was friendly, helpful, and she knew what she was doing. She could work with men and keep a proper professional distance. She was assured, confident, and comfortable in her life. She loved her home, and her job, and she didn't need to prove anything to anyone.

Bull, she thought. The truth was, she was a coward, she accused herself. Afraid to take a chance again. Still, she'd learned a good lesson from it all. She'd learned to be careful.

Play it safe, be austere, flirt, dance, form friendships . . . and keep it all right on the surface. Don't care too much, and you can't lose too much.

She fitted the key into Marnie's lock, then hesitated, knocked hard, rang the bell.

She waited. Nothing. She rang the bell again and again. Pounded. Still nothing. Even if Marnie had been dead asleep, she should have awakened.

Dead asleep.

Dead.

Don't! Sam warned herself. She turned the key, opened the door, and stepped inside Marnie's foyer. It was quiet. She hesitated again, closed the door, and leaned back against it, chiding herself for being a chicken.

Even as she did so, an odd feeling of unease suddenly wrapped around her.

"Marnie!"

Her voice was just a croak.

Dunce! she accused herself.

"Marnie!" she called more loudly.

The foyer echoed the sound of her voice, and it seemed that the house itself was alive in a strange and haunting manner.

She was tempted to run.

No.

She had to do what she could to find out where Marnie was.

Chapter 3

The houses here were really three stories, but because it was a flood zone, only two of the floors actually counted. The bottom area, code-wise, could be built up only illegally, but that didn't seem to matter to most of the homeowners. A builder couldn't put a bathroom on the lower level, but when buyers moved in, they could add a bath. The bottom, or flood level, was usually on a plane with the pool, and most people wanted a cabana bath. Rowan's house had been lovingly planned by the previous owners, and his flood-level floor had been finished with indoor-outdoor carpeting and high shelving, along with patio furniture, a wet bar, small refrigerator and barbecue, a big bath with a sauna and Jacuzzi, and a built-up area for an entertainment system. He had added his own touch—instruments acquired through the years, a piano, keyboards, drum set, two bass guitars, three lead guitars, and a sound system that could highlight, diminish, play loud, play soft, play with computer enhancement, and be turned off altogether for acoustic work. He had designated one corner of the room for his scuba-diving equipment.

He had just reached into the small refrigerator for a bottle of beer when he heard his name called.

"Mr. Rowan? Mr. Rowan?"

"What is it, Adelia?" he replied. His eternally pleasant and efficient housekeeper had poked her head down the stairway. He'd tried to tell her she could call him Rowan, but no matter what he said, she still had to put the "Mr." on it.

"Telefono!" She made a face. "That reporter. I told her you weren't here, and she said that she'd come here and stake the house, or something like that. I say, you come to his *casa,* I call the police! But then I think I'd better ask you."

Rowan grinned. He wished the young reporter dogging him would fall into the bay, but Adelia was priceless. Marnie had sent her. She came at nine in the morning, let herself in, kept the place immaculate, and left precisely at five, leaving him a cooked meal if he planned to be in. She had apparently decided she liked him, because she was being as ferocious as a bulldog in his defense.

"Adelia, it's all right, I'll take it. Maybe I can say the right thing and she'll really leave us alone."

Adelia nodded gravely. Her head disappeared. He could hear her once again busy at her task of putting dishes away.

"Hello?"

"Rowan!" His name came out in an annoying gush. The reporter was young, aggressive, and attractive. She seemed to think that they had become best buddies.

"Beth, Beth Bellamy. Now, what on earth could you still need to know?"

"Rowan, I am sorry to bother you again, but I'm trying to be complete and correct in everything that I write about you. Totally accurate. Now, I know it's a sore spot, but we never really talked about the accident that killed Billy Marshall, the drummer. And you didn't tell me if his death was the reason you didn't want to go on—"

"Billy hit a cargo van and died. Yes, it's damned hard to have a group without a drummer. We had a good run of several years. To me, it was over. Anything else?"

"Well, you might have been killed as well. And I heard

that there was a big argument before he got behind the wheel. That you followed them. And you dragged Connie Marshall out of the vehicle—"

"Billy is dead, it's over. That's that."

"But—"

Beth was still talking; he had ceased to listen.

Billy had been gone now for more than three years. It was really time that he was allowed to rest in peace. He had tried to keep Billy out of the driver's seat that night, but Billy had eluded him. He'd done the best he could, racing after him. At least Connie had survived. Could he have changed things, no matter what? Like Dina, Billy had been set on a path of destruction and there was probably nothing that would have altered that.

So much for new beginnings. Back home, the reporters had left him alone. He'd been old news there.

"Beth, sorry, gotta go. I've given you everything I can think of to give you, and that should be plenty."

"But, Rowan, Rowan, you don't understand, I want it to be right, from your side—"

A massive surge of irritation welled within him. "You write whatever you feel you have to write," he said, and hung up.

Sam took a deep breath. She smiled after a moment. There was nothing spooky about the house. She was making it up in her own mind. The house was beautiful. It had all come together now. The massive chandelier above her head was dazzling in the sunlight that filtered in from the long windows. The light fell against the majestic stairway, touched the paintings on the walls, highlighted the ages-old tile and marble accents on the floors. From where she stood, she could look up the graceful stairway, or to her right or left, to the living room with the grand fireplace and high ceilings, to the library. She knew the layout of the house; she'd been in it time and again.

Marnie's excitement had been that of a child—yes, look at her new toy. It was magnificent.

Was there any way that Marnie could still be sleeping? Sam decided to call out again. "Marnie! Hey, Marnie! It's Sam. Are you here?"

She should stop yelling. That was what was making her feel so funny. The sound of her voice was echoing hollowly through the house. She knew that it was empty.

She moved through the house, into the living room, then back through the foyer, and out to the back, the kitchen. She looked out at the patio, over the crystal-clear water of the pool, and on to the blue depths of the bay beyond it. A bright, perfect Saturday morning in May. Lots of boaters were out there. Sails rode the breeze. The water sparkled as if the sun had cast down a shimmering, jeweled carpet on it.

Sam slowly looked around the kitchen. There were no wineglasses left sitting on the counter, as if a date had come for her. Sam opened the refrigerator. Wineglasses and a bottle of 1980-something California Chablis waited on the middle shelf. There was also a tray of cheeses and vegetables in plastic wrap on a lower shelf. She had meant to entertain or so it seemed.

Sam turned around again, frowning. There was a servants stairway in a hall behind the kitchen. She started quickly up the steps, which reached the second level right by the guest wing. "Marnie?"

Silly. She knew Marnie wasn't going to answer her now. So what did she think she was doing, snooping around her friend's house?

Looking for clues as to where Marnie might be. No, just trying to reassure myself that Marnie is out somewhere and okay.

No sign of Marnie or anyone else in the guest rooms. Everything was perfect. Brand-new, smelling of fresh paint. Everything had a clean and almost too perfect look about it.

She came back out and looked down the hallway. Marnie's room. *If something had happened,* she suddenly thought, *it would have happened there.*

"Oh, jeez, come on!" she chastised herself out loud. *Nothing had happened.* Marnie would show up any minute, and she might be angry at first that Sam was there, but then she would be all excited, thrilled that Sam was finally her audience for a tour through the almost absolutely completed renovation.

Smiling to herself, Sam started down the hallway. At Marnie's door, she paused again, holding on to the door frame. She looked into the bedroom.

It was clean, neat as a pin. There wasn't the slightest wrinkle in the Ralph Lauren spread that graced Marnie's big bed. There wasn't a bit of dust on the carpet, the least smudge on a wall. The place was perfectly clean. No sign of a struggle whatsoever.

She breathed, letting out a long sigh, unaware until she did so that she'd been holding her breath.

Yet just as she exhaled, she noted the dressing table.

Like everything else in the room, it was neat as a pin. Perfect—if you didn't know Marnie. But she did know Marnie. Marnie was a fanatic, a perfectionist, in many ways. Nothing was ever out of order, not even her makeup. And though it was arranged as usual in perfect rows . . .

The beige lipstick didn't line up with the beige nail polish.

"The Devil's Own Red" nail polish was next to "Barely There" lipstick.

She frowned, shaking her head. No big thing—it was all still in perfect order. To most people. Except Marnie. Maybe Marnie had been in a hurry. Maybe she'd actually

gotten so involved in what she was doing that she'd forgotten to be perfect.

Still frowning, Sam suddenly dropped down and
looked under the bed. Nothing, not even a dust bunny.

She rose, then stared at the closet. She opened it. Already full. Marnie's tailored work clothing, her wilder
evening wear. *Something really wild,* Sam thought, curiously reaching out to touch the fabric of a risqué bra and
panty set with spangles, sparkles, and fur. She couldn't
help a smile. Marnie did plan some wild dates. Yes, that
she did. Well, in college she'd done some fairly wild
things for income, Sam reminded herself. Then she realized she was intruding, looking through her friend's closet,
and she stepped back quickly, closing the door again.

She walked across to the windows, remembering how
excited Marnie had been to explain the way that she
would be able to see the sun coming up in the morning. It
meant so much to her. Maybe Marnie made her feel guilty
at times. She'd had such a normal life. She'd grown up in
the house that was hers now—she'd been blessed with
sunrises and sunsets all her life. It had been terrible when
her father had died, a pain like the severing of her soul.
He was a wonderful man, he'd have cut off his own arm
rather than hurt her, he loved her mother, and he'd never
raised a hand against either of them. After his death,
learning to work with her mother had been therapy for
them both. It had made them closer.

Marnie had never really known what it was to be loved
unconditionally.

Staring out the window, Sam frowned suddenly, feeling a cold tension seize her. Why? Something . . .

A sound.

Yes. She thought she'd heard a sound from downstairs.
"Ma—"

She opened her mouth to call out, then closed it

quickly. Some sixth sense warned her that it wasn't Marnie who had walked into the house.

She held dead still. Listening.

Not a sound.

She waited. Looking down, she realized that her fingers were curled hard over the tiled windowsill. She made a point of relaxing them.

Still nothing. She had imagined it.

Then she heard something again. At least she thought she did. A sound, coming, fading, gone. What had it been? A creaking?

And then she realized . . .

Someone was coming up the stairs.

Someone moving with such tremendous silence on purpose. Furtive.

Certainly *not* Marnie.

Sam started to rush out into the hall. Then she realized that if a burglar was in the house, she would run right into him. She stood frozen. No, she couldn't go running into the hall. So where? The balcony? No, someone could just look out . . . The closet.

He was coming closer. Coming straight for Marnie's bedroom.

She spun around, tried to silently open Marnie's closet door. Thank God everything was so new—the door didn't creak. She stepped into the closet, quickly closed the door behind her.

Shit! Big closet, but with the door closed, it was dark as Hades.

Now she could feel his footsteps through the floor. She groped blindly in front of her. Marnie, what do you have in here, what kind of a weapon? Is there anything here, anything at all?

Her fingers grasped something. Something wooden . . . and woven.

A tennis racket.

She felt around frantically in the same area. Something else, long and hard and strangely clothlike.

An umbrella.

She gripped it tightly in her hands, making a bat of it. Better than the tennis racket. She prayed that she wouldn't have to use it. That whoever it was would just look around the bedroom and leave.

She waited, barely breathing. She heard nothing. Nothing at all. He must have gone.

Then suddenly, just when she was relaxing her stance, breathing deeply, easily, the door was flung open wide.

"No!"

She screamed the word in panic. And she started to swing the umbrella with all her might.

"Son of a bitch!"

She heard the deep swearing, yet was only barely aware of it in her frantic desire to escape. The man had his arms up, protecting his face from her blows. She slammed the umbrella down again and tried to catapult herself past the invader.

"Oh, no, you don't!"

She was caught by her hair at first. Shrieking, she tried to break free. Marnie had been murdered. She was suddenly certain.

The killer often came back to the scene of the crime. Teddy had told her so. Cold sweat broke out all over her body.

"Hey!"

Her hair was suddenly free, but fingers wound around her arm. She tried to strike out again, but the umbrella was caught. She struggled to keep it, and free herself. Stepping backward, she tripped. She went down as the umbrella was wrenched from her hands.

He fell on top of her!

She screamed, struggled, striking out. She was a strong woman; he was stronger. She was blinded by her hair. She kicked, writhed . . .

Her hands were caught, pinned beside her head. Her hair was moved from her eyes.

Then . . .

"Jesus! Sam!"

She looked up, stunned to immobility.

"Oh, my God! Rowan?" she said incredulously.

Yes, Rowan. Rowan Dillon. He'd closed a door against her, and she'd walked out of his life more then five years ago. And now he was on top of her in Marnie's house. He hadn't changed. Well, maybe a little. The lines around his eyes were a little more deeply grooved; strands of gray were starting to dust his hair.

Rowan. She blinked. Oh, God. *He* had to be the new neighbor.

Oh, but he was still tall, dark, and handsome, just as Laura had described him when she had seen nothing but his height and his coloring and back the day they'd just missed the new neighbor as he was walking into his new house.

Tall, broad-shouldered, a large, powerful man, he was here now, in Marnie's house. He had known Marnie, of course, when they had lived in Gainesville.

Where he had been accused of murder!

Ridiculously so, of course.

Rowan. Rowan Dillon was here.

She'd never believed it, not for a minute. But then, she had loved him. She had been the cast-aside lover. The foolish "other woman." She had believed him, believed that he had been finished with Dina. Yeah, the cops had believed that, too. Believed he had a hot enough temper, maybe even a good enough reason to kill . . .

"Sam."

He said her name very softly. His dark hair was mussed, of course. She'd just beaten him with an umbrella. He'd just tackled her to the floor. He didn't seem any the worse for wear from the beating. He was just staring at her. Studying her.

"Rowan!" she repeated, angry now. She'd been caught off guard. She'd never thought to see him again. "Damn you, what—?"

"I bought the house next door," he explained.

His voice, just hearing his voice, caused a strange sensation to snake up her spine. Great voice, naturally. He loved the guitar, and the drums, but it had been his voice that had taken the group to the top of the charts. Deep, with a touch of huskiness, his voice could make every woman listening think he was singing to her, make every man feel as if he were the one with the thoughts.

"How could you?" she accused without thinking. She was so . . . furious!

"How could I buy a house?" he inquired incredulously. He stared at her, then said, "Well, I'm sorry, at the time I didn't know that you lived here. I didn't even know that Marnie had this house—"

"You didn't know?"

"No! I didn't know."

"So what the hell are you doing now? What in God's name are you doing skulking around in Marnie's house?"

He arched a brow, easing back slightly. But his features were tense, jaw locked, at the sound of her voice. She was still pinned down, she realized. And he was not really backing off, not responding to the sound of anger in her voice. It wasn't his way to back down.

"Excuse me," he said, actually leaning closer. "What were *you* doing, hiding in Marnie's closet?"

"I have a key to this house," she snapped back.

"And that explains why you're in her closet?" He rose suddenly, reaching down to her. She realized that she'd just lain there like an idiot, that she hadn't even asked him to get off her. She grasped his hand, rising. Her hand felt as if it had been burned.

"Well?" he inquired.

"I—was worried about Marnie."

"Why?"

"She hasn't come home."

"Since when?"

"Last night."

His brow arched slightly higher. Okay, he thought she was a fool for worrying about a woman who'd been gone less than twenty-four hours. Or did he? How well could she really know a man she hadn't seen in five years? How well had she ever really known him? *Every inch of him, I thought I knew every inch, inside and out, but I guess I didn't, because he didn't want me.*

"So what are you doing here?" she demanded.

He smiled, running his fingers through his umbrella-mussed hair, smoothing it back from his face. "I thought someone was breaking in. I came to check up on the prowler I thought was in here, to keep the house from being burglarized."

"Oh?"

He was studying her intently and she felt acutely uneasy. He was in swim trunks, cutoff denims. Shoulders and chest were still muscled and tanned. Teeth were still white against the bronze of his face, his eyes amber-green. Hazel eyes, taking on different colors at different times, with different emotions. He'd always been quick to smile. Quick to anger, quick to passion.

She had to get away. She was entirely too off balance. Five years, and now she was alone with him. He'd just had to be half naked here in cutoffs, too, of course, and he'd had to touch her, tackle her, straddle her, and. . .

And he was still studying her, those amber eyes so

intent, physical form so imposing and male. She could smell him, for God's sake, and he smelled so *sexy*—no, she would not be such a fool!

"God, Sam, it's good to see you," he said quietly. He stepped back, giving her plenty of space. Arms crossed over his chest, feet well apart, legs sturdy. Great legs.

She couldn't believe the things she was thinking, the way her mind was working. Maybe Marnie was right, telling Sam that she needed a real life, sex now and then.

He was waiting for a reply.

"Oh, yeah, Great, yeah, right. Good, great, absolutely, right. Wonderful to see you, too. Just wonderful. If you'll excuse me . . ."

She pushed past him, started out. But at the doorway to Marnie's room, she looked back, finding a modicum of dignity.

"No, it isn't wonderful to see you. I had never wanted to see you again. And I don't want to see you now. Okay, it's a free world, you bought a house—near mine. I still don't want to see you. More than ever, I don't want to see you, unless we're both out on our lawns picking up our newspapers, and we wave to one another, just to be civil."

He stared at her, giving her a slow smile. "Sam, there's no law saying that neighbors have to be civil. Hell, don't wave if you don't want to."

She didn't bother to respond. She turned again and started out of the house. Calmly. With dignity.

Even *slowly,* at first. Oddly, all she could think of at that moment was diving class. *If you run into a shark, never try to swim quickly away. Never let the animal know that you're in distress . . .*

Just like diving class. She walked down the hall slowly . . .

A shark recognizes distress. Distress makes a victim look like easy prey.

By the time she reached the stairs, she was walking faster.

By the time she reached the bottom, she was running.

And she didn't give a damn. All she wanted was out of that house.

Chapter 4

"Hey, Sam!"

Laura came into the glassed-in Florida room. Sam was sitting on an upholstered wicker chair, staring toward the bay, as she had been doing ever since she'd walked back into her house.

"Sam!" Laura stared down at her. "You're not dressed, you're not ready!"

Sam looked at her. "I know who the new neighbor is."

"Oh, really? Who?"

"Rowan Dillon."

"What?" Laura said incredulously.

Sam nodded. Laura stared at her.

"You went over there? He came over here? You met him?"

"No, we were both in Marnie's house. I was trying to find her, to see if something was wrong, and I heard noises . . . and it was him."

"Rowan?" Laura repeated.

"Rowan."

Laura spun around, heading purposefully for the front door. Sam jumped to her feet. "Where are you going? What are you doing?"

"Well, you're not ready to go out. I'm going to go over and say hi to him."

"*What?*"

"I'm going to go and welcome him to the neighbor-hood."

"Laura, I don't believe you!"

Laura stopped, turning to her. "Why? What's the matter?"

"Laura, you're my cousin, remember?" Sam said in-credulously. "The man devastated me! Broke my heart, destroyed my life—"

"Sam, Sam! That's a bit dramatic, isn't it? He was go-ing through some terrible times. And your father dying is what broke your heart, and your life isn't destroyed. It's a little boring at times, but that's because you refuse—"

"Rowan practically *threw* me out of his life," Sam said angrily.

"He was going through a bad time."

"And maybe he's still going through a bad time! Laura, I don't want to be neighbors with him. I don't want him dropping in on me on a casual basis now! Dammit, you're the one always telling me that I don't go out, that I don't give relationships a chance. Well, that's the man who ru-ined any real relationships for me!"

"If I may interrupt this sorry-for-myself fest—"

"Sorry-for-myself fest? Excuse me. Who's dragged you out of every morbid mood you've been in for the last decade?"

"If he ruined other men for you, it makes sense. He's incredible, he's handsome, intense, talented, determined, sexy . . . Naturally, it's tough for other guys to stand up against all that."

"Laura, excuse me! I wound up in dozens of tabloids because of him! I was grocery-store-checkout-line read-ing because of him. I was vilified, notorious—"

"Lots of women might have enjoyed the attention and media."

"Laura—"

"Don't you remember? Marnie always said that she wished it had been her."

Sam let out a snort of total frustration.

"Besides, what do you care what people think or say?"

"Forget all that! You're right. He hurt me. Badly. You weren't there at the end—"

"That's right. So I have no argument with him."

"I don't believe this!"

Laura rubbed a hand over her forehead. "All right. If you really, really, really don't want me going over there, I won't."

"I really, really don't want you going over there."

"You're not acting like yourself. You're supposed to be all mature and reasonable and dignified."

"Yes, and I like to be that way."

Laura turned and started toward the door again.

"What are you doing?"Sam demanded.

"I'm going to call on your new neighbor."

"You just said you wouldn't!"

"I lied."

"Laura!"

At the door Laura spun around again. "Sorry, my son's a struggling musician and Rowan may not be playing anymore himself, but I'm willing to bet he's still got some great connections."

"If you go over there now, you're not my cousin anymore!" Sam told her, arms crossed over her chest.

Laura grinned. "It doesn't work that way. Genetics, you know. You can choose your friends, but you can't choose your relatives. Sorry."

Laura walked out of the house. Sam stared after her. "Son of a bitch!" she exclaimed in Laura's wake.

She spun around and headed for the kitchen. She thought she'd actually made it back to her house fairly reasonably. She hadn't thrown herself on her lawn kicking and screaming, nor had she attempted to tear her hair out. She hadn't even made herself a drink. She didn't drink a great deal, she reminded herself. She was a fitness expert and physical therapist, moderate in all things. Like hell.

She made herself a stiff gin and tonic with lots of ice and tons of lime. The clinking of the ice into the glass seemed like a good, rational, normal sound. She stared at the drink. Dammit. She'd built herself a nice life. A *safe* life, she mocked herself. She lifted her glass. "Moderate in all things, including living!"

He had hurt her. It was that simple. She should have known better. She should never have fallen for a married man, even if he had been separated for months. Even if he was devastating, the best time she'd ever had, even if it had seemed that they were closer than any two people could possibly be . . .

One day the door had shut in her face. She'd come to support him, to offer her love, her devotion against all odds, and he'd closed the door in her face and told his security people to make sure that she didn't bother him anymore.

Well, she wasn't going to have anything to do with him. She was going to go upstairs and get dressed and look her best for another man.

She swallowed the last of her gin and tonic in a long gulp, then dashed up the stairs. So, they were going shopping, and then clubbing. A black cocktail dress for a stroll around the mall? Sure, they were going to Cocowalk, an open-air mall in the heart of Coconut Grove with shops, restaurants, and clubs. Some people wore tank tops over bathing suits, and others dressed up, depending on which way they were headed. She would just straddle the two extremes. Black cocktail dress, killer heels—it could be a pain in the butt being short, or medium-short, as Laura called her.

She discarded her clothes along the hallway, dove into

the shower, and dressed in a matter of minutes, wearing
the highest heels she had. She viewed them in the mirror
as she brushed her hair with furious strokes. Great shoes.
They added the dimension she needed. The kind of shoes
that enhanced muscle tone if you had it and made it appear that you had great calves even if you didn't. She
smiled for a minute. One of her friends, a writer who
worked out at the gym, classified dress shoes in two
ways—those with wild, tough heels were fuck-you shoes.
Delicate sandals and high spikes were fuck-me shoes.

These, she reasoned, were somewhere in between.

The doorbell rang. For a moment her heart seemed to
hammer, heat, and then freeze. None of these things
really happened, she knew. Her adrenaline was simply in
a rush.

She put the brush down, eyeing herself in the mirror.
She hated to feel like this. Going crazy over a long-dead
affair was ridiculous.

The doorbell rang again. She tore down the stairs and
through the house, throwing the door open before she
could think more or panic in any way. As she opened the
door, she saw a man standing in the shadow. *He'd rejected her. When she had thought that he would need her
most, he had rejected her.*

The man standing on her doorstep was tall and dark,
but he wasn't Rowan. He was thirty-something with a
leathered complexion and look of someone accustomed
to working in the sun. She blinked for a minute, then realized that she was looking at Marnie's contractor, Phil
Jenkins.

"Phil!"

He looked her up and down before answering, so much
so that she wondered if she'd gotten a little carried away
with the dress and the shoes.

"Yeah, uh, sorry to bother you, Samantha, but I was . . .
uh, you look great, you know," he said.

She flushed. "Thanks. You were saying?"

"Yeah, I haven't been able to reach Marnie all day. I thought maybe she was with you."

"No, I'm sorry. I'm actually a little concerned."

The look he gave her assured her that he wasn't exactly *concerned*.

"Well, you know our Miss Newcastle—better than I do, I'm sure. But I don't suppose I'd waste my time being too concerned. That lady does seem to have the world by the balls—whoops, sorry, excuse my French!"

"Marnie can be very determined and stubborn. She has to be, in her position," Sam said, irritated that she sounded so defensive. "It's a tough world out there. She's worked very hard, and she works with a lot of hard types."

"Yeah, well, some people kind of have a knack for making the old world tougher themselves, know what I mean? Never mind. Sorry. She's your friend. Hey, when you get around to redoing this old place, make sure you give me a call. It's a beauty. I'll give you a great deal."

"Thanks."

"I can work on credit, too. Have you seen Marnie's place yet?"

"Several times. You've done beautiful work."

He was still staring at her, hovering on her porch. Her fault. It was the shoes.

He grinned, showing perfect teeth. He made good money as a contractor; he had obviously invested some of it in his mouth.

"You could invite me in and we could discuss all that I could do on credit."

"Well, you know, I'm just not ready to get into any renovations yet, Phil. And knowing Marnie, I'm willing to bet that she's not quite through with you."

His smiled broadened. "Yeah, well, she is one tough broad, for certain. But then again, she's a wild one, and I reckon maybe you're right. Maybe she's not quite through with me. She's a stickler for perfection, but she sure knows a good thing when she, er, sees it."

Now she was decidedly uncomfortable. She was about to pull the door closed, but she hesitated, seeing a sleek Lincoln pull up in front of Marnie's house. Not Marnie's car, but maybe Marnie was in it.

"Look maybe that's her now," Sam said. Her concern caused her to ignore Phil and step around him. She crossed her small front yard as quickly as she could in her heels.

A man was emerging from the car. He was lean, moving with an easy, fluid motion. His wavy dark hair was styled in a traditional cut that was enhanced by the perfectly tailored designer suit he was wearing. He got out of the car alone, looking up at the house, smoothing back his hair as he did so.

"Hello," Sam called.

The man turned to her. He recognized her and smiled. "Samantha. Hi, how are you?"

Yes, she knew him. Nice-looking guy, smooth as silk. He worked at Marnie's firm. In fact, he frequently worked with Marnie, but they were also competitors in a way— both pushing for the next partnership.

He extended his hand. "Sam, it's Kevin, Kevin Madigan. I'm hurt, I must say. You don't remember me."

"Yes, of course, I remember you," she told him. He hadn't meant it. He probably believed that no woman ever forgot him. "Kevin, hello, how are you?"

"Very good, thank you. And you?"

"Well, thanks. I . . . I do admit, though, I was rather hoping that you were coming here with Marnie."

"Yes, I gathered you were worried."

"You did?" Sam inquired, startled.

He smiled. Another man who had put a lot of money

into his teeth. "You called the office today. Loretta told me."

"Loretta?"

"Marnie's secretary. You spoke with her earlier."

"Oh. Oh, yes, of course. She must have been the one who answered the phone when I called the main number."

"Yes." He just smiled, looking at her.

"Well," she murmured, "I still haven't seen Marnie. Have you?"

"Not since you called. But we were in court together on Friday. It's a little early to be getting worried about a grown woman like Marnie, don't you think?"

His tone was great. Not condescending, just logical. Of course, he *was* an attorney.

She smiled in return. "But then again, you're out here."

"Well, having heard that you called, Mr. Daly just wanted to see if Marnie had gotten home."

"Mr. Daly?"

"Of course. Mr. *Daly*."

He indicated an older man with snow-white hair sitting in the passenger seat of the car. The man made no effort to get out, but he nodded gravely to Sam as she looked his way. She nodded in return. Mr. Daly. Marnie's firm was Daly, Simpkins, and Smith. Daly was a senior partner.

"Has she come home yet?"

"Not that I know of."

"She hasn't come home."

Sam swung around. Phil had come up to stand behind her. He stared at Kevin Madigan. Madigan stared back.

She could almost smell the testosterone on the air. The two men were so very different—Phil so rugged, Kevin Madigan almost elegant and yet so assured. Confident. They were both macho men each in his own way.

And Marnie had slept with both of them. Sam was suddenly certain of that fact.

"Sam, Sam! Is Marnie back, then?"

Sam groaned inwardly. Laura was now on her way up to the group, hurrying anxiously over to the Lincoln parked in front of Marnie's house.

"No, she's not back. But Phil and Kevin are looking for her, too," Sam said.

"Oh, hi, Phil!" Laura had seen Phil around the place often enough. She hadn't been to Marnie's office very often, so she just smiled at Kevin Madigan, who smiled back at her.

Sam felt a strange, creeping sensation as she realized that Laura wasn't alone. She had been followed out of Rowan's house. By Rowan.

"Rowan, Kevin Ma—"

"Yes, I know Kevin," Rowan said, shaking hands with the man.

"Rowan purchased his property here through our firm," Kevin said.

"Of course. I knew that," Laura said. "Well, then, Rowan, meet Phil Jenkins—"

"Yes, actually, we've met, too," Rowan said, shaking hands with Phil.

Sam watched the exchange, feeling as if a pit were being dug in her stomach. Yes, they had all met. Through Marnie.

The testosterone quotient seemed even greater now.

The tough-man contractor, the suave attorney . . . and Rowan. Somewhere between the two. Skin bronzed by the sun, features given character by the passage of life, somehow all the more striking for the lines weathered into his face around his eyes. Dark hair a little longer than that of the others. He wasn't as casually dressed as Phil, nor was he as elegantly decked out as Kevin. He wore a black knit polo shirt, black jeans, and a dinner jacket. He smelled clean, his hair was damp; to Sam he seemed to reek masculinity. His simple presence seemed to call out to every natural instinct in her body.

Old Mr. Daly chose that moment to exit the car. "If Marnie isn't here, she isn't here. We've left messages on her machine. If she doesn't show up by Monday morning, we'll call the police."

"Perhaps we should go in—" Kevin suggested.

"Despite a key, that would be breaking and entering," Mr. Daly said indignantly.

"Oh, no, not really! Both Sam and Rowan have already been in the house!" Laura announced cheerfully.

Sam and Rowan stared at her simultaneously. Sam realized that she and Rowan were sharing a common emotion at the moment; they were both ready to box Laura's ears.

"You were in the house?"Daly inquired, looking from one of them to the other.

"Marnie is a friend. I have a key to check up on her."

"I was afraid someone had broken into the house," Rowan explained.

"You have a key, too?" Daly asked.

Sam thought that Rowan hesitated for a split second. Then he simply said, "Yes."

She lowered her head, feeling ill again. Hands clammy. A sickness in her stomach. An awful, painful jealousy.

They had all slept with Marnie. In fact, it was like one big Marnie slumber party out here.

Of course, she could be wrong, but . . .

"If half of us have already been in the house, perhaps someone should use his or her key to let us in so we can make sure that Marnie isn't lying hurt somewhere. Maybe she tried to fix something, got up on a ladder, fell," Kevin said.

"I looked. Marnie wasn't here at all," Sam said.

"Should we just check?" Kevin asked gently.

"All right. My key is in the house—" she began.

"Mine is in my pocket," Rowan said. He swept past all of them heading up the walk. One by one they followed.

Entering the residence, they all paused in the foyer, looking around. "Marnie!" Laura called. "Hey, Marnie!"

No response. Even now, with all of them in the foyer, the way Laura's voice bounced back sounded eerie to Sam. She walked around the foyer.

"Shall we check upstairs?" Kevin asked.

"Sure," Phil said. He, Kevin, and Rowan started up the stairs. Kevin and Rowan both headed down the hall toward the guest rooms. Phil entered Marnie's room. Sam followed him.

He bumped into her on his way out. "Nothing!" he said.

"Umm," she murmured, but she walked on by him. She'd already been in the room. She walked back to the dressing table. Nothing. In perfect alignment. To most people, it couldn't be more perfect.

Marnie wasn't most people. And still . . .

Who could she possibly convince that this was awry? Just because colors weren't matching up . . .

Maybe it was nothing. Nothing at all.

She suddenly swung around, sensing that someone was behind her. Rowan. He looked at her, around the room, and back to her again. "What's wrong?"

"Nothing, really—"

"Nothing?" he queried, eyes sharp, aware that she was hesitating.

"Her make up is out of order."

He frowned, coming toward her. "I've never seen anything left so neatly in my life."

"The colors don't match up," she said.

He frowned.

"Never mind," she murmured. He was standing too close to her. She didn't want to be this close.

"We've been here before," he reminded her quietly. "No blood and guts."

"No blood and guts," she agreed, and she turned quickly, heading out of the room.

She walked briskly back to the hallway. Rowan didn't follow. She bit her lip, wondering just how familiar he was with Marnie's bedroom.

She could hear Phil and Kevin, down the hall, still checking out closets and bathrooms. She started back down the stairs, certain that they would find the rest of the upstairs in perfect order.

Mr. Daly, who walked with a cane, stood at the foot of the stairway.

"She isn't here, is she?" Daly asked Sam, staring hard at her. *He might be old,* she thought, *but his eyes are sharp as glass.* He was tall and despite the cane, it appeared that he had maintained broad shoulders and good muscle tone into his twilight years. His hands were large, and she imagined that they might be quite powerful. He was still a very handsome and dignified man.

"I don't believe she's here, no," Sam said.

"And you're worried."

"She was so thrilled with this house, I have to be worried if she isn't here to show it off to everyone."

Daly nodded. "Still, she's a bold and impetuous young woman. If she did decide to take off somewhere with someone, she would have done so, not giving a damn that others might be worried about her."

Sam frowned. "It doesn't sound as if you like her very much, Mr. Daly."

"On the contrary. She is a woman after my own heart. She is, quite frankly, a barracuda, and I admire her tremendously." He smiled, and Sam couldn't help but think, *Oh my God, it sounds as if he knows Marnie really well, too. Really, really—intimately!—well, too!*

Laura returned from the kitchen. The men came back down the stairs, Kevin in the lead, Rowan behind him, Phil bringing up the rear.

"Nothing," Kevin said. "No sign of Marnie."

"And no sigh of any disturbance," Phil added.

"Her car is gone, right?" Rowan asked slowly.

"Yes, her car is gone," Laura said. She turned to Sam. "Honestly, Sammy, she's just gone off, and if she were to come home now, she'd probably be furious with the lot of us!"

At that moment the front door suddenly burst open. In a group they spun around, startled—guilty.

Expecting Marnie.

But it wasn't Marnie. An odor swept into the house along with the grizzled old man who burst in. He was unshaven, gray-haired, both fierce and frightening in appearance. He was wearing a suit, but it had been slept in. Often, over many nights, so it appeared.

His teeth were crooked and yellowed. A shame, because Sam knew that Marnie gave him plenty of money for dentistry and doctor's visits.

"Where the hell is my daughter, that bitch? And what are you yellow-bellied leeches doing here?"

Sam felt Mr. Daly stiffening by her side. She realized that most of them knew Colin Newcastle, Marnie's father.

"I'll find her myself! What's she doing, whoring around in her brand-new bedroom?" he demanded, starting up the stairs. He teetered dangerously, but when Kevin took a step after him, he turned around, furious. "Get back! What is this down here, a line? Where is my daughter?"

"Someone should get him down," Mr. Daly said. "Before he kills himself."

"Yeah, well, maybe Marnie would thank us all if he did!" Kevin muttered.

No one objected to his statement, but Rowan took a step toward the stairs. "You're right; he's totally inebriated and he will kill himself on the stairs."

But before Rowan could move, Colin Newcastle came

running back down. He missed a step but recovered. Sam thought that God did indeed look after fools and drunks.

"Where the hell is she?" he shouted, looking at them all one by one.

"Marnie isn't here, Mr. Newcastle," Kevin said, his voice rich with contempt.

"Then what are you doing here? I oughta call the police," Newcastle spit out.

"Pop!"

Newcastle went still.

A young man appeared in the doorway. He was twenty-something, Sam decided. She realized that although she hadn't seen him in a long time, she did know him. Thayer Newcastle, Marnie's baby brother. Marnie often said that she tried to help him, but he didn't want to help himself. He had long, dark hair, a thin, aesthetic face. Strangely, he also looked a lot like Marnie, beautiful in a masculine way. He spoke so softly. So differently from Marnie.

"Pop, you're drunk as a skunk." The young man looked at the faces around him. He recognized Sam and smiled. "Hi, Sam, good to see you, though I'm sorry for the intrusion. I've been following him around for a while . . . I'll get him out of here. Is my sister here?"

"No," Sam said.

"Where is she?"

She shook her head. "We don't know. She isn't here."

He arched a brow, looking around at all of them. "Then maybe none of us should be here, either." he said softly. "Pop, come on, before you fall down."

"He's right," Rowan said firmly. "None of us should be here."

Thayer strode across the room for his father, took him by the arm, and started out with him.

Colin Newcastle shook off his son's hand. "Leave me be, boy."

"That's Marnie's boss, Dad."

"Hell, I know who it is! You think he's any better than the rest of them?"

"You want to get her fired? There'd be no more money at all then. Let's go."

Colin Newcastle squared his shoulders and turned toward them. He lifted his chin in a semblance of dignity.

"Get out of my daughter's house!" he ordered.

Sam was startled when Rowan was the one to answer him again.

"From what I understand," Rowan said, his eyes narrowed sharply on Colin Newcastle, "you don't have any right to be anywhere near your daughter, period. You gave up that right years ago. You're lucky she hasn't prosecuted you."

"What?" Colin Newcastle looked as if he wanted to charge Rowan.

And Rowan might have been waiting for him to do just that. Sam felt an intense desire to defuse the situation. Before there were blows.

"Mr. Newcastle, the reason we're in Marnie's house is because we're worried about her," Sam said.

Colin Newcastle said, "You think something happened to Marnie?"

"I'm just worried. She didn't tell me she was going away," Sam explained. Despite his manner, she tried to speak patiently. He was Marnie's father, after all.

Newcastle smirked. "If something has happened to Marnie, then this place is mine. Get out of my house!" he demanded.

Sam's heart seemed to twist. People who thought that Marnie was hard didn't begin to understand just where she had come from. Sam glanced at Laura and saw that her cousin seemed stricken. Everyone in the house, even old Mr. Daly, seemed stunned.

It was Thayer Newcastle who broke the silence.

"Pop, let's go! Nothing has happened to Marnie."

He clutched his father by the arm and started to drag him out of the house.

But Marnie's father turned back. "There had better not be a thing out of place here. Nothing. Nothing gone. I'll sue you. I don't care if you are a bunch of attorneys. I'll get better attorneys. I'll sue you to the bones, I'll have you jailed for breaking and entry—"

"Pop!" Thayer said.

But Colin wasn't about to go in silence. He smiled suddenly, wagging a finger at all of them. "If something has happened to Marnie, it's my place. You remember that. My place. Sam, honey, I'll be your new neighbor. Won't that be cozy?"

Sam didn't have to reply. Thayer had finally managed to drag him out. The door closed behind the two of them.

For long moments they were all silent.

"My God!" Laura breathed then. "My God! Sam, feel free to hit me anytime I say anything bad about Marnie from now on, okay?"

"Get me home, Kevin. I think I've had enough local color for the night," Mr. Daly said. "Watch out for our girl now, Miss Miller," he said to Sam. She started. She hadn't been certain that Daly knew she had ever been in the office, much less her name.

"I'm going to leave her a note in the kitchen, telling her that we're all worried," Sam assured him.

Daly was heading toward the door on his own. Kevin Madigan paused briefly, taking her hands. "Please, feel free to call us if you hear anything, find out anything . . . or if we can do anything at all."

"Thanks." She withdrew her hands uneasily, aware that everyone was watching. "I'll write the note now."

"Want me to stick around?" Phil asked.

"No, thanks . . . Laura is with me. I can lock up," Sam said.

She turned around and hurried into the kitchen, feeling as if she were being watched every step of the way. As she dug into one of Marnie's drawers, she heard the front door open and close. She found paper and a pencil and wrote, *Marnie! Call me, first thing, now, not later! Sam. P.S. Immediately. Don't go to sleep, don't pass go, don't collect two hundred dollars! Call me!*

Marnie didn't have any refrigerator magnets. She couldn't stand clutter. She would never put cute little pictures drawn by a kindergarten child facing her by the ice machine. Sam found heavy tape and secured her note.

She turned around. Laura and Rowan had followed her into the kitchen.

"The others are gone," Laura said. She shivered. "I don't like this house. It may be beautiful, it may be high tech, but it gives me the shakes. Like it's evil. Like the house itself did something to Marnie."

"Laura! Sam said, shaking her head. "Marnie's going to be mad as hell that I've gotten sticky stuff all over her refrigerator," she commented.

"Let's lock it up," Rowan said, obviously impatient to be gone.

"I can really manage—" Sam began, simply because she felt a need to protest anything he had to say.

"There's nothing more to do here. Unless you want to tape another note to the front door—just in case she isn't hungry when she comes home," Rowan said.

She stared at him, then felt a tremendous urge to grit her teeth. Of all the times for Rowan to step into her life.

"That's a good idea," Laura agreed.

Of course it was a good idea. She turned around, found more paper, wrote another note. When she was done, she reached for the tape. Rowan had already gone for it. His fingers brushed hers. She despised the sensations that leapt through her body.

Going without, that's what caused it. Marnie had told

her once that it wasn't natural to go without. Everyone needed sex, no matter how smart or sophisticated. We were just animals, and sex was instinct.

Maybe Marnie had been right.

Her hormones seemed to be flying. Yes, she had a vivid memory. Just from his touch. His thumb moving against her lips, fingers brushing her cheeks. Tall, taut, whipcord lean, he lent an air of power to the space around him. Once it had been her space. No, it hadn't ever really been hers. That had been illusion. Now, they were strangers, by chance cast together. She stepped away. *Damn Laura!* He might have stayed in his own house if it hadn't been for her wretched cousin.

Rowan was moving ahead of her. She hurried after him, eager to get out of the house. Laura was on her heels, unaware of the tension. Sam brushed past Rowan again on her way out. She decided not to wait, aware that he was taping the second note to the door and that Laura hovered on the elegant porch. "Sammy!"

"Laura, it doesn't take more than one person to tape a note to a door!" she said, then determined that she was going to have her wits about her and behave like a normal functioning person. "Thanks, Rowan. Good night."

"But, Sam . . ."

Laura came hurrying after her, catching her on the street between the two houses. "Sam, Rowan is going to come with us. Can you believe that? He's going to come and see Aidan play!"

Sam, felt as if she'd been hit in the chest. But Laura was so excited. It meant so much to her.

"Of course, he'll come to see Aidan. I'm sure he remembers what it was like to be a struggling musician. And Aidan is good; he'll do himself proud. But you know what? You know how I hate clubs and being out so late. Since Rowan is going, please, can I bow out?"

Laura frowned. "But we were going shopping first!"

"You look like a million bucks already," Sam assured her. It was true. Laura was in a little white sundress that showed off her tan, her hair, her legs. She looked great. "Go get some dinner or something first. Honestly."

Honestly? She was lying like a rug. She suddenly wanted nothing more in the world that to go with them. All she could remember was the way she had landed on the floor, the way he had straddled her, chest bare, thighs so strong, the hair on them teasing her flesh.

Oh, good God, that was exactly why she couldn't go!

"But, Sam—"

"And if Teddy shows up, he'll think you have a really hot date!" she said, smiling.

"Yeah, maybe."

"Go, girl. Go do it!"

She kissed her cousin on the cheek and fled into her own house.

Fifteen minutes later, she was sitting by her pool, sipping Merlot and damning herself for feeling sorry for herself.

All dressed up in her fuck-you shoes and everything, and no place to go!

Well, what had she thought, that they would come barging in and demand that she go with them? That Rowan would walk in and say that he had only said he would go so he could be with her?

She walked to the small, rustic dock on the edge of her property. Her little dinghy—nothing more than a rowboat with a weak motor, really—was tied there. As she looked into the water, no more than five or six feet from behind the house here, she smiled, feeling her heart lighten a bit.

"Mollie!"

The neighborhood sea cow was right below her dock. Mollie the manatee was one of the reasons she would never dream of selling her property, not even if her house caved in on top of her. Mollie had once gotten too close to the propellers of a boat, and she still carried the scar. Wounded, she had remained close to the shallows here in the bay, by the homes on this little peninsula. She had been fed and pampered by the sea-loving people in the area.

"Hungry?" Sam asked. "Sure, you're hungry."

She hurried inside, rummaged in the refrigerator, found a new head of lettuce. She hurried back out with it—barefoot now. She sat down on the dock, splitting the head of lettuce, tossing the leaves in. Moonlight reflected on the water, and the stars were shining above her. Mollie munched happily on lettuce, allowing Sam to scratch her head. Sam smiled. Most people felt about manatees the way they did about bulldogs—the creatures were just so ugly that they were cute. Hundreds of pounds of cute, in Mollie's case. And she was so wonderful She had made her peace with man. Sometimes that was bad for the animals. Most were hurt simply because boaters were careless. But sometimes manatees just wanted to be close to their human neighbors.

Luckily, Mollie stayed close to the neighborhood, close to those who looked out for her. Mollie was more careful than most women, Sam thought ruefully.

Where the hell was Marnie?

She stood up, staring at Marnie's place.

She suddenly thought of what Laura had said. The house itself seemed evil. Dark, looming.

She looked back to the water. Mollie was gone. The manatee had swum away.

Chapter 5

They called her the Goddess of Grace.

She loved to dance.

Lord, but she loved to dance.

Swing, dip, strut, stretch, swirl. Dance was in the mind as much as in the body. It was feeling, thought, and emotion. The body was the tool, music the impetus. She knew that she felt the music, the flow, that it touched her in a way that sent her into a different dimension. She was good. Good enough that her dreams had real flight. In her dreams she soared. She was on Broadway. Maybe doing *Cats*. Maybe a revival of *West Side Story*. She was a decent singer, and excellent dancer. She loved to feel the music, feel it invade her body, do the moving for her . . .

Her dance ended. The audience broke into applause. She felt the lights, felt the acclaim, for a moment felt the dream.

Then she opened her eyes.

And saw her audience.

All men. They were disgusting. Old, hairy, middle-aged guys. The kind with gray, grizzled faces, who belched and watched football while guzzling beer and scratching their balls.

"Go, Goddess, go!" someone called.

"Ooh, baby!"

"Closer, closer!"

Closer was the way to get them to stick bills into her

G-string—the last garment she was wearing, other than the long red wig that concealed her natural hair. It was the way to make real money here. Once or twice, when they hadn't been too bad-looking, she had managed to let it happen.

Not tonight. She made enough dancing. She was one of the best the place had ever had.

She grabbed the pole at her side, and fled behind the curtain.

Twenty minutes later, Lacey Henley was sitting at a rear table at Joffrey's, a coffee shop in Coconut Grove, wondering whether or not any of her friends would be appearing. She was much later than she had expected to be. In fact, she was surprised to have found her table free. Though it was late and a lot of the afternoon crowd that often frequented the coffee shop had moved into the bars and clubs for drinks or entertainment, this place was always crowded. Kids loved it; adults loved it. The coffees were really good, and they also made one heck of a milkshake.

She was sipping a milkshake. At twenty, she wasn't old enough to buy a drink in the state of Florida. Though she'd lied about her name on her application at the strip joint, she hadn't lied about her age. Go figure. It was legal for a twenty-year-old to serve drinks or strip, but not to buy a beer herself. Funny, her mom might have understood. Laura had told her about growing up in the last days of Vietnam. They had changed the drinking age to eighteen back then. "Kids were dying, fighting as ordered by their country. It was the right thing to do."

"But no more?" Lacey had asked her.

"You are over eighteen. That means you're adult enough to think on your own. But I heard an idea once that's really important. Responsible freedom. If you're going to drink, you need to be with a designated driver. If you're going to be out late, you need to be careful about where, and who you're with. Make sense?"

It made sense, yes, but what did sense have to do with the law?

Everyone broke the law, of course. Kids out of high school—and in it—could get booze.

And strip.

She took a long sip of her milkshake, ready to burst into tears. Yes, she had made money. But she didn't feel very free, or very responsible.

She shivered then, feeling slightly ill. It was okay, because no one knew. It was the kind of money that would eventually get her to New York, where she could audition to really dance.

If her father didn't catch her.

If he found out what she was up to, he'd kill her.

He would never find out, she assured herself. He never went to the club, his friends never went to the club, no one he knew would ever go to the club. And even if they did, she would never be recognized. Never in a million years. Not with the wig she wore and the makeup she caked on.

"Why, hello! Goddess of Grace, isn't it?"

Stunned, Lacey looked up. A tall, full-figured woman with fluffy long brown hair was looking down at her. The woman held a cup of steaming coffee. She was attractive—thirty-something, Lacey thought, without a stitch of makeup. She was in stretch pants and an oversized shirt, looking comfortable and very sweet.

"Goddess of Grace?" Lacey repeated blankly.

The brunette smiled, taking the chair opposite Lacey. "Honey, I nailed you right away, but I guess you don't recognize me. I'm Tiger Lilly, from the club."

"Ohmygod!" Lacey breathed, all in one word. Tiger Lilly—of course. She did a great little number, Indian fashion. Like Lacey, she covered her hair with a long wig when she danced. And her features were far from innocent at the club. It was amazing what a difference makeup could create in a woman's appearance.

Lacey looked around quickly, feeling her cheeks flame with color. No one knew what she did. No one. Not even Aidan, and she told him almost everything. He took the role of big brother to heart. He would want to drag her off the stage, slug any man looking at her.

"I-I-I—" she began to stutter.

"Oh, honey, I'm sorry!" Tiger Lilly told her softly. Then she giggled. "Don't worry. Your secret is safe with me. I even know your real name—Lacey Henley—and I don't believe it, but you really don't recognize me, do you?"

Lacey stared at her and shook her head.

The woman grinned. She had a cute, mischievous quality to her. A truly friendly smile. Different, of course, from the smile she wore onstage.

"Loretta."

"Loretta?"

The woman lowered her voice again. "Sweetie, you've come into the law office a few times with your mother and Sam to pick Marnie up for lunch. I'm Marnie's assistant."

"Ohmygod," Lacey breathed again, staring hard. Loretta Anderson. Yes. Marnie's efficient, polite, charming assistant. She wore perfectly tailored suits, a smooth chignon, and an aura of serenity and professional calm that was eminently dignified and . . . almost asexual!

"No, I hadn't recognized you, I wouldn't have, I . . ." She broke off, moistening her lips, leaning forward. "Oh, Loretta, please, you mustn't ever say that you know me. I mean, if my family found out—"

"No one will find out!" Loretta promised quickly. She reached across the table, taking Lacey's hands, squeezing them. "Do you think I put my real name on my job application?" She inquired, sitting back, a bit amused now.

"No . . . I . . . guess not," Lacey said. She shook her head. "But you're old!"

"Thanks a lot, kid," Loretta said dryly.

"Oh, God, I'm sorry, I didn't mean that. I mean, I'm not even twenty-one. You have a great job. You can do what you choose to do. And you must be pretty well paid—"

"Yeah, pretty well," Loretta agreed, smiling again. Then she shrugged. "Once, though, I wanted to be a dancer. A real dancer. I was with the ballet, in Cincinnati. And don't go knocking Ohio. It was a great ballet troupe, and I was darned good."

"I believe you. What happened?"

"I broke my ankle. It was never going to go back quite right. Anyway, I couldn't really dance anymore, so I started taking a few law courses, some computer classes . . . and I landed the job with the firm down here."

Lacey shook her head. "But still . . ."

"Why the club? Is that what you're about to ask?"

Lacey grimaced, then smiled. "Yeah. How do you go from *Swan Lake* to Tiger Lilly?"

"How do you think? The same way you did."

"Oh, no, I haven't given up yet!"

Loretta smiled, but looked sad. "Honey, I didn't give up—it was just over. But that's not what I meant. I got my job at the club through the same party, I'm sure, who suggested it to you."

Lacey inhaled sharply. "Marnie?"

"Yep. Marnie."

"I thought no one else knew how she made most of her law school money. She told me she stripped in clubs in Gainesville when she was there with Sam and that Sam didn't even know what she'd really been up to."

Loretta grinned. "You know, one of the nicest things about Marnie—and trust me, she can be a regular witch to work for at times—is that she can be extremely honest.

And funny. When we talked once, I told her that I'd like to finish law school myself. That's when Marnie told me about the club—and that she'd been a stripper at that particular club herself." She paused, was about to say something but stopped herself. Then she went on. "The only way to make the money you really need without giving away hours and hours of labor you can't afford. There's always a method to Marnie's madness, you know."

Lacey laughed, stirring her milkshake with her straw. "That's exactly what she told me. I was complaining once that I'd never get to New York, that I just couldn't afford living there. My mother kept giving me the same old story, you know—try out locally, get a basic education, then go for the dream. She can't comprehend just how old a dancer can get! Marnie came to me and told me about the stripping, saying that she didn't advertise it—wasn't good for her image—but she wasn't ashamed of it either. It got her through law school."

"Are you ashamed of what you're doing?" Loretta asked her.

"No," Lacey said, then reddened. "Yes. Well, I'm not comfortable, let me put it that way. But I don't want to give it up. In a year I might have some real money. You know, it's not that my folks won't help me, but my mother . . . well, she was a mother most of her life, she didn't really make much money and she's just now learning how to make it and handle it herself. And my dad, well, he's a cop, and cops don't make great money. So . . ."

Loretta sipped her coffee. "I've seen you, honey. You've got nothing to be ashamed of. You're putting on a performance, and that's it. You don't go anywhere near those guys."

"I try not to," Lacey admitted. Then she laughed ruefully. "Well, sometimes I go near. When they're not too repulsive." She sighed and felt her cheeks redden again. "You make more money if you let them touch you."

"Yes," Loretta said, sitting back and studying Lacey. "But I do understand what you mean. Sometimes the men and the women. But then . . ." She broke off, hesitating, studying Lacey. "Well, sweet thing, they are just too old and ugly and rotten for you most of the time. Still . . ."

"Still what?" Lacey asked curiously.

"Sometimes I work private parties. There's a man who calls me about them—totally on the up and up. Birthday parties, stag parties, that sort of thing. Nothing any more intimate than what we're up to now, but usually with a clientele that you don't mind having touch a garter— especially when they're touching it with large denominations in good old American green."

"You work a lot of private parties?" Lacey asked.

"Um . . . yes, actually, I prefer the private parties."

"And no one asks you to . . . to do anything other than strip?"

Loretta sat back, shaking her head. "I didn't say they didn't ask. Men will always ask. But they do take no for an answer and accept it. Honey, half the old-timers in the audience couldn't get it up in ten years, but they're men. They feel compelled to ask, to pretend that they're studs. That's life, I suppose. But I've never been pressured to do anything. I've . . ."

"You've what?" Lacey asked innocently.

She was surprised when Loretta was the one to flush then. "Once or twice, when I've been really intrigued . . . I've . . . well, hell, I've said yes. But always on my own terms. You say no, honey, to any of it. You remember that. You are still young. And innocent. You may dance on that stage, but you're as clean as a whistle. There are tens of thousands of women making money that way, and some of them are married and loyal and devoted to their husbands and just as sweet as you."

Lacey just nodded.

"Well, I'm going to get on home. I live just down the

street here. And don't you worry—I swear it. Your secret is entirely safe with me."

"Thanks. And I'll never tell a soul about you, either!" Lacey assured her.

Loretta smiled, rose, and started out of the shop.

"Wait!" Lacey called after her.

Loretta hesitated, then walked back to the table. "What is it, sweetie?"

"When you know about a—a good private party, let me know?"

"Sure thing, kid. Sure thing." Loretta smiled and left.

Lacey stayed at the table. She was still sitting there, when she felt someone shake her shoulder. She looked up. It was Jennie Allen, one of her friends from school. "Earth to Lacey!"

"Jennie!" she exclaimed. With a short-cropped hairstyle, pedal pushers and a midriff sweater, Jennie looked no more than fifteen. Something about her friend's appearance suddenly made Lacey feel strangely old—and not innocent or decent at all.

"Hey!" Jennie said. "Hugh Norman was just telling me that your brother is playing at the Hot Patootie tonight."

"Oh, Lord! That's right! He told me. I was supposed to show up there, and I forgot."

"It's all right. We were thinking about riding out now."

"It's so late—"

"He's with the closing band," Jennie told her. "We'll still be early, actually! Do you have your car here?"

"Yeah, I do—"

"Good. It's the best car between us. You can drive, and bring Hugh and me back here to pick up our cars. Okay?"

"Sounds great."

Aidan nearly fell off the stage.

At first it had seemed that the night was going straight

to the dogs. They were the last band to play—and another local group, Fungus, playing ahead of them, made it all run even later. They'd had trouble with their sound system, and then they'd just played and played. Even on a Saturday night on South Beach, people eventually tired out. Young marrieds had to get home to baby-sitters, teens with fake I.D.'s had to arrive in time for some kind of curfew, and even the legal singles began to wear thin.

His father had come with one of his friends, another cop. Sally Hewitt, a sweet lady who was a detective with homicide as well. She was very slim, short, a waiflike woman with platinum-blond hair. She looked way too delicate to bring down murderers. But then, Aidan knew that it was hard to judge people.

Like the tall, lean, dark guy with the longish hair in the corner. He knew him; he'd seen him before, talked to him before . . . but couldn't quite place him.

His sister had shown up with some friends, and she had smiled in support and he had smiled back.

The real problem was Nellie Green. "Nellie Nightlife," as she styled herself in the papers, did a section on local talent. She dressed bizarrely and rushed around to all the clubs on the beach. There were a few other local newspaper people doing the club beat and local talent as well, and most of the time, they had good words—or at least a decent opinion—for Beowulf, his band. Not Nellie.

Nellie had dated Hogan Landon, their bass guitarist, and she hated Hogan now. Hadn't been Hogan's fault, he had said, and Hogan hated Nellie with a passion as well. So they were in trouble whenever Nellie showed up to cover the band.

Then his mom walked in.

And he very nearly fell off the stage.

She arrived with Rowan Dillon.

He'd met the guy. Once, a long time ago. He'd still been in middle school, he was pretty sure. They'd gone up to Gainesville, where Sam was going to the university, and they'd gone out to dinner with him because Sam had been in love. Then, of course, Rowan had gone back to his wife.

So Aidan had never in a thousand years expected to see Rowan Dillon, once of the famous group Blackhawk, standing in the audience *with his mother,* ready to cheer him on.

The song they were doing ended; there was a smattering of applause—his mother and sister among the most enthusiastic, along with the heavyset drunk at the corner of the bar.

And Rowan Dillon. He lifted a hand to Aidan, a gesture like a friend might make, a longtime friend.

Alex Hernandez, lead guitar, nudged him. He burst back to life, gripping the microphone, thanking the crowd. He hesitated just a minute. Introduce Rowan? No. He didn't know how the guy had gotten here, but he was here, and he was just going to be grateful for it and not tempt fate.

He announced "Bereft," their next song, one he had written with Alex, one of his favorites and, he hoped, one of their best.

The bass started with the hook, the drums popped to life, and the guitars revved up for his vocals. He was still in the middle of the second bridge when ol' Nellie Nightlife made her way over to Rowan Dillon. He wasn't sure what Rowan Dillon said to her, but he spoke quickly, then indicated that he wanted to give his attention to the band. He gave Aidan a thumbs-up sign.

And Aidan smiled, his belief in God suddenly renewed.

"Rowan, I can't thank you enough!" Laura told him sincerely. She was seated in the passenger seat of his

Navigator, her eyes bright, her face illuminated. She twisted toward him. "I mean it."

He smiled, watching the lights as he moved along the causeway. Beautiful. The night was beautiful, with the bridges, the islands, the water reflecting the light in shimmering diamond patterns.

"Laura, honestly, I was happy to come."

She was silent for a moment, then she said, "You were happy to come when you thought Sam was coming."

"It would have been nice," he acknowledged.

"I don't care if you did come just because of Sam—I'm still so grateful."

He laughed. "Laura, look, I'd like a chance to talk to Sam sometime, really talk to her, but I came with you because you're a wonderful promoter—and I really wanted to see your son play. I remember what it's like to start out. I got help now and then. If I can do anything for Aidan—great."

"Oh, but you don't know what you did!" she told him, wide-eyed. "I can't help but be grateful. I mean, Teddy was almost jealous!"

"Well, now, I didn't come to make trouble—"

"Trouble? We're divorced, Rowan."

"I know, but unfortunately a divorce doesn't necessarily mean feelings are neatly resolved. I don't want to play a pawn between you and your ex-husband."

"Don't be silly. I would never do anything like that to you." She grinned. "It was just great to be with someone so sexy and so famous."

"Infamous," he murmured.

"How did my silly cousin ever let you get away? Oh, that's right," Laura said, looking at him innocently, "you were still married. You threw her out."

He looked at Laura, shaking his head. She was an attractive woman, and he really liked her very much. She'd always been straightforward with him.

"It wasn't that simple, and you know it," he told her.

"Of course not."

He glanced at her, arching a brow.

"No, I mean it. Nothing is ever that simple. And you two—you were like a pair of Shakespearean tragedians, determined to do the right thing. But she'll never forgive you, you know. Because however not simple it was, you did turn your back on her, make her feel like a fool. And she really loved you, you know. Humiliation is even more painful when you really love someone. Believe me, I know."

"Laura, I can't undo what happened."

"No, I don't suppose you can. But you realize, she thought, when she first started seeing you, that you were divorced. Sammy has always been so . . ."

"So . . . ?"

"Moral," Laura said, after thinking a moment. "Being the bad guy in the whole thing was so mortifying for her."

"I honestly tried to keep her from getting hurt. Don't you understand? I thought that if I stayed away from her, the media would stay away from her. I tried—"

"You tried too hard. You threw her away."

He gritted his teeth, saying nothing.

"And you were still married. And you went back to your wife."

"Yep."

"And then she died anyway."

"Laura—"

"I'm sorry. We won't get into all that. You were so wonderful tonight. That nasty Nellie girl was there, and you told her that you thought Aidan's group was great. That will make her change her wretched little write-ups!"

"Well, I hope so."

"And I sure hope they have a future. Are they really good, Rowan?"

"Yes, I think so. They're writing some good lyrics, and

it seems as if the group really knows how to play as well. There's a lot of heart in what they're doing. There's nothing manufactured about them. They just need one really catchy song to get played at some stations, and they may hit the charts."

They reached his house. Pulling into the drive, he got out, came around, opened the door for Laura. He walked with her to her car, parked in front of Sam's.

Laura kissed him on the cheek and whispered, "I hope she's going to be jealous as hell."

"Sam?"

"Of course, Sam! She should have come with us tonight."

"But you said she'd never forgive me," he whispered back.

"I don't know. How well can you grovel?"

"I don't grovel; it can never really change anything. I'm sorry as hell that I hurt Sam, but going back, don't you see—I couldn't have changed things. I thought that maybe Dina's life was in my hands. I had no idea at all that I had no power whatsoever," he told her. "I can't beg Sam to understand the position I felt I was in."

"If you'd only managed to really talk to her—"

"Laura, you forget everything that was going on back then."

"Oh, I remember you being arrested—"

"Actually, I was taken in for questioning," he interrupted.

"You got into a big fight with the cops."

He felt a tick in his jaw. "One of those cops is still a good buddy of mine. I got into a fight with two of them who were being assholes, yes, but I honestly didn't mean to do that. I was worried sick, and they were insisting I had to know what had happened to Dina. I guarantee you, I got no apologies when she came back.

Laura chewed on her lower lip. "Remember how Sam

used to love the drums? How natural she was, what a good player?"

"Yeah."

"She hasn't touched them since she left Gainesville."

"That's too bad. No one should ever lose his or her love for music."

"She lost an awful lot. You, her father, the drums."

"I heard about her father. I was so sorry. But as to her music, well, maybe she's only misplaced it."

"Oh, Rowan, I guess I'm being selfish, I would have loved to have had you for a relative. How did you manage to leave it all behind?"

He shrugged, then told her, "I guess I thought I could change the world."

"But you found out that you can't change the world."

"No. I found out that you *can* change the world. What you *can't* change is people."

Laura nodded slowly and smiled with a new understanding.

Rowan looked toward Sam's house. It was quiet and dark. So was Marnie's.

He walked to his own house, fit his key into the lock. He turned back, feeling an odd sensation of being watched.

The night was so still. So dark . . . and ominously silent.

He let himself in.

From out on the water, *he* watched.

It was so intriguing . . . watching people. And he could see so much from the water. People who lived on the bay loved the water, and though they protected themselves with walls in front and gated entries, they would never dream of protecting themselves from the water they loved.

So he could see . . .

Yes . . .

He could see. Into their windows.

Into their lives.

He felt such power. Like a god, omniscient. He did have power. He'd proven it already. Power was the ability to bend others to your will.

Power was life . . .

And death.

The breeze moved so softly, the moon played on the water with gentle, beaming kisses. And looking to the land, he could see . . .

Sam. A silhouette in her window, lithe, slim, watching for something. He couldn't see her features, of course. Just her slender and shapely form as she looked out into the night.

Worried about Marnie?

Or the return of . . .

Her lover.

He moved his binoculars, focusing them on Rowan Dillon's house. It was darkened. He couldn't see. It made him angry. He was strangely disturbed.

He needed to leave; he had business awaiting him, the most entertaining business. And yet . . .

He lingered.

Watching.

She seemed so forlorn. Awake at this late hour. As if she sensed something. Why, it even looked as if she turned . . .

To see him.

But of course she could not. He watched from the darkness. He loved darkness, he had learned to accustom himself to see against ebony shadows. He'd always known that his had to be a realm of shadows.

And still, she searched. He saw the incline of her head, the way she stood. She was a beautiful woman. So intuitive, intelligent, and aware. Watching . . .

As he watched.

Oh, Sam! he thought. *I can see you! I am watching . . .*
Take care, Sam. Take care!

He thought he had come that night to watch Marnie Newcastle's house. To see if there was any commotion yet.

But no . . .

He realized suddenly that he had not come to watch Marnie's house at all. He had come to watch Sam.

Chapter 6

There was something odd about the scene.

Rowan walked out to his front yard to get the paper, and there was a boy. He was perhaps eight to ten years old, a handsome kid with dark hair and a striking face. He stood in front of Marnie's house, in the side yard closer to Sam's place. The boy rocked, back and forth, staring at the house. Curious, Rowan forgot his paper, and sipped from his coffee cup, watching the boy. There seemed to be no real recognition in his eyes; the lad just stood there, watching.

"Hey, you all right, son?" he called.

He might as well have been talking to the moon. The boy continued to stand there, just rocking sideways on the balls of his feet.

"Hey, you okay?" he called again.

And again, no answer. He just stared at Marnie's house.

Had Marnie returned? Rowan doubted it. Watching the boy, he walked to Marnie's door and banged on it. "Marnie! Hey Marnie, you home yet?"

Inside, he knew that she wouldn't respond.

But what was the boy looking at?

Who was the kid? Sam wasn't married, but he had to be Sam's guest—unless he had wandered down from one of the other houses farther along the canal. That would be a long way for such a kid to come.

A short way, he realized, if the boy were a normal eight- to ten-year-old. But this one had something wrong. His heart suddenly went out to the boy. His brother, Ewan, hadn't suffered from the type of neuro disorder that seemed to afflict this child. His difficulties had been physical, and yet, watching this boy, Rowan felt something of the same pull on his soul. The boy looked lost, out of this world, in need of a friendly hand.

The boy's gaze remained fixated on the house.

Rowan started walking to him. "Hey, hello?"

The boy still didn't look at him. He just kept staring at Marnie's place. It was as if he saw something that wasn't there, as if he knew something . . .

"Hey."

Rowan had come right up to him. The lad still didn't respond. Rowan waved a hand in front of his face. Even that gesture went unacknowledged.

But at that moment the door to Rowan's house, left ajar when he had come outside, swung open on a gust of ocean breeze. The sounds of his stereo filtered out to the street, and to the beat of drums and a twang of guitar, the boy turned at last.

He started walking toward Rowan's.

"Music. You like music. All right, that makes you a good man in my book already, son. Come on, there's lots of music in the house. We'll give Sam a call and tell her you're over here. Whoever you are."

Sam sighed with frustration and hung up the phone. An Officer Aldridge had taken her call regarding her request to file a missing-persons report on Marnie. Officer Aldridge had seemed irritated that she had called. He told her she couldn't file a report until the person had been missing for forty-eight hours. Call back tomorrow.

That wasn't good enough. Taking a stab in the dark, she asked if Detective Ted Henley happened to be in.

He was. Teddy told her not to be so worried, that he would come out himself, do the paperwork beforehand and make sure that her concerns were taken seriously the next morning. She thanked him, hung up the phone, kicked the leg of the table, and sighed, still angry with Aldridge.

"Gregory, it's so frustrating!"

Her young friend was back with her because his mother had gone into the hospital—apologetically—for an emergency appendectomy. The phone had rung at eleven—late enough, but since she hadn't slept until the wee hours of the morning, it had seemed like a rude awakening. Gregory had arrived fifteen minutes later. She didn't mind. Despite the fact that he didn't speak, he was good company. She felt like a time bomb, ready to explode. Marnie was gone, no one seemed to listen, and Rowan had moved into the neighborhood and gone clubbing with her cousin. She felt mad enough to throw things.

"Gregory?"

She put the phone down and looked toward the television. He wasn't seated in the chair before it. Her heart leaped instantly into her throat. "Gregory?"

In a panic, she tore through the house, running upstairs and back downstairs. It was then that she realized he had opened the door. Her body froze with fear. The water.

He can swim, he can swim, she reminded herself. Water was a therapy that Gregory loved. Getting him out of the water was sometimes difficult. He had tremendous strength for a boy his age, and when his mind was set and he wanted to stay in the water, it was difficult to convince him that it was time to get out.

But the whole bay was there, endless water where a boy could easily drown . . .

She sped out back. Barely daring to breathe, she looked into the pool. No sight of him. She hurried to the water's edge, terrified that she would see his body, floating face-down. But he wasn't there. She raced around to the front of the house. "Gregory!"

Frightened, she screamed his name. Gregory wasn't just any child; he was more vulnerable than most.

"Gregory!"

She screamed the name again, suddenly feeling a sense of the unreal. First Marnie, now Gregory, disappearing . . .

She looked toward Marnie's house again, thinking of an old episode of *The Twilight Zone* in which a child had fallen beneath his bed and from there been swept into a fifth dimension. His parents could hear his cries, but they couldn't see him, couldn't find him; he had drifted into oblivion.

"Hey!"

She swung around. The call didn't come from Marnie's house, but from next door to it.

Rowan was in his doorway. Again, he was in cutoffs, hair tousled, coffee cup in his hand. "The boy is here."

"What?" she demanded blankly.

"The boy—you're looking for a boy, right? He came over here."

She walked to his house, furious. "How dare you? What the hell is the matter with you, taking an autistic child—"

"Whoa!" he countered, snapping back. "Your autistic child was wandering around by himself. Where were you? I take it you were supposed to be watching him?"

So charged, she caught her breath, backing away. "I was on the phone. With the police," she added defensively.

He arched a brow. "So, anything new?"

She shook her head. "No. The officer I spoke with said that I can't file a report until forty-eight hours have passed." Rowan didn't respond, so she switched back to the original subject.

"I'm sorry to have bothered you. Gregory must have wandered out. He never does. I mean, really, he never does. And you have to understand the child. When he watches a videotape, he doesn't move. I mean, he has never moved. Until—"

"Until today," Rowan supplied. He stood in his doorway, watching her. She felt at a disadvantage, and hated feeling that way. He had just woken up, she thought; he'd showered, slipped on the cutoffs, and run a comb through wet hair. He was relaxed. Unperturbed, sipping coffee. She was a basket case. Showered, yes. Dressed in a comfortable old knit halter dress that was great for the heat. Nearly threadbare. She didn't have on a stitch of makeup. Not the way she wanted to look to see Rowan Dillon.

"You don't understand the child," she said stubbornly, feeling somewhat like a sulky child herself. Her fingers curled into fists at her side. "Well, I apologize. He is my responsibility. I'll take him back now—"

Rowan shrugged. "Fine. Come in and get him."

She stared at him. He backed away from the door and grinned.

" 'Come into my house, said the spider to the fly!' " he taunted softly. Then he asked more seriously, "Are you afraid of me, Sam?"

"No, of course not!" she snapped. But then she shook her head. "Yes, maybe I am. A little time with you and suddenly my name is mud, and to the whole world, at that."

"I'm sorry. I did try to keep that from happening."

"Did you?" she murmured. Then she was sorry she'd voiced the question because she didn't want to discuss the answer. "It seemed that once my name was mud, all you did was scrape me off your boots."

"That wasn't the case at all, Sam, damn it. I—"

"Look, please, sorry, I shouldn't have spoken. It

doesn't matter, it's in the past. I'll just get Gregory and be on my way."

"Stay and have some coffee," he suggested.

"No, thanks."

"Why not? We are neighbors."

"Yes, but you're the one who pointed out that I didn't even need to wave from the lawn if I didn't want to."

"But Gregory is enjoying himself. Have some coffee."

"Look, I—"

"Take a chance," he taunted. "What are you afraid of? That you won't be able to resist my raw sexuality and we'll simply start back where we left off?"

"No!"

"Good," he said, and grinned. "There is a child in the house."

"You're impossible. Rude and conceited—"

"Then you'll have no trouble resisting me, and a cup of coffee will be fine."

She let out a sigh of exasperation and stepped into the foyer.

The house was nice. Paneled with warm woods, decorated with earthtones. It was much bigger than her own, yet it somehow had the same quality. Her parents had always made the house a home, not a showplace. Children could play at her house. Rowan's place, though wonderfully neat—far neater than her own—still had a comfortable feeling. He hadn't been here long, but it already bore a mark of his personality.

"Cream, sugar—" he began.

"No!" she said, almost barking out the word. She didn't want to think that his house was comfortable, that there was anything nice about it. She was afraid of him, afraid that it felt far too natural to be near him.

"Sorry," he said, ignoring her tone. "I should have remembered the way you like your coffee—"

"No, you shouldn't have remembered anything!" she

assured him. She tried to keep her voice and tone low, aware that her tension was growing. "Really, I don't want to stay, I don't want to talk. I want to get Gregory and go home. And honestly, Rowan, I'm not sure how to say this without being rude, so I will be rude. You made my life hell. I really don't want to know you again, I really wish you had bought property elsewhere."

He stood still, watching her. His eyes seemed shaded, a look she had seen before. "I'm sorry. I didn't know that I was ruining your neighborhood. No one mentioned that you lived here until I'd moved in." His tone was far from apologetic.

"Well, perhaps you'll discover a real dream house somewhere else now that you're down here."

"No, I don't think so. I like my house just fine." He smiled. "Maybe you'll move," he said politely.

She gritted her teeth. "Perhaps you could just take me to Gregory."

"Fine," he said softly. "Come this way."

He walked downstairs to the basement of the house, the level facing onto the pool. He had a drum set and keyboards in a large room, along with all manner of amplifiers, guitars, recording devices, and a grand piano. Rowan, she remembered with a pang, could play anything, though he liked the piano best. He wrote music on his piano, an old one. It had been his mother's, she knew, and he had brought it with him from Scotland.

Gregory was sitting at the piano. Seeing him there immediately sent a wave of guilt rushing through Sam. It was Rowan's beloved piano, one of the few material items he really cherished. And he had allowed Gregory to play it.

The boy's fingers were moving lovingly over the keys. He was playing one of Aidan's songs. As always the fact that he could listen to a piece and instantly pick it up amazed her. So often he didn't respond to his own name.

His parents thought themselves blessed. Autism covered
such a wide range of behavioral problems, the Lacatas
were just grateful that Gregory had music as a language.
He was so beautiful when he played. She knew that his
parents went through terrible times of frustration. He
would learn a few words, he would forget them. He
would like a certain food, then he would refuse to eat it.
Certain days he functioned well, other days he didn't. But
he always loved his music.

And he was enjoying himself—just as Rowan had said.
She had been blunt and rude—her right, of course—but
she was suddenly remorseful, anxious that Rowan like
Gregory, and continue being kind to him.

"He—he really won't hurt your equipment," she heard
herself explaining. "He loves music. Honestly, he won't
hurt—"

"Obviously," Rowan interrupted firmly.

Startled, she found herself trying to explain the situation again. "He's autistic, but he's what they call a—"

"Savant," Rowan supplied.

"Yes," she murmured. Gregory hadn't given any indication that he had noticed the arrival of either of them. He
looked perfectly normal playing the piano.

"One out of about ten thousand," he said.

"What?"

"Autistics. People tend to think that more of them
should be savants, that because of their disorder they
have greater powers of concentration. Maybe they all do.
No one knows yet. But the statistics state that only one
out of every ten thousand children afflicted with autism is
a true savant. This lad seems to be one of the few."

Startled that Rowan understood Gregory's condition,
she felt grudgingly compelled to give him an apology. Not
that she wanted him to think she had any desire to create

so much as a casual friendship between the two of them again, but this fell in the category of common decency.

"You should watch your instruments down here. If we have any kind of a storm with flooding, this level of the house does sometimes get drenched."

He nodded, watching her. "So I've heard. I'll be sure to pull this all out if we get any kind of a weather warning. Thanks."

Sure."

She stood awkwardly, wondering how she was going to get Gregory away from an instrument he so obviously loved. She needed to be in control here.

"He's welcome to stay here for a while."

"He's my responsibility."

"His folks are relatives or friends?"

"Friends. His mother is in the hospital. Emergency surgery."

"Look, you may not like me, but I am dependable with children. He's welcome to stay and play the piano until he tires of it."

She exhaled on a long breath, possessively wanting to keep an eye on Gregory but equally concerned regarding Marnie. "I just want to file a report on Marnie."

"She still hasn't shown up?"

"No."

"Well, it is still the weekend."

"I don't care. I know Marnie."

She watched Gregory, and she suddenly wanted the same freedom. She wanted to walk over to the drum set and play. Her fingers itched to play the drums. She wanted to touch . . .

She wanted to be touched.

Arguing was better. Safer. The urge to do so was irrational and immature, but it was sure there. "You're sure it's all right if he stays a while? He's different—"

"It'll be all right."

"I won't be long."

"Take your time. We'll both be fine."

"You'll bring him back the moment he loses interest?"

"Yes."

"All right." She hesitated uncomfortably; it was obvious to them both that she didn't want to be indebted to Rowan in any way. His features remained implacable. "Thanks," Sam said at last, and she turned and started toward her own house.

Gregory had never noticed that she had come or gone.

Ted Henley drummed his fingers on the desk, feeling tension knot every muscle in his body. Sam was all concerned, but she knew Marnie. Hell, Marnie was the type of woman who lived by her own rules. She might be anywhere, go anywhere, with anyone—on the slightest whim.

He'd told Sam that he would come out to her place himself, fill out the report himself, make sure that the force paid attention. It wasn't his job. He was in homicide. But he'd worked a lot of different types of investigations before he'd become homicide. He'd been a detective with the domestic abuse unit, he'd worked with larceny, and he'd worked missing persons as well. Missing persons could be such a crapshoot. All too often, worried relatives reported a person who was just off on a joyride. Maybe it was the modern world. Stress got to a banker, and he left everything to go off surfing in California for a week, even though he'd never surfed before. Teens disappeared by the dozens. Sometimes they were runaways. Sometimes they came home. Sometimes they were victims of violence, and they were never found, and their parents spent the rest of their lives wondering, praying, hoping, and always fearing the worst.

The station was quiet. He didn't usually work on Sundays, unless something unexpected came up on one of his team's specific cases, but after last night, seeing Laura at the club with Rowan Dillon, he'd been so restless, he had needed something to do.

And he had plenty of work waiting for him.

Specifically, he had some paperwork to fill out on the last case they'd presented to the D.A.'s office. Simon Ridley had killed his common-law wife and stuffed her in the dumpster. He'd thought himself free and clear of the crime. Despite the fact that his prints had been found on the dumpster, the prints weren't out of place there—the dumpster belonged to his apartment complex. And at first they hadn't been able to get any prints off the black plastic garbage bags he had taped around the corpse. But Sally had known about a technique being used by the Royal Canadian Mounted Police. Their captain had sent the bags up to Canada for help from the Mounties—and voila! The Canadians had gotten them a good set of latent prints, and now the D.A. had plenty of evidence to take Simon Ridley to court.

Ridley had been so smug. Teddy Henley felt a slight shiver snake along his spine. Normally, it was dismal to think about how hard the cops worked and how many criminals got away anyhow. Because of lawyers like Marnie.

No matter what, she was trouble.

Just like that office of hers was trouble. There was a specialist for everything at Marnie's firm. A guy for real estate, for divorce, for taxes, for traffic violations, personal injury, rape, robbery, and murder. Marnie herself dealt with the worst of the lot. He'd warned her time and again to watch out for her clients.

But then, talking to Marnie had always been useless. She was a lawyer. She knew how to insinuate, and how to threaten. And how to make a man do just about anything.

He pushed his chair back, stood, reached for his jacket,

and braced himself. He would be asking Sam a lot of questions.

Unfortunately, he was rather afraid of the answers regarding Marnie Newcastle that he harbored in his own heart.

Chapter 7

When Sam returned to her house, she was surprised to see that Laura was there, leaning against her car, waiting for her to reappear. She was wearing sunglasses, a hat, a cool top and shorts.

"Hey!" Laura said, rising, noting the direction from which Sam had come, and smiling. "Ah, at last! You brought the neighborhood welcome wagon to Rowan's house."

Sam opened her front door and walked through, Laura following her. "No," she said flatly, heading on into the kitchen and mechanically putting coffee on to brew.

"You were at Rowan's?"

Sam measured out some coffee. "Gregory slipped out when I was on the phone. Somehow, he wound up over at Rowan's."

"He must have heard music," Laura said.

Sam shrugged. "It's something they have in common. Oh, by the way, your ex is on his way over here."

"Why?" Laura asked, frowning.

Sam felt a little guilty. "He's going to take a missing persons report on Marnie for me."

"Teddy is going to do that?" Laura inquired incredulously.

"Yes. Why? I mean, he's still a cop. He did work missing persons at one time."

"Yes, but now he's too cool for anything minor. He works homicide."

"Well, he's here," Sam said, as the doorbell rang.

Laura stiffened. "Already?" she said.

"I imagine."

Laura forced a smooth smile to her face. She floated to the front door and threw it open. "Teddy! This is so sweet of you. You know, of course, Sam is so concerned about Marnie, though personally, I'm not sure why."

"Hey, Laura," Teddy said, taking his ex-wife's hands and kissing her cheeks. He nodded past her to Sam, who had come out to greet him as well. "Hey, Sam."

"Hey, Teddy," she returned. "And thanks for coming. Aldridge was a jerk."

Teddy shrugged. "He's really not being such a jerk. It's just the forty-eight-hour rule. Tell me why you're so worried, then I'll start with the paperwork, okay?"

"Sure. Coffee?"

"Sure, I can always use a cup of coffee, I'm a cop, right?"

"Hmm. Let's get some donuts, and he can really feel as if he's working hard!" Laura said dryly.

Teddy frowned, cocking his head as he studied her. "And I was about to say that you look like a million bucks."

"Really?" Laura asked pleasantly. "You look good, too. But then, you're a man, and men don't age the same, huh? Those pooching guts don't begin to compare with cellulite thighs."

"My gut doesn't pooch," Teddy said.

"And my thighs are becoming toothpicks."

"I told you, I was about to say that you look good today."

"Right. Because yesterday I looked like crap."

"Children!" They were bickering like a pair of kids.

Maybe they had married too young. "Children . . ." Sam repeated with a mock sigh.

Then she remember how she had felt at Rowan's. Sometimes it was easier to fight than to feel. It was just natural instinct to strike back when you'd been hurt.

"Speaking of children, where were you last night?" Teddy asked Sam. "You're usually always there, moral support for our children, and you didn't come out to see Aidan last night."

"I—" Sam began, then broke off. She liked Teddy, and he was doing her a favor, but he had, at one time, badly insulted his wife and cheated on her. Few breakups were one-sided, but she had to stand behind Laura on this one. Sam smiled sweetly. "Well, Laura had a date who was knowledgeable about music and ready for a night out at the beach. She didn't need me."

"Did you sleep here—at Sam's?" she heard Teddy ask Laura. It was amazing how they could both continue to be so jealous of one another.

"No. Not at Sam's," Laura said and came on into the kitchen ahead of Teddy. "Aidan was just great, wasn't he?"

"Yeah. Our son was great," Teddy said flatly. He was irritated. Laura must be loving it. "Okay, Sam, let's get down to business. When did you last talk to Marnie?"

"Friday night," Sam said, pouring coffee. Then she hesitated, looking at her cousin. "Actually, it's a good thing you're here, Laura. You were the one who talked to her last."

"Me?"

"Yes, on the phone, remember?"

"Oh, of course!"

"Well, then, Laura, what did she say? Think hard. Was there any indication she might be going away? Did she tell you her plans—was she going to come over, was she going out?"

Laura related what they'd said, that Marnie couldn't come over because she had a date that night.

"She already had plans?"

"That's what she said."

"With who?" Teddy asked, staring at his ex-wife, loosening his tie and collar.

"I don't know," Laura told him. "She wouldn't say. I think some workmen arrived while we were talking—oh, man, I'm not sure exactly what she said at all anymore. I think she told me she was going to go yell at someone— her date, the workmen, I don't know. Because in the end, she just hung up on me."

Teddy lifted a hand and looked at Sam. "Sam, I'm writing down all the specifics, and I'll take a cruise through her house, I'll put out bulletins, and I'll see that a couple of good guys are put on this investigation, but honestly, don't you think she might have gone out with some guy, found out that he was the hunk she's looked for all her life, and spent the weekend with him?"

Sam sipped coffee. She shook her head. "Teddy, you don't know Marnie."

"Sam, we all know Marnie."

"It's frightening just how many people seem to know Marnie," Laura said.

"She adores that house. Like you said, we all know Marnie. She would have made her date, no matter how hot and heavy, come back to her house."

"Maybe, Sam, maybe not," Teddy said. "Look, where can I work, fill out some papers?"

"Right there."

She directed him to her desk, and Teddy took papers out of his jacket and sat down. He began to fill in the simple statistics of Marnie's life—her name, age, address, height, weight, eye color, hair color, and so on and so on.

"Okay, Laura, talk to me again," Teddy told his ex-wife.

"Why?"

"Because you may have forgotten something."

Despite her aggravation, he made Laura describe her conversation with Marnie over and over again. "You know, come to think of it, at the time I thought she was maybe yelling at Phil Jenkins, her contractor or, like I said, one of the workers . . . or someone. I don't know if she said good-bye to me, or just left me on hold, or completely forgot I was there. But in the end, she hung up on me."

"You're sure that the connection was broken?" Teddy asked.

"Yes."

"So you think that someone was definitely in the house with her?" Teddy said sharply.

"Well . . . I guess. I mean, someone must have been. Even if she just went out for her date, he would have come for her, right? Maybe there were a number of people in the house. One of her workers . . . a few of her workers, and her date. I don't know," Laura said. She threw up her hands. "I guess someone came for her."

"Or," Sam said, "someone came after her." She hesitated for a minute. "Teddy, this may sound silly to a man, but her makeup was out of order."

"You mean, knocked down, thrown around the room?" Teddy said.

"No . . . it was, well it was all perfectly arranged, but out of order. 'The Devil's Own Red' wasn't in the right place." He was just staring at her. "Marnie aligns everything, Teddy."

He stared at her. "All right. 'The Devil's Own Red' was out of order."

She gritted her teeth, ready to slam her head against the wall. He was patronizing her. Men just didn't get it.

"Someone came after her!" she repeated softly, and the way Teddy looked at her then, she wondered if he did understand.

Gregory played for an hour, song after song.

Rowan sat at the drums, just keeping a beat, and followed his lead.

Gregory completed every work that he started, but the order of his songs didn't seem to follow any pattern. He played some things Rowan recognized as Aidan's original music from the night before, and he played a bunch of old-time hits by the Beach Boys and then Queen. Then he played Americana songs, "The Star-Spangled Banner" and "Battle Hymn of the Republic." He played a Christmas carol. Then, just as suddenly as he started, he stopped. Throughout his playing his face had never shown emotion. He had just gone from song to song—and then stopped.

"That was nice," Rowan told him. He didn't know if Gregory had heard him or not.

The boy stood up, turned toward the back of the house, the pool, and the bay beyond. He started walking out. Rowan followed him.

He came to the docks and stared down. For a moment Rowan was afraid that he was going to jump in. He didn't jump; he just waited. Rowan stood next to him, not touching him but ready to grab for him if he made any attempt to go in. He didn't know if the boy could swim or not, and he didn't want to take any chances.

"The water is great, huh?" Rowan said to him.

Then he was startled when Gregory spoke, pointing at the water. "Mollie," he said.

Looking down into the water, Rowan saw the sea cow. "Wow!" he said to Gregory, and bending down, Rowan flattened himself on the small wooden dock. The sea cow was a fair size, long and weighing several hundred pounds. She appeared as if she should be an awkward creature, gray, bloated-looking, with whiskers and huge dark eyes. She swam in and out around the pilings, in no hurry to get away.

"Mollie!" he said, rolling to look up at Gregory. "She's great, just great, really beautiful. I didn't know that my place came with a personal sea cow!"

Gregory didn't smile, but he still seemed to realize that Rowan was there with him and that Rowan liked the sea cow as well. He stared into Rowan's eyes.

"Mollie," Gregory said. He closed his eyes.

"Yes, Mollie. Mollie is the sea cow, right?"

Gregory looked out across the bay. "Marnie," he said then. It was almost a whisper, so softly spoken it might not have been real.

And still Rowan felt as if his heart skipped a beat. "Marnie? I thought you were showing me the sea cow. And you called her Mollie."

Gregory slowly lifted an arm and pointed. He pointed across the bay. He opened his mouth as if he were about to say something.

But he didn't. His arm lowered. His head lowered. He looked into the bay. "Mollie!" he said distinctly.

"Mollie, not Marnie," Rowan said. "Marnie lives next door. In that house. Have you seen Marnie, Gregory?"

But Gregory wasn't looking at Rowan anymore. He started walking back across the yard, then through the side yard to the front of the houses. Rowan followed him.

"Time to go back to Sam's," Rowan said.

Gregory moved at a brisk pace through his yard and across Marnie's front yard. He had very nearly reached Sam's place when he stopped dead.

And he stared up at Marnie's house.

"No, no, we're not going to Marnie's house. We're going to Sam's," Rowan said.

Gregory continued to stand stock-still, staring at the house.

"Come on, time to go back to Sam's."

He touched the boy's arm.

And then Gregory pointed at the house and began to scream. It was a terrible, high-pitched sound, like an alien being from *Invasion of the Body Snatchers*. He just kept pointing and screaming.

"Gregory, Gregory! It's all right—"

Sam, Laura, and Teddy came flying out Sam's front door, all rushing over.

"Christ Almighty!" Teddy swore. "What did you do to the boy?"

"What?" Rowan demanded, astonished and outraged. "I didn't touch him. He just started screaming."

"Gregory, Gregory!" Sam said, approaching him. She put her arms around him. He struggled wildly, with such strength that Rowan thought he would hurt her. But Sam was strong herself, far more powerful than her slim build implied. She held Gregory tightly until he went limp in her arms.

"You must have done something to him!" Teddy said.

"I didn't do anything. He started back toward Sam's on his own, then stopped here and started screaming. I tried to take him by the hand to urge him on toward Sam's," Rowan explained, trying to hold his temper. Teddy was studying him suspiciously. Laura had stopped some distance back, not willing to interfere.

"Come on, Gregory," Sam soothed. "Come on, we'll go on in. We'll turn on the *Lion King,* we'll take out your crayons. We'll get your pillow."

Sam looked at Rowan over Gregory's head. He couldn't read her gaze. Was she accusing him of having hurt the boy somehow as well? He felt a stabbing sensation in his gut and forced himself to return her stare. She had absolutely unique eyes. Their color was ever-changing.

Yellow, gold, amber . . . then, at times, surprisingly green. And they still seemed so amazingly clear, honest—and demanding of honesty in return. She looked young, innocent, fragile, in a tank top and shorts.

She wanted no assurances from him. She'd made that very clear.

He turned away from her.

"Were you able to take down the report on Marnie Newcastle?" he asked Teddy.

"Yeah," Teddy said, then added flatly, "Of course, I— or someone else—will need to get a statement from you."

"I thought you were homicide."

"I am."

"But you've got a special concern here?"

"Marnie was a friend."

"Was?"

Teddy flushed. "Marnie is a friend. Yes, I've got a special concern here. Sam is very upset, and she's family—"

"*Was* family," Rowan suggested.

"I'll be talking to you. That's a guarantee."

"Oh?"

"Oh, yeah. About the last time you saw her, if anything suspicious went on around here, you know, the usual."

"Yeah, right," Rowan said. "I haven't lived here all that long."

"Sure. But you did know Marnie, right? You must have known her—fairly well."

"Yeah. I knew Marnie," he said. "Come talk to me anytime you want."

He turned away, fully irritated now, and started across Marnie's yard toward his own with long, angry strides.

"Ro-wan!"

The calling of his name stopped him. It wasn't pronounced clearly, but rather was drawn out, with the *w* totally silent. He turned back, startled that Gregory had mouthed his name at all.

To his amazement, the boy came to him and hugged him. He hugged the boy back. After a moment Gregory let him go.

Sam walked over and took Gregory by the hand. She eyed Rowan curiously. For once, she was so surprised that her hostility was gone. Her eyes were very wide and green, searching. "He doesn't even say my name," she admitted ruefully.

He shrugged, absurdly pleased. "Well, he knows the sea cow, Mollie."

She arched a brow. "You saw Mollie? And Gregory—said her name?"

"Yes, why, has he never done that before?"

She shook her head. "No, no, he has said Mollie's name before. There was a time when he talked a little for a while . . . then he just stopped. He did say Mollie's name before."

"What about Marnie's?"

"What?"

"Did he ever call Marnie by name? He must have known her, right?"

"Yes, he knew her," Sam said. "Why?" she asked, frowning. "Was he saying her name today?"

What did he say now? Rowan wondered. Had he really heard Gregory say "Marnie," or had he just thought he had heard the name when the boy had really been talking about the sea cow?

But then again, Gregory had pointed at Marnie's house and started screaming.

"Sam," Teddy said, walking up. "Sam, don't go getting ideas because this poor little retard is staring at her house. He stares for hours at all kinds of things!"

"Teddy, I hope to hell that you don't have political aspirations!" Sam returned angrily. "That has to be one of the most insensitive statements I've ever heard."

"Sam—" Teddy began sheepishly.

"Was he saying her name?" Sam demanded of Rowan.

Rowan saw a ray of hope in Sam's eyes. She had instinctively defended Gregory, but she was hoping as well that the boy could help her find Marnie. Rowan felt a strange tightening in his stomach. God, but he could remember that look in her eyes. The light that shone in them, the innocence, the belief, the simple beauty. He didn't want her to start thinking that Gregory could point the way to a magical answer, either.

"Gregory is autistic, Sam. Different. No, he didn't say Marnie's name."

Sam's lashes swept her cheeks. "Thanks for watching him," she said briefly.

"My pleasure. Honestly. I enjoyed having him. I even played along with him for a while. He's a great guy to jam with, a fine musician. No trouble at all."

"Come on, Gregory, Laura." Then, while speaking to the boy, she looked first at Rowan, and then at Teddy Henley. "Personally, Gregory," she said, curling her fingers into his, "I think that you, the young autistic child, are far brighter than any of the grown, so-called mentally able men around here!"

She walked firmly across the lawn, the boy's hand in hers, Laura following in her wake. They disappeared into Sam's house, Laura looking back apologetically as she closed the door behind them.

Teddy stared at Rowan again. Rowan stared back. Rowan smiled suddenly.

"We both knew Marnie, didn't we?" he asked quietly.

Ted Henley flushed. "Knew her?" he queried. "Do you know something I don't know?"

"No. No, I don't."

"Maybe you should know this—I am a cop. Push me too far, and I'll push back. I can take you down for questioning."

"Can you? Great. Good for you. Hey, go right ahead, arrest me."

"If it winds up there's a homicide here, you can bet I will."

"Are you suggesting that there was a homicide?"

"Maybe there are a lot of people who wouldn't want Marnie talking," Ted said.

"Are you one of them?" Rowan asked steadily.

Ted Henley stood very tensely, staring at Rowan. "Fuck you," he said at last.

"Are we going to have a brawl, right here on Marnie's lawn?"

"You'd be assaulting an officer."

Rowan grinned. "Well, I've been taken in before on far more ridiculous charges."

"I'm a cop. I'm in damn good shape."

"So am I, though I'm a musician, not a cop. You'd be surprised. Never really wanted to get into a fight, but then, there's life for you. I've been in plenty of fights before. Maybe it's a Scottish thing."

Teddy waved a hand at him. "Fuck you!" He stared maliciously at Rowan a moment longer. Then he, too, walked back toward Sam's house.

He entered where Rowan knew he himself wasn't welcome, and the door slammed in his wake.

Chapter 8

Sam tried calling Marnie's that night and then again when she rose at six the next morning. If Marnie had come home from a wild, late weekend, she would have a few choice words for Sam. That would be fine. Same would live with it. But Marnie didn't answer her phone. She could have come in and gone right to sleep, but Sam knew that hadn't happened. As rude as Marnie could be, she would have called Sam once she'd seen her notes.

Teddy would already have the paperwork going. There was little else she could do. She went to work early, and she was glad. She had a Peter Hubert to work with, his first day of walking therapy after a bout with colon cancer. He was a distinguished-looking fellow of about sixty-five, cheerful, grateful that it appeared his cancer had been caught. She spent half an hour on a walker next to him, leading him through an easy, continuous pace. He did fine. In the days to come, they would add more distance.

Next was Jodie Larson, a beautiful sixteen-year-old whose leg had been mangled in a car crash. She'd gone through a dozen painful surgeries to save the limb, and now she worked with the same determination to see that she was able to keep it. Jodie had been in therapy a while. They ran a good mile together, went on to a bike, then to the stair machine.

She hated the stair machine. She never did it unless a

client needed to build leg muscle. In her opinion, walking, bikes, and a number of the new multifunction machines were much better for slimming legs than stair machines.

But long after Jodie had left, she was still on her stair machine. She didn't even realize it until she heard a voice break in on her thoughts.

"Honey, give yourself another hour, and you'll disappear into thin air. What in God's name are you doing?"

She turned to see Joe Taylor, her partner at the Energy Workout and Physical Therapy Center, leaning against the next machine over. No, he wasn't exactly leaning. He was posing. He looked casual enough, but she knew Joe. He was a good-looking guy with the kind of brown hair he described as *sable,* powder-blue eyes, a ruggedly square jaw, and a body to die for—if you didn't mind the fact that the magnitude of his muscles seemed to leave him with no neck.

Not fair, she told herself. She loved medical therapy herself. To her, the body was the most fantastic machine, with more amazing features than anything mechanical that man could ever make. She loved the healing process, and she loved to see people who had been terribly sick grow strong and confident again. But she did like to make a decent living, and Joe's charm brought young women flocking in for his tutelage. He also could be a no-nonsense ball-buster when giving someone the facts about losing weight and getting in shape. They sold all kinds of energy drinks and food bars, but to his credit, Joe pushed water. He pushed *free* water out of their fountain. No fluid on earth was better at cleansing the body. Drink, drink, drink, always drink while working out.

"I'm not likely to disappear," she said, but she grabbed her towel from the bars of the machine, threw it around her shoulders, and stepped down.

"Then you'll simply drown us all in sweat!" Joe said,

grimacing. "Your hair is plastered to you. What's up? I have never seen you stay on a step machine so long. Never."

"I'm worried about Marnie."

"What?"

He didn't say "who," she noticed. He said "what"?

"I'm worried about Marnie."

"Marnie Newcastle?"

"Yeah."

"Why?"

"Well, I talked to her Friday night, but not since."

"Friday night? So?"

She sighed. It seemed that no one understood. "Marnie loves her new place. She's as proud as a peacock over it—"

"She's as proud as a peacock over the simple matter of being Marnie Newcastle!"

Sam arched a brow, then decided that it wouldn't be tactful to suggest that his comment was like the pot calling the kettle black.

"She probably had a hot date Friday night," Joe continued.

"How do you know? Did she go out with you?"

Impatiently, he shook his head.

"Then what makes you think she had a hot date?"

"Because she's Marnie Newcastle. And men are disposable. They should be used, then spit out, flushed down the john of the past."

"Joe, I thought the two of you—"

"Yeah, we got along fine—until she realized that I really meant nothing to you."

"Oh, Joe!" Sam protested, but he put up a hand. "Listen, kid, we're good partners, good friends, and you're a real beauty, baby, but we didn't have the chemistry, huh? That's good, 'cause we're in this place together for the long haul. But I'm telling you, I think your friend did want to take something away from you. That's the kind of woman she is."

"Joe!"

"Sorry, but that's how I feel. Shut your jaw—our clients will start to notice. Oh, by the way, you got a phone call."

"Who was it?"

"Said her name was Loretta. She's Marnie's assistant. The one with the great boobs. And real ones at that."

"Thanks, Joe."

Sam shook her head in bewilderment and started for her office. Once inside, she swept the towel over her face again, picked up the phone, and called a familiar number. "Hello, this is Samantha Miller."

"Hi, Miss Miller. This is Loretta Anderson. You know, Miss Newcastle's assistant."

"Yes, of course. Hi, Loretta. Has Marnie come in yet?"

"No, and I'm getting worried. She never misses her appointments. She had a ten o'clock with Mr. Chapman this morning—you know, the fellow who *allegedly* shot down three of his business associates?"

"Yes," Sam said. "I've seen the case in the news."

"Well, she just never fails to show up. You haven't seen her or heard from her, have you?"

"No, I'm afraid I haven't. But I had a missing-person report filled out on her yesterday. My cousin's ex-husband, who is a detective from way back, took the information. I'm sure that someone from the police will be in to see you about the situation soon."

"I'll call them," Loretta said determinedly.

"Actually," Sam said, "I wish you would. Everyone keeps telling me that Marnie probably went off on a lark. If you stress the fact that I've tried to press home—that Marnie's just too ambitious to go off on a lark—it may make them pay more attention."

"Of course, I will! Oh, dear, do you mean to tell me the police won't take this situation seriously?"

"No, no, I'm not saying that exactly," Sam murmured. "Ah, Loretta, I know I'm imposing . . . but could you possibly meet me for lunch? Maybe if I talked to you, I could see things more clearly."

"Things?" Loretta said.

"Things . . . like the things that went on last Friday," Sam said.

"I'd be delighted to meet you for lunch. When? Where?"

"Monty's on Bayshore. Outside? In an hour?"

"Sure."

"Bye," Sam said.

She checked her calendar for her afternoon appointments. Jill Landers, Sandy Oakmen, both workout sessions, nothing medical, or critical, about them. She punched in her receptionist's line. "Didi, reschedule my afternoon for me, will you?"

"Sure," Didi Sugarman said. The name sounded right for a teenybopper who smacked gum. Didi was sixty-three, slim, silver-haired, and dependable as the earth turning on its axis. She was a great asset, and Sam prayed that she wouldn't want to retire until she was very, very old.

"Thanks, Didi."

She hung up. A few minutes later, she had showered, dressed, and left the facility. The gym wasn't far from her home, and Monty's wasn't far from the gym. In fact, she could see the back of her house across the water from Monty's.

It didn't take her long to find a parking place. She glanced at her watch as she got out of her car, and saw that she was almost exactly on time.

Once inside, she easily spotted Loretta sitting alone at a table. She was a big woman, both tall and built. Stacked. She had a Jayne Mansfield figure. Pretty features. But then again, she dressed sedately. No makeup, and her hair was knotted into a severe twist at the back of her head. Sam thought that the look was strategic. Because of the way she was shaped, if she freed her hair and wore slightly daring clothing she would look . . . very sexy.

A young waitress appeared as Sam sat down.

"Hi. Iced tea for me, please," Sam said.

"I have one," Loretta told the girl.

"I know," the girl said, hiding her boredom. "Just let me know when you want to order."

"The fresh fish sandwich for me, honey."

"I'll take the same," Sam said quickly. She didn't care what she had to eat. She wanted to hear what Loretta had to say.

The waitress smiled, told them that she'd get Sam's tea right away and put their order in, and left them.

The two women talked for a bit, exchanging pleasantries, until Loretta said, "So, what did you want to know?"

"I'd like to know what happened on Friday. I talked to Marnie—no, actually, my cousin talked to her—about dinnertime that night. So whatever happened . . ."

"Yeah, whatever happened had to happen after that. So you want to know what happened during the day? We had a big lunch celebration, I remember that."

"What was the celebration for?"

"The real estate deal."

"What real estate deal? Marnie doesn't do real estate."

"The one by your place, the house next door to Marnie's. Eddie Harlin had done all the work, of course, but Marnie had suggested that he show the place to Rowan Dillon when she'd first heard that Rowan was looking for property down here. She'd known him. They were old friends. Did you know that?"

Somehow Loretta had missed the tabloids when Sam's

own picture had been slapped on a page alongside Rowan's.

"Yes, I knew that."

"Well, anyway, it was a big sale. Eddie came to lunch, and Mr. Daly, because he was so proud of Eddie. And Kevin, Kevin Madigan, of course, because he works with Marnie so often."

"And Marnie was at lunch?"

"Right, and Rowan Dillon, and—"

"Rowan Dillon went to lunch on Friday with Marnie?"

"Yes, of course, along with all the others I'm telling you about—he was the one who had bought the property."

"So, did anything odd happen, that you saw?"

"No, things were fine. It was a little false, because it was business, but I didn't notice anything."

Sam was frustrated. This was getting her nowhere. "Loretta, do you happen to know if Marnie had planned on going out on Friday night?"

"She likes to party on the weekend, you know that."

"But did she have any specific plans? With any man in particular?"

Loretta hesitated, then shook her head. "Sorry, she didn't say anything."

"Well, well, if it isn't two lovely ladies . . ."

Loretta was startled by the deep voice. It sounded like . . . She spun around and saw who was coming toward them. No, it wasn't the same.

Sam turned to see as well. It was Joe. He was in cutoffs and a tank top, an outfit that made him look ready for a photo shoot for summer casuals. He was tanned and sleek, and muscles bulged everywhere.

"Joe!" she said blankly.

"So we're both playing hooky from work." He made a face. "Actually, I heard you tell Didi you were running over here. I was hoping I could find you and join you. I

just didn't feel like eating alone. I'm sorry. I didn't realize
you were meeting a friend."

"It's okay. You're not intruding," Sam lied. She wondered if her cheeks were as red as they felt.

But Joe had already turned toward Loretta. "Why,
Miss Anderson, I have seen you before, at your office."

"You have?" Loretta asked, flustered. "I've seen you,
of course. But I hadn't realized you'd ever noticed me."

"How could I not notice you?"

Joe smiled. He was being very charming. Sam didn't
know whether to be amused or exasperated.

"Well, meeting you again—formally—has made it a
true pleasure that I came here for lunch!" Joe said.

"No, no . . . it's a true pleasure for me."

"Thanks."

Their eyes locked. Sam inhaled patiently.

"Do sit down," Loretta said.

"My pleasure," Joe assured her. "What's good?"

"The fish."

He leaned closer to her. "Which fish?"

"The dolphin," Loretta supplied. They continued to
stare at one another.

"Well . . ." Sam murmured. Neither of them noticed
her.

She had eaten only half of her sandwich, but she was
full. It seemed that Loretta didn't have anything else she
felt it terribly important to say to her.

"Well . . ." she said again.

"I think it's wonderful, both of you," Loretta said, at
last remembering she had met *Sam* for lunch, "working in
a gym. Keeping your bodies in such great shape."

"Seems to me," Joe said, "your body has an even better
shape."

"Oh, how sweet . . . well, there's a lot of me."

"In all the right places."

That did it. Sam decided it was time to go. She stood. "I guess I should be getting back. Joe, no hurry."

"Oh, Sam!" Loretta said, looking up guiltily. "I, um, I wanted to tell you. I was actually thinking of joining the gym, you know. I mean, everyone at my office belongs—"

"Yes, and we appreciate it," Sam said. She looked sternly at Joe. "Marnie made everyone join when Joe and I were starting out."

"She knew a good thing," Joe said with a smile.

Sam forced a smile. "Well, why don't you two just finish lunch, and when you're through, come on back to the gym, and we'll be all set!"

"Sam, I can come with you now—" Loretta said.

"And leave Joe to finish by himself? I wouldn't hear of it. He can, however, pay the check." Sam gave a wave, then determinedly left them.

She wasn't really ready to head straight back to work, but she had no particular aim in mind. Driving south, she saw the facade of the Cocowalk Mall ahead of her, and on a whim, she made a right onto Main Street, then turned down Virginia to head into the parking garage.

Once parked, she wasn't sure what she was doing there. Shopping, Laura had told her once, was a surefire cure for any restlessness. There was a store here that carried great workout clothes. She could always use more.

She stopped at a kiosk for a cappuccino, then wandered around the second floor of the mall in a circle, heading for the store. Halfway around, she paused.

An iron-railed balcony looked over the front of Main Street. The tables of an open-air bar lined the railing.

Rowan was there, dark hair swept smoothly back, sunglasses in place, bronze good looks shaded by a baseball cap. He was casually seated, sipping a beer. He was there with Kevin Madigan and two other men.

She slipped quickly behind the standing menu to one of

the mall's restaurants—trying to hide without being obvious—to see who else was with Rowan and Kevin.

The one man she quickly recognized as Eddie Harlin, the nondescript real estate attorney. Slim, with thick, black-rimmed glasses, he looked very young, except for his wispy, thinning hair. He might have been the college brain, the valedictorian. The other man . . .

She knew him. She'd seen him before. She couldn't place where, or when. And he was definitely a striking individual, one who would be noticed. He was bald, but not by chance; he had a clean-shaven head. His eyes were large, dark, deep blue. He was big and husky—even sitting, he looked tall.

Then it hit her, like a brick. Lee Chapman! She had seen his face in the paper dozens of times. He was reputed to have Mob connections, though he was supposed to have done the killing himself in the shootings with which he had been charged. He shouldn't have been walking the streets, but his lawyers had gotten him out on bail.

"Hey, there's Sam!" Kevin said suddenly. As always, he was pristine, suave, and totally smooth in a designer suit. The heat didn't get to him—he never seemed to sweat. He stood, waving at her, and she realized that once she had recognized Chapman, she had come out from behind her hiding place. She was there, all right, in front of them—gaping. Nowhere to run, that was for sure.

"Kevin!" she said, trying hard to sound casual. He stood up and pulled out a chair for her. "Come on over, have a drink with us!"

"Thanks, but . . ."

The four of them were standing politely. She couldn't see Rowan's eyes; they were shaded by his dark glasses. He didn't move. Kevin came around to take her elbow and walk her toward the table. "Sam you know Eddie, right? Eddie, you've met Sam Miller—"

"Of course," Eddie said, taking her hand. "Hi, Sam, good to see you. Join us?"

"And Sam, Lee Chapman. Lee, a friend, Sam Miller."

She nodded, not trusting her voice. He smiled, aware that she knew him by reputation—and didn't approve.

"It's nice to see you all, but—"

"Sit down, Miss Miller, please," Rowan said.

"No, thank you. I don't want to interrupt your business—"

"You're not interrupting any business," Rowan said flatly, still an enigma behind his dark glasses. "Eddie and I were talking about property earlier—you did suggest that there might be other spectacular places around, remember?"

"Yes," she told him.

He smiled. She couldn't see his eyes, but she knew that smile didn't touch them.

"In fact," he continued, "our discussion at the moment will surely interest you. We were talking about our mutual next-door neighbor. You haven't seen her yet?"

"No, but the police—"

"Yes, of course, they're on the case," Rowan said. "What would you like, Miss Miller?"

"What?"

"To drink, Miss Miller."

"Nothing, really. I have to go back to work myself."

"But you own your own business, don't you?" Lee Chapman asked, leaning forward.

"Yes." She wondered how he knew.

"So . . . you can be late if you choose," he said.

"*And* go back with beer breath if you so desire," Kevin said cheerfully. "It's a great gym, Lee. Best place in town."

"Thank you," she murmured and determinedly remained standing. "It's a great place because both Joe and I show up for work—without beer breath!" She tried to say the words lightly, without sounding like a self-righteous prude. No good. She could see the small smile that flitted across Chapman's face. Even Eddie Harlin was smirking. "It was good to see you all," she added lamely. The men all stood as well. Kevin bent to kiss her cheek.

Cheek kissing. It was big in Miami. Maybe because of the Latin American influences. She prayed that Chapman wouldn't come near her. He didn't. Neither did Rowan.

"Good day, Miss Miller," he said.

She nodded, and started off, feeling ridiculously awkward. She almost stumbled over a chair behind her. She recovered and walked quickly away, heading for the elevators to the parking garage. She hit the wrong floor, wandered around, realized her mistake, and entered the elevator once more.

When she came out into the gloom, she saw her car right away. Yet as she headed toward it, she heard footsteps behind her.

She swung around.

Chapman. Goose bumps shot up her arms.

"Miss Miller," he said casually, "how nice to run into you again."

"I, uh, I lost my car."

"Lost it?"

"Misplaced it for a minute."

"But you've found it."

She was suddenly loath to point out her car.

Chapman grinned. He was indeed striking—in a rather evil fashion, she thought.

"I'm not in the least dangerous to you," he said quietly. He came closer to her. She was tempted to turn and run.

"Ah, Sam! There you are!"

She was startled to hear Rowan's voice. And there he was, casually walking toward her. She was startled when he slipped an arm around her. If Chapman hadn't been there, she would have wrenched away.

But she didn't. And Rowan, a bit taller than Chapman, gave his enigmatic, sunglasses-shadowed smile. "I was hoping to catch up with you, my love."

"Ah . . ." Chapman murmured. "I'd heard there was something . . ."

"There is," Rowan said flatly.

"Well, then, you must convince her that I'm not the evil demon I'm pointed out to be!" Chapman said. "Just a good old Southern boy, a hunter, fisherman—why, honey, I even have a license to hunt gators. I just wanted you to know that if I can help in any way, call on me. I need your friend back. More than anyone."

He smiled. They smiled back. Waited for him to leave. He didn't.

Then he lifted his hand, indicating the Jaquar behind them. "That's my car," he explained politely.

"Oh!"

Sam moved away from it; Rowan came with her, his arm still around her. Chapman slipped into his car. He gunned the motor and drove away.

She could breathe in Rowan. Feel him from head to toe. It was more than she could handle. She pulled away quickly. "What was that all about?" she asked. She meant to be indignant, but she just sounded breathless.

Rowan stepped easily away. Here, in the shadows of the garage, his expression was more fathomless than ever. "I just thought that it would be a good idea for him to think that you're protected."

"Why?" she demanded. "Do you think—"

"I don't think anything. There's your car. I'll watch you drive out."

"I come here all the time. I can manage—"

"Fine."

She started toward her car, wishing she didn't feel so awkward. Lost. She felt as if she faltered every single time she spoke with him.

She opened her car door, stepped in. He was right beside her, arm on the top of the car, leaning down. "I noticed you didn't protest while Chapman was around."

"I didn't want to make a liar out of you," she said.

"Why not?"

She lifted a hand vaguely. "All right, next time I'll make a liar out of you."

She thought he might have smiled. "Drive safely," was all he said. He closed her car door and walked away.

Chapter 9

Loretta sat in Sam Miller's office waiting. She was glad to have had lunch with Joe—it had been so much fun. She'd thought he was about to ask her out, but maybe he was a little shy, waiting. And then again, she had told him she'd only feel right if she had Sam show her around the gym. Maybe he'd been planning to ask her out after the tour; she was thinking that maybe she should have gone ahead and let him do his spiel, but she had felt her conscience nagging at her ever since lunch, and so she knew she had to talk to Sam again. Why Sam had taken so long to get back, she didn't know, but she would just have to wait at this point.

She needed to get back to work herself. She was perhaps the only employee at the law firm who didn't belong to the gym; it was true, Marnie could be a mover and a shaker when she chose, and she had set fires beneath everyone to join when Sam had first bought into and opened the place. If Loretta wasn't careful, she'd be out here on a very extended lunch hour, and she would run smack into one of her bosses.

She grew restless and stood up. Sam's office was a great little place, with one-way smoked glass, a simple pine desk, matching file cabinets, comfortable swivel chairs, and pictures everywhere. A handsome older couple. Mother and father, Loretta assumed. Her own were fine, decent, hardworking farm people from Georgia, but once each of their nine children had hit the age of eighteen, they'd been out of the house and on their own. Her parents had never smiled quite like that in any picture. Another picture on the wall showed the three of them together. There were pictures of another couple, pictures of children.

Lacey. Lacey Henley with her folks at about two. With her brother and Santa Claus a few years later. Lacey Henley graduating from high school. Her brother playing with his group. Four Henleys together. Family pictures all over the walls, the desk, the filing cabinet. A beautiful little boy with blue eyes and blond hair.

Lacey Henley again.

Loretta bit her lower lip. What had she done? she wondered. Nothing wrong. Really, nothing wrong.

Suddenly she stopped in her tracks at what she saw through the smoked-glass window. There was Mr. Daly. Mr. Lawrence T. Daly, head of the whole law firm now that his partners had chosen retirement. An older man, but one with eagle eyes and striking energy. He was on a treadmill, going hard and fast. He seemed to be walking off his frustrations.

His eyes rose to the glass. For a moment Loretta thought he was looking straight at her. Then she remembered the glass was smoked.

The door opened. She swung around, ready to jump out of her skin. It was Sam at last, who jumped herself, at seeing Loretta. She'd come in looking a bit perplexed, her beautiful hair tousled, her eyes very green and troubled.

"Loretta!"

"I'm so sorry, I startled you."

"I had no idea that you'd wait for me."

"I needed to see you again."

"What is it?" Sam asked, throwing her shoulder bag

into a file drawer. She had shaken off her worried look and was smiling, embarrassed at being so startled.

Loretta hesitated. She wished she'd gotten to this at lunch. It would have been easier once they were involved in conversation. As it was, she had so little time.

"I waited for you to see the gym—"

"Oh, of course. Come on!"

Sam had opened the door again. Daly was right outside. She couldn't talk now.

"I . . ."

Sam saw Daly. "Oh! This way!"

She pulled Loretta down a hall. "Treadmills and step machines, bikes are all that way. And trust me, no one can stay on a Stairmaster like your Mr. Daly."

"Oh, I believe you."

"This is the weight room . . ." Sam said, and her voice trailed off. Loretta quickly saw why. Phil Jenkins and Teddy Henley were both in there, one spotting the other as they worked bars for their biceps and triceps—appreciable muscles on both men.

Phil was spotting Teddy at the moment. He looked up, saw them both.

"Hello, there, Samantha, Loretta," he said gravely.

Ted Henley quickly set the bar on the rests, turned, and rose from the bench where he'd been working. He grabbed his towel, staring at them.

Loretta had the feeling they'd both just been waiting for Sam to show up.

"Hi, ladies," Ted said.

"I haven't seen you here in the daytime in ages," Sam said.

Ted shrugged. Phil answered. "He's here questioning people. He asked me who was supposed to be working at Marnie's Friday night, but no one was. He's got the phone numbers of all my subcontractors anyway."

"I'm just trying to find out if anyone has seen Marnie. Has she appeared anywhere that you might know about?"

"No," Sam answered him. "Have you done anything, gotten anyone to work the case?"

"Yes, of course. And I'm giving it my own free time as well," Teddy assured her. He smiled at Loretta. "You haven't heard from her, right? Have you any ideas, anything at all?"

Loretta shook her head, wondering if he could see the flush that was spreading over her body. She couldn't tell Ted Henley what she meant to tell Sam.

"Um . . . well, you know, there was a plainclothes man in the office this morning, Detective Henley. He said that he was handling the case, since it was a missing-persons situation."

"I'm just pitching in because it means so much to Sam here."

"And because of your own friendship with Marnie, I should hope!" Loretta said innocently.

Teddy was wearing very dark glasses. They didn't hide the tick in the vein at his throat. She felt a sudden sense of deep unease. She would never betray Lacey to her father!

"Of course," he said.

"He's grilling the hell out of me!" Phil Jenkins announced. Buff, sweating, macho-looking, and a little scary himself, Phil seemed to be staring at her as if he knew too much. *About what?* Loretta wondered. She was becoming paranoid of everyone.

"Questions, questions, questions," Phil said. "This guy earns his paycheck, all right."

"And I'm sure you're trying to help," Sam said.

"Damn right."

"Well, I'm glad."

Phil grinned. "Marnie Newcastle owes me money."

"Oh, I see," Sam murmured. Sam didn't care much for

Phil, Loretta thought, watching them. Then she started, realizing that Detective Ted Henley was watching her.

"Didn't know you two girls were friends," he said.

"We met one another at lunch, and we realized that Loretta didn't belong to the gym and that she wanted to. And we've got to get going—Loretta has to get back to work," Sam said. "Thanks for the interest and hard work, Teddy."

Loretta felt Sam's hand on her shoulder as Sam ushered her quickly along. "I really do have to get back to work, but I need to tell you something quickly."

"What?"

"Not here."

"My office—"

"Mr. Daly is right outside."

"I'll walk you out to the parking lot."

And still, when they were in the parking lot at Loretta's car, she found herself tongue-tied again. What she was doing came near to being a breach of trust. Not to mention the fact that now, with hindsight, she was a bit dismayed about some of the things she had done herself. But as far as Lacey Henley went, she had already set things in motion.

Sam leaned against Loretta's car, amber-specked eyes on her, waiting patiently.

"I just . . . well did you know that . . . well, you do know Marnie. She thinks you didn't know, but when she was trying to get through school—"

"She was a stripper. Yes, I knew."

Loretta paused. "She thought you didn't know."

Sam shrugged. "She didn't want me to know. Why would I talk about it?"

"Well, when she was starting out, she worked at a place down here, too. On the highway."

"Was she working there recently?" Sam asked, frowning.

Loretta hesitated. "She has an interest in it." Again Loretta hesitated, then she plunged in. "You see, I got a job there, rather anonymous, just part-time, after work. Then Marnie looked in my bag one afternoon, thinking someone had left it, and saw my outfit. I was so afraid that she was going to fire me. But she started to laugh. And she came back in to the club one afternoon. Since then, well, she has an interest in it I think."

"You're still working there?"

Loretta flushed. "It's honest money—"

"Loretta, I never said it wasn't!"

"It's a very nice place, of course."

"Of course. Why are you telling me about it?"

"Well . . . a girl named Eva Larson worked there once, too."

"So?"

"So, Eva supposedly ran off. But her folks never believed it."

Sam frowned deeply then. "Eva was the secretary who disappeared?"

Loretta nodded gravely. "She was in love, though. Deeply in love. She never told me with whom, but she would talk about the way she would do anything to be with him."

Sam touched her shoulder. "Loretta, then she's probably with him."

Loretta nodded. "I do think I'm being a bit paranoid—"

"Why don't you talk to the police about this place if you're worried about it?"

"That's the funny thing. I'm not, not really. I only work a few nights, and everything is great. The manager, Steven Doran, is a great guy. The bouncers are there to protect the girls. Sometimes the clients are scuzzies, sometimes they're preppy college kids, sometimes nicely dressed businessmen. It's an on-the-level place. I've seen doctors—and lawyers—in there." She giggled suddenly. "Lawyers from our firm—they never recognize me. And do we get cops! Tons of them! Blue-collar guys, white-collar guys, rich guys, a lot of them. Married, single. The clientele is mainly men, naturally, but we get couples, too. And women. Women who . . . like women. Which is great. A couple of the girls prefer their own sex, anyway. But don't get the wrong idea. The drinks are good, there's jazz night, swing night . . ." Her voice trailed off. Was it possible to make a striptease establishment sound dignified?

"Then . . . ?" Sam persisted, frowning. Naturally. If it was all on the up-and-up, why would she feel so compelled to tell Sam about it? Loretta did feel a bit ridiculous. Sam—compact, together, beautiful, logical, kind, and caring Sam—was still trying to understand her fear.

"Well, you see, I never knew it for a fact, but there was a rumor among the girls that Chloe Lowenstein liked to dress up in disguise and work at the club. Well, I mean, she was in the scandal sheets often enough, but for a woman like her to actually become a stripper . . . Well, of course, it would have to be a major secret. And I don't know if it was true or not."

"Loretta, tell this to the cops. They'll interview every girl there."

"I can't go to the cops."

"Why?"

"It's secret work for most of us."

"Then why did you tell me?" Sam asked.

"I just thought that . . . I don't know."

"I should go there," Sam mused. "See the place for myself."

"That would be good. You're so . . ."

"Prudish?" Sam asked dryly.

Loretta laughed. "No, I was going to say 'classy.' You

might be able to tell if anything out of the ordinary is going on."

Sam seemed amused—not judgmental. "I don't know if I'm familiar enough with strip joints to know what is and isn't on the up-and-up. But I do think that I should go there. If Marnie was involved there . . . But Loretta, if I see anything I don't like, I will go to the cops."

"Deal. But see if you don't think it's legit yourself. I mean, what could I say?" But she hesitated, then shrugged. "All right, well . . . yes, I think Marnie has a hand in the till and the management, also, well . . . every once in a while—a rare while!—Marnie comes in to strip."

"She does?"

"Yeah. Not often. But she kind of gets her kicks—stripping, you know. She likes to be this powerful, dignified woman at work . . . but she likes the power of sex as well. So, like I said, every once in a rare while she comes in. But I still don't think it means anything about the place. I think that the rumors about Chloe Lowenstein stripping might have been just that—rumors. And as for Eva, well, like I said, she was in love, and everyone but her mom thinks she ran off. No one who works there works more than a few nights a week, and almost everyone appears in some kind of a disguise. No one uses a real name. There's nothing at all I could prove. The cops would laugh me right out of the station if I went down to report trouble, and besides . . . I . . ."

"You what?"

Loretta lowered her head. "I don't want to make trouble there. I'm . . ."

"Yes, Loretta, please?"

She looked at Sam. "I'm afraid. Not of working—only of making trouble. Marnie was in the management, but I don't know who else." There was so much sympathy in the other woman's eyes that Loretta felt warmed. Sam impulsively reached for her, kissing her cheek. "I've really got to go!"

Loretta crawled into her car, glanced at the clock, winced. She waved to Sam and revved her engine.

She had to get back to work.

Well, she'd told Sam Miller about the club. She hadn't betrayed anyone. Lacey was safe.

Yet as she drove, she was suddenly sorry . . .

She had already given Lacey's name to the husky-voiced man who planned the private parties.

Maybe she shouldn't have.

Maybe she *should* have told Sam.

No . . .

She couldn't betray a trust.

Yet a strange question was haunting her.

Not even when it might mean . . .

Life or death?

"Let me get this straight," Laura said, sounding very puzzled. "You want me to go with you to a strip joint."

"Yes," Sam said simply, drumming her fingers on the desk in her Florida room. She had brooded over Loretta's words all night and throughout the next day. Now it was Tuesday evening, and nothing had changed. Marnie hadn't shown, the police had done nothing but take statements, and she felt compelled to do something.

"With *you*."

"Yes."

"*You're* going to a strip joint."

"A nice one," Sam said defensively.

"A male strip joint?"

"No."

Laura was quiet for a long time. Sam inhaled to try to find a way to explain, but while she was inhaling, Laura began to speak again.

"You know, I've heard it before. Women turn to women

because they've had such a rotten time with men. But Sam—"

"I'm not turning to women. I just need to go to this place, and I don't want to go alone. Will you come with me, or not?"

"A strip joint?"

"Laura, I have gone to seedy clubs with you and been all but assaulted by beer-guzzling geezers with no teeth, just to hear Aidan play. Now, are you coming with me or not?"

"I . . . well, I guess so."

"Why do you sound as if you don't mean it?"

"I do mean it! It's just kind of like being invited to an orgy by the Flying Nun, that's all."

"Oh, really!"

Laura sighed. "Where is this place? Maybe it will be good for you."

Sam gritted her teeth. "It's the place on the highway with the red neon lights."

"Fine. I'll have to meet you there—I have volunteer night with my adopt-a-grandparent group."

"Laura! I don't want to go in alone!" Sam said with dismay.

"Don't worry—it's adopt-a-grandparent night. Our adoptees go to bed by eight. I'll be in the parking lot at nine."

"Not a second later!" Sam warned.

Laura agreed. Sam hung up, worried. Was it enough, going with Laura? Why was she so afraid? Loretta worked on the stage, and she wasn't afraid. She could have asked Joe to go with her, but she would have felt uncomfortable. She thought about calling Teddy, but Loretta didn't want the cops involved. She even thought about calling Kevin Madigan, but without explaining, it would look as if she were interested in an affair.

There was Rowan, of course . . .

Oh, never, never, never. She would die in a strip joint with him.

Ladies' night out, she decided. It would have to be her and Laura.

She hurried on upstairs, glancing at her watch. Since she had plenty of time, she decided on a long bath, and after she had filled the tub, she sank in, hoping for some relaxation. Didn't work. She sat in the tub a while, then decided to bring in a glass of wine. The whole thing was crazy. She had to admit that the evening would be out of character for her—even though she definitely resented the Flying Nun comment.

What did one wear to a strip joint? She'd never been in one. Her only knowledge about such places came from cable television. Still, though, if she was honest with herself, she had to admit she was intrigued. This realization disturbed her all over again. She opted for a second glass of wine. She was in the tub until the water turned cold.

At eight-thirty she was studying her closet. What was proper attire for a heterosexual young woman in a strip joint? Maybe she'd get lucky and it would be jazz night and the band would be great and there would be lots of couples.

Black.

Once again she decided on black. She ruled out anything too dressy and anything too plain. Anything too sexy and anything too prim. That left a long-sleeved Donna Karan sheath.

"Ah, yes!" she told her reflection. The dress was fine. Now, for shoes . . .

"Fuck-you shoes, or fuck-me shoes?" she asked her reflection. "Oh, my God, what am I saying? Pumps, low pumps! *Sexless* pumps."

Hair brushed, ready to leave at last, she decided on

calling a taxi rather than driving herself. A bit too much wine in the tub.

At 8:45 she was in the parking lot. She exited her cab, anxious to see if Laura had arrived.

"Hey, honey, you coming in?" A short, bleary-eyed businessman, his tie askew, wandered up to her. He looked her up and down. "You gonna strip? If so, I'm getting a ringside seat!"

"No, I don't strip," she told him. He inched closer, ignoring the fact that she was searching the parking lot.

"You can strip for me here. In the parking lot. The cops will never bust you—we can pay them off!" he said hopefully.

She looked at him. She wasn't really afraid of him. He was drunk, and she had a good right hook, even had taken a few lessons in kick boxing. "No. I'm definitely not stripping in your parking lot. Now, if you'll excuse me—"

"You like women, huh?"

"What?"

"You swing toward women?"

"I—no, I—"

She broke off. He was almost on top of her. Yes, she could deck him, but she didn't particularly want to. The idea was to be discreet.

She thought she saw Laura getting out of the passenger side of a car across the lot. She looked at the short, chubby, hopeful drunk. "Yes! That's it. Sorry, sir, but I do like women. If you'll excuse me . . ."

She left the drunk and started across the lot. It was Laura. But as she reached her cousin, she came to a halt, just staring, wishing she were far more sober herself.

Laura hadn't come alone. She had brought Rowan.

He was coming along behind her, devastating in a black suit and tieless black tailored shirt. As he got near,

Sam caught the faint scent of his aftershave. She felt shaky—and furious with Laura.

"What's he doing here?" she hissed to her cousin.

Laura gazed at her with wide, innocent eyes. "Well, Sam, honestly, I couldn't tell you no, I wouldn't come, but I'd have been a little scared here, just you and me. And I even thought about asking Aidan to come with us, but that was just a wee bit too sick."

"What about Teddy?" she grated, even though she had decided against Teddy herself.

"I did call him, and he was trying to come, but he was busy. Some drug lord got himself shot up. He said he'd try to show, but . . ."

"Sorry, Sam," Rowan said smoothly. "I was all that was left." His eyes seemed gold tonight. Devil eyes, she thought. No. the wine had simply demonized his eyes to a glittering shade. She ignored him, swung around, and started toward the door to the establishment. Laura got ahead of her just a bit.

Rowan's fingers suddenly wound around her arm. He pulled her back, bent slightly, and whispered in her ear, "What are we doing here?"

She pulled away from him. "I just had a sudden desire to see a strip show, that's all."

"The Chippendales don't dance here."

"Maybe I've decided to go for women."

His eyes brushed hers. "You? Never."

"How on earth would you know?"

He arched a brow, his lips forming a strange, small smile. "I know," he said softly. "So come clean—why are we here?"

"Can we please just go in?" she asked impatiently.

He shrugged. "You will tell me," he said. He kept his hand on her arm, urging her forward. Laura was waiting for them at the door.

"I'm sure as hell not going in alone," she declared.

Then she giggled. "I don't believe I'm doing this. And with Sam, of all people!"

Sam gritted her teeth. At least Laura hadn't referred to her as the Flying Nun again.

Rowan opened the door. There was a bouncer there, watching those who entered. He didn't seem surprised to see a man with two women. He did assess them a bit curiously, and Sam felt her face sting. The bouncer seemed to be smirking. As if the three would stay a while, get buzzed, heated up—and depart for a heavy-duty threesome.

"Twenty-dollar cover charge apiece," the bouncer told them.

Rowan reached for his wallet, but as he dipped into it he whispered to Sam, "Are we trying to get close to the stage and the action?"

"No!" she gasped, looking at him with alarm. "No, no, we need the back of the room!"

"Okay, okay! It just matters for how much I tip this guy, that's all!" he informed her softly.

"I take it you've been to places like this before," she whispered back.

"Most red-blooded American males have," he told her dryly.

The bouncer looked at the money in his hand. "Sir, where—"

"Back there, please. The dark corner table over there."

The bouncer laughed, looking them over again. "Sure thing, sir."

A few minutes later they were seated in the back. Sam was served a very decent Merlot, and she started sipping it quickly. She felt like shrinking into the corner.

Laura was staring unabashedly at the stage.

"Wow, will you look at that!" she breathed. Sam looked. The dancer's chest seemed to be forty-five inches at the minimum—bare, except for the tassels streaming

from her red-rouged nipples. She was young and pretty
good, lithe, nimble. She moved like a gymnast, around a
large silver pole. She threw her head back, leapt around
the pole, straddled it, gyrated . . .

"My God, I've never seen anyone have an orgasm with
a pole before!" Laura gasped.

"Laura," Sam murmured.

Rowan leaned back in his chair, arms crossed over his
chest. Sam sensed that he was watching her rather than
the stage.

The dancer suddenly fell to the floor. She arched her
head back, meeting her toes, her breasts bulging toward
the gentlemen seated by the stage.

"Like twin torpedoes!" Laura said.

Rowan was silent.

The dancer swirled to her back, lifted her legs, parted
them. Slowly. Her G-string was the size of a shoelace. It
was nothing but a slender silk ribbon, and others, in different hues, were tied about various parts of her body.

"Oh, my God!" Laura said.

Sam assumed that she was referring to the dancer
again. She wasn't. Teddy was standing by the door, by the
bouncer.

"He made it!" Laura said. She lifted a hand.

Teddy saw them and started across the room to them.

He kissed his ex-wife's cheek, then Sam's. He looked
at Rowan, then the two of them shook hands. He pulled
up a chair, ordered a beer, then raised his eyebrow,
glancing toward the stage and back at Sam. "This is
definitely an interesting outing, but . . . what are we doing here?"

Sam hesitated. Teddy was a cop. Loretta hadn't wanted
her telling the cops anything yet.

"I thought it was jazz night," she tried blandly.

Laura gave her away. "What?"

Sam wasn't accustomed to lying, and yet she was

amazed now at how quickly a better lie came to her lips. "I . . . I read a really interesting article today about strippers. Something about there being several hundred thousand women in the U.S. who do this and that it's amazing how fit most of them are. I was really curious. I . . ." She leaned forward, groping for words, then jumping headlong into her fabrication. "I couldn't believe that any really fit and beautiful young woman would want to do this. I mean, she should really dance, or go into modeling, or the movies. But I . . ."

The dancer had arched up. The majority of her was plainly visible. And she was a beautiful young woman. "I . . . well, I guess I was wrong. There is some pull to this, a lure . . ."

"Money," Laura said sagely.

Teddy shrugged. He seemed to buy Sam's story.

Rowan was watching her. He hadn't believed a single word. He lifted his wineglass to her, sipped from it. She quickly looked away.

"She is gorgeous," Laura said of the dancer.

Teddy looked at his ex-wife. He smiled suddenly. "Money, the lure of danger, and decadence. This is kind of fun, being in a place like this with you."

"Really?"

"You used to be so uptight."

"Was I?" She had ordered a rum and Coke. She brought her swizzle stick to her mouth, liking the tip of it. "Well, you know, hanging around with my decadent cousin has just made me a wild thing."

"Wild and wicked," Sam agreed, settling back in her chair. Her wineglass was empty. She didn't know why, but she glanced at Rowan. He waited a moment, then poured her more wine from the bottle. He leaned forward. "You'd better leave your car here until morning."

She looked away. "My car isn't here."

"Teddy, Teddy!" Laura said suddenly. "Look! Isn't that . . . that criminal?"

Teddy twisted around. "*Alleged* criminal," he agreed.

Sam tensed. Laura was right. Down at a table almost dead center before the stage sat Lee Chapman, his bald head gleaming. The dancer was playing to the whole of her audience then, twisting, turning . . . spreading again. But she was also playing to Chapman.

"What do you think he's doing here?" Laura whispered, though the man couldn't possibly have heard her.

Teddy looked at his wife. "Getting turned on?" he suggested.

"Teddy, that's not at all what I meant!" Laura said.

Teddy smiled slightly. "He's out on bail—his attorneys arranged it. And, speaking of his attorneys . . ."

Sam leaned forward and saw what Teddy meant. Chapman wasn't alone at his table. Kevin Madigan and Eddie Harlin were with him.

"Are they entertaining their client?" Sam asked Rowan softly.

"So I would assume," he said with a shrug.

"Well, you're kind of best buddies with them, aren't you?" she persisted.

He gave her a long, hard stare, then looked at her glass. Empty again. She met his eyes, feeling defiant. She plucked up the wine bottle herself, refilled her own glass. Neither Teddy nor Laura noticed.

Rowan did.

Another woman, this one dressed in a feather mantle, came on the stage. The first girl went into a coil. Feather Woman swirled and dipped; her headdress was fantastic.

Then she shed the mantle. She was down to bands of feathers.

She strutted down the runway, where the first woman rose to meet her. They began to move in unison, beautiful bodies fluid and sensual. They came down to their knees together, rolled, twisted, and sat with their backs together, legs extended.

There had been whoops and hollers now and then. Now the room was silent. The women worked together in a stunning symmetry of movement, entirely wanton movement. They rose together. The first stripped the second of her feathers. The second stripped the first of her ribbons. They embraced in a curiously beautiful pose, then turned. Walked the stage, reached silver poles at the same point and began making sexual movements against the poles—both now completely naked.

Sam found that her eyes were glued to the dancers. She wasn't sure she wanted to watch them, but she didn't want to look at anyone else.

"I would say that's fairly erotic," Laura murmured.

"Yep," Teddy agreed.

"They're both really pretty," Laura said.

"Yeah, I could jump their bones," Teddy said casually.

Sam couldn't turn. They were definitely erotic; she also felt as if she had walked in on someone in the shower. It seemed one thing to watch, another to be seen watching. She felt strangely disturbed, and also ready to crawl beneath the table.

"Just their bones?" Laura murmured softly.

"Well, you know, there's something . . ." Teddy replied.

"I must say . . . stimulating."

"Think so?" Teddy asked. He'd moved closer, much closer, to Laura. Sam was aware of him, dipping his head to her and whispering discreetly, "Want to leave?"

"Maybe." Laura tossed her head. "Although . . . well, I don't want to start anything . . ."

"Neither do I. But . . ."

"I mean, we don't want to get back together. Really."

"No."

"But then, we were married once."

"That we were. Ready?"

"You betcha!" Laura agreed.

The two of them suddenly rose.

Sam felt an awful sense of panic. "You're leaving?" she said with dismay.

Teddy frowned at her. "Yes."

"But—"

She told herself that her feeling mainly had to do with Laura. Sure, she trusted Teddy, she called Teddy when she needed help, but . . .

Should Laura be leaving with him?

Was it fear for her cousin—or terror for herself? She'd never thought that she would be left here alone with Rowan and—naked people.

"Good night, folks. Thanks, Rowan. Call me, Sam," Laura said, and then they were gone.

Sam groped for the wine bottle. Rowan had it. "Did you want to just chug straight from the bottle? I could order you something harder. Or, since you're so uncomfortable, we could just leave." His amber eyes were on her. She lowered her own quickly. She didn't need more wine. Her head was spinning. Absurdly, she suddenly felt herself smiling. She looked up at him. "So . . . could you jump their bones?"

"Depends on the circumstances," he said.

"Oh?"

"At the moment, no. Did you get what you came here for? If so, let's go. If you drink any more, I can almost guarantee you'll throw up all over my car."

"I would never!" she protested.

But when he helped her to her feet, the room was spinning. Badly. Yet, oddly enough, her sense of panic was gone. He didn't escort her out, he more or less held her up. She leaned against him, giggling, touching the fabric of his suit, appreciating the scent of his aftershave.

"Why do people go to places like that?" she asked.

"Um. Gee, I wonder," he muttered, folding her into the passenger seat of his car. He slammed the door and walked around to the driver's side.

"Seriously, does it get men going?" she asked him.

He shifted the car into gear and glanced at her. "Does it get women going?"

"It apparently got Teddy and Laura going." She frowned. "Do you think they're all right?"

"They were married once."

"Yes, I know, but now . . ."

"Now what?"

"I don't know."

"They left in full view of dozens of witnesses. I'm sure your cousin will be all right."

She met his eyes in the rearview mirror and felt her face flush. "I didn't mean, Teddy wouldn't . . . I don't know what I'm saying."

She felt his gaze again, but he said nothing more. She leaned her head back and closed her eyes against the spinning.

A few minutes later he was nudging her. She started, realizing that she had dozed off.

"Sam!"

She jumped, stepped out of the car, wavered. He came around quickly and caught her before she could topple over.

"I'm all right."

"I'll get you to the door." He swept her up, walked the few steps to her front door.

"Got your key?"

"Of course."

She fumbled in her purse, found her key. He took it from her fingers. "You know, really, I'm all right, this is so . . ."

"Shut up, Sam." He twisted the key in the lock and they were inside. "I'll put you to bed."

"No . . ."

"I didn't say I'd *take* you to bed. I said I'd *put* you to bed."

Her arms slipped around his neck. He took the stairs quickly. She stared at him, feeling queasy, yet aware of the texture of his cheeks, the width of his mouth, the length of his hair beneath her fingers.

A few moments later, he set her down on her bed and took off her shoes. The feel of his hands on her feet seemed incredibly erotic.

He pulled the covers over her. She caught his hand.

"Rowan . . ."

"Um."

"Didn't you feel . . . something in there? I mean, it was so . . . something. Teddy grabbed Laura and ran out of there . . ."

"Sexy?"

"I . . ."

"Sam, are you asking me to take advantage of you?"

"No!"

"Good. Not tonight."

"What?"

"Not tonight. And by the way, what were we doing there?"

"Why, you don't think that on a crazy whim I might just want to go to a strip joint?"

"No."

"I'm really very sophisticated, and a tremendous amount of fun."

"I didn't say you weren't. But we were there for a reason."

"We were just out for a wild, reckless night, that's all. For the thrill of it."

"You and Laura together?"

"Well, there were single men there, of course."

"Oh, I see. You wanted to go to a strip joint with Laura just to pick up men?"

"Maybe."

"Teddy definitely wanted a woman fast enough." He smiled. "Eventually you'll tell me the truth."

"I have a life, you know."

"I'm glad. Now, good night, Sam."

"Were you going . . . somewhere else?"

"Are you asking me if I'm going to go sleep with someone else?"

"No! Of course not!" she lied.

He was still for a moment, watching her, a small smile curving his lips. Then he sat at her side and smoothed back her hair. "Sam, in a million years, I would never touch you tonight, give you more fuel for your anger. I'm going home. Were the dancers erotic? Yes? A turn-on? Yes, quite. Would I want them . . . or anyone else? Yes— if you weren't in the world right now. Am I turned on by you? You know it." He rose, leaving her. The world was still spinning, and yet she was strangely on fire. He came back a second later with water and aspirin. "Take these. It will help."

She did.

"I have to key in the alarm. Can you remember your code?"

She frowned at him, then found herself smiling. Oh, Lord, had she overdone it! "You're really leaving?"

"That I am. Why? Did you want me to stay?"

"No, of course not!"

"Because you're in no condition to deal with me."

"You flatter yourself."

"You can hardly keep your eyes open."

"Oh, really?" she said. But it was true, she was very tired. She wanted to close her eyes, block out the world.

"Be a good kid, tell me the alarm number and go to sleep."

She mumbled the number.

Closed her eyes. And remembered nothing more.

Chapter 10

L acey had never expected a call to come so quickly.
On Wednesday afternoon, she'd barely gotten home from school when her mother told her there was a Mr. Snowden on the phone.

She didn't know a Mr. Snowden, but she grimaced, took the receiver from her mother, and said a curious "Hello?"

"Hi, honey. I hear you're a party girl."

"What?"

"Are you alone?"

"No!"

"Then just listen. Friday night there is a fabulous opportunity for a new girl, bright, with good moves. A mutual friend said you're that girl and that I should give this opportunity to you."

Then it hit her. This was the business Loretta had told her about, and she was setting her up for some on-the-side stripping. Her throat constricted. She was afraid. But she was compelled to listen. Maybe it was the very danger of the thing that attracted her.

"Tell me, please."

Mr. Snowden read off an address in Gables Estates, a very pricey area indeed. He told Lacey to arrive fairly early. It was an ad exec's birthday, and all she had to do was hop out of the cake and bare a little flesh.

"Sounds like a great sale!" Lacey said, flashing a

glance and a smile at her mother, her fingers tightening around the phone cord. "How much?"

"Five hundred, plus tips, if there are any."

Her jaw nearly dropped. Five hundred dollars. Double—no, quadruple—what she usually made in a night.

"Do you want the job? It will be a trial night for you—and the agency, of course. We're trusting you with an important event because you come so highly recommended."

"Great. Yes, yes, of course, I want to come."

Mr. Snowden repeated the address, and by the time Lacey hung up the phone, her mother was looking at her with wide, sorrowful eyes. Had she heard? Lacey's heart began to pound.

"Mom—"

"Oh, honey, I'm so sorry! You look so excited about going to that sale, and I'm almost dead broke. I didn't go shopping the other night. Good thing I didn't. I had no idea just how low I'd let my checking account get. I don't understand it. I didn't write that many checks."

Lacey started laughing with sheer relief. She hugged her mother. "Mom, it's that thing called an ATM. The money that comes out isn't free. You have to put money in to get money out. You seem to think that if you don't write it down, it's not really gone."

"It's just so annoying!" Laura agreed with a sigh. "I haven't done very well for either of you, have I?"

Impulsively, Lacey hugged her mother tightly. "You've been wonderful. Don't worry about money. Daddy slipped me some money last week."

Laura's eyes clouded and Lacey was sorry she had mentioned her father.

"Mom—"

But her mother didn't say anything disparaging about her father. "You know, your father doesn't mean to be cheap. Cops really don't make all that much money. If he could afford to send you to one of those swank places in New York, he would, you know."

Why did she have to feel so guilty? Lacey wondered.

"I know, Mom." She hugged her mother again. A little too fiercely.

Laura didn't seem to mind. "I love you, baby. I love you so much."

"You, too, Mom. Honest."

As they hugged, the phone began to ring again. Lacey nearly jumped through the roof.

"It's just the phone!" Laura said with a laugh.

"Yeah, yeah, the phone. I'll get it," Lacey said and made a dive for it.

"Lacey!"

"Yeah!" Her heart began to thud with relief. It was just Janet, a good friend she'd known for years and years, a friend with the same dreams for the future.

"Guess what?"

"What?"

"They're casting a national tour of *When the Wind Blows* in New York—this weekend. It's an open casting call. No big-shot agent needed."

Lacey frowned. "Gee, that must be just great for New York wannabees."

"We're getting a small group together. You, me, Sara, and Kasey. We're going to hop a late-nighter—gives Kasey time to close up that community show she's doing—and we're going on that new cheapie airline out of MIA Friday. Midnight flight. It's only one hundred and fifty—round trip! Our room will break down to one hundred a girl. Another hundred for meals, and we've got it made. Are you in?"

"I would be, but—"

She broke off. She didn't have the money, and she didn't want to ask her mother for it.

But she would have the money. By late Friday night, she'd have more than enough.

"A midnight flight, did you say? I didn't know there were midnight flights to New York."

"Yes, it's that new airline—you're not afraid of it, are you? Under the old name, they had a big-time serious crash, but now they're supposed to be the safest in the air. The FAA jumped all over them, of course."

"No, no, I'm not afraid," Lacey said quickly. "Midnight. I think I can make midnight."

"So you're in!" Janet said, sighing with relief. "Oh, thank God! The finances work much better with the four of us sharing a room and taxis." She giggled. "I had to swear on a Bible to my mother that I wouldn't take the subway in New York City. Like, we live in Miami, right? As if we don't have our own vice and dens of iniquity!"

"I'm in, I'm in, yes—" She broke off, aware that her mother was staring at her with concern in her eyes. "I'll call you back."

She hung up. "Mom, I'm going to fly to New York with the girls on Friday night, okay?"

"Well, wait—"

"We'll be perfectly safe. We'll stick together. Kasey knows the city; her family only moved down here a few years ago. Honest to God, Mom, we'll be safe, we'll be good. I'll give you the number to the hotel—"

"Well, honey, I wouldn't want to check up on you, but—"

"They're casting a road show. A really good musical."

Lacey saw tears start to form in her mother's eyes. Laura had always told her that she had to do what was best for her. Laura even encouraged her to go away to school, should she choose to do so. But she knew as well that her mother was afraid. Losing her children was hard now that she was alone.

Laura frowned. "We'll have to get the money from

your father. I just really don't have it at the moment, and I'm always asking Sam for a loan, and it's terrible. I always repay her so slowly, I'm so very bad with money—"

"Mom, I've got it. I've been saving, I told you." She moistened her lips, deciding to lie just a bit. "The flight is only ninety-nine bucks and we can share a decent room for about a hundred and fifty. And even taking taxis, we share four ways and it's just a bit more than a dollar a person to get from place to place."

Laura hugged her again. "Oh, honey, I am so excited for you. What a weekend you're going to have!"

"Thanks." She frowned suddenly, hugging her mother again. "You look so tired. Are you upset? Didn't I hear Daddy here this morning?"

"Um . . . yeah, he came by," Laura said.

"Are you two fighting again?"

"No, I'm just tired. You're not going to believe this, but Sam got it into her head to go to a strip club last night."

Lacey felt the blood drain from her face. "What?"

"Out of the blue! And she always comes with me, wherever I drag her, you know, for Aidan, or you, when you're in a show. So . . . we were out late."

"Where—where did you go?"

"The place on the highway."

"My God."

"Oh, honey, it wasn't that terrible. It was . . . interesting. Don't be so shocked—we are over twenty-one."

Lacey thought she was going to die.

"Daddy came too."

"Daddy?" She was so afraid that her voice was a squeak.

"I wasn't sure what Sam was up to . . . I was a bit chicken. I called your father. At first he didn't think he could make it, but he did and . . ."

"And?" Lacey breathed.

"That's it. He made it."

"Oh, my God! He slept here! He came back here!"

Laura blushed. Lacey knew she had discovered the truth. She almost fell on her knees, ready to thank God that she hadn't worked the night before.

Her parents had gone to the club—and come back here together! She was going to faint, pass out, throw up. It was sick, sick, sick . . .

Her father at the club.

Her mother . . .

"You wouldn't go back—would you?"

"Are you all right, honey? You're looking a little fevered," Laura said worriedly.

"Mom!"

"What, dear?"

"Never mind, never mind. I—uh, love you, Mom. I've got homework."

Lacey gave her mother another kiss on the cheek and fled to her bedroom. She doubled over, breathing hard. She needed a paper bag. She was going to hyperventilate.

No, she was going to call the club and quit. No, she needed money. No, she was quitting. Right now. Lord, what if she'd been on stage last night? If her folks had watched and not known they were watching their own daughter and gotten all heated up and . . .

She was going to call and quit right away. She'd be all right.

After all, she could work the private parties. They would pay so much better.

And be *so* much safer.

Mollie was back. A ray of hope that just made Sam feel better.

She'd been lucky not to wake up with a killer headache, she knew, and yet, by Wednesday afternoon, she was feeling very concerned and totally frustrated.

What had going to the club proved? Nothing, except that she was a chicken and capable of drinking far too much wine. And she'd made a fool of herself with Rowan. And the thought had tormented her all day, so she'd tried to concentrate on work.

Two officers, now showing more and more attention to the matter—although they still told her that this was no great amount of time for a grown woman to be missing—had been assigned to Marnie's case. Detectives Lawrence and Ostermann. They had shown up at the gym, too. They reminded Sam of Laurel and Hardy, the one being very tall and slim and the other being as round as a department-store Santa. They were both friends with Teddy, who assured her he had seen to it that the best men were on the case. The detectives were concentrating on the law firm, delving into the people Marnie was defending.

She wondered if she should mention the strip club, but she didn't know what to say. She had promised Loretta that she wouldn't, and she wouldn't—not without a reason! She didn't really have one. Maybe the police were right to concentrate on Marnie's clients.

It was sunset now. She'd come out, seen that Mollie was cruising her waters, and gone back into the house for a head of lettuce. When she returned, she sat and fed the manatee, coaxing Mollie close, scratching her head, talking to her.

The night was still. The colors over the bay were glorious. It all appeared very peaceful, and beautiful.

She felt Rowan's presence before she turned to see him. Actually she didn't exactly sense *Rowan's* presence, but she realized that *someone* was standing behind her, and when she turned, it was him.

She looked back to the water. "You're not supposed to just appear in someone's backyard. You might have knocked on the front door."

"I did. You didn't answer."

"That probably meant I didn't want to be disturbed."

"I thought I'd take a chance and come around back here."

She was trying to think of the right words to tell him that she wanted him to go away. Except that she didn't want him to go away. She stared straight out across the bay, her feet dangling in the water. He sat down beside her. He was in cutoffs and a polo shirt, barefoot, and he dangled his feet over the dock, then reached down as she had done to pat the manatee. She wished that Mollie would recognize him as a stranger and swim away, lifting her sea cow nose into the air. Mollie did no such thing. She kept sweeping back and forth by Rowan, accepting his touch.

"She's incredible," he said.

"Yes," she murmured coolly.

"Friendly."

"Maybe too friendly. She'll catch another propeller one day. We probably shouldn't feed her the way we all do."

"Oh, I think she seldom leaves this area. She probably learned her lesson about boats."

"Well, sometimes we can all be amazingly dense about learning lessons in life."

"Are you referring to me, or yourself?"

"Maybe both of us."

He sat up, shaking the sea water from his hands. "I never wanted to hurt you."

"Be that as it may, you did a darn good job."

"You might consider the idea of forgiving me."

"I might," she said, looking his way at last. "But somehow . . . the desire to do so just eludes me." Then she flushed, realizing how horrible she sounded—and just how decent he had been the night before. "I—I just don't think that . . . that people can go back. That we could like or trust one another again."

"Well, then, there's not too much I can do," he said, but he didn't move. It was the most beautiful time of the day. Both sky and bay gleamed with a soft crimson glow, and orange streaked the skies. Across the waves, the buildings out on Key Biscayne glittered like ancient palaces.

She kept staring at the bay. "You left last night. You could have stayed. I was in no shape to protest."

"That's exactly why I didn't stay. But, yes, I could have."

"I owe you for last night, that's for certain."

"All right. This is the truth, and I swear it, and I don't beg people to believe me, no matter how much I want them to. Dina was self-destructive, and I knew it. When she returned, she was in sorry shape. I had married her. I could never have lived with myself if I hadn't tried to help her."

"You might have said that to me then."

"At the time? Exactly what should I have said. 'Oh, excuse me, thank you, you've been a fabulous lover, but they've found my wife, I didn't do away with her after all, but she's a drug addict and I need to be with her'?"

She swung on him then. "Yes!"

He shook his head. "I didn't love her anymore. Oh, God knows, I did care. But I didn't love her. When she ran off—before I was accused of having done something to her, of course—I was actually relieved. She . . . God, she clung. I don't know if she knew what she was doing to herself or not, but she was so needy. When she first ran off, all I could think was that I was so grateful—I could breathe. Then I met you. And I was in love with you. You were everything that Dina couldn't be—strong, independent, you knew who you were. You didn't need pills to sleep, or pills to wake up, or alcohol to make it through to sunset. You were fresh air and starshine, and we laughed, and you listened when I played, and you were so sincere in everything you did.

So she was right. I didn't love her. But I had to try. I thought that I could make her stronger. That I could build her up so she could live her own life. I was wrong. But I still couldn't have done anything differently. I don't know if I did things the right way, but I couldn't have done them any differently."

Sam hugged her knees to her chest. "I don't know what you want me to say. When we first met, I thought you were divorced—"

"I told you that we had split up," he interrupted quietly. "I didn't lie. I didn't tell you that I was legally divorced."

She shrugged. "All right, maybe I believed what I wanted to believe. But I loved you. When you were arrested—"

"Actually, I was simply taken in."

"Whatever. The police cuffed you and took you away. It didn't matter to me. I knew you were innocent, I loved you. I knew better. I adored you. I was like a stricken groupie. When I look back now, I was pathetic. But . . . but I went away. What else was there to do? So you went back with your wife, and . . . and my folks were in an accident, my father died, and my mother was terribly injured. It was a wretched time of my life. I'm through with it. I don't want to take giant steps backward. I don't want to fall in love with you again."

He had turned toward her. There was a rueful smile curling his lips. He reached out, stroking her hair, brushing a knuckle down her cheeks. "Don't fall in love with me, then. Just let me be a neighbor—a friend."

"A friend?"

His smile deepened. He looked out to sea. "All right, well, sex is an instinct in life. I mean, we all usually want to have sex with someone . . . and well, we've practiced before, there's both a certain excitement and a comfort in knowing what you're going to get . . . ."

"You have incredible nerve."

"Do I? You would have been as easy as sliding into silk last night."

"Oh, my God—"

He laughed. "We could head back to the club, see how you feel today."

"You're being horrible."

"I'm being anxious. Well . . . what do you think?"

"I think you should dunk yourself in the bay!" she told him.

"Actually, that doesn't sound like such a bad idea. Do you ever dunk yourself in the bay? I have a ton of scuba equipment."

She hesitated, then shrugged, realizing that he'd completely changed the subject. "Yeah, I go in now and then. Especially when Mollie is around. She loves to swim with people."

"Does she?"

Sam took a look at him. He appeared comfortable, at ease. She knew that whatever her own bitterness against him, she was still terribly attracted to him—and that life hadn't dealt him an easy hand at times either. Dina and then Billy. She thought about how painful it had been to lose her father, then she wondered what it would have been like if she'd had police and reporters demanding explanations for her every move along the way as well.

But she was sober now, and she didn't want to ride the roller coaster again. Yet it was good to sit beside him, and good to talk.

"Sam," he said quietly, "why did you go to that club?"

"Marnie used to work there," she said, glancing at him. "I thought I could learn something . . . but I failed miserably."

Rowan was very concerned. "Sam, don't go getting involved with a bunch of creeps, thinking you're going to help a friend. You've called the police. There's nothing more that you can do. Except put yourself in danger."

"There's got to be more that I can do—"

"There isn't. If something bad did happen to her, you could be putting yourself in the same kind of danger."

Sam looked at him. "You're the one who's buddy-buddy with the law firm. You should try to find out what goes on down there."

"Maybe I will."

Before Sam could reply, an anxious voice interrupted them.

"Mr. Rowan, Señor Rowan . . . ."

They both spun around. Sam saw a middle-aged, slightly rounded Hispanic woman in a maid's outfit making her way toward them. Croton leaves and hibiscus flowers were sticking out of her clothing. She had obviously dug her way through the foliage to reach them.

"Adelia!" Rowan said, surprised, rising to meet her. "What happened? Are you all right? What's the matter?" He walked to her quickly, taking her hands, studying her from head to toe.

But the woman shook her head quickly. "No, no, you needn't worry for me, Mister Rowan, but she's back! That awful woman is back."

"Marnie?" Sam said, leaping to her feet.

Adelia looked her way, frowning. "No, no, that reporter woman," Adelia explained quickly. "She came to the door, rang, and banged! I didn't answer the door to her, and do you know what she did? She dared walk right into the back—around the house. She was going to the pool to look for you, or to sneak into the basement area, where you keep your music."

Rowan glanced at Sam. "Must be an epidemic in this neighborhood of people running through private property to reach people they want to see."

"She is coming after you now, Mr. Rowan," Adelia warned. "I think that she saw me, that she is following me right through the bushes!"

Rowan was silent.

Sam looked down at her hands—they were shaking. Damn, she didn't want to do this. She looked up at him. "Do you want to come in?"

"Yes," he said simply.

She stood up, dusting off her hands and walking to the house. She entered on the basement level, allowing the two of them to follow her. She closed the door and looked out just in time to see a young woman in a tailored pantsuit come crashing through the bushes.

The hedges were close to the pool. The young woman nearly plummeted in. She was attractive, mid- to late twenties, with short, cleanly cropped dark hair that swung in an angle around her features. She regained her balance and looked around suspiciously.

"Where did that old bitch go?" the young woman said, loud enough to be heard behind the closed door.

Adelia swore in Spanish.

"I really should go give her a piece of my mind—" Rowan began.

"Umm, and she'll write it right up," Sam warned. "Shh!" She watched as the young woman walked around her yard, down to the dock. She stared out at the water, looked into it. Then she came back, walking around the pool area.

"This is ridiculous—" Rowan muttered.

"Rowan, stop, or she'll hear you."

At length the woman turned and started walking around to the front of Sam's yard. Maybe she figured that she had lost her quarry, and it would be useless to subject herself to the tall crotons and hibiscus again.

"Let's see where she goes."

Sam led the way up the stairs to her ground level, carefully pulling the front drapes to the side of the living room window. The reporter had gone to her red Jeep, opened the door, and crawled in. Sam waited for her to start the motor. She didn't. She twisted around, and Sam saw that there was a man seated in the back of the car. He got out and headed toward Rowan's front door.

Adelia started to mutter threateningly in Spanish.

"She's really after you, isn't she?" Sam murmured.

"So it seems."

"Why?"

"Same old story. You'd think that I would be very old news. We'll go back the way we came, Adelia," he told his maid.

She nodded, but turned to Sam. "Thank you, *gracias.* It's so kind of you, letting us in like this."

"So graciously!" Rowan added.

He turned then, heading back to the steps to the basement level, to the French doors to the patio, and on out. Adelia followed along behind, and Sam followed them.

"Shit!" Rowan swore, stopping. The bushes were moving again.

"Well, you wanted to try out the water," Sam suggested.

"What?"

"The water. There's a little more gas and fuel on the shore here, but it's really not so bad. Nowhere near as bad as by the marinas."

"Good thinking."

"Oh, no! No, no, no! I am not going into the water!" Adelia protested.

"No, you just stay here with me for a while," Sam said. "Rowan, you'd better hustle—"

But he was already gone. He moved with the silence and grace of an athlete, shooting across her yard, onto the dock, and into the water.

A second later the man appeared. He stopped just by Marnie's bushes. Then Adelia started to swear again in Spanish—and her words were punctuated with references to the *polizia.* The man retreated into the bushes.

Sam couldn't help it. She started laughing. She put a hand on Adelia's shoulder. "Come in. We'll have a glass of wine together." Wine. Maybe she shouldn't. No, it would be all right. She wouldn't be staring at naked people tonight—she wouldn't be tempted to guzzle.

"Oh, no, no, no, thank you, but I'm working, I work for Señor Rowan—"

"You work for him all night?"

"Oh, no!" Adelia said with wide eyes. "Oh, no, he is easy, the nicest man I have worked for ever." Her eyes rolled. "At first I was afraid. I meet Miss Newcastle, and I think, no, Adelia, I scrub sidewalks before I work for her. I worked at the law office, you see, but they hired a new company, and the companies, they . . ." she paused, sniffing scornfully, "they make money off my knees, you understand?"

"I'm afraid I do."

"But Mr. Rowan . . . he tells me to go home early, he thanks me for what I do—and he give me what he calls 'bonus' already. I love him! I work when he needs me. Next time I will take a rolling pin to the head of that reporter woman!"

Sam laughed again, certain that Rowan would be in good hands. She could just picture Adelia, dark Latin eyes flashing, as she went after the chic brunette.

"The next time, she goes into your pool, eh? She is the one who will be all wet."

"Here, here! Now that certainly deserves a glass of wine."

Adelia was confused and protested again, but Sam urged her on in. She poured them both wine, then found herself cooking pasta.

She enjoyed Adelia. And sipping the wine carefully actually did seem to help.

Adelia told her about her nieces and nephews back

home in Cuba. She was trying to earn enough money to help her sister bring the family over.

"Can they legally come?" Sam asked.

"You don't understand Cuba. Laws are for sale. Maybe I can get them out legally, maybe I will need more money for people to turn their heads. Even here, money talks loudly, you know? Mr. Rowan, he will help, I know that."

"But you worked at the law firm—"

"Yes, there is a man there for immigration. Miss Newcastle, though, she is the one who tells me to help myself, and then God, and others, will help too!" She crossed herself.

Sam lowered her head for a moment. Yes. Marnie would help Adelia. Marnie could be cold, self-centered, and ambitious as hell, but she could be stubborn and determined, and she would admire Adelia's work ethic and her determination.

She served simple pasta with marinara to herself and Rowan's protesting maid; she forced Adelia to remain seated while she put out the plates and poured the wine. Adelia grew giggly, and described Cuba when she had been a little girl. She'd had a husband once, but they had locked him up years and years ago in a Cuban prison, and she didn't even know if he was alive anymore, if she was really a wife or a widow.

"And there's nothing you can do about that?"

"Maybe. Maybe now that Mr. Rowan has gone to Mr. Daly. Mr. Daly can make things happen. He knows men in politics, and sometimes . . ."

"Your husband may very well be dead, Adelia."

"I know."

"But you should know, in case you wish to remarry—"

"No," Adelia said, turning the wedding band on her finger. "Mario and I were deeply in love. He would not recognize me now—I am chubby, *si*? But once I was slim, so pretty, and he was so handsome. Proud—he had to say what he believed. So they took him away, but I will always love him. I will just keep praying. Am I silly? A silly old chubby woman?"

"No, Adelia, you're beautiful, and your thoughts are beautiful," Sam told her. She hesitated, thinking about Adelia's words, about the man she had married—locked away now for years, if he still lived.

But life was standing up for what you thought, or believed. Or for people. No matter what others said or thought.

"Adelia, would you excuse me for just one minute? I need to run up and make a phone call."

"*Si,* I pick up."

"No!"

"I pick up, or I never come over again."

Sam sighed with exasperation. "Okay, just set the dishes on the counter. You're not here to work. You're—hiding out."

"*Si,* Miss Sam," Adelia agreed.

As Sam started up the stairs to her desk phone, she could hear Adelia picking up the dishes—and scraping them. She shook her head. By the time she got back downstairs, Adelia would have the dishes washed and dried and probably put away.

But it suddenly seemed important for her to call Teddy. She could call the missing-persons officers, but if they had learned anything at Marnie's office, it was unlikely that they would share their information with her.

The evening was wearing on, but she knew that Teddy had a tendency to work very late hours, so she tried his private office phone first. Yet even as it began to ring, she looked outside and noticed that there was someone standing on Marnie's lawn. The reporter?

No, she didn't think so. This fellow was almost in the bushes.

The phone was still ringing; Teddy wasn't picking up.

His answering machine came on. He gave his other numbers, his beeper number if it was an emergency, and then allowed for a message. It wasn't an emergency. "Teddy," she said, still staring down at the figure in the bushes, "it's Sam. Call me. Please. As soon as possible."

She hung up, then moved around to the front window to look out and see if the reporters were still out there by the Jeep.

The red Jeep was gone.

She paused, then jumped as her phone began to ring. She made a dive for it, surprised that Teddy would be calling her back so quickly.

"Hello?"

"Are you holding my maid hostage?"

"No! We had dinner."

"Really?" He sounded wistful.

"Why, is that a problem for you?"

"My God, you are one testy woman. No, Adelia is more than welcome to have dinner with you. She is a warm and wonderful human being, and I hope you made her something delicious. It's just that the thought of it makes me hungry. Actually, I just wanted to make sure that everything was all right."

"Everything is fine, except—" She broke off.

"What?"

"The reporters are gone, I think. The red Jeep is gone. I don't see another car—but there's someone standing by Marnie's big croton in the front."

"Someone? A him or a her?"

"I don't know."

"I'll go and find out."

"No, Rowan, wait. We should just call the police. Rowan—"

"You can't call the police on people just for standing by a bush."

"Maybe it's whoever took Marnie."

"We don't know that anyone took Marnie."

"I think someone made her leave," Sam said stubbornly. "I know Marnie."

She heard him sigh. Then he said, "If someone took Marnie, why would he be back now?"

"Because criminals . . . return to the scene of the crime, don't they?"

"Am I supposed to answer that from experience?" he asked dryly.

"No, I just—"

"I'll go down. We'll find out."

"No—"

"Sam, it's all right. I'll be careful."

"No, Rowan, no!"

But he'd already hung up the phone.

Chapter 11

Rowan quietly exited his house by the basement, moving slowly. It had been a ridiculous night, he mused. He'd jumped into the bay to get away from a reporter. And now he was sneaking around in the dark to try to find a trespasser on Marnie's property.

He came silently along the side of his house, hugging the bushes closest to his own property. Sam was right. There was someone there. Just standing, staring up at the house. He was far back against the bushes.

Rowan inched closer, then he paused, frowning.

He had reached a distance at which he could see the nocturnal visitor fairly clearly. The fellow was dressed in black Levi's and a chocolate-colored polo shirt, which made him blend in well with the night. He appeared fairly tall, not too heavy, but in the shadows it was hard to discern his true size.

Rowan decided not to take any chances.

He could handle himself in a fight. Other kids had made fun of Ewan, and he had never allowed an attack on his brother to go unanswered. After one brawl when he was about ten, a feisty old teacher had taken him in hand, telling him that if he felt the urge to fight, he should be doing it for the school's boxing and wrestling teams.

Now he judged the distance of his enemy, and his size and weight the best he could. Speed meant as much as

strength; if the fellow did have a weapon, he had to take
him down before he could use it.

Rowan swept along the back of the property line and
hedges, came around Sam's side of Marnie's property. He
was close to his quarry now—any closer and he took a
chance of being heard. He bolted from his position, flying
with all the speed he could muster.

He had the element of surprise. He caught hold of the
shadowy trespasser, tackled him, and knocked him down.
The fellow's breath expelled in a long whoosh. Then he
gasped for air and protested:

"Hey, please!"

The voice was familiar. Rowan rolled him over. It was
Marnie's brother.

"Thayer?"

"Yes, it's Thayer . . . please, I don't mean any harm.
Could I possibly get up?"

Rowan stood, reaching down a hand to the young man.
Thayer grasped it and rose. He grimaced at Rowan and
began dusting off his jeans and polo shirt. "Thanks. Hey,
for a musician, you tackle pretty well."

"Sorry. Thayer, what are you doing out here, skulking around in the bushes?" Thayer looked across Marnie's
yard, swallowed. Guiltily, Rowan thought. He kept looking at the young man who stood awkwardly before him.
Then he asked again. "Thayer, what are you doing out
here like this?"

"I came to see if Marnie was back yet, but she didn't
answer when I knocked. I know half the world has a key
to her house, but I'm afraid I'm not among that half."

"I don't think she's come back. I admit to being worried about her myself now."

"Yeah, I'm worried, too."

"So why were you hiding in the bushes?"

"I wasn't."

Rowan arched a brow.

"Honestly . . ." He looked around himself and laughed. He did look a lot like Marnie. He was an interesting young man. So good-looking he was almost pretty, and yet, despite his looks and his thinness, he didn't seem effeminate. "I guess it looks strange," he said. "But after no one answered the door, I came back here to study the house. I was just looking at its architecture."

"You like architecture?"

"Art. I love art. My sister thinks I'm a fool because I paint and sell my stuff off the sidewalk down in the Grove, or out on the beach. But I'm happy. She can't seem to accept that. I make a decent income."

"Well, if you're happy and surviving, that's great."

"Yeah, I'm great, really, but I'm honestly worried about Marnie now."

"I guess we're all getting more and more concerned. It's hard to imagine Marnie missing work on purpose, isn't it?"

"Yes," Thayer agreed flatly. "And my father . . ."

"What?"

Thayer shook his head. Then he looked at Rowan with a shrug. "My father is a drunken asshole, and he wants to talk to Marnie, or have her declared legally dead."

"What?"

"Sick, isn't it?"

"Well, thankfully, it'll be a very long time before he can declare her legally dead."

"Yeah. Don't repeat that, please. I try to look after him, kind of—he is my old man. But he's a wretched old alcoholic. Marnie hates him—and he hates her. He's got it in his head that Marnie had life because of him and so she owes him anything that she makes. Marnie thinks that she made a life despite him and he should do us both a favor and drop dead. It's terrible. Talk about your dysfunctional family."

Rowan didn't get to reply. The thought had begun to

form in his head that although tragic events had happened in his life, his family had never been that dysfunctional. He'd known about Colin Newcastle already. Marnie had told him.

"Rowan?"

He heard his name called and realized that Sam had come out her front door. He winced, making a mental note to remind her that she'd been inside for safety—stepping out when she didn't hear from him immediately wasn't a good idea.

"Yeah, Sam, I'm here—at Marnie's. With Thayer."

"Thayer?"

Sam came around her front yard to the property line and found them both by the hedge. "Thayer! Hi, what are you doing here?"

"Checking on my sister."

"She hasn't come back," Sam said softly, obviously concerned for the young man.

"I know. Rowan told me."

"The police are working on it." She tried to sound cheerful.

"Oh, yeah, I know. They grilled me endlessly. As if I would hurt my own sister."

Rowan cleared his throat. "Well, you did say it was your basic dysfunctional family."

Thayer glowered at him, eyes both furious and hurt. "I love Marnie!" he said stubbornly. "You don't understand. She may not approve of me, but growing up, we were all each other had. Don't you understand that? No, maybe you can't understand!" he added, looking down. "It was a strange house," he said gruffly.

"Thayer, why don't you come on in my house? Adelia and I just had pasta. There's plenty left."

"I didn't come to bother anyone—"

"You won't be bothering anyone. You're one of my best friend's little brother. You come on in."

Rowan stared at Sam. She was about to take the young man in her arms and smother him with feminine concern. He looked at Thayer again. Definitely the artistic type. Slim, wiry, slightly long, really good hair. Big eyes.

But he'd tackled the kid. He might be skinny, but he was strong. He might be just a young man struggling for his own identity against a harrowing past—or the past might have made him just a little bit psychotic.

"Thayer, please, come on in," Sam insisted. Her hazel eyes were bright, green and gold. She looked like a waif, feet bare, long legs perfect as they stretched from her shorts, hair just swept up with a pin, light tendrils framing her delicate face.

Rowan cleared his throat. "Hey, I could sure go for some pasta. Am I invited as well?" He glared at Sam. He forced a smile. "After all, it seems that you have been keeping my domestic assistant hostage over there."

As if startled—just realizing that he really was there—she looked back at him. "I've been keeping your domestic assistant hostage?"

"Adelia," he reminded her.

"Oh. Yes. Well, I—umm—of course, I suppose."

Yes, it would be rude if she just ignored him after having talked to him previously about their unknown nocturnal visitor.

"Thanks."

Only in America. He was slipping in through the graces of his maid.

As they walked across the lawns, they saw the lights of a car driving down the street toward the three houses at the tip of their little peninsula. Sam shaded her eyes. "I wonder who . . ."

Marnie.

They could all tell she was hoping against hope that it was Marnie.

But it wasn't Marnie's car. Hers was a black BMW. This car was light.

"May be that reporter coming back after you, Rowan," she warned.

"Maybe we should hurry," he said, feeling tension slipping back into his every muscle. He set a hand on Sam's shoulder, thinking he could urge her along. But she resisted.

"No, no, it's all right. It's just my cousin."

"Who?"

But she had already started forward. A little yellow Honda pulled into the drive and he saw Lacey Henley stepping out. Sam gave her a hug.

"Laura Henley's daughter?" Thayer asked Rowan softly.

"Yeah."

"Wow."

The kid was pretty wow. Young, graceful, like a doe. A dancer, Laura had told him. A good one. He could believe it. He'd seen her moving around the floor while her brother had been playing on the beach.

Thayer Newcastle stepped on past Rowan, walking toward the car. He shrugged and followed.

"I have a terrible crick in my neck," Lacey was saying. "I was going to call you, but Mom said just to get in the car and come on over. She said you'd be here. And I'm . . . I'm restless tonight, I guess. I just needed to get out for a while—Mom said that you hadn't called her for any wild activities, so you must be home."

Rowan lowered his head, trying not to smile. He saw Sam's face turn beet-red.

"You heard about the club, huh?" Rowan said. Sam cast him a warning glare.

"Yeah," Lacey said, and for some reason she looked more uncomfortable than Sam.

"Um, I'll be happy to work on your crick," Sam said. "Let's go on in."

But Lacey wasn't listening. She was staring at Rowan, and she seemed a little less uneasy as she smiled. "Mr. Dillon. It's really great to see you again. Mom says you come right to the rescue when you're asked. And you were so wonderful about my brother the other night. I can't tell you what it meant to him, that you came to watch him play and said such great things about him and the group."

"They are good. I wouldn't have said so if they weren't."

"But still . . . you just being there . . ."

The tone of her voice was so grateful and adoring that he felt his own face turning red. But he remembered. It was a tough world. Until you had a record label, until you were recognized by the radio stations and MTV, you were just another player. It was a rocky road.

"I had a great night," he said simply.

Sam cleared her throat. "Okay, Lacey, he's great, we all adore him. Maybe we could go in now? Oh, and have you met—"

But she didn't need to introduce the young man hovering just behind Rowan.

"Hi. Lacey, right?" Thayer said, stepping forward.

Lacey's eyes widened, and she smiled curiously as she let Thayer take her hand. "Yeah, hi, I'm Lacey, but we've met before, right—?"

"I'm Thayer, Marnie's brother."

"Yeah! You come to see my brother play a lot. That's great. You know, when you're just starting out, it makes such a difference if you can really get an audience at the local clubs."

"Yeah, I know. I'm an artist, and getting the galleries to pay attention is just about the same."

"I have friends who have gone off to New York or L.A.

just to get hired to come back and work shows here!"
Lacey said. "In fact, guess what I'm doing this weekend,
Sam?"

"What?"

"Just that! A friend of mine found out about a show
that's being cast, and a group of us are going to share
the expenses and go up and give it a fling. Imagine! We
have to go to New York to try to get cast in a show that
will play right here!"

"Well, good luck, Lacey. We know you're good."

"I can tell," Thayer interrupted. "You are good. Really
good. The best."

"How can you tell?"

Lacey's innocent smile was all for Thayer then.

"I've seen you move," he told her. And grinned. "Pure
poetry."

Lacey kept smiling. She and Thayer seemed to have
forgotten that they weren't alone.

Rowan looked at Sam. She stared back at him. He
shrugged. "Still want to do the pasta thing? I could take
you out somewhere. We could leave them standing in the
yard for a while. They might not notice that we've gone
until we get back."

She smiled sourly. "You're forgetting I have that crick
thing to take care of."

He grinned. She flushed, lowering her lashes briefly, as
if to hide some emotion from him. Was she as determined
as she claimed not to get involved again? Yes, she'd made
that obvious.

Maybe not. There had been last night . . .

Right. Too much to drink, and a strip show.

Today, she seemed more alarmed, as if she had discovered that whatever had been between them hadn't
changed. It had always been so easy to talk. He felt a twist
in his heart, thinking about the first time he'd met her. It
had been at a small coffeehouse in Gainesville. He hadn't

been with the group that night; some friends had talked him into doing an acoustic set with one of the owner's guitars. She had come to him afterward, telling him how much she had enjoyed the power of his voice. It was great with the group, but she'd seen him in concert once and she had to admit the amplifiers had been bad and the drums had been overpowering. "It's easy for that to happen, I know. I love the drums myself," she had told him.

And later that night, he had heard her play. At his house. She hadn't slept there that night, or with him. He had kissed her good-bye. And she had stared at him with her beautiful eyes, innocent eyes that were yet strangely wise. "You're married—"

"No more," he had assured her. "No more."

It hadn't been a lie. Yet it hadn't been the truth. And it had come back to haunt him.

Sam, he realized, had started for the house. He quickly snapped back to the present and followed. Lacey and Thayer must have remembered that Sam and Rowan did exist, because they followed as well.

Adelia, worried, met them at the front door. "Mr. Rowan, everything is all right?"

"Yes, Adelia, things are fine. This is Marnie Newcastle's brother, Thayer, and Sam's second cousin, Lacey Henley. Thayer, Lacey, Adelia Garcia."

"But who was in the bushes?" Adelia asked.

"Guilty," Thayer told her. "I didn't intend to be in the bushes—I was just staring up at the house, wondering where my sister could be."

"She'll show up, sooner or later," Lacey said with false cheerfulness.

"Yeah, you know Marnie, she's a wild woman," Thayer agreed.

"And her car is gone, her purse is gone, right? That's what my dad said," Lacey added encouragingly.

"Speaking of cars . . ." Sam murmured suddenly. "Where is yours, Thayer? How did you get here?"

"Oh—I didn't bring my car."

"You walked down here?" Sam asked, frowning.

"No, I came by boat."

"Boat?" Rowan said sharply. Once again, he looked at Sam, and she at him. It suddenly occurred to them both that someone could have come by boat, taken Marnie, her purse, and her car, and driven off, then returned via the water—or even on foot—to retrieve the boat.

And Thayer had come by boat.

"You like boats?" Lacey asked Thayer.

"Boats, water, on it, in it, diving, sea creatures, you name it."

"That's great."

"And you?" Thayer asked her.

"I adore the water. Next to dancing, it's the most wonderful thing in the world."

Arm in arm, the two wandered on toward the rear of the house. Adelia looked at them, then at Rowan and Sam.

"It's possible, isn't it?" Sam said.

"Sure, of course, almost all things are possible," Rowan said.

"I'll put water on to boil for more pasta," Adelia said.

"No, no, you sit, relax—" Sam said, turning to her quickly.

"No, you sit, relax," Adelia advised. She walked on back toward the kitchen.

Rowan was glad to see that Sam seemed to be regarding him with a shade less suspicion and hostility. Except that he felt the same unease she did. Their little tip of the peninsula had seemed entirely private and secure. Easy to see a car come in or out. But the bay stretched behind them, made even more elusive by the darkness of night.

"Sam," Rowan said, looking at her, "we have no way of knowing that Marnie even disappeared from here."

"I thought you were convinced she was off on a weekend fling."

"I was."

"Well?"

"The weekend has been over," he said quietly.

She turned around, heading for the kitchen, aware that he followed her. She didn't try to take over from Adelia, who was stirring sauce while water bubbled in a pot. Lacey and Thayer were seated in wicker chairs by the doors, leaning toward one another, deep in conversation. They'd found the red wine, which Sam picked up to pour for Rowan.

"Red again?" he queried pleasantly.

"Shut up, and don't tease me when I'm being sober and logical," she said, handing him a glass of the wine.

He drank his wine, watching her. She cared, really cared. Naturally, he cared as well, but if something had happened to Marnie, it wouldn't affect his life the way it would hers. The only people who would really care about her as a person would be Sam and maybe her brother.

If he hadn't been instrumental in her disappearance.

"I'm sure the police will be doing more and more now that time is going by," Rowan said. It was a lame assurance. "You have to trust their methods."

She swallowed her wine suddenly as if it were a shot of tequila. Tonight it didn't seem to faze her. "Everyone was convinced that she was off for a wild weekend."

He swirled the wine in his glass. "Sam, the police are on it."

"But maybe the police just don't see all the possibilities. Maybe somebody came in by boat, kidnapped her with her purse and car, and then—"

He put a hand on hers. She stared down at it. For a moment he thought she would jerk her hand away. "You can't make yourself insane over this."

She kept staring at his hand. He wanted to tighten his

hold on her, but he didn't dare. There was such a pulse of life to her, such a warmth. Just touching her so, he felt a white-hot poignancy tearing through him, a sense of déjâ vu. He felt a yearning to enfold her in comfort and assurances, and he also felt alive with a desire to physically retrace the past, really remember, lie down with her, be with her. It was frightening how he could remember her scent, the feel of her flesh, the way she moved, the things she did. It would be incredibly easy to forget that time had passed at all, to touch her cheek, stroke her lips with his thumb, give up the present, let the darkness and the night hide them from all that plagued them.

That, and the pure forgetfulness of sexual gratification. If only . . .

God, he still loved her.

"I, uh, dinner," she said.

She freed her hand and, turning, pulled plates from cabinets and called to Lacey and Thayer to come serve themselves.

At least she hadn't forgotten him. She piled pasta high on a plate—a little too high—and brought it over to the counter.

"Aren't you going to eat?"

"I ate with Adelia."

The pasta was delicious. And thankfully, the conversation did turn from Marnie. Lacey was elated because she and her friends were going off on their New York jaunt. Thayer talked about some of his works, and then they plagued Rowan about when he was going to play again himself.

"I'm retired," he said, curious to find that Sam seemed to be studying him intently.

"You can't just retire!" Lacey told him. She was a stunning girl, filled with the beauty of her enthusiasm and love for life. "Artists—of any kind—don't just retire! You have to die in the creation of art, surely you know that! But you do, of course. My mom said your house is full of musical instruments."

"I'm writing. I just don't want to go back to the circuit your brother is getting into now. You know, it's one of those 'been there, done that' kind of deals."

"You really had a great group. A great group. The Blackhawks!" Thayer told him earnestly.

"*Group.* We were a great group. The group can no longer exist."

"Your drummer died," Lacey said. "Surely there are other great drummers around! Sam, I remember when you used to play the drums. We all loved it. My brother thought you were the coolest relative that it was possible to have. You were so little and yet so awesome with those drums!"

Sam looked frozen. She answered casually, "Well, I've retired, too. And I can retire. I never thought of myself as a great artist. I like what I do now . . . Whoa, look at the time, will you? It's getting late, you know. Adelia, no more washing dishes. I can do that myself. Lacey, you've got school tomorrow, don't you?"

"Yeah, I've got to go," Lacey said regretfully, looking at Thayer. "Thanks for the pasta, Sam. Thayer, it was great to get to know you."

"You, too, Lacey. You, too."

"Rowan . . . thanks!" Lacey said and kissed him on the cheek.

"Oh, Lacey! What about your neck?" Sam asked.

"It's . . ." She shrugged, smiling. "It's fine now!"

They started for the door. Adelia was still trying to wash dishes, but Sam stopped her firmly. "No more work! Go home. And if I can help you with anything, with your husband, with anything at all, you let me know."

"*Gracias, muchas gracias!*" Adelia said. "I can finish these dishes—"

"No! Doesn't that retired musician you work for now ever wash a few of his own dishes?"

Rowan smiled, determined not to take offense. So Sam was touchy about not playing the drums anymore. If she felt that way, why had she quit?

"Alas, poor Adelia! Come back to your wretched place of employment, get your things, and be gone for the night!" Rowan said.

Adelia laughed, her cheeks were rosy. She'd had a good time, so it seemed.

Lacey was already out the front door. Thayer saw her to her car. "I'll just go get my things and go home for the night," Adelia said.

"Come see me anytime!" Sam called to her.

"*Si*. Maybe I come to the gym and you make me a skinny girl again, eh?"

"Hey, we can do it if you want."

Lacey's car was backing out. Thayer had a hand up, waving to them as he started off toward his sister's yard.

"I'll be back in a minute," Rowan said, determined to follow Thayer out back and get a look at his boat.

"That's all right—I'm going in, locking up," Sam told him quickly. "Thanks for scouring the bushes. Good night—"

"No. Lock your door, but wait for me," he said firmly.

He didn't let her answer but quickly followed after Thayer. He moved slowly, quietly. Thayer walked along the edge of Marnie's property, along the hedge line. At the dock, he slipped the rope on a small motorboat.

The motor revved, and Thayer was gone, shooting across the bay.

Rowan walked on over to the dock. It was larger than Sam's. At low tide you could probably slip a couple of small boats beneath it and they'd never even be seen.

Of course, once out on the bay . . .

But most of the time, even at night, there were boats

out on the bay. On a sunny day there were dozens at any given time. On a Friday night . . .

Yes, even on a Friday night, a boat could easily come and go from anywhere in this area and barely be noticed.

Fine. A boat could have come and gone. Great. What did that mean? Had Marnie disappeared from the house? Or had she kept a date with someone and then disappeared? And if so, and if she had met with foul play, why hadn't her car been found? Or her purse? Or . . .

Her body.

Adelia came around the back of the house and stepped into it, humming. She'd had such a nice evening. Once, she had dreamed that she would have a nice house herself, children underfoot, and a life of cleaning and cooking for her husband, Julio. But soon after they were married, Julio had been arrested for his public dissidence, and when the opportunity had come about in 1981 for her to slip aboard a boat, he had insisted that she leave, swearing he would be right behind her.

But now no one in Cuba knew where he was. The people who had tried to help her from the United States had been able to discover very little. She was really not that old, not forty yet. There had been a time when she could have gone out with other men. Now she never thought about it. She had loved her Julio, and maybe it was best just to remember those good times.

She walked through the kitchen and picked up her old leather handbag. It was so big, and so nice. She had bought it at a church fund-raiser. America. She loved this country.

Her compact was in her purse. She took it out, opened it, and checked her nose. Shiny. She had gotten a little round. Maybe she would take Miss Sam up on her invitation to come to her exercise place. Maybe one day Julio would come home.

Suddenly, out of the blue, she felt as if ice water had been poured down her spine. Was that a shadow that flashed past the mirror? A moment's blackness, someone there . . .

Instinctively she spun around.

Nothing.

The house seemed empty. Silent. Still. Dead still.

And yet . . .

She was frightened. Her mouth was dry, and her palms were all sweaty.

She had to get out of the house. Her mind began working. Even here, on this private little piece of peninsula, they always kept the doors locked. But Mr. Rowan had come out just to see who was next door. He must have left the house without locking up.

Panic seized her. She didn't want to know if someone was or wasn't in the house. She snapped her compact shut, thrust it into her purse, and went straight to the front door. She unbolted it quickly and hurried out.

Once she was outside, the urgent sense of fear began to fade. She was no longer trapped with the shadows of what might or might not be. Starting for her car, she thought about telling Mr. Rowan that she'd imagined that maybe someone had slipped into his house while they were both out. Then she felt silly, like a coward; chicken, as the Americans liked to say. She didn't want him to think that she was silly and scared. And she had already said good night. She walked on resolutely to her little red Honda.

The night wind began to whisper through the trees and the bushes. She looked up and around her, afraid of the shadows once again.

She felt as if someone were watching her.

Just watching . . .

Waiting.

Breathing . . .

Eyes in the night.

"Mr. Rowan? Mr. Rowan?" she called out.

No answer.

She slid behind the wheel. And she did something that a matronly Hispanic lady never did—she jerked into gear, slammed on the gas, and burned rubber.

Rowan walked along the hedges out of Marnie's yard and around the front of Sam's house. He tapped lightly on the door. No answer. He tapped harder. Still no answer.

He hesitated.

Well, he could hang around a while longer. Bang on the door, create more of a disturbance. He had told her he was coming back.

And that was probably why the door was locked and bolted, he thought. Apparently, tonight, sober, and without benefit of outside stimulation, she just hadn't felt that same undeniable spark of electricity that had zapped him, that longing to touch again, feel again, breathe again . . .

Go home, he told himself.

If and when she was ready, she would call.

He lifted his hand, tempted to knock one last time. He knotted his fingers into his fist, but he didn't knock.

He turned around, crossed Marnie's yard, and came to his own front door.

He'd left by the back.

He tried the knob, noticing that Adelia's compact car was gone. To his surprise, he found that she had left the front door unlocked. He opened the door hesitantly, thinking that it was unlike her not to lock the door. But then, they had both left the house by way of the back, and so that had been open—why lock the front?

Still, he walked into the house uneasily, disturbed by a gut feeling that things just weren't quite right. How to search it out? he asked himself. The problem with a fairly large house was seeing it all at once. Top to bottom, he decided.

Treading softly, he took the stairs to the top. He went to his room first, glad for once that he had a bag of golf clubs. He had a set of Pings sitting just inside his closet. There was nothing like a good golf club in his hand to make him feel a little safer.

He walked through the upstairs rooms in the darkness, his eyes adjusting, daring the shadows. That level was clear. Down to the kitchen and public rooms. All clear as well.

So much for gut feelings.

Finally he headed down to the basement level. There, all of his instruments stood in shadow, wrapped in a strange silence.

There was nothing so silent as an instrument waiting to be played.

And nothing so quiet as shadows that only hinted of a noise that might have been.

But there was nothing here. No one lurking in those silent shadows. He walked around the entire area, making certain that no one was waiting silently, protected by darkness and the night.

His house was empty.

But it hadn't been.

The last time he had played the drums, he had left his drumsticks sitting on the stool. They now rested on the snare.

How could he be so sure where he had left them?

He knew, he just knew.

As he pondered the problem, the phone began to ring.

She had been certain that it would be Rowan, and so she had answered the phone. At first she hadn't been going to do so. She didn't want to talk to him, to hear his voice, to let herself be swayed . . .

To become involved.

But after it had rung a few times, she told herself that

she had to pick up the phone. It wouldn't be fair to let him worry about her.

And so Sam answered her phone on the fourth ring, right before the answering machine would pick up.

"Hello?"

Nothing. She almost hung up. Then . . .

Breathing. And a soft warning: "I can see you."

"Rowan?"

"I can see you."

"Who is this?"

"Leave it alone. Do you hear me? Leave it alone."

"Leave what alone? Who is this?"

"Leave it alone. Just leave it alone." The voice was husky, hoarse, a croak. Disguised.

A prankster?

No, she didn't think so.

Not the way fear seemed to touch her. Like the tip of an icicle drawn down her spine, so sharp, so cold it burned . . .

A whisper now, barely discernible. "I can see you. Leave it be. I can see you."

"Who is this? What are you talking about?"

"Just remember that I know what you do, and where you go. Leave it alone."

"Who are you?"

"I'll be watching."

"Damn you—"

The phone went dead in her hand.

For a moment she was afraid. More than afraid. The icy chills continued to race along her spine, then sped throughout her limbs. Her throat was constricted, her breathing sounded like the wind in a hurricane.

Then she was suddenly furious, thinking it might well have been a prankster, or someone who had been trespassing, running around the houses. Someone try-

ing to scare her. She hated being afraid, hated people
who did things like that . . .

Being angry had brought warmth. Strength. Indignation.
But not enough.

Her anger and warmth were fickle; they began to fade.

The chills started up again. Like icy-cold fingers, slipping around her neck, stroking downward along her collar-
bone, touching her spine with tentacles of fear.

Then the phone started to ring again . . .

Chapter 12

She let it go, waiting for the answering machine to pick up

It wouldn't be him again, she told herself. Teddy had informed her once that hundreds of people received obscene and threatening phone calls every day. There was little the police could do about it, not unless they got persistent, not unless . . .

The machine picked up. She heard Rowan's voice.

"Sam, are you all right? Did you just call here? Damn, Sam, answer me, are you all right? Hell, I'll be going insane here all night worrying."

It was the sound of his voice as well as the exaggerated quality of the last that caused her to pick up the phone.

"Hello!" She knew she was breathless.

"Sam?"

"Yes, yes, of course. What's wrong?"

"Nothing is wrong. I had just thought that . . . did you just call here?"

"Did I just call there?" Sam said. "No! Did you just call me?"

"No. Yes. I mean, I just called now, and I'm talking to you, but I didn't call before. Why? What's wrong there?"

With him on the phone, she didn't feel quite so scared. In fact, she felt her warmth coming back, and her anger. His voice could do that for her.

It had been a prank call. A call made just to scare her. Someone angry with her? A random number?

"Nothing. Nothing at all. Just a silly prank. Why were you so worried about me?"

"I don't know. I just . . . I don't know." He was quiet for a minute. "Have you ever considered buying a German shepherd or a rottweiler?"

She laughed. "No. I like dogs—I just work a lot."

"Really? Lacey made it sound like you were Ma Kettle, always at the good old homestead. Well, except for those wild nights when you're at strip clubs."

"How amusing. Well, Lacey is wrong. And she should have never said such a thing. It's her mother who spends half her life dragging me from place to place," she said before thinking. Then she winced. It was probably painfully clear that she didn't lead a very exciting life, not by jet-setting, club-hopping standards, that was for sure.

"I think I should come over."

"No! I don't think that would be wise."

"I'm not worried about being wise."

"You're really not far from me at all, you know."

"Neither was Marnie."

Neither of them chose to correct the grammatical tense.

"You can just think of me as a large rottweiler," he said.

She hesitated. She wanted to hang up on him. She wanted to say thanks, that he'd been decent, but he was out of her life, she was moving forward, and she never wanted to see him again.

But it wasn't true.

And if she hung up on him, she'd be awake all night. Awake, and afraid. And then she might find herself calling him back. That would be worse.

She sighed as deeply as she could without being overly dramatic. "All right, fine, but I don't understand why you're so worried." She hesitated. "I mean, you really are worried. Not just . . ."

"Hungry?" he queried softly.

"Rowan—"

"I am worried."

"Why?"

"I'll tell you when I get there."

"All right."

He was there within five minutes, his keys in his hands. He seemed tense. As soon as he had entered her front door, he turned around and locked it. "Key in the alarm."

"What is the matter?" she pursued.

He shrugged. "I don't know . . . exactly. I just . . ."

"What?"

"I just had an odd feeling that someone was in my house while I was at yours."

"What?"

"I think someone was in my house."

"Was anything stolen? Destroyed—"

"No."

She hesitated, looking at him. Had this been an excuse to come over? No, he seemed to be wound as tight as piano wire. And . . .

She had the same uneasy feelings. That someone was watching. That someone was near. That someone . . .

I can see you, the voice had said.

"Besides a gut feeling, is there any other reason at all to believe that someone might have been in your house?" she asked, trying to sound very calm and rational.

"The drumsticks."

"I'm sorry?"

"My drumsticks. They were moved. I'd set them on the stool; they were on the snare."

"Maybe you just forgot where you left them."

"No."

"Maybe."

He lifted a hand. "Maybe, but it's so unlikely. And still, there is that maybe. So you tell me—just what do I say when I call the police? I think there was an intruder in my house. Did he take anything? No. Disturb anything? No. Leave obscene messages? No. He just broke in and moved my drumsticks."

She stared at him and then turned and started walking toward the back of the house. He was right behind. "I just made tea," she said.

"I'll have a bourbon."

"So will I."

"You don't like bourbon."

"Maybe I've acquired a taste."

"You've definitely acquired a taste for wine."

"Oh, that is cruel! I don't want any more wine this evening."

"Sorry—I need a drink. Join me. A gin and tonic? Or has that changed?"

"And you didn't remember the black coffee, huh?"

"I'm beginning to think I like you best when you're a wee bit tipsy."

"Funny."

He passed her on the way to the kitchen. It was uncanny, the way he seemed to know her cabinets. Of course, he'd been there earlier. Eating pasta. He'd seen where things were stored. He found the liquor cabinet, poured himself a bourbon, and gathered the makings of a gin and tonic for her.

"Are you trying to get me really smashed?"

He stared at her.

She flushed.

"Hardly likely," he said. "Because maybe tonight I don't want to be in such a hurry to leave." He set the drink in front of her, then stood there, challenging her. "Tipsy, so you're more mellow. You have a tongue that can cut like a knife. Drunk, no. I have my standards for seduction. If you're really anxious that I leave tonight, why did you let me come over?"

She lifted her drink, paused, slowly grimaced. "I didn't think you'd take no for an answer."

"Gee, you've gotten easy."

"You were absolutely insistent!"

He shook his head. "I don't believe you—that's not the only reason you let me come."

"Oh?"

"You're scared," he accused her.

"Really?"

"Unnerved about something."

"You're the one convinced that someone was in your house because your drumsticks were moved!"

"Why did you stop playing the drums?" he asked, his change of subject so abrupt and demanding that she was caught off guard.

"I—I—"

"You were good."

"Oh! You think I stopped the drums because of you? What an ego! Well, you're wrong. My father played, I told you that. He played through high school and college, and he and his group still played, except that he loved to teach as well, so he played as a sideline. But he was the one who taught me. I quit because my father died, and believe me, it had nothing to do with you."

He lowered his head slightly, rolling the ice in his Jack Black on the rocks. Then he looked at her again, eyes intense. "Your father would have wanted you to quit playing the drums?"

"Never mind—it's none of your business!" she snapped. She slipped off her counter seat, picked up her glass, and took a big swallow of the gin and tonic.

A mistake. She swore silently to herself, but too late.

She was off balance, and to her horror, she wavered. He reached out immediately to steady her.

She would have jerked her wrist free except that she was afraid she might fall. "I'm fine."

"You'd better be."

"You made the drink."

"Stick to one."

"Hey!"

"You heard me."

She had, and the way he was watching her was making her very uneasy. Flashes of the night before came to her mind's eye.

She shook her head. "I'm really tired. I think I need to go to bed."

He paused, eyeing her. "Do you want me to leave?"

"Were you planning on staying—I mean, through the night? I mean, last night . . . you couldn't wait to get out of here."

"That was last night. Actually, yeah, I was planning on staying tonight."

"In—in what way?"

He smiled very slowly. "In what way would you like me to stay?"

"Rowan—"

"Sam! What's up? You're not at all inebriated, and you're still as prickly as a porcupine when sober, so . . . ?"

She hesitated. His gaze was so intense. His hand was still on her arm. She looked up at him, and her eyes fell. "All right, I'm afraid."

Dark lashes closed over his eyes for a moment, and she detected a faint tick at his throat. Then he was looking at her again, speaking levelly. "I knew that you were afraid, but it would be nice if you'd be a bit more specific about exactly why you're afraid."

She moistened her lips. "All right, the phone call."

"What phone call?"

She shrugged. His grip had tightened until it was almost painful. She heard the grating in his voice. Did he know something that she didn't?

Was there someone he suspected of all this?

She shook her head, a little afraid of his tension. "I kind of told you before. I got a phone call. It was really—I'm certain—just a stupid phone call. Maybe even a bored kid playing, you know? It was someone who whispered. Some jerk."

His hold on her grew even tighter. "Someone who whispered what?"

"Really . . . not a lot."

"Sam, what did he say?"

"That . . ." She let her voice trail off as she met his eyes. "That he could see me."

"And you thought it was *me*?" he inquired incredulously.

"I . . . no. I—"

"Great."

He released his hold on her.

She pulled her thoughts together, her own temper flaring. "Look, you idiot, obviously I didn't think it was you—I let you in here, right?"

He walked past her toward the phone. "I'm going to call the cops so you can tell them about the phone call. And you don't need to worry about me being around here. If you don't want to. You don't have to be friendly or polite. You don't even have to acknowledge me. Just think of me as a large rottweiler."

Sam gave him Teddy's number.

"I got an answering machine," he said after a moment.

"Try his home number," she said, and give him another set of digits.

A minute later she was talking to Teddy, trying to remember the call she'd had word for word. Oddly enough, all she could really remember well then was the whispering, husky quality of the voice. Thinking about it brought renewed chills.

"He said that he could see you?" Teddy asked for the second time.

"Yes . . . I'm quite certain that's what he said. That he could see me."

"Did he threaten you?"

"Yes! He kept telling me to 'leave it be.' I think I remember that right."

"But he never said anything like, what happened to Marnie, or what happened to your neighbor, might happen to you?"

"No."

"It might just have been a crank."

"Yes, I know that."

Apparently Rowan, standing a few feet from her, could hear what Teddy was saying.

"And it might not have been a crank!" he said firmly.

There was silence at Teddy's end. Then, "Tell the rock star I'm aware of that fact."

Sam inhaled deeply. She didn't need to tell Rowan anything; he had heard. He took the phone receiver from her. "Aren't the police supposed to protect and serve?"

Sam wasn't sure why, but Teddy must have backed down somewhat. She couldn't hear him, but after a moment she saw Rowan smiling ruefully. "He said to ask you if you have that star-six-nine service from the phone company. You might have traced the call yourself right away."

"Yes, I do have that option," she admitted. "I—I didn't think to use it."

"It was probably a blocked number anyway," Rowan said with a shrug. He talked with Teddy again for a few minutes, listening mostly. A look of surprise crossed his features. After a moment he said, "Yeah, sure."

Then he hung up.

"What?"

"Well, as we all know, there are way more crank calls than any police force could possibly handle. And this guy didn't actually promise to slit your throat or come seize your person or anything of the sort. Teddy said to wait. If you get another call, he'll discuss the options."

"Doesn't he think this might be related to Marnie's disappearance?"

"I don't know. But it's true that there's not too much he can do about one phone call that was vaguely threatening."

"What happened at the end of the call? Why did you look so surprised?"

"Because he asked me to go fishing with him tomorrow."

"Teddy asked you to go fishing?"

"Yeah. We actually were out together last night, you know. Before he and Laura so quickly left us." He was smiling, then he sobered. "He said he was sorry for the crack about my being a rock star the other day, that he was grateful for the help I'd given his son, and he's going out to the Everglades fishing tomorrow and he'd like me to join him."

"And you're going?"

"Why not? I love the Everglades. And I'd like to know Ted Henley better as well."

"Why?"

"Why? Damn, you are suspicious."

"You don't suspect Teddy of anything, do you?"

"Why? Do you?"

She shook her head emphatically."Of course not! He was married to Laura. He's Lacey's father, and Aidan's father. He's a cop."

"Right. He's a cop."

She knew from his tone of voice that he didn't automatically exonerate all cops. Maybe she couldn't blame him.

"Well, good," she murmured, looking down. "I . . . I'm really tired. Frankly, yes, I was afraid, uneasy, and I'm glad you're staying, but—"

"But?"

"I am sober. And we're talking to each other very nicely, but in truth, I'm still bitter. I'm not ready to sleep with you."

He grinned. "I didn't ask."

"I really should slap you, you wretch! You've insinu-ated—"

"Because I would like to sleep with you."

She remembered last night. The feeling that she wanted to touch him, be touched, feel warmth . . .

Excitement.

"But—" she began.

"But you're going to sleep. Fine. Go to sleep. I'm go-ing to check your windows and doors, all right?"

"Go right ahead. The guest room is at the top of the stairs to your left. There are clean towels and all kinds of extra stuff in the bathroom closet. Help yourself."

"Thanks."

Hands on his hips, he watched her as she walked toward the stairs.

He just watched her go. Strange things were happen-ing, and he was back here, in her house, just watching her go up the stairs.

Strange things were happening, yes, and she wanted him here. For safety, that was all.

Ah, but it was her heart in danger tonight.

The right thing to do, of course, would be to go straight to bed, clad in the ugliest, most ragged flannel pajamas she possessed. And she did have a few ugly, ragged pairs of pajamas—great for when she visited her mom in winter. She should have put them right on and crawled right into bed. She should have.

But she didn't.

She stripped off her clothing and stepped into a steaming shower. She told herself not to wash her hair or shave her legs. Why bother? She wasn't planning anything intimate.

He was in her house. He had left last night because she'd had too much to drink.

Not tonight.

She used her favorite perfumed soap, shaved carefully, scrubbed and conditioned her hair. When she stepped out of the shower, she toweled her hair energetically, considering which lotion she wanted to use on her skin. Just because it could be dry, of course.

But as she studied her favorite bottles of talcs and lotions, the phone began to ring. Knotting her terry robe and speedily winding a towel around her hair, she hurried to the bedroom phone, about to pick up the receiver.

NO.

She needed to hear the caller first.

She raced out of the bathroom and down the stairs toward the answering machine.

Rowan was already there, waiting, listening.

The machine came on. She heard her own voice.

Then silence.

More silence.

A long moment of silence.

And then . . .

Softly . . .

A click.

Chapter 13

S am stared at Rowan. She shrugged, not wanting him
to see that her chills had begun again. It was amazing,
how much fear a moment of silence could make her feel.

But he was with her. And they were looking at one another. And suddenly they both smiled.

"Star sixty-nine!" they exclaimed together, and she
dove forward, hitting the phone buttons. A second later,
an operator's voice informed them that the service was
denied on the number that had called.

"I figured as much," Rowan told her.

"Do you think . . . ?"

"That it was your caller again? Why would he hang up
this time?"

"I answered the phone last time. This time he got a machine. Maybe he doesn't want his voice recorded."

"Maybe it was a telemarketer."

"This late?"

He smiled. "They can get pretty desperate. In any case,
I don't think he can see you anymore—if he ever saw you
to begin with."

She spun around, realizing that he must be right. He
had closed all the curtains and drapes in the house. Even
over the French doors, where the glass panes on the upper
half had no draperies or curtains, he had hooked dish
towels.

"Thanks," she murmured. He was right about the

hang-up. Lots of people didn't leave messages. Just that thought made her more relieved.

"Don't mention it."

He was walking toward her as he spoke, she realized. She thought about beating a hasty retreat, running back up the stairs. But her feet were like concrete. And her legs were jelly. She didn't want to move, she didn't want to go anywhere. It didn't matter that somewhere deep inside she was swearing away at herself. She was a fool. The flesh was so pathetically weak. She really didn't want to become involved again. It had simply hurt too much. Thoughts spun through her head as he approached her. It should be different. Different time, different circumstances . . .

And yet . . .

There simply were no guarantees. And so she was afraid.

But she wanted him. With a sweet, slow-burning hunger that was far greater than her fear. She didn't want him to speak, she didn't want him to ask permission. She just wanted to pretend that it was all darkness, no questions, no answers, no . . .

He touched her. Her face first, fingers moving over her cheeks, knuckles brushing her forehead, the tip of his thumb running over her lower lip. There was something about this . . . this way he had of touching her face. Of course, he had other ways of touching her more intimately, sometimes, just the brush of his fingers, the tip of his tongue . . . the lightest caress. There were ways, yes, that he could touch her, ways that could bring her to a climax in a matter of minutes. Ways that she had always loved. And yet this . . .

The feel of his fingertips, the tenderness in them as he brushed her face . . . It had been a long dry spell since she had known him. A barren desert in time, because she had known this touch, this feeling, and so, always, from the depths of her being, she had craved no less. Better to sleep alone. But now . . .

He smiled at her. "You know, you have always been incredibly sexy."

"I, um, I try," she said flippantly. Sexy with wet hair—in terry. "I'm not exactly a dancer . . . stripper . . ."

"Thank God."

"But they were beautiful. You even said that you could want them under the right circumstances—"

"If you weren't in my life. There's no one I want, when I can see you."

"You know, you've always had a great line."

"Not a line, the truth. And I'm pretty good at getting rid of clothing on a woman. And thankfully, you're not burdened with too many pieces."

She shouldn't have smiled.

She did.

"And there's no one I know who looks better without clothing. Actually, there's no one I've ever seen who looks better. No one. Not a stripper in the world. Although, I must admit, they did make me think. About you. Naked."

He kissed her. He never did anything hesitantly, or halfheartedly. His mouth formed over hers, never questioning, simply deciding. Her lips parted swiftly, instinctively, to the passionate demand of his. She burned to the simple pleasure of his tongue, wet, hot, probing deeply into her mouth. She wanted to be analytical: *Sex, yes, simply sex, a basic instinct, something we all need or at least crave, as simple as breathing, I don't have to fall so fast, become so involved, make this an emotional thing . . .*

Instinct, yes. She'd waited a long time. He could do all the right things, had a way of *knowing,* how and where to touch, when to tease, when to take . . .

He kissed her deeply. No way to be analytical. He kissed in a way that demanded emotion, and commitment to the deed and nothing more. Kissed in a way that touched her all the way through, elicited sweet hot fire, a roiling in her blood, an intimate rise of desire where he did touch, a craving where he didn't.

So she kissed him back.

Tasted his lips, delved into his mouth, slipped her arms around him and held him as he held her, felt the hard-muscled pressure of his body against her own. And the world seemed to explode in a riot of sweet, wet beauty as it seemed that she came alive.

He touched her cheek, calloused fingers both gentle and sensual. His soft stroke moved along her throat. Her robe parted.

She hadn't tied it very well.

His hand, large and encompassing, cupped her breast. His fingers curled around her, thumb tip playing erotically against her nipple. She felt her knees give, liquid fill her, limbs and flesh, a searing in her blood. His mouth lifted from hers; he stepped back. Her robe remained parted and he looked at her, then stepped forward, slid it from her shoulders until it fell to the floor. Again he stepped back, and she was tempted to cover herself, embarrassed, afraid, yet suddenly her limbs seemed frozen.

"You look so . . . wonderful," he murmured.

"I feel so cold!" she whispered.

His lips curled into a half smile. "In such a hot city. We'll have to do something about that."

Teasing words, but she shivered, suddenly looking around.

"I've closed everything," Rowan said quickly.

"I still . . ."

I can see you!

Perhaps Rowan remembered the phone call at the same time. He stepped forward, taking her into his arms. She felt the rich, provocative heat as his hands stroked her back, her buttocks, drawing her nearer. She could feel his erection through his clothing. "Trust me, I learned how to hide from the world. Look around you. I've closed everything. Tightly. No one can see anything. You're safe."

"Safe?" she queried.

"Safe . . . from everything and everyone!" he assured her. His fingers feathered through her hair. Like a cat, she wanted nothing more than just to rub against him.

"From everyone and everything—except you," she told him, and prayed that she managed to say it somewhat lightly, and not with the vulnerability she was feeling. There was no stepping back. There was so much that should be said. She wanted some kind of an assurance, and yet she knew that couldn't be. Life didn't work that way.

So what was it?

She wanted the moment?

Yes, and more . . .

He pulled away slightly, studying her eyes. His fingers brushed her chin, touched her cheeks. His gaze was intense. His smile came very slowly. "Maybe you're right. What I want to offer may not be safety. But is that really what you want?"

"Ah, the very question I've been asking myself!"

His eyes remained steadily on her, flecked with their gold, so challenging. He wasn't going to try to explain anymore. He had already done so.

Well, she had accepted the challenge before. Loved and lost.

"I should want safety," she told him gravely. She should. But all she wanted was him naked too. What had happened to her? No decorum, no dignity at all. It had been that awful club!

"I think it's too late for safety," he told her. "And I also think you're a liar."

"Oh?"

He was grinning. "What you want is sex."

"And you know what I want so clearly?"

"Well, you were fairly clear last night," he said blandly.

"Oh, was I?"

"And you did just come racing down here in a bathrobe."

"Last night—"

"I was a complete gentleman. But now . . . I think you're just dying for sex, and you're going to have it."

"And the papers have always claimed that you're not egotistical! Well, you might be wrong. Perhaps I just wanted to remind you of all that you gave up. Me. I could turn away now. Maybe you mean nothing to me, and I really do go around casually nude on a day-to-day basis. You could just go on home again."

"I could." He waited. "Perhaps I even should. So turn away. I'll have no choice." He waited. She felt as if the night had wrapped around her, and the air held her where she stood. It was his eyes, she thought, that kept her there. After a moment he said softly, "You're not turning around."

"I'm taking my time. Deciding," she told him.

"Well, I have suggested that it's your call."

"I wish it were that simple. Easy for you to say when I'm already standing here . . . as I'm standing here."

"Trust me, walking away would be much, much harder for me!" His tone changed; it was suddenly harsh. "My God, I hurt you, but you can't begin to understand what it was like for me before—"

"No, you can't understand what it felt like for me!" she charged him.

"Then. The past. But it's now, and . . . you're so . . . unbelievably wonderful," he murmured, and his voice was a breeze of rich, husky seduction against her ear. "More

beautiful than ever, then even I remembered, and in
memory, you know, you were beyond all human beauty."

"Untrue," she charged him.

"I wouldn't lie."

"Then how could you have ever turned away from me
so completely?" she asked, a strange little sob catching in
her throat.

He didn't answer her. He kissed her throat, and slid
along her length, his hands molding the form of her body,
head burrowing against her abdomen as he came to his
knees. Her fingers threaded into his hair; she was going to
fall. So much for conversation, recriminations, the past.
He was here, now, mouth hot and open against the vulnerable flesh of her belly, fingers curving her hips and
buttocks. He nuzzled against her, touched her, teased,
coaxed. Her fingers tightened in his hair. She murmured
something, protested, gasped, encouraged. His knuckles
brushed her inner thighs, his lips touched there, light,
feathering, harder, fingers stroking higher and higher. A
circle within seemed to wind tighter and tighter, hungry,
tantalizing, whirling around a center that ached and
yearned and longed, and oh, God, just itched to be
stroked, touched, taken . . .

Touched, taken. The subtle, then not so subtle, probe of
his fingers. A stroke that teased, elicited. Then the touch
of his tongue, a caress that found the ardent center of all
of her hunger and desire and seduced unbearably. She
cried out something unintelligible, still wanting so badly
to tell him that she didn't want him, that he should just go
straight to hell, while at the same time she was certain that
she would die if he went away . . .

"Stop, please!" She begged then, fingers taut in his ink
dark hair, body trembling wildly, flesh on fire yet cold in
the air, burning here, shivering here.

"Please . . ."

It was building in her, something so delicious she

couldn't stand it, a mercury rising. Her cheeks were flushed, her breath came in pants, she needed to pull away; she could do nothing but press closer, feel, wait, build, shake and tremble and beg him not to touch her anymore even as she arched against that touch until . . .

She screamed, cried out, felt the warmth of intense pleasure fill her, even with the realization that she hated the light, wanted the darkness, a place to curl away, to remember this, both ecstasy and embarrassment. For a moment she couldn't begin to understand Marnie, who could do this so easily, accept any intimacy, from so many different people, when she felt so vulnerable. She closed her eyes and lowered her head as he rose, but he caught her chin, lifted it, and kissed her lips again, and when she opened her eyes, he was smiling. His eyes, so close, were green and gold, and more intimate even than what had happened between them. "Still so shy, the primmest wanton I've ever known. My God, you've known me, know me well, and you're just dying to turn away."

"Maybe it's all an act," she murmured, forcing herself to meet his eyes. "I know you—maybe you don't know me so well . . ."

He pressed his finger against her lips. "Shut up," he said softly.

She shook her head, challenging him. "So you think I've just been waiting for you all my life? Pining for you, that you'd come find me?"

"Have you?" he asked her, smiling.

"Don't be an ass!"

He wasn't offended; his smile never faded. "Why? I've always looked for you."

"I can imagine!" she whispered. "You looked hard, scrutinizing every woman."

"I didn't say I became celibate."

"You talk far too much."

His grin deepened. He slipped an arm beneath her and

picked her up. Easy. He was large, she was small. "I can see the stairs. Or—are you still deciding?"

"I'm going to hit you any second."

She wished that it wasn't quite so wonderful. Being with him again. There was something so familiar. The way he held her . . . his strength, his ease, and always, his lack of pretense. But it had been wonderful before.

Wonderful . . .

The hall light cast a gentle glow into her room. He laid her down on the bed, and she could see his face in the shadows, and his bronzed shoulders and chest as he stripped off his shirt. Shoes cast aside, cutoffs and briefs, and he crawled over. *Wonderful.* The feel of the length of his naked flesh against her own. *Fire!* A warmth she hadn't known in forever. She wanted to reach for him, touch him, forget all the talk she had tried to use to deny herself. She itched, she yearned. She tried to draw him to her, but he pushed her back, and drew away, and his voice seemed strangely harsh as he told her, "Never completely, you know."

"What?" She could feel him so vibrantly, the sound of his breathing, the pulse of his heartbeats. The line of his jaw was so close, she knew the texture of his skin, the scent of him, each ripple of muscle, the titillatingly erotic feel of his erection against her flesh. The pulse of his heartbeat surged there as well, and she wanted only the magic of the darkness and the night.

"I could never push you away completely."

"It doesn't matter. Not now . . . this isn't—isn't a commitment," she whispered a little desperately. "Just a little sex between neighbors."

"It does matter," he told her insistently. "It matters. You were always with me. When I was with Dina, with anyone, you were there, in my memory, always there, always. She knew it. She never believed that I loved her when I tried to help her. God help me, it might have been a mistake. But you should know, if I could go back, I would still have to try."

"Fine!" she told him. "And stop, please, stop, just . . ." She curled her arms around his neck, drawing him to her again. She found his mouth, kissed him, teased his lips with her tongue, arched her length against him. She felt his muscles tense. She writhed to be closer, touched his face as she kissed him feverishly, passionately, drew her fingers over his shoulders, his back, down to his buttocks. She stroked, teased with her fingernails, kneaded, feathered, pressed. She brought her hand between them, drew a line down his middle, stroked over the tightly knotted muscles of his belly until she touched his sex, encompassed, teased, and stroked. She heard sounds thundering in his chest, emitting in a groan, and then she was the aggressor no more, for her hand was pressed aside, his weight and length wedged between her thighs. She felt his thumb, stroking, rotating, wetting, preparing, finding the exact place where the madness of desire was throbbing within her. She choked something against his shoulder, and the fullness of his sex was suddenly within her. Slow, oh, so agonizingly slow as he first sank inside, deeper, more, more . . . Her fingers tore into his back, her body arched, slammed. He withdrew . . . then moved again, deeper, deeper . . . Lord . . . deeper. She gripped his shoulders, tossed her head . . .

She felt his eyes. Knew he was watching her. She couldn't meet his gaze. She whispered something, demanded, frantic. And then . . . she received. He moved with force and power, arms wrapped around her hard, hands sliding down her back, encompassing her buttocks, pressing her closer and closer. She felt him through the length of her, in her blood, her limbs, her body, in the center of her being, between her legs, the juncture of her thighs where the spiraling tightened to a coil of desperate ecstasy. She clung to him, slick, shaking, writhing, and climax seized her again with a grip as powerful as the man above her, and she cried out, tossed into the soul of the darkness, shaking anew as little seizures of after pleasure rippled through her center, and on throughout the length and breadth of her.

Seconds later, she felt his constrictions as he climaxed within her. Explosive warmth encompassed her. Seconds ticked by in which the shadow magic of satiation swept them both. Then night fell again. Night, in the darkness, with the past between. Too fast. She had let it come all too fast. She had wanted him. Just as before. She had loved everything about him, his size, his build, the way his shoulders were tanned, the patterns of his chest hair, his scent, his eyes, his voice, the way he touched her . . .

Now, fingers stroking her cheeks. She had wanted him, did want him. But she had loved him, still loved him, and it was a selfish wanting, and for some reason she couldn't quite seem to let herself have him easily. The past remained. And so she said, "Was it still difficult to push me away completely . . . when you were with Marnie?"

She bit her lower lip as soon as the words left her mouth. It had been the wrong thing to say.

He rose. Naked, graceful, restless. He walked to her window, slightly shifting the drape. He could see the bay from that window, she knew.

And Marnie's house as well.

He didn't answer. She stared at his back. Straight, defined. Fine, muscled buttocks, good long sturdy legs. Handsome even from the back. She found herself pulling up the comforter and sheets, slipping beneath them. She sat up, hugging her knees and all the bedding to her chest. "You did sleep with Marnie, didn't you?" she persisted softly.

He turned around and stared at her. In the darkness and

shadows, she couldn't read his eyes. Neither, she thought, could he read hers.

She wanted him back. She wanted to pretend she had never spoken. She wanted his answer to be no.

"Yes," he said simply.

"I see."

"No, you don't. You don't see at all."

"What's really to see?" she asked, and tried to sound as if she spoke offhandedly.

"I've looked for you. I've looked for you in everything I've done. I wanted all the traits and virtues—and yes, even the faults—I'd found in you. But you were right. I had pushed you out of my life. I didn't expect you to be somewhere in the world waiting for me. I didn't stop living."

"Marnie is a beautiful woman," she said, shrugging.

"No. Marnie was—"

"Is! Marnie is!" she interrupted passionately.

He hesitated, and she knew that he hadn't realized he had spoken in the past tense. "Marnie is a wounded girl, with scars that run so deep they'll never heal."

Sam plucked at the sheets. "I know that Marnie was hurt. I suspected that—"

"She was abused, sexually, from the time she was about ten. Like any little kid, she was looking for affection. What she got was betrayal of the worst kind, the most heinous kind. You've met her father. Can you imagine her life?"

Sam closed her eyes, amazed to feel ashamed. "She's my friend," she said. "And yes, I have imagined her life."

"She loved you, you know," he told her.

"My God, stop! Stop talking about her as if she's gone—"

"She is gone."

Sam moistened her lips. "I can't believe it, I won't believe it. She's out there somewhere, and she needs help."

Leave it alone, the voice had said.

Why? Could Marnie be found? *Or was she dead already and what the voice warned was that Sam would wind up that way, too?*

Rowan walked back to her, dark hair tousled over his forehead, a vein pulsing in his throat. He paused at her side, fingers winding into a fist, unwinding. "Sam, leave it alone."

Leave it alone, the voice had said.

She lifted her hands. "What can I really do?"

"The police are on it, and believe it or not, they know what they're doing."

She shook her head, hugging her knees more tightly. "Do you know how many murders there are in this city every year? Dozens. And people disappear all the time. And it's not that I believe the police are incompetent, I don't. I know that most of them work very hard, it's just . . ." She paused and looked at him. "It's just that they do have dozens of murders to solve, and there are no clues, Marnie is just gone—"

"There are clues. There are always clues. Give them a chance." It was his turn to hesitate. "If not the police, give me a chance. I won't let anyone forget that she's missing. Until she's found."

"Dead or alive, right?" she asked bitterly.

"Dead or alive."

They were both silent for a while.

"Am I allowed back in there?" he asked after a moment.

"What if I were to say no?"

"Well, I'd probably be rude and forceful at the moment. Long day, I'm tired and somewhat irritable."

"I wouldn't dream of stopping you."

"I'll take that as a wonderfully passionate invitation."

He lifted the sheets and slid in beside her. His arms

came out, strong, warm, powerful. She braced instinctively, hating her own defensiveness.

"Sam!" he murmured.

She eased against him. Then sighed, turned, and curled against his chest.

"That's better," he murmured, soothing back her hair. "I was beginning to wonder where we could go from here."

"We have to find Marnie before we go anywhere."

"We will find Marnie." He sounded as if he believed his determination.

"But then, of course . . ."

"But then?"

"Well, what if Marnie wants you back?"

He lifted her from his chest, forced her back on the pillows, and crawled over her. Hazel eyes bright and sharp as gold, he stared at her. "You want it all dragged out, right? Described in minute detail? All right. I had no idea you lived here when I bought this house. I wound up being with Marnie, talking. We had some drinks. We started really talking. She told me about growing up. I told her about watching people die. I listened to her horror tales about sexual abuse. She listened to my guilt about my inability to ever really help anyone I loved. We wound up comforting each other with a little bit too much alcohol in our veins. Which wasn't really so terrible, just in itself. We're both of age, single, and sure as hell a bit bruised and battered by the things gone by in life."

Something about his emotion touched her deeply. As involved as they had just become, as much as the past had hurt her, she realized that she had trodden where she hadn't really had a right to go, and she felt painfully intrusive now. "Don't!" Sam said. "It's none of my business, I'm sorry—"

"Don't be. Because that was when I found out about you. That you were here, right next door. That you were my neighbor, and I would see you again. And I barely knew Marnie was there anymore, I just up and withered like a tree in winter, and we got into quite an argument— with Marnie telling me I was useless, which I was, at that moment, to Marnie. So, you see, I sincerely doubt that Marnie has any interest in me. Are you happy now?"

"I—no, of course not, I really didn't mean to pry—"

"Bull!"

She tried to twist beneath him; he would have none of it, firmly flipping her back over again and pinning her down this time, his face close to hers.

"Anything else you want to know?"

"No, damn you, leave me alone, stop it—"

He kissed her. Legs splayed against hers, the pressure of his hips and chest on her, the coarse texture of his body hair a tease against the softness of her flesh. His tongue roughly invaded and aroused, his hands held her wrists prisoners still, and the force of his body was intoxicating. He lifted his lips from hers. "I ask again—anything else you want to know?"

She moistened her lips, smiling. "You really withered? With Marnie? Because of me?"

"Cross my heart," he said solemnly.

"You're not withered now."

"I know. Because of you. See what power you have?"

Her smiled deepened. "I really have all that power?"

"You do. Want to see?"

Later, she lay there with him.

The bulk of his body was a stalwart warmth against her; his arm, around her, was a feeling of comfort she had barely dared remember. His breath whispered against her neck, and she thought that he slept.

This . . . this was so wonderful. There was nothing so special in the world, she thought, as this feeling of being so . . . so . . .

She wasn't exactly sure what the feeling was. Sex itself was great. Wonderful. Marnie could assure the world of that. But there was more, and no matter how many men Marnie had, Sam had the feeling that she had never really known what it was like to feel more. This was the more. A feeling of being cherished, secure, protected—without feeling in the least diminished for all that protective care. Maybe that was one of the qualities that had drawn her to Rowan from the very beginning. He had never needed to be adored, or even admired. He loved his music, he loved to play. But he loved music in general, loved to see and applaud other musicians. He had encouraged her. He had loved to hear her play, to play with her. He had told her that she could definitely make a living with her drumming—girl drummers, especially good ones, were in high demand. She'd told him about her father, about how he loved his drumming but loved teaching more.

There had been so much between them.

Then the headlines.

Dina Dillon had been reported missing. Rowan had been surly with the police, telling them that they'd been separated a long time. He'd been hauled down to jail.

He had tried to protect her, but he had gone back with his wife. Yet she had a feeling that he had told her the truth. He had thought that he could save Dina. Still, could they change all the pain that had come before with a night's lovemaking?

No.

Sex was good, sex was great. But there was more.

And maybe it was the more that would eventually heal them. And it was the more that Marnie had never known. Maybe the possibility of ever having the more had been stolen from Marnie when she was a child.

Sam set her fingers over Rowan's hand where it rested on her flesh. She tightened them.

She closed her eyes. There were no guarantees in life. Marnie had disappeared. She feared for her friend more every day.

A husky, menacing voice had whispered threats. *I can see you, I can see you . . . watching you . . . I can see . . .*

So much out there was frightening.

Chilling.

And yet, tonight, she was warmed.

And for the night, the warmth was good.

Chapter 14

Come the morning, Rowan was gone.

He had, however, left her a note. "Thanks for a wonderful evening. Coffee is on downstairs. Alarm back on—I'm getting ready to head off to the jungles with Teddy. Talk to you tonight? Rowan."

She read the note, held it, curled it into a ball in her hand. The words were easy, casual, comfortable. She had missed him in her life so very much.

And yet . . .

It had been too easy, and too fast. Circumstances. People slept with people all the time. On the first date. It was a liberated world they were living in. But she didn't let people into her intimate world often. She had never fallen out of love with him, and that was what meant so much, because it was the emotion that ripped people to shreds, and she didn't dare take the risk again too quickly. She had to be so careful of involvement.

Right. As if she hadn't involved herself right up to the neck last night.

She needed to slow things down.

She showered and dressed, then went downstairs for coffee. She was glad last night that Rowan had pulled the draperies. She had been afraid, unnerved by the phone call, and desperately glad of the privacy. Not to mention all that it had afforded them. But by day she wanted the sun coming back in, and she wasn't nearly as frightened as she had been.

With the drapes pulled back, the sun warm on the window glass, and a spectacular view of the sparkling bay hers once again, she poured herself a cup of coffee, surveyed the beautiful day for a moment, then went back upstairs to her bedroom to finish getting ready. Setting her coffee on the dressing table, she told herself she was just going to put on a little makeup before Teddy arrived.

She wasn't going to go over and stare at Marnie's house. She had done that enough.

But it didn't matter. As she did every morning, and every night, she went to the window, and she stared out. The house remained still and silent, keeping its secrets. Yet even as she sipped her coffee, watching, she saw someone going up the steps.

Her heart quickened. She heard a knocking at the door, then someone calling Marnie's name. Not certain who it was, she set her coffee cup down and ran the stairs two at a time before bursting out on her lawn and racing over to Marnie's.

No one remained at the door. She spun around. Nor did she see a car anywhere. Had the visitor come by boat?

A creepy feeling assailed her as she looked around. There was a gentle breeze; trees rustled and bent, and there seemed to be a whisper through the foliage.

I can see you!

For a moment, she felt a repeat of the chills that had danced along her spine. She gave herself a shake. It was broad daylight.

But no one was around on the little peninsula. No one. Her house was empty.

She hoped. She had run out the front door to see who was looking for Marnie, and she'd left her own door open.

For God's sake! she chastised herself. She could still

see her front door! Yes, but she had turned her back on it, hadn't she?

No one could have snuck in that quickly, she told herself. And there wasn't a single car around.

And besides, it was a Thursday. Early. Teddy might not have come for Rowan yet; he might still be in his house, and if not, Adelia had probably come in for the day.

She wasn't really alone.

And still she felt that icy sensation.

I can see you . . .

Angry, she gave herself a shake. Someone had come here, calling out Marnie's name. Loudly. There had been nothing furtive about it.

She squared her shoulders and walked around the house. "Hello? Can I help you? Who's there?"

No answer.

She came around to Marnie's beautifully manicured backyard. The breeze skimmed over the crystal water of the pool. Crotons and hibiscus continued to whisper softly. Out on the bay, the blue-green sea rippled and shimmered.

I can see you . . .

She groaned softly to herself. No one was here. And yet the very bushes and trees seemed to have eyes. They watched her.

It's broad daylight, she told herself.

"Hey! Is anybody here? Can I help you?"

No answer.

She realized that she still felt the icicles. She didn't want to go back into her own house. She was afraid.

She gritted her teeth. She had to go back into her own house. It was the only way to get her purse and keys, take her car out of the garage, and head on in to work. "Marnie," she murmured, "if you are just off on some kind of joyride, I'm going to beat you black and blue!"

She started around the foliage to reach her house, wishing she could shake the feeling that the bushes were watching her. She began to quicken her pace, walking faster.

Faster.

Then she was running.

She came around the huge crotons that separated her yard from Marnie's in a full-blown panic. Her hair flew into her face.

And she plowed right into someone.

Her momentum was so great that she started to fall. Hands reached out for her. She screamed, fighting, slamming her fists in a crazed fury. The grip on her loosened; she fell, dragging down the body she had encountered.

"Sam, Sam, Sam!"

He landed halfway on top of her, groaning and letting out a slight *woof* of pain as he twisted and fell hard to avoid crushing her with his weight.

She blinked; he was trying to move the tendrils of hair from her eyes.

She looked up. Rowan. A slight smile curving his lips, a slightly concerned look in his glittering gold eyes.

"Rowan!" she whispered.

Then she pounded his chest with her knotted fists. "Damn it! You scared me to death."

"I scared you to death? You just slammed into me."

'What are you doing in the bushes?"

"I just came from your house."

She frowned. "Why were you at my house?"

"Well, I had been looking for you. Then I heard you calling out, and I came around to see what you were doing."

He rose, offering her a hand, pulling her to her feet. She accepted his assistance, dusting croton leaves off her knit pants as she did so.

"You didn't see who was at Marnie's?" she asked.

"Someone was at Marnie's?"

"I heard someone at Marnie's door, calling out to her. If you were on your way to my house, you must have heard him. Or her. No, I'm pretty sure it was a him."

"Sam, I didn't see anyone."

"You must have!"

"But I didn't. I heard you, I came around here, you flew into me."

He was frowning, concerned, she thought. Because there might have been someone in Marnie's yard, or because she might be losing her mind?

She stared at him, then threw up her hands. "There is someone here! And why would he suddenly be hiding? He was calling out—loudly. And we were both around. I mean, no one could have assumed that neither you nor I would hear him calling."

"And if he was calling, trying to find Marnie, he's probably not someone who had anything to do with her disappearance."

"But he's just disappeared!" she exclaimed with frustration. Then she said softly, "My house!"

"What?" he asked, his frown deepening.

"I left my door open—"

"You what?"

It was said with reproach. Definite male "you idiot female" reproach.

"Hey! That's not an appropriate tone! All I did was run out of the house—" she began, but he had already turned and was hurrying toward the front door of her house. "Rowan, wait a minute! If someone is in there, someone dangerous . . . maybe we should just wait for Teddy."

He had already reached the house. He opened the door and stepped in.

Sam followed close behind him.

Loretta liked to get to work early. It didn't matter if she'd had class—or even her other, highly lucrative work—the night before. She was a go-getter, and a lucky woman. She didn't need much sleep.

And now, with Marnie missing . . .

She made coffee, just as she always did.

And she put a cup of steaming black coffee on Marnie's desk, just as she always did. Maybe it was silly. But she kept hoping, every day, that Marnie would reappear.

She didn't put coffee on Kevin Madigan's desk. Kevin had to have his hot. And he complained when it wasn't. Not that she really cared, but she hated being yelled at in front of other people.

She thought with a smirk that Kevin had better get his tight, handsome, little buns in to work—Lee Chapman was coming in again this morning. He was growing very impatient with Marnie's disappearance, and he was threatening to look for a lawyer elsewhere. He claimed he was innocent, of course. And he could afford to pay for the best possible attorneys to prove it.

Loretta always brought coffee to Mr. Daly as well. He had his own private secretaries—assistants, as they called themselves—but he liked her coffee. And she liked Mr. Daly. He could be a cantankerous old goat, but he was usually an honest and a just one.

But Mr. Daly hadn't come in yet, either.

Sitting at her desk again, Loretta shook her head worriedly. What was happening here? People just didn't show up where and when they were supposed to anymore.

The phone rang and she picked it up quickly, answering in her most professional voice. Naturally, her voice was recognized.

"Are you available to party Friday night?" It was the man who liked to be called "the arranger." He "arranged" entertainment. He sounded strange, though. And he didn't usually call her here. Of course, he never left a message on a machine. "Friday. Um, yes."

"You're a definite?" The voice was sharp.

"Yes," she said more firmly.

"All right, make sure you're there. Don't ever make a fool of me. I've called your young friend for a job as well. Two important parties this Friday. She'd better show, or you're in trouble, too."

Her young friend? Oh, yes, of course. Lacey.

"My friend will show."

"She'd better. And by the way, there were interesting guests at the club the other night."

"Interesting guests?" she echoed.

"Watch your mouth, Loretta. You talk too much."

"I . . . I don't know what you're talking about—" she said faltering. Had she given away too much?

Had Sam gone there?

"I think you do. I see you talking. I see you all the time."

"You can't possibly see me—"

"But I can. I can see you. So take care. Now, take this address, and don't screw up again. Do you know what happens to people when they screw up?"

"They disappear?" she whispered.

His voice was silky. "They get fired. Now take the damn address."

Loretta jotted down an address, then hung up the phone, angry and unnerved.

Forget him! But . . . who had shown up at the club? Sam would never have gone there alone.

She picked up her own coffee cup and sipped the brew. She did make good coffee.

How strange. She wanted to be like her mentor, Marnie Newcastle. Strong, determined, a woman to break all rules and go her own way.

And yet . . .

For a moment she felt wrong about it all, no matter how some might say that the goal justified the means. She winced, thinking that she had set another woman on this path. The very pretty, very wide-eyed young Miss Lacey Henley. It was something she should never have done, she thought.

Never. But it was too late now.

Someone *was* in Sam's house.

Rowan knew it the moment he walked in.

Someone was in the back. In the family—or Florida—room just behind the kitchen. The room leading out to the pool and the dock beyond. He heard a soft sound . . . of movement . . . like a shifting. A quiet, nearby silent step . . . So light. Like a slipper touching the floor, over and over again, with almost perfect rhythm.

Rowan stood just in the entry, listening. Sam was at his back, not touching him, yet so close that he could feel her breathing.

He motioned her to stay behind him. He felt her shake her head.

He motioned her firmly to keep a slight distance. Then he lowered himself to a crouch, remaining tight against the wall as he moved closer and closer, tension building within him. He moved around the wall, and through the large arch into the kitchen area, where an open counter looked over the Florida room.

Then he saw the person who was making that ever-so-slight noise.

And he stood up, drawing Sam along with him.

It was Gregory. In jeans and a neat, short-sleeved plaid shirt, the boy stood in her family room, facing the television/VCR but not watching the empty screen. He was just staring out.

Sam had opened the drapes again in the back, and sunshine poured in through the windows. The sunlight touched the boy's pitch-black hair and his handsome young features. Rowan felt a strange pain in his heart from a distant past. His brother had been blessed with features so fine. His hair had been dark, but the deformity in his thyroid that had taken such a toll on his heart and lungs and normal growth hadn't been visible in his face at all. Gregory was strong physically. Gregory's abnormality was within his mind. Yet Rowan sensed the same soul within the child—a knowledge, a beauty, something unique and wonderful. Ewan had loved paintings; with Gregory, it was music. And even now, his movement was a rocking set to a silent beat. He felt a rhythm in his heart, and moved to it, even as he looked out on the world, searching . . .

For what?

"Gregory!" Sam said at last.

The boy didn't turn. He just kept looking out. Toward Marnie's house.

"Gregory!" she repeated. Leaving Rowan in the kitchen, she walked to the boy. She stood directly in front of him, making a sign with her fingers to indicate that he was to look into her eyes. At last he did so. "How did you get here? Where are your folks?"

He didn't answer, but he did meet her eyes. Sam reached out and gently touched his cheek. He took her hand. Sam looked at Rowan. "I don't know how he got here. I wasn't expecting him today."

"Could he have been the person you heard at Marnie's?"

Sam hesitated, looking at Gregory. She shook her head. "No."

"You're certain?"

"He doesn't talk," she said softly.

"I've heard him say names," Rowan reminded her.

She stared at him wryly. "He's autistic, remember? Yes, he does say names, we both know it. But not in the way that I heard. Sometimes, every so often, he even says words in a string. In a sentence. Sometimes he responds to a touch, or to his own name. But he could never call out the way I heard, and I can't imagine him going right to Marnie's door and saying her name under any circumstances."

"And yet," Rowan reminded her, "he is always staring at Marnie's house."

Yes, he was, Sam thought. And suddenly she remembered dinner at her house the night that Laura had been talking to Marnie—right before she had disappeared.

"What?" Rowan asked sharply.

"Well . . . the night we last talked to Marnie on the phone . . . Gregory was staring at the house then."

Rowan looked at Gregory thoughtfully. "Let's go to Marnie's. With Gregory."

"Rowan, should we—"

"Yes."

Sam was still uneasy, afraid of hurting the fragile child in some way.

"Sam, I'd never hurt him," Rowan said.

"But we don't know, maybe there's something psychological—"

"Aren't you the one always telling me I'm not seeing what's right before my eyes?"

Had she told him that? Maybe, in frustration, when he—like others—refused to see the significance in something like the disorder of Marnie's makeup.

"Let's go," she said.

She slipped her arm through Gregory's and met Rowan's eyes. He led the way across the lawns, to the house.

He used his key to enter.

As they walked into the house, they both studied Gregory. First, he walked to the rear of the house. They followed him there, looking at one another. Then, suddenly, he turned and headed up the stairs, going to Marnie's bedroom.

The sun was shining in through the windows that offered the sensational view. Gregory stood stock-still in the center of the room, then walked to Marnie's dressing table and stared at it. Sam felt her heart beat hard. Marnie was not a gusher at all when it came to children, and Gregory actually made her uncomfortable at times. But when he was in Sam's care, Marnie was decent to him. She'd shown him her house as enthusiastically as she had shown it to others.

Gregory, she realized, knew that the makeup had changed position.

"You know it's different!" she whispered, slipping her arms around him, hugging him as he stared at the tray. He reached out—as if he knew how to put it back properly and would do so.

She caught his hand. "No, sweetie, we may be looking for prints soon!"

She turned to see that Rowan was staring at the bed. The way the sun shone in, it lightened the dark mahogany of the furniture. Suddenly he bent down. He started to reach out, then stopped himself.

"Rowan?"

She hunched down beside him. He pointed to a tiny patch of shining . . . something on the bed leg.

"What is it?" she asked.

"It may be blood," he told her.

"Oh, my God."

"Sam, take it easy, it's a trickle if it is, no more. Marnie could have cut her own leg shaving—"

"She shaves her legs in the bathroom!"

"What I'm saying is that it's just a little bit of blood."

"The police need to see it."

"Yes. Well, Teddy's on his way."

Sam rose, suddenly feeling chilled. "Let's get Gregory out of here."

They did so. They had barely returned to her home before her bell started ringing.

Opening the door, they found Teddy standing on the front step.

Teddy was frowning. "I thought you were going to be at your house!" he said somewhat irritably to Rowan.

"There's something you need to see," Rowan told him flatly and ushered him back out the door, leaving Sam alone with Gregory.

The men were gone for a while. She waited anxiously, putting on a tape for Gregory. A bit of blood. It didn't mean that Marnie was . . .

The bell rang again. She hurried to it. Rowan and Teddy had reappeared. "There will be a forensics team in, would have been anyway," he said.

"So—"

"So nothing!" Teddy said firmly to Sam. "Don't go getting panicky. And I hear that you're going to join us."

"What?" Sam said.

"You're coming fishing with us."

"This is the first I'm hearing of it," Sam said, looking at Rowan. "I do have a place of business. I work."

"It is your place of business, and that's exactly why you can call in and skip a day," Rowan said.

"I've been skipping a little too much lately," she reminded him.

"So what's one more day?" Teddy said.

She thought he sounded a little sarcastic. Of course, the whole thing was a little strange. Why was Teddy so determined to get Rowan off to the Everglades? He had appeared to resent Rowan thus far. She felt suspicious, yet her ideas were ridiculous. What, had Teddy intended to take Rowan out in the Everglades, hit him over the head, and throw him into the swamp? No, Teddy was a cop.

Bodies could disappear in the Everglades. They disappeared in places far less uninhabitable than the dense Florida swamp.

But Teddy was a cop. He valued his job. He knew that little telltale clues were often what convicted a criminal.

Not only that, but Teddy wasn't a killer! He might fight with Rowan, but . . .

"Yes, I think I'll go," she said suddenly.

"You will?" Rowan spun on her, surprised.

"Well, I thought you said you came over to invite me!"

"I did, but . . ."

"Gregory!" she said suddenly.

"Gregory," Rowan agreed.

"What the hell are you two talking about?" Teddy demanded.

"Gregory is here. I was outside, and apparently he wandered in from somewhere." She waved at them. "You two go on. I'll wait with Gregory, start trying to reach his folks," Sam said.

"No, we've got time. The swamp isn't going away," Rowan said.

"Actually," Teddy told him unhappily, "it is. Progress, you know. Half the homesites to the west side of Broward were recently built on swampland."

"Teddy, half our area in general is built up and man-enhanced."

"Yes, but the swamp is dwindling!" The environment was a big issue with Teddy. Not that he was an animal lover. He was a hunter. He kept a license for fish—and alligators. He was one of the first people out there every season. "The sugar interests tear up the swamp, the developers don't give a damn if there's nothing left for the wildlife. What they don't realize is that we're destroying our water and our entire ecosystem. It's great out there, beautiful. You'll see."

"I've been there," Rowan told him.

"Out in the swamp?"

Rowan shrugged. "Out on an airboat. Fishing."

"But we're going deep into the swamp today," Teddy told him. He grinned. "An old area, off the beaten track."

"Teddy, all of the swamp is old," Sam said.

Teddy laughed. "True, but I mean an area not many people know well these days. Years ago, it was kind of an oasis. There are a lot of waterways and high hammocks. Men went out there and built weekend retreats—"

"Manly men, of course. Weekend warriors," Sam interjected.

Teddy made a face at her. "I've taken you lots of times."

"Did you own the land?" Rowan asked.

"No, no, it was government land, so our 'manly' weekend lodges got demolished. Torn down, overgrown. Such a pity. But then, years ago, the world down here was smaller, you know? Miami wasn't always so international. Hundreds of thousands of people live here and never see the Everglades. Ah, for the old days, when any good old South Florida redneck had a truck, a pit bull, a boat—and a weekend warrior retreat in the Glades."

"Yeah, yeah, Teddy," Sam said.

"Her father had the truck, and the boat, and the retreat in the Glades."

"All we were missing was the pit bull. My dad ruined it all. He had a little Chihuahua he adored," Sam explained.

"Don't knock a man's love for the great outdoors!" Teddy said.

"Maybe you'd best go on—" Sam began.

"We can wait," Rowan said firmly. She sighed. "That okay with you, Teddy?"

"Sure. You got coffee?"

"Yeah, we got coffee. Help yourself. I'm going to call, if you'll both excuse me."

Sam walked toward the back of the house, and the phone on the little wicker desk in the Florida room.

She should call the Lacata house and leave a message there, at the least, that Gregory was with her. She didn't think that she'd find anyone in—if Gregory was here, one or both of his parents was near.

Still, she called the house, left the message. She had just hung up when the doorbell began to ring. She ran through the house, followed by Rowan and Teddy. She reached for the door and threw it open.

Harry Lacata, looking very worried, was standing there. "Sam, I'm so sorry to disturb you, but I was up the street at a business coffee, and Gregory was with me. He was standing right next to me, and then he was gone—"

"He's here," Sam said. "I just tried your house."

Harry sighed with relief, the tension leaving his face. "Annie is home, but she's in bed, and this was a small affair, so I thought I'd be fine taking Gregory with me. Then I turned around, and he was just gone."

"Well, you were right, he came here, and he's just fine. Come on in," Sam said.

Harry, handsome in a business suit, entered the house. He said hello to Teddy and looked at Rowan, politely waiting. Sam realized they hadn't met, and introduced him. "I was hoping I'd get to meet you," Harry said. "I have to admit, I wasn't all that familiar with your music, but my son actually comes home at night and says your name."

"Really? That's nice. I have a houseful of musical instruments. I think that's what he likes."

"You've been great to him. We're grateful."

Rowan shrugged. "I enjoy his company. He reminds me of someone who was once very close to me. And my God, what a talent. Perhaps he'll be able to make good use of it eventually."

"I don't know," Harry said, lifting his hands. "Once he

talked a bit. Then he backtracked, and he seldom talks at all anymore. It's such a tough condition. We take a few steps forward, and a few more steps back. He may not ever be strong enough to face the public, but it won't really matter. My wife and I adore him. All we want for him is the best that he can be. Well, thanks again. I'd better get my boy and let you folks get on with your day."

He went to the Florida room and soon emerged, his son in tow.

As they walked out, Gregory suddenly stopped. He stared at Rowan, then smiled. "Ro-wan!" he said.

"Hi, kid. You'll come over and play the piano again soon, okay?"

Gregory didn't answer. "Ro-wan!" he said again.

"Thanks again," Harry said.

"Please believe me, he's a pleasure."

"Gregory?" Harry Lacata said. He took his son's arm. Gregory's lashes fell over his beautiful eyes. He turned with his father and walked out.

"Should we go now?" Sam asked. "Shall I bring anything? Drinks, potato chips, sandwiches? Are we having a picnic—"

"Yeah, we should go. Now. And don't bother with food and drinks, Sam. We'll never get out of here. We'll stop at our friendly local 7-Eleven store," Teddy said. "You ready, Rowan?"

"Yeah, I'm ready."

Teddy spun around and started out. In the lead, he threw open the door. He jumped back in surprise when we found a person standing there.

Phil Jenkins.

In a T-shirt and jeans, Phil was all macho man. His skin, tinted by years in the sun, was a pure, rugged bronze. His clothes were clean; his jeans were blue, his T-shirt was white, his pack of Marlboros was secured in the rolled-up left sleeve of his shirt.

"Hey, there, it's Detective Henley."

There seemed to be a bit of mockery in Phil's voice.

Teddy reacted curtly. "Hey, yeah, in the flesh. What can I do for you?"

"I just came by to see if anyone had learned anything more about Marn—about Miss Newcastle."

"There's nothing new on actually finding her, Phil. I'm sorry," Teddy said. He shook his head, looking back at Marnie's house.

"I've still got things to do. Can't do 'em without her approval." Phil looked at Marnie's house, then back at the three of them. "Not to mention the fact that she owes me money."

"Phil, were you looking for her earlier—at her house?" Sam asked.

His soft blue eyes touched hers. He smiled slowly. She remembered the way Marnie used to talk about him. *Yes, Marnie had slept with him. Had there been more? Something . . . a touch of evil, perhaps? She was going nuts! Hearing something more in every word spoken!*

Yet she suddenly felt uneasy. Ever so slightly assessed. As if he were weighing her every attribute. Marnie was gone, but here she was.

"No," he said at last. He folded his well-rounded biceps over his chest. "No, I wasn't here earlier."

"You're sure?" Rowan said sharply.

Phil turned to Rowan. The look in his eyes was different. "I just got here. My truck is right outside," Phil said, challengingly.

Sam couldn't help peeking around. He was telling the truth.

"There's nothing new on her whereabouts," Teddy said.

"When you do find her—or find out what happened to her—you will let me know right away, right?"

"Everyone will be informed," Teddy said.

"Yeah. All right. Fine," Phil said. He stared at the three of them again, pulled a cigarette from the pack rolled at his sleeve, and turned around.

Then he spun back to face Teddy, tapping his cigarette on a thumbnail. "What do you think happened to her, Detective Henley?"

The question seemed charged, as if Phil were making an implication.

"*I* don't know what happened to her," Teddy said.

"But you're a cop. You should know something by now," Phil said.

Teddy leaned back, crossing his arms over his chest in a macho gesture to match Phil's. "All right, yeah, maybe I do know something. Haven't had a chance to tell you two yet, but I might as well, since things are going to start heating up," Teddy said to Rowan and Sam. He looked back at Phil. "Marnie was getting calls the night she disappeared. Calls on her house phone. Some of them came from Sam's phone. And do you know where the others came from?"

Sam shook her head. The men just stared at Teddy.

"Marnie's cellular phone. She was receiving calls on her house phone from her own cellular. And guess what? That phone has now disappeared, just as cleanly as Marnie."

Chapter 15

The intercom buzzed. Loretta pressed the blinking button.

"Loretta, it's Kevin. Coffee, now." A second later, as if annoyed with his own afterthought, he added, "Please."

"Coming right up, Kevin."

She poured coffee and walked into his office. It was big, beautifully furnished, with windows that looked out over the Miami skyline. The offices were located on Brickell Avenue and had some of the most beautiful views in the city. Kevin's back windows faced the water.

Marnie's office was nicer. Her back and side windows faced the water. They'd had big fights over the offices. Kevin had wanted Marnie's office. She hadn't been about to give it up.

Marnie had won.

Remembering that made it easier to trot in here when he called, demanding coffee. Really, for God's sake, she wasn't his personal servant!

"Here you are, nice and hot!" she said, setting it down.

He could have gotten his own coffee. He wasn't very busy. In fact, he was leaning back in his expensive leather swivel chair, hands laced behind his head, just looking out the window at the beautiful day.

"Thanks, Loretta. You make great coffee, you know?"

"Thanks. Anything else?" she asked somewhat sharply.

He shrugged. "Yeah, actually. There will be a memo going around again, and I'm willing to bet the cops will be in for another round of questioning."

"About what?"

He had looked relaxed. Suddenly he was watching her, with eyes as sharp as an owl's. "Marnie's cellular phone."

Loretta stared at him blankly. "What about her phone?"

His eyes narrowed on her. "It's missing."

"So what? Her purse is gone, too. I imagine it's in her purse."

He shook his head slowly. "So what?" he repeated. He unlaced his fingers and stood up, coming around behind her. He still gazed out the window, but she had the uneasy feeling he could pounce at any minute. Strange. She'd never felt afraid of him before.

"There were a umber of calls made to Marnie on Friday night."

"Well, I know that her friend Sam tried to invite he over—"

"Calls made *to* Marnie's house, *from* Marnie's cellular phone."

"What? That's ridiculous—"

"Yes, it would be. If the police even began to imagine that Marnie was calling herself!"

Loretta's mouth opened and formed into a large *O*. Kevin shook his head with disgust. "Come on, Loretta, that took you long enough!"

"Well—well . . ." She was irritated to find herself stuttering. She longed to tell him exactly what to do with himself.

She refrained.

"I suppose I was hoping that nothing bad had happened to Marnie. And with this information you've made it obvious that someone was in the house with her, someone calling her—on her cellular phone to her house—before somehow abducting her! Excuse me for not wanting to think that she is in real trouble, or . . . or . . ."

"Dead?" he asked softly.

"You want her dead, don't you? She gets what you think should be your office. She gets what you think should be your raises!"

Loretta didn't realize just how high her voice was going until he suddenly gripped her shoulders and shook her. "Shut up!" he hissed at her. He was strong, and insistent. His fingers bit into her flesh, and his handsome face was knotted with tension. "Damn it, shut up! No, I don't want her dead! My God, yes, she's a bitch, she's the goddam Wicked Witch of the West. But you're her secretary—"

"Assistant," Loretta informed him coolly, though she was shaking. "And I assist you, too."

"Yeah, yeah, assistant," he said.

"And I'm good!"

"Sure."

"Damn good."

He grinned suddenly, his hold on her easing. His eyes were different, a strange light was in them. "Oh, yeah. Come to think of it, I have heard that you're good. Damn good."

"What's that supposed to mean?" she asked.

He kept smiling. "Just that I've heard—you're good. At everything you do."

She took a step back, looking at him warily. "Just what is it that you want from me, Kevin?"

"I want to know if you know where Marnie's cellular phone might be."

"I don't have it. And if someone was playing games with her, calling her from her own phone, then he—"

"Or she."

"Fine! He or she has Marnie's phone."

"But that's just the point, don't you see? *When* did he or she get Marnie's phone?"

"I don't know."

"Because you haven't thought about it. But think. Think back. Think about the whole day. If you do, maybe you'll remember the last time you saw Marnie with her phone. Who was with her then, who was with her after? The police are going to want to know, too."

"Then I'll tell the police."

"I want to know, Loretta, if you remember."

She was shaking inside, but she meant to do Marnie proud on this one. "Let me give it some thought . . . " She smiled and started out of the office.

To her surprise, he opened his door after she had closed it and called after her softly. "Loretta, honey, I'll bet that you are damn good at your second career. Damn good, honey. You just never know. Maybe one of these days I'll just find out for myself."

Her skin was crawling. How could anybody so good-looking be such a nasty bastard? She couldn't help but wonder, What did he know about her? And just what did he intend to do about it?

He asked, "Do you enjoy your nights at the club, Loretta?"

"I don't know what—"

"Yes, you do."

"No—"

"Loretta, you idiot, I have a financial interest in the club."

She was so stunned that she gasped.

He smiled. "Oh, we're legal, honey. All legal. You're the only one who . . . well, who might not look so good around here if all the truth were told. Well . . . go back to work. You do have a full day ahead of you, huh?"

Chuckling, he went back into his office.

She returned to her desk, shaking. How was she ever

going to work? She should lay low. Yes, that's exactly what she would do.

But then she remembered the phone call she had just received. Had that been from Kevin, was Kevin the voice? She closed her eyes tightly, trying to think.

She was afraid.

"Teddy, if you know that someone was calling Marnie on Marnie's own phone from inside Marnie's house, and then we find a blood smear—"

"Sam, don't start telling me how to do police work!"

They had stopped at Big Al's Gatorland and Bait Shop, a place right of Tamiami Trail. After the discovery of the blood smear, Teddy had called in crime-scene specialists. Yet he couldn't work the case himself; he'd known Marnie personally. So there was no point hanging around, as Sam insisted. Once the police lab came up with results on the smear, Teddy would be notified immediately.

Still, Teddy was in a foul mood now. All he'd wanted was to spend his day off fishing.

Sam fell silent. She was in jeans and a long-sleeved shirt, with the sleeves of a windbreaker tied around her waist. Her hair was tied up neatly in a knot at her nape, and she looked both petite and delicate and ready and able. In the store, she picked her own bait. She was as good a fisherman as any guy. When he and Laura had first been married, Sam had been with them often when they'd come out to the Glades.

She had given Rowan some slimy stuff to keep the insects off. He couldn't claim Teddy's rough-and-ready familiarity with the swampland, but he had been out in the Everglades before. He'd come south and gone on Miccosukee airboat rides. He' been north of here, too, up to the Big Cypress area, coordinating some play dates with a group of Seminole musicians that had been damn good.

Sam got what she wanted and went out to the car. No

sooner had the door closed behind her than Teddy turned
to Rowan.

"What is it with you and that weird kid?" Teddy
demanded.

"What?"

"You know, that Gregory. He hardly ever talks, but
then you show up and he's always saying your name.
Why is that?"

"To start off with, I don't think of him as a 'weird'
kid!" Rowan snapped. Teddy was staring at him as if he'd
like to cuff him—or shoot him— and be done with it.
"All right, Henley," he said, keeping his voice low. "You
don't like me, don't trust me. Why the hell did you agree
to let me come fishing?"

Teddy looked away from him, smoothing back his
brown hair. "I owe you."

"What?"

"I owe you . . . for my boy."

"You don't owe me a damn thing," Rowan assured
him. "Your son is good. I didn't support him for you."

"All right, then, fine. I don't trust you. You show up in
town, Marnie disappears. And that simple boy—
Gregory—every time you're around, things get spookier
with him. It looks like he saw something, so why is he
saying 'Ro-wan, Ro-wan'?"

"You're right. It is as if he saw something. But doesn't
it seem to you that he isn't afraid of me, that I'm actually
the one he trusts?"

"Are you hypnotizing him, or something?"

"Oh, Christ!"

"But Marnie is gone. You moved next door—Marnie is
gone. You had a wife disappear once, too, huh?"

"She reappeared," Rowan reminded him. Rowan felt
his temper rising. His palms were getting slick, and a knot
of tension was sliding up his neck.

"Yeah, I guess you're right," Teddy said, more subdued.

"Dammit, it's just that you were sleeping with Marnie, and she did disappear."

Rowan stared at him, surprised that he had backed down. He shook his head. They might as well have it out. "Yeah, but you were sleeping with her, too."

Teddy hefted a bag of the groceries in his hands. "Not really," he said softly. "She only slept with me so she could flaunt it to Laura at some future date." He let out a long, bitter sigh. "She laughed at me. No challenge. Sex was like breathing for Marnie, no big deal. And yet . . . "

"Yeah? And yet?"

"I still felt bad. She used me. She pissed me off big time. Can you understand?"

"Yeah," Rowan said.

Teddy shrugged, looking beyond Rowan. "Maybe. Who knows, maybe you're right." He hesitated. "I think that both Sam and Laura suspected I was seeing someone when it broke up the second time. But they didn't know who. As far as I know, Marnie never let on. I think she meant to at first; I mean, she thought it was funny. But then, she was smart enough to value Sam's friendship. I don't think she ever said anything."

"Is that what this is all about? I sure as hell never intended to say anything," Rowan said, adding, "It isn't my place, Ted. If you decide to talk it out at some time, it might be your best bet. But, hey, that's your decision."

Teddy nodded thoughtfully. "Thanks. Let's go. Sam must be thinking we're talking about her. Hell, there she is, staring at us, thinking we're arguing or something."

"Damn, why would she think that?" Rowan muttered.

His sarcasm was lost on Teddy.

By noon Loretta was frustrated. The police kept calling— and no one was in. She could only speak to the officers herself, going over and over the events of that Friday. When had she last seen Marnie with her cellular phone?

Kevin Madigan had left early, and Mr. Daly didn't come in. She decided to head on out herself for an extended lunch. Who would know?

She started out driving toward one of her favorite restaurants, then decided maybe she should avoid the place. She'd been putting on a little too much in the middle lately. Instead of lunch—exercise!

She'd joined the gym, and it seemed a good idea to use her time taking off rather than putting on. And besides, it would be great to see Samantha Miller again.

But when she got there, she found that Sam wasn't in. Though disappointed, she was still determined to work out. She started off on one of the walkers at a brisk pace.

A few minutes later, she heard a soft, pleasant wolf whistle, followed by "Hi, there! Glad to see you using your membership."

She turned slightly to see Joe Taylor, Sam's partner. She couldn't help but smile. She was sure that he'd almost asked her out on a date that day she'd run into him at lunch with Samantha. What a hunk of a man. Tall and muscled. Wow, was he muscled! Bulging biceps, a six-pack stomach that belonged on a blow-up poster, legs of pure steel.

She almost giggled. Marnie had told her once that he was big all over. Nothing was sacred to Marnie—she shared all. Too bad guys didn't know that when they fell under her spell. Guilt for the disloyalty of her feeling plagued Loretta, and her smile faded.

"Hi, Joe. Thanks. I was hoping to see Sam, but I guess I've missed her."

"She didn't have any appointments today, so she went off fishing in the Everglades."

Loretta shivered at the idea. "Not a place for me, I assure you!"

Joe smiled. "No, I guess not. Not my favorite hangout anymore, either."

She laughed, flushed and feeling a little deliciously fevered, enjoying the conversation. "You mean you used to love the swamps?"

"Oh . . . before the laws changed, way back when we were kids, lots of guys used to hunt and fish and we'd build shacks and cabins. They're all torn down now, though." He made a face. "Progress, you know."

"Yeah, sure . . . well, progress is fine by me. I don't like bugs and snakes and things that chew in the night."

He moved closer to her. "Not even a little nibble?" he asked softly. There was something very sexy in his voice.

She laughed again. Was he going to ask her out? "It depends on who's doing the nibbling," she replied.

Behind them, someone came into the room. She saw the body in the mirror in front of the walker, but whoever it was, his head was cut off from her vision.

"Hey, Joe!"

"Hey!" Joe called back, but he didn't look pleased. "Talk to you again, Loretta. Maybe we can . . ."

"Yes?"

"Um, yeah. Sometime. Soon. Maybe we can get together."

"That would be great."

"Hey, Joe!"

In the mirror, Loretta saw headless torsos and long masculine legs.

Walking away.

Strange, she realized, in afterthought. Just her luck. A client would come bug Joe right then . . .

She'd recognized the voice. She couldn't quite place it, but she recognized it.

Then she knew. *Another of Marnie's lovers. Had her boss slept with the whole damn world?*

She felt suddenly chilled again, as she had outside Kevin's office.

She was in broad daylight; the gym was busy. She was being silly.

And as to Kevin, well . . . He could be a jerk, but just a jerk. He liked to harass people, but he was all hot air.

And still, Marnie had challenged them all, made them all look like jerks.

And had she paid for it . . . with the ultimate price?

Loretta stopped walking. She was dripping with sweat. And she was very cold.

She swore to herself that she'd be careful. So very careful.

Chapter 16

"I used to really love it out here!" Teddy said with conviction. "Years ago. When things were still all wild and free."

Rowan liked wilderness himself. Mountains, rugged shorelines, crags, cairns, crashing waves, a landscape where all that could be seen for miles was earth, sea, and sky.

There were few major highways through the Everglades. Farther north, in Broward, was Alligator Alley, now part of I-75. Here there was the Tamiami Trail. Toward the city, houses now lined the road. But coming farther and farther west, civilization slowly faded away.

The great rivers of grass began, sawgrass rising over water and muck, canals in between, and here and there, hammocks of high ground. It was a vast no-man's-land. Some considered it a horrible place filled with vile creatures. To others, such as the Seminole and Miccosukee Indians who had fled here during the decimation campaigns of the military in the nineteenth century, it was a haven.

To anyone, it was a place to be knowledgeable and wary.

They had taken a small motorboat from Big Al's, and were being careful to follow the canals. There were dangers in not knowing where you were going with such a boat—water lilies with thick, tangling vines, shallow water over knotted roots, sudden bars of land in what looked like a fairly deep waterway. But Teddy had assured them he knew what he was doing. And Sam was familiar with the area as well. "Through the years, we've gone out from Big Al's a lot," she'd told Rowan.

"Ted, I've got to admit, I'm an outsider, but things around here are looking pretty wild to me," Rowan said. Sam, sitting across from him, grinned.

"We're still not that far from Big Al's," Teddy assured him.

"Oh, and you know where you are?" Rowan asked Sam, shouting above the motor.

She nodded back. "See the hammock straight ahead?"

He twisted around to see what straight ahead meant to her. Sure, he could see the hammock. Kind of. It looked like everything else around him.

"There are still some old rotten wood picnic tables out there. Should we have lunch there?"

"Sure, why not?"

Sam didn't mind getting her sneakers wet, and the slimy stuff seemed to work well against the insects. "Avon Skin-So-Soft," she told him as he followed her out of the boat, carrying grocery bags. "Help me spread out this comforter. The tables look as if they haven't been used for a long time."

They laid down the comforter she'd brought—thicker than a sheet, but unlike a fuzzy blanket, it wouldn't pick up all the twigs and grass when they left. "You do have to be careful out here—snakes!" she reminded him.

He nodded, helped her, then stretched out on the blanket. Snakes, hell, yes, but it sure was beautiful. They were surrounded by pines on a small spit of high, dry land. The trees rustled, and he could hear the forlorn call of a bird. The sky above him was powder blue, lightly dusted with clouds. Sam began to set out their food and drinks. Teddy came by, grabbed a beer, and went back to check on his fishing gear. After a moment Sam stretched out beside him. Her hair was back in a ponytail; she wore little makeup and especially that afternoon she seemed as natural in her beauty as the surroundings.

"My dad loved to come out here when I was a kid," she said. "Teddy's family were really considered farmers back then, living way out here."

Rowan thought she would go on, but she lapsed back into silence. A large bug flew near his face—before deciding it didn't like Skin-So-Soft—and flew away. Rowan was idly watching Teddy fiddle with his fishing pole when Sam blocked his view, rising up on an elbow to study him with grave eyes. "Marnie never mentioned you to me. She must have known for some time that you were buying that house. But she never once thought to warn me—"

"Maybe she didn't see me as someone you should be warned about."

She flushed. "Oh, you're very dangerous. Apparently, she just wanted you for herself. What is it, I wonder? Are you simply a pied piper? With everyone Marnie had, she wanted you. My own cousin would readily throw me beneath your feet to be near you. Even the neighborhood sea cow throws us all over to be near you and . . . and Gregory says your name when he barely knows you. What do you think it is?"

He lifted his hands. "Pure seduction!" he said, mocking himself.

She shook her head. "I don't know what to think. Gregory never says my name."

"You believe that I could have something to do with Marnie—"

"No, I was just wondering why Gregory kept saying your name like that."

He rolled toward her, both irritated and amused, then paused when he saw the look in her eyes. She was serious, very serious. "What do you want me to say? That I'm some kind of a demon, that I've special powers?"

"Of course not."

"The kid probably connects with me because I connect with him! Listen to people like your ex-cousin-in-law, our great swamp escort over there, and he'll tell you that kids like that are slow. He doesn't see them as real people, he doesn't understand—"

"And you do?"

"Yes, yes, I do."

"How?"

"What does it matter?"

"It's something."

"Yeah, well, maybe . . ."

"Maybe what?"

He exhaled in frustration. "I told you long ago that I'd had a brother who died."

"Yes, as a child, but you didn't tell me—"

"I told Dina about him once, and she was horrified. She told me I had convinced her that we should never have children."

"My God, that's horrible, what could—"

"They thought that Ewan was autistic—new term to us back then—because it took him so long to talk. Then he had an operation. He could talk; he was very bright. But the defect that had damaged his vocal cords had damaged other organs too. His heart was too small, his thyroid was bad. He grew like a miniature hunchback, and he endured years of torture from his classmates before he died. But I was his brother. I always understood him, even when he couldn't talk. So maybe this kid just senses that I've had some practice with seeing inside, I don't know. I know that my brother was deformed on the outside, but he was a better soul inside than anyone I've met since."

He stopped abruptly, wondering what had brought on such a long speech. It should have been sweet and simple.

I had a close relative who had problems, so perhaps I'm more attuned to the difficulties of such children.

Her eyes were shielded, her thick lashes falling over them. "I suppose that's true enough. What Dina said to you was cruel—no one really knows yet what causes autism. It may be genetic, it may not—and it might have been a combination of genes. And yes, a child like Gregory is a responsibility, but he is also a wonderful little human being with every right to life." Her eyes flew open, meeting his. Then she flushed and sat up, quickly trying to lighten up. "God, it is a spectacular day. And they say we don't have seasons here! It's a perfect spring—"

"Now you tell me something," he said, pinning her with his gaze. "Why were we at a strip joint the other night?"

She shook her head. "I wanted to see—"

"Sam, come on—the truth."

She inhaled deeply. "The women who have disappeared—Marnie, Chloe Lowenstein, that young secretary—they all had associations with that place."

"Did you tell Teddy about this?"

"No, not yet. I learned this in confidence. Well, and the thing with Chloe might not have even been real. There was a rumor that she liked to disguise herself and, er, get down and dirty, I guess."

"You stay away from there."

"Excuse me?"

"Sam, really."

"Rowan, it's not like I was ready to apply for a job myself, but still . . . Hey, Teddy!" she shouted suddenly. "Let's eat these sandwiches and start fishing. I don't want to be here when it turns dark, okay?"

"Why not?" Ted asked, grinning, putting down the pole he'd been rigging to come over to their picnic area. "Afraid of the creepy crawlies?"

"Turkey, salami, or tuna?" Sam asked, ignoring him.

"One of each. I'm starving," he said. He seemed relaxed out here. Watching him, Rowan thought that he really did love the Everglades.

"You really like it here," Rowan commented out loud, accepting a sandwich from Sam. Odd what people remembered. He preferred turkey. She'd handed him a turkey sandwich on wheat, light mayonnaise, lettuce and tomato, and a slim wedge of Swiss cheese.

Teddy grinned, chewing, then talking. "Yeah, I do. It still feels like you can get away from it all out here. Of course, things were different years ago. When we came out here when I was a kid, it was really like being at the end of the earth. There used to be more canals—and the gators would get into them, and the snapping turtles—"

"The gators get into the canals often enough now," Sam said.

"They're just natural predators, and they help to keep the balance in nature. They feed on the weak and the slow."

"And children and pets, when they get in the developed areas," Sam argued.

"Maybe we shouldn't have developed those areas," Teddy said.

Sam sighed, eyeing him sideways. "And maybe we were so concerned about the gators that we went a little too far, and they should be hunted more often!"

Teddy smiled at her, enjoying the fight. "They're such perfect predators!"

"One would think you deal with enough predators," Sam said sharply.

Teddy grinned again. "Ah, but these guys are different."

"They just *look* evil," Rowan offered.

"They do, huh?" Teddy, surprisingly, agreed. "Those

dark, beady eyes. Just at the water's edge. Those jaws . . ."

"Speaking of which," Sam commented quickly, "look across the canal over there, toward the other hammock. There's at least seven of them sunning on that embankment." She shuddered. "Maybe we should get going now, don't you think?" She started picking up the sandwich wrappers, stuffing all their trash back in the paper bags to go with them—there was no garbage pickup out here.

"Sure," Teddy said. "Hey, Rowan, want to see the hulk of a burned-out cabin?"

"Why not?" He grimaced at Sam, stood up, and offered her a hand.

"I've seen plenty of the cabins—standing, halfway torn down, burned down. Go with him, get him moving. I'll get the last of this stuff picked up."

Rowan went over to where Teddy was standing. There wasn't much to see. Nature reclaimed her own quickly. The base of a structure remained, little more, a few burned logs here and there, now encrusted with vines and roots. "Watch where you walk—you can run into some mean rattlers out here."

Rowan did watch, wondering if Ted Henley had invited him along in hopes that he would step on a rattler. But Teddy seemed different out here, more like a big kid than a city homicide cop.

"Hey! Are we fishing, or what?" Sam called. She was standing at the water's edge, by the boat. Their grocery bags, repacked, were in it, along with the ice chest.

Five minutes later, they pushed off from the hammock. Sam was still watching across the canal where at least half a dozen alligators had congregated. Rowan felt strangely as if the gators were watching them back. The dark eyes seemed to follow their every movement.

"Don't worry, they have a natural food supply out here," Teddy said, amused.

"I wasn't really worried—you weren't planning on pushing me in, were you?" Rowan said. He'd taken the seat next to Sam. He leaned forward, grinning. "I'd damn well take you with me, you know."

Teddy grinned. "Yeah?"

"You bet."

"Guys!" Sam groaned. "Are we fishing or not? How about that little lagoon area over there, Teddy? I don't think we've ever been in there, have we?"

Teddy revved the little engine and twisted the tiller. "Looks good!"

He motored over, killed the engine. "Here?"

"Here," Sam agreed.

Keeping low in the boat, she expertly baited her line and cast it into the water. The men followed suit. They all started off basically paying attention, but as time passed, they sprawled out more in the boat, finding comfortable positions against the cushions.

"So you've always lived here?" Rowan said.

"Always." Teddy nodded toward Sam. "Just like Sam. And Laura. And their families. We were kind of pioneers. Well, our folks and their folks were, at any rate."

His voice had a friendly tone to it—and yet a strange warning note. As if he were saying, *We belong here. You don't.*

"Scotland," Teddy said. "Cold there, huh?"

Rowan shrugged. "Yeah, a lot of the time."

"Hey, you know, tell me—do you *really* like bagpipe music? I mean, you know, after a while, doesn't it start to sound like a million cats wailing?"

Rowan lowered his baseball cap so that it better shaded his eyes. "I kind of do like the pipes, though I'm not a great player myself."

"Will you two shut up?" Sam said. "We'll never get any fish."

But just then Rowan had a good solid tug on his line.

He gave it a jerk, securely hooking the fish. Then he let the creature play out the battle, encouraged by the other two.

A minute later, his fish was in the boat.

"A beauty," Sam applauded.

"A little small," Teddy commented.

"Small, my ass," Rowan contradicted him. Teddy grinned, not arguing.

Five minutes after that, Sam sat up sharply.

"You've got something?" Teddy asked.

"Something . . ."

"Well, did you hook it?" Teddy asked.

"Yeah . . . but it's not fighting."

"Well, damn, then, you've got bottom!" Teddy said.

"No, I haven't, I know when I've got bottom. Ted Henley, I've been fishing since I was a little kid, I know what I'm doing."

"Then bring it in."

She shot him an evil glance, then frowned and began to work at her line again. Rowan leaned forward to help her. She grimaced. "I seem to have snagged onto a tree limb or something floating . . . I guess I should just break the line and start over."

"Here, let me see the pole for a minute."

Rowan took her fishing pole, reeling in, trying to get a feel for what was on the other end. He couldn't loosen the hook; it was solidly caught in something.

He brought in more of the line.

"I see it. I've caught a . . . a big pile of branches and leaves, I think," Sam said. "I think I can get my hook and bait back." She leaned out of the boat as he reeled in, reaching for the pile of floating debris. Her fingers started to curl around the end of the line.

Then she stiffened, going dead still.

"Sam . . . ?"

She pulled away, scrambling, trying to come to her feet

in an effort to get away, her eyes still hard on the water. The boat began to rock dangerously.

"Sam, what the hell . . . ? Have you lost your mind?" Teddy demanded.

"Sam!" Rowan said, reaching for her, drawing her against him. She felt like ice, stiff and shaking at the same time. "Sam, what—"

"Oh, God!" she gasped.

He pressed her behind him—down. He could still picture the gators on the shore not so far away from them, and though he didn't have a special fear of the creatures, he had no desire to tempt fate. But he'd never seen Sam react as she had just now, with such terror.

He reached over the side of the boat.

He saw.

He touched.

He started, and jerked back in horror.

"God damn, what the hell is it?" Teddy said impatiently. "What on earth did she catch?"

Rowan felt bile rising in his throat. An odor was wafting up to him now. Fetid as the swamp at its worst. An odor of rot and decay and death.

"Not what—who," he said flatly.

"What?" Teddy repeated. "What did she catch?"

Rowan gritted his teeth and calmly turned toward Teddy. "A body."

"A body?"

"Well, a torso . . . and a bit more," Rowan said. He forced himself to look back at the remains covered in algae and black, oozing muck. *Breathe through your mouth,* he reminded himself. "It's—it's real, certainly. Dismembered . . . or all that remains of a body. There's just . . . it's hard to say. A torso, part of a pelvis, the stump of a leg . . ."

"A man? A woman?"

He had to take a good look. Some strips of muddy

cloth remained on the body. The bone appeared to have been . . .

Bitten.

Oh, Lord.

He swallowed. He could see the chest, and despite the condition of what they had of the corpse, he was pretty sure he could tell the sex.

Or could he? *Had those lumps possibly been breasts at one time? There was no flesh at all in places, just shining bone. But then . . . then he could see tissue. Muscle? Flesh?*

A fly buzzed around him, landed on the lump that had once been a life.

"I think it's a woman's torso," he said.

"Oh, God . . ." He heard Sam breathing again.

"Is it Marnie?"

Chapter 17

Sam was sick. She wanted more than anything in the world to jump overboard and swim away as fast as possible. Somehow she stayed in the boat.

But at one point an odor crawled into her nostrils just as she looked at the mud-and-growth-encrusted remains.

And she was sick.

Later she managed to produce her cellular phone when Teddy asked her for it. She listened to his official codes and jargon as he called in their grisly discovery.

She felt Rowan's arms around her. But God, she was cold. So cold. Dripping with sweat, frozen inside.

Could it be Marnie?

The first person to join them was a Miccosukee cop, Jimmy Puma. Right behind him, led by him to the scene, was a man named Dr. Rick Mira. He was an assistant Miami–Dade County medical examiner. Small world. He'd happened to be out fishing that afternoon, the same as them.

He inspected the remains of the corpse in the water, then instructed Jimmy and Teddy on how to bring it in carefully so that no evidence was lost. Even then, when the body was bagged and brought into Big Al's to await the arrival of the meat wagon, as Teddy referred to the county hearse, Mira told them, "A woman, yes, late twenties, early thirties—the pelvic bone is there, so we'll know more certainly on that, but as to helpful evidence as to how and when she got here and who she was . . . well, we've got no hands, no face, no teeth. A torso and hips . . ."

"Well, I guess we can safely say that we have a woman who was murdered and her killer dismembered her," Jimmy Puma said.

"Well, we can't say that for sure," Mira corrected.

"Then what can we say for sure? That she's dead?" Rowan demanded.

"Don't get testy," Mira said. "She was down in that muck for a long time. Buried in it." He realized they were all staring at him. "Well, you see, alligators often drown their victims. Drag 'em down until they quit struggling. Keeps the gators from getting injured by their prey, not that it's easy to injure a gator. Of course, lots of predators are like that. Killer whales do the same, toss their prey around, stun them, demoralize them, take all the fight out of them. Make it so they can't fight back. Instinct, you know, self-preservation."

"Instinct," Rowan repeated softly. He must have been aware that Sam was hovering right behind him, feeling very ill again, and very green. "However she died, can you tell us . . . how long she's been in the water?"

"Can't really say yet," Mira assured them, trying to be as cheerful as he could manage. "This will be a hard case to solve, to crack. A really hard one. Although," he added, brightening, "nothing is unsolvable. There was the case of the maggots."

"The maggots?"

"Oh, yeah. In this one case, maggots completely consumed the flesh of a woman, and the detective on the case—a bright fellow—was certain the husband had been poisoning her. A specialist collected the maggots, swirled them into a soup in the blender, and tested the maggot soup for poison. The detective was right. The little buggers were full of cyanide. Can you beat that?"

She was going to be sick again.

Maggot soup.

The body, floating, filled with muck, algae, green . . . headless . . .

No, no. Breathe through your mouth, that's what Rowan had told her. Breathe through your mouth.

Although Teddy had discovered the body, he wasn't given the case. Another team that was on duty was called in, and one of those men, a fellow named Rolf Lunden, was made lead investigator. At first Teddy wasn't pleased. He had found the body. It might become a major case, depending on just who the body parts had once belonged to.

All Sam wanted to do was leave. She was tired; she felt filthy from the heat and the swamp—and from the proximity of the body. She was feeling a lot stronger than she had right after her discovery. No one could enjoy finding a body, but after the first shock, she didn't feel the need to be coddled or protected. She did, however, want to go home.

But Teddy had been driving. He was over by the refrigerated section; she could see him arguing with one of the cops who had come to Big Al's, and she heard someone say that reporters had gotten wind of the find, and they'd be showing up soon.

Rowan went to Teddy. "We're getting Sam out of here."

"I'm okay," Sam said.

He stared at her. "Want to be around when the reporters show up?"

"No," she admitted.

"But—" Teddy began.

"Hey, we're about wrapped up for the night anyway," Rolf Lunden said. He seemed such an easygoing man to be a homicide cop. "Teddy, don't worry, I'll keep you informed every step of the way."

"Yeah, please, do that, Rolf. I can't help but be interested in this one."

"Yeah, I know. This area means a lot to you," Rolf said.

They had been talking about diving the next day, but it was pitch-dark out in the swamp now. There were a lot of night feeders out there. There would be little they could discover in the blackness of the Everglades.

At last they left Big Al's behind them. Sam was grateful.

"What will happen now?" Rowan asked when they were seated in Teddy's Jeep, headed back east along the Tamiami Trail, Teddy's boat securely hitched behind them.

"Well, what we found will go to the morgue; they'll take what tissue samples they can scrape together—" he said, then broke off. "Sorry. Anyway, there will be an autopsy on what they do have of the body."

"Will they be able to find out anything from—from what we discovered?" Sam asked.

"Sure. You heard the M.E. It's amazing what they can discover. Of course, they don't have a lot to work with, but . . . well, they'll know approximate age, height, weight. Maybe, if there are enough of the lungs left, they'll be able to tell if the victim drowned. They'll study the bones to see if—" He stopped again for a minute, meeting Sam's eyes in the rearview mirror.

"Go on," she said flatly.

"If her limbs were cut off or . . ."

"Chewed off?" Sam demanded.

"Yes," Teddy answered quietly. "Tomorrow, when it's light, police divers will go down in the area. We'll see if we can find any more body pa— any more evidence."

"Oh, God," Sam breathed.

"Are you going to be sick again, Sam?" Teddy asked.

"Damn it, Henley, just drive!" Rowan said protectively.

"I'm not going to be sick," Sam said. She hoped she was telling the truth. She swallowed hard and breathed through her mouth.

"That would be one interesting dive," Rowan said.

This time Teddy met Rowan's eyes in the mirror. "You think so?"

"Yes. Very. I'm a licensed diver, you know."

"Is that right?"

There wasn't much more conversation between them until they reached the house. As Teddy drove into Sam's driveway, they saw that there were two police cars and an old beige BMW parked in front of Marnie's house. Quickly exiting the car, Teddy narrowed his eyes toward Marnie's and said, "I wonder what the hell is going on over there. I'm going to go on over and see."

Rowan crawled out of the car and reached in to help Sam out. "I'm all right," she said.

He didn't seem to be paying much attention to her. He was looking at Marnie's house as well. As they looked, someone stepped out of the house and walked toward the BMW.

"Thayer," Rowan said quietly.

"Marnie's brother. Oh, God, I wonder if . . ."

"Don't start wondering things!" Rowan said firmly.

Teddy stopped Thayer briefly. Then Teddy kept moving toward the house. Thayer continued toward his car.

"Thayer!" Rowan called out.

"Hi, there!" Thayer called back cheerfully.

He would never have sounded so light and carefree if they had just found his sister's body somewhere, would he? Sam wondered.

"What's going on?"

Thayer reached the car. He looked handsome in a thin, dark, artistic way, Sam thought. He was in pressed linen trousers and a silk shirt. "I don't know. The police won't tell me. Teddy said they might have fingerprint experts in there . . . serologists . . . they're trying to see what they can find, I guess."

He obviously didn't know about the blood smear. "At least they're trying to do something," Sam said.

"Yeah, sure," Thayer said. He tried to sound encouraging.

"How did you happen to be here?" Rowan asked.

Thayer shrugged. "I haven't seen my father in a few days now. I thought he could be here."

"You look really nice," Sam said. "Very nicely dressed to go looking for your father." The moment the words were out of her mouth, she wished that she hadn't said them. They sounded so suspicious, as if she were accusing him of something.

He didn't take offense. "I have an appointment with a gallery owner. I'm going to show some of my work to this fellow who has two places, one in the Grove and one up at Aventura."

"That's great," Sam said. "Your sister would be so proud of you."

He laughed. "Do you think? I'm not so sure. I don't think Marnie believes in art."

"I'm sure she does—"

"Oh, come on, now, we all know Marnie here. Unless I were to sell a piece for an ungodly sum, Marnie would never care one way or the other. Hey, want to see my stuff?"

"I'd love to," Sam said. "Except that I really need a shower—"

"Let's see it," Rowan said.

"Sure!"

Pleased, Thayer went around to his trunk and took out a large portfolio. Sam followed Rowan.

Thayer opened the zipper on the leather portfolio.

A street lamp shone down upon his first painting.

Sam almost screamed out loud. Her fingers dug into Rowan's arm.

It was an oil painting, a beautiful, fascinating painting. Of the swamp.

It might have been the very place they had just left.

There were the hammocks, the water . . . the beautiful birds, with their multicolored plumage. In the darkness, the eyes of the alligators peered above the surface of the water. In the sky beyond was the surreal glory of a sunset.

"My God!" Sam breathed. She felt weak.

"There are more!" Thayer said, pleased with her reaction. "This is one of my favorites." He slid his fingers carefully around the canvas to display the next painting, of the sun shining on a heron. In the next, an old Indian man fished in the water; the work on his face was wonderful. There was a painting of a panther in the brush. And then, a scene on the water again. This time a woman walked out of the swamp to the shore. Water sluiced from her back. She was elegant, graceful, and, other than the jewelry she wore, she was naked, cast in night and shadow, smiling. Offering the same allure, somehow, as the swamp. Beauty, and danger.

"They're excellent paintings," Rowan said.

"Do you think so? Thanks. Thanks so much."

They were talking so casually, Sam wanted to scream. They had just come from the swamp.

They had found a body there.

And now it seemed that Thayer had re-created that very spot.

With a woman walking out of the water, she told herself. He hadn't painted any corpses.

Just a woman.

Naked in the swamp.

"Did you manage to get a live model, naked out in the swamp, to pose for that painting?" Sam asked.

Thayer laughed. "No. I was in the swamp. I've even

been in the swamp with a few women. But no, no one posed for this. She was from memory; the swamp was real." He offered her a boyish smile.

"There's something so familiar . . ." Rowan murmured.

"What?" Thayer asked sharply.

"She's really intriguing," Rowan said. "Anyone we know?"

"I would never kiss and tell! Well, I've got to go," Thayer said cheerfully. "I'm late for my appointment as it is." He gazed at Sam, frowning. "Are you all right? You're pale as a ghost!"

She jerked her head in a nod.

"Long day fishing," Rowan explained.

"Oh, where?" Thayer asked, his frown deepening. "Out on the bay? You usually get burned out there—"

"In the Glades," Rowan said. "A place kind of like the one you pictured in all your paintings."

"Oh, yeah? I love the Glades. I still go out whenever I can, despite the fact that so many people think the really 'natural' beauty has been so compromised. Why, there are places out there I'm willing to bet will never be really civilized. Talk about being alone, communing with nature . . . well, you can't beat it."

Sam ground her teeth together hard. "No, you can't beat it."

Thayer grinned at Rowan. "What a place to take a date, huh?"

"Oh, yeah. What a place."

"Did you find something out there. Is that why you look so strange?" he queried suddenly.

"Find something—" Sam began.

"A body," Rowan said flatly, watching Thayer. *Did he think . . . ?*

They didn't even know whose body they had found! Not

Marnie's! Thayer couldn't have had anything to do with the body they'd found . . .

So why did she feel so uneasy, so afraid?

Because he'd painted the exact hammock where they'd been. Or was it? The hammocks could look so much alike. Dark, overgrown, with beautiful birds . . .

And the deadly eyes of predators.

"A body!" Thayer exclaimed.

"Yeah." Rowan folded his arms over his chest and leaned against Thayer's car, watching him. "Sam was fishing. She snagged a body."

"Oh, my God!" Thayer stared at them. He seemed stricken. "Not—my God, not Marnie!"

"No, not Marnie."

"Thank God!"

"What made you think it would be your sister?" Sam demanded. "She hated the swamp."

"Oh, yeah, I know, but my father—"

"Your father what?" Rowan demanded.

"Oh, when we were kids, he'd drag us out there sometimes. I always loved it. Marnie hated it. He still goes out there. When he's really hungry, and can't find Marnie or me to give him a handout." He offered them a grimace. "We both give my father money. He drinks it."

"But you give him more?" Sam said.

"Well, he's my father."

"You think he might have gotten mad and dragged your sister out there somewhere?" Rowan asked.

"God, no!" Thayer said, horrified.

"But you asked if we had found Marnie."

Thayer lifted his hands. "I'm just glad that you didn't. Sam, are you sure you're all right?"

"Fine," she told him.

He looked at Rowan. "Well, I really gotta go. Good night. Wish me luck."

He zipped up his portfolio and walked around to the driver's seat of his car. Sam and Rowan stood back.

Thayer waved and drove off.

As he did so, Teddy came out of Marnie's house. "Boy, if she is all right and comes back soon, she is going to be royally pissed off!" Teddy said. "Her place is a real mess."

Sam saw that Rowan had turned. An officer was coming out of Marnie's house. His hands were still gloved in plastic.

"Rowan, this is Officer Aldridge. Aldridge—"

"We've met," Rowan said icily.

"Yeah, well, I guess we're going to have a few questions again, Mr. Dillon—" Aldridge began.

"Why? You'll get the same answers."

"Yeah, well, we'd like you to cooperate. We're going to need some samples of—"

"I'll cooperate. You can have whatever samples you want, but you've already got your answers. Yes, I had a relationship with Ms. Newcastle. No, I had nothing to do with her disappearance. No, it wasn't serious. It was friendship."

Aldridge looked at Sam, as if telling her she was into a bad thing. He looked back at Rowan. "A one-nighter, huh?"

"A friendship," Rowan repeated.

"I hear you were with Detective Henley today—and found a body."

"I fished up the body," Sam said.

"Well, we will be talking to you," Aldridge told Rowan.

"I'm easy to find," Rowan told him.

"Don't leave town."

"I wouldn't dream of it."

"Well, then . . . and hey, all of you—stay out of that house now."

Aldridge walked away.

"Asshole!" Teddy said under his breath.

"Well . . . Teddy," Sam said. "Thanks for the fishing trip. It's been one hell of a day."

"Yeah. Sorry, both of you. Thought we'd be frying up catfish. I didn't mean to get you involved in something like this."

He slid into the driver's seat of his Jeep and looked out at Sam. "You all right?"

She nodded.

"I'll be talking to you," he told Rowan.

They stood together in the driveway as Teddy left. When his car was gone, Sam said, "I really have to take a shower."

"Yeah, so do I."

She turned, starting toward her house. "Wait a minute," he said. "I'll just go in with you for a minute."

"I'm all right," Sam said, fitting her key into the lock, then tapping in her alarm code.

"I'll be the judge of that," Rowan tried to sound teasing. He walked in with her, walked through the house, ran upstairs. He came back down after a minute. "It's empty."

"What were you expecting?"

"Nothing. But it's better to be safe than sorry."

He didn't seem to have any intention of leaving.

"Rowan, I've really got to take a shower." In her mind's eye, the vision of the corpse was beginning to become just a bit surreal. They hadn't found Marnie. Life had to go on. They might never know who they had found. Or how she had gotten there.

Still, he hesitated. "Sam . . . you need to understand."

She felt a strange tension. "Oh, yeah. About you and Marnie. It was just one of those things."

He shook his head. "No. She was hurt. Really hurt. It happened. It wouldn't happen again."

"Rowan, it isn't any of my business."

"Yes, it is."

"Rowan, please—"

"Yeah, I have to take a shower, too. I need clean clothes badly. I'll call you."

"Sure."

He started out.

"Rowan?"

"What?" He hesitated at the door.

"Do you think that Thayer is a homicidal maniac who hangs out in the swamp and waits for naked women to walk out of it?"

"I don't know what to think. Do you?"

He opened and closed the door, leaving her.

Laura Henley came in from shopping and heard music coming from her son's room. Surprised, she frowned. Aidan was never home at this time of night.

She walked to his room. Yes, Aidan was home. She tapped on the door, then tapped louder. He came and opened the door. He was on the phone, but smiling away. He beckoned her in.

"Yes, yes. No, it's fine, we don't mind the short notice. No, we'll be there. I'll get people there, I promise."

He hung up the phone, then let out a cry of joy, throwing his arms around Laura. "Mom!"

"What?" she demanded, pleased that he was so happy.

"Mom, Mom—we've been asked to open for a big free concert in the Grove this Sunday!"

"That's great, Aidan."

"So great! Except, oh, Mom, help me, please—I've just got to get people there."

"We'll get people there. Your sister will work on it, Sam—"

"And one of you can get Rowan Dillon to show up, right?"

"Probably."

Aidan kissed her on the cheek. "Everyone. I need everyone we know. Maybe Sam can get all her clients to come. And all the people from Marnie's law office."

"Maybe."

"And Lacey will help me, of course. Except that Lacey is leaving tomorrow."

"Oh, yeah, I forgot."

"Man, big opportunities for both of us, huh, Mom?"

"Yep." She talked with him a while longer. She was so pleased for both her children. She really loved them; she really wanted the best for both of them. Sometimes, though, it felt so lonely. Their lives were just beginning. Hers was . . .

Well, when they were gone . . .

Hers would just be alone.

She lifted her chin, told him again how happy she was, and headed out. Lacey would be off tomorrow.

She paused at her daughter's door, then tapped on it.

"Come in!"

She went on in. Lacey was just sitting on her bed in a pair of baby doll pajamas, looking very young.

And lost. And frightened.

"Did you hear about your brother?" Laura asked.

"Yeah, isn't it great?" Lacey gave her a big smile. Yet it faded so quickly.

"And you—going off to New York!"

Lacey smiled again. She looked a little pale. Laura sat down by her side. "Honey, are you sure you're all right with money for this? I can get my hands on a little more—"

"No! I'm fine, Mom, honest. I'm fine."

"Okay. You look pale."

"I'm just tired. And excited. I guess."

"Okay, sorry I disturbed you—get some sleep."

Laura started out of the room.

"Mom!" Lacey came running after her. She threw her

arms around her. "I really love you. So much, you know?"

Laura hugged her back. "Oh, sweetheart. I love you so much!"

"I want you to be proud of me."

"I'll always be proud of you!"

"I hope so," Lacey whispered.

"Get some sleep, baby. You've got a big day tomorrow."

Lacey kissed her on the cheek. "You can't begin to imagine."

Rowan stood by the plate-glass windows at the back of his house, staring out at the bay. Next door, the police were still inside Marnie's house.

Finding that body had been disturbing. Yet he was bothered by more than that.

He closed his eyes. Pictures, voices, sounds, all seemed to spin before him. Thayer's paintings had been uncanny. Paintings of the swamp . . .

Of the woman.

She had seemed so familiar . . .

He turned quickly, suddenly afraid. He didn't want Sam to be alone.

The phone started ringing. He answered it quickly, thinking it might be Sam. "Hello?"

There was silence. For a moment he thought about Sam's strange caller. But who . . .

"Rowan."

It was Teddy.

"Yeah?"

"Rolf definitely has police divers going down tomorrow."

"That's probably a good idea."

"I'm going."

"Good. You wanted to be involved."

"Yeah, I did. You really have certificates?"

"Yes."

"Want to go down?"

"Will they let me?" Rowan asked. *What a fool! Why would he want to dive in such a place—and look for more body parts? He wasn't a cop; he wasn't responsible or obliged in any way. It would be a wretched dive!*

"We're low on divers. I told Rolf about you. He said okay, as long as you know it may be no picnic."

"I'm aware of that."

"You want in?"

"Sure."

"It's not a hundred percent certain yet. Rolf has to get a few okays, but then we can hire you as an outside diver. Won't be the kind of pay you're used to, I'm sure."

"I've never been paid to dive."

"It won't be any hotshot rock star money, you know what I mean."

"I don't need the money."

"I'll see you first thing in the morning, then," Teddy said.

"Yeah. I'll be ready." He hesitated a moment; something had occurred to him. "I need some information—think you can get it for me?"

"On what?"

"I want to know who owns the strip joint we went to the other night."

"I can tell you that already."

"You can?"

"Sure. Sam doesn't know?"

"No, I don't think so."

"Funny, I thought that was why we were there the other night. The place is owned by a corporation fronted by Lee Chapman. I don't know that much about financing and silent partners and all that, but I think Marnie was in. Along with Kevin Madigan."

"Interesting. You think the place could have had anything to do with these disappearances?"

"I suppose it would be worth checking out. If it was associated . . . where does that get us? Half the red-blooded males in town go there. It's a popular place."

"But if it had to do with the owner," Rowan told him. "That would narrow Marnie's disappearance down, wouldn't it?"

"I suppose. It's hard for me to get excited without some hard evidence. I'll see you tomorrow for the trip back to the swamp."

Rowan hung up.

He swung around, thinking he saw a shadow passing his windows. He shook his head, disgusted. He couldn't let himself get so easily spooked.

And yet . . .

Out on the water. A boat. A small boat. No big deal—it was the bay, after all. People lived on boats in the bay. Day and night, there were boats on the bay.

And yet . . .

He felt as if someone was watching . . .

Someone was out there. He was certain of it. Someone in the night . . .

Eyes . . .

Watching what? Watching whom?

I can see you, a voice had told Sam.

He turned from his view of the bay, feeling an urgent need to reach her.

Chapter 18

The phone was ringing. Sam knew it was Rowan. She picked it up right before the machine could kick in.

"Rowan?"

"Hey, yeah, it's me."

"Everything all right at your house?"

"Just like I left it. Your door is locked, right?"

"Yes."

"I found out something rather interesting."

"Oh?"

"Yeah, Teddy told me right off—he knows who owns the club. The strip club. It's Lee Chapman."

She gasped softly. "Well, there you are!"

"Not that simple. He has backing. From the law firm—and Marnie herself."

Sam was silent.

"You didn't know, did you?"

"No, but I can't say I'm surprised."

"I'm coming over, but I have a few errands to run. You are okay?"

"Yes."

"Fine. Keep that door locked. I'll see you soon."

Rowan hung up. Sam picked up the receiver and started to dial Loretta at work.

Too late. Way too late.

She tried Loretta's house. No answer. She hesitated a long time, then decided that she couldn't wait. Chapman was dangerous. Loretta needed to be out of the club. She dressed quickly and headed out the door, locking up, nervously looking around. Rowan was gone.

Rowan would be furious.

No matter. She had to go.

It didn't take him long at all to get to the club. He wasn't sure exactly what he intended to say to Chapman, but he was anxious to confront him. Maybe just to let him know that he was being watched.

He started to get out of his car, but then he realized he recognized a car in the parking lot. A little yellow Honda. Lacey Henley's.

Then he saw a woman hurrying toward the car. From the club. It wasn't Lacey. Yes, it was. He got out of his car and reached the yellow Honda before the woman did. The hair was all wrong; it wasn't Lacey. And the face . . . so much makeup.

But it was Lacey, and she knew he recognized her the minute her eyes met his.

"Oh, my God!" she breathed.

"Yeah, oh, my God."

"Rowan, Rowan, please . . . my folks, you can't—my father, oh, God!"

"Lacey, your father has been here."

"He doesn't know that I work here."

Rowan shook his head. "Lacey, I'm not going to tell anyone, but you've got to get out of this place. Marnie Newcastle has disappeared, and the associations with other women who disappeared might have come from right here."

"My real name has never been down on anything. No one knows who I really am. Well, one other girl knows, but—"

"Lacey, you have to leave here and not come back."

"I just quit. Well, I tried to quit, but they want me to finish out next week—"

He took her by the shoulders. "Lacey, get out of here, and don't look back. I'll take care of it. Don't come back here, do you understand?"

She stared at him, then nodded. Tears filled her eyes. "You'll never tell my family?"

"Never."

She kissed his cheek and jumped into her car. He watched her drive away.

Well, he'd been wondering what he would say to Chapman. Now he knew. He walked into the club, pushing his way past the bouncer.

"Sir—"

"I'm not staying for the show."

He saw Chapman down at his center table watching a busty brunette as she gyrated. He walked straight to the table and stood in front of Chapman. Chapman looked up at him. He smiled. "Well, hail the conquering rock hero. What can I do for you, Mr. Dillon? Have a seat. Can I get you a drink? Have you taken a good look at this baby? I do get the most beautiful women in here."

Rowan sat. "Beautiful women in—and out."

"What's that supposed to mean?" Chapman asked, scowling.

"They disappear from here."

Chapman was silent for a moment, then rubbed his clean-shaven head. "Let me tell you something—I haven't hurt any woman. I like women. I really like them. But I like them alive."

"So you say—"

Chapman leaned toward him. "If—and I am saying if—I wanted someone dead, why, I'd just shoot the fucker." He smiled.

"All right, then let me just tell you this—one of your women just tried to quit. Someone told her she had to work next week. She won't be working next week, and no one will bother her again. Do you understand?"

Chapman studied him. "Are you threatening me?"

"Yes."

Chapman waved his hand in the air. "I guess the girl can go. She was good, though. Really good."

"That's what I wanted to hear."

Rowan rose. He turned and left Chapman.

Sam, not wanting her car seen in the parking lot, left it next door in a space intended for a nearby coffee shop.

She walked over to the building, wondering if there wasn't an entrance for staff. She didn't want to go past the bouncer.

She watched the building for a few minutes. When she saw a woman go in a side door, she hurried to it and slipped inside.

She entered a hallway. She could hear women talking and laughing, and she hurried down the hall.

A huge, handsome black man barred her way. Arms crossed over his chest, a fierce scowl on his face, he demanded, "Hey, what are you doing here?" Then he suddenly smiled. "Sorry—you just starting tonight?"

"Yes," she lied. "Is that the dressing room?"

"Go right on in. Hey, what are you calling yourself?" he asked.

"What?"

"Your act, what are you going by?"

"Oh, um . . . Water Woman," she fabricated quickly.

"Cute. Weird, but cute," he said and waved her on in.

She entered the dressing room. Half a dozen women were sitting around in different stages of undress. They were before mirrors, applying makeup, adjusting wigs.

"Hey, Chrissy, how's your little girl?" a brunette called to a redhead across the room.

The one called Chrissy smiled. "She's nearly walking. Can you believe it? After the accident, they said she'd never walk again, but she's doing it."

"Boy, those hospital bills must be something!" a blonde muttered.

The brunette giggled. "Yeah, thank God Chrissy did the surgeon."

"I did not! I went to dinner with him!" Chrissy protested.

"Hell, I'd do him. I've probably done worse!" the brunette said. Then she caught sight of Sam in the mirror. Their eyes met. "Hey," she said suspiciously, "you a new girl?"

Sam shook her head. "I was looking for a friend."

"You have a friend here?"

"Yes. Her name's—" Sam broke off, realizing that she didn't know what name Loretta used.

"Yeah?"

"Well, she's about so tall, pretty face—and she's very big . . . breasted."

The brunette laughed. "We're all big-breasted." Sitting there stark naked, she indicated her ample cleavage. Then her hostility faded. "We're the crew working tonight. There's one girl onstage, but she's brand-new. Can I help you in any other way?"

"No, no, I guess not, thank you," Sam said. She started to back out of the room. She backed into a body. Spinning around, she felt as if her blood had congealed.

Chapman.

"Well, hello! Are you coming to work here, Miss Miller? You'll be quite welcome, you know."

She shook her head. "I was—"

"Slumming?" he inquired.

"Just looking for—"

"A friend? Someone I know? Someone I must know, I imagine."

"I was just leaving."

"Why don't you stay awhile? Drinks on the house."

He reached for her arm. She backed away, almost screaming.

"Hey!"

Her eyes spun to the door. Rowan was there. She wasn't sure whether she should be stunned or relieved.

"Sam, get out here."

She didn't like his tone of voice. Neither did she like the way Chapman was looking at her.

"Sam!" Rowan grated. Then he looked at Chapman. "If you ever so much as touch her—"

"Hey!" Chapman lifted both his arms. "Go, Miss Miller, Please do go. But as I told your, er, friend here, I like women. I don't hurt them—I enjoy them."

Sam fled past him, taking Rowan's hand. His fingers wound painfully around hers. He jerked her down the hallway. Then they were outside, and he swung her around. "You fool! What the hell are you doing here?"

"What the hell are you doing here?"

"Damn you, Sam! It was dangerous for you to be here. I came to ask a few questions."

"Maybe I was working here."

"Oh, Sam."

"Rowan, you can't tell me what to do!"

"Great! I can just try damn hard to keep you from getting into trouble."

"Rowan."

"Get in the car."

"I have my own car."

"I'll follow you."

"Sure, fine."

She drove her car; he drove his. He parked in his own garage, but he was in her yard, following her to the door, before she could fit her key into her lock.

She hesitated. He wasn't talking anymore. He was still tense. So was she.

"I have to work tomorrow. I mean, I really have to work tomorrow."

"Good for you."

"Maybe—"

"I'm not going home."

"But I really have to work."

"I'll be out of your hair. The police are going down to the swamp tomorrow—to look for more evidence."

"Body parts. What does that have to do with you and me?"

"I'm going back out with Teddy."

"Why?" she asked. She opened the door. He followed her in. She turned around to stare at him.

"I'm going to dive with them."

"You're not a police diver."

"But I'm certified. They hire outside divers under certain circumstances."

"There are snakes and alligators out there—you saw where we were!"

"I'll be all right. But you—you need to go to work and stay there, understand?"

She looked down, wanting to argue with him. But maybe slipping into the club through the employees' door had been a bit reckless. And thankfully, he didn't really know why she had gone there. He had told her who owned the club, and he seemed to assume that information alone had sent her snooping.

She didn't want to tell him about Loretta.

"I think I'll make tea," she said, a little awkwardly. "Want some?"

"Tea. Yeah, sure."

He followed her into the back of the house. She put the teakettle on.

"This diving thing, Rowan. It's insane. What if you find something?"

"I'll be all right. It's you I'm worried about. Stay away from that club."

"Rowan—"

"Sam, I mean it. Swear to me that you'll stay away from it."

She poured tea for them both, then stared down at her cup. "Is Teddy diving?" she asked.

"So he says. It's not certain for either of us yet. It's up to the lead investigator. He's the one who decided that area of swamp should be explored for more . . . should be explored."

"I found the damn thing—just say it!" Sam whispered.

"Evidence. Body parts, clothing, jewelry, a weapon. At this point, anything could have happened. The medical examiner doesn't seem optimistic that he can discover much with what he has."

"Then does he know—"

"It's not Marnie? It's definitely not Marnie. The blood types don't match."

She swallowed her tea and set it down.

"Where the hell is she?"

His eyes were steady on hers. "I don't know. But we will find her. I won't stop until she's found, I promise you that."

"Oh, why?"

He leaned on the counter, a strange smile curling his lips. "Because you're never really going to let there be an us until Marnie is found."

She looked away from his gaze. "I really want her found."

A few beats of silence fell before he asked quietly, "Are you all right after this afternoon?"

"I'm fine. Honestly."

His hazel eyes, sharp as gold tacks, studied her own. "You're sure."

"I'm sure."

"Enough to . . ."

"Ah . . . fool around?" she whispered.

"Yeah, this is what I meant." Walking to her, he took her teacup from her hand, set it on the counter. He threaded his fingers into her hair, feathering out the soft strands. He cupped her chin and kissed her. Slowly. Then more deeply, more sensually, his tongue doing exotic things in the warmth of her mouth. She kissed him back. Moved into his arms. Felt his heartbeat, the fire of the heat within him.

Felt his hands stroking her bare flesh beneath the hem of her knit dress. Moving. Touching, manipulating.

Slipping the dress over her head, finding the hook on her bra. It fell between them, and they were back together again.

And his hands . . .

Were everywhere.

High against her breasts.

Low . . .

She moaned softly into his kiss. Her fingers slipped into the waistband of his pants. Button fly. One by one, she unbuttoned . . .

He watched.

Because always he watched. He could see so much, and he knew so much. No one knew, no one understood that everything he did was deserved and just.

Take the two of them . . .

The wretched snoops . . .

They'd been out there. A piece of body had risen . . .

Her fault.

And she wouldn't stop. Finding a body wasn't enough; she had to pry.

He'd never wanted it to be her. Because she was different.

Not so different. What was she doing right now? Showing what she really wanted, just like the rest of them.

He watched . . .

The man's body, her body. She moved like a cat against the man, rubbing against him, sliding against him. She was on her knees, she was up, he was down. Her back was arched, her head cast back. She was so very perfect in her form. He could see what she did, how her lips moved, almost the words that tumbled from them. He could hear her every cry and whisper . . .

He felt a sudden, agonizing cramp.

She was the same. Not different. Just the same. He'd known it. Known that she wouldn't leave it be. But tonight . . .

He wanted her.

They said that his crimes were crimes of violence, not love, not sex. Yet they were so foolish; they didn't begin to understand the rush, the ultimate climax, when the two combined. They didn't even understand that he only punished those who sinned. In a different time, in a different age, he might well have been applauded.

Ah, Samantha.

It shouldn't have been you.

You were different, but you wouldn't let it be. You pretended such purity, but you're sullied. Just like the rest. I sensed it before, and now . . . yes, now I want you.

And you have sinned.

I've been watching.

And you must be punished . . .

Sam really did go in to work early. Rowan woke her with a nuzzled kiss, making her get up to come lock the door—he was leaving. Once he was gone, she hurriedly showered and dressed and headed on in to work. She caught up with bills and correspondence, watching the clock all the while. The minute nine o'clock arrived, she called the law firm. She was anxious when Loretta didn't answer the phone, except that the cheerful receptionist told her that she had talked with Loretta, who was taking a sick day—she seemed to have a terrible cold.

Good. A cold would keep her out of the club.

Then Sam was glad in a way that she hadn't gotten to Loretta. She didn't want anyone wanting to know why she was trying to reach Kevin Madigan, or even that she was doing so. But the girl who answered the phone was a temp who gave her information without even asking her name or her business; she put Sam right through to Kevin Madigan's office. Sam worried about leaving a message, but Kevin answered his own phone impatiently.

"Kevin?"

"Yes, who the hell is this?"

"Sam. Samantha Miller. You left me a message at my house last night. Something about having lunch."

"Oh, yeah, great! Are you available?"

"Well, I—"

"I was hoping we could put our heads together on Marnie. You know, maybe think of some little thing that might trigger something. I know you were her best friend. I can't claim the same, but I sure want her to be found."

"I think lunch would be a great idea."

"Where would you like to go? I haven't much time; things are crazy here."

"Mm. Things are crazy," she murmured. She couldn't help but think about Thayer Newcastle's beautiful paintings, the body in the swamp—and the fact that people at the law firm were connected with the strip club.

"I'll come by the gym," Kevin said. "I could use a half hour on the treadmill anyway. When I can get away, I'll come in. Then, when you can get away, we'll just go."

"Fine, sounds great," she said, glad that he meant to accommodate her schedule.

The only question was, why was he being so accommodating?

Rolf Lunden, the lead investigator on the case, was actually a friend of Teddy's, and he was a nice guy, willing to bend the rules. There had been a killing on the beach the night before, plus two major execution-style killings, the victims dropped into the bay. So there were only two police divers who could be spared. Lunden had told Teddy hell, yes, he was welcome to go on down. He'd been more hesitant about Rowan, but Rowan had come armed with his diving credentials, and after Lunden had studied them for a minute, he shrugged. "Hey, well, you know, this is considered about the worst duty you can draw, going down out here in the muck, so if you're determined . . . just watch out for any evidence, huh?"

"Absolutely," Rowan assured him.

So now he was down.

And he had learned why it was considered like diving into hell.

Though the day was hot, he'd chosen a fairly thick skin—Teddy's suggestion. God alone knew just what all might come against you down in the water.

They weren't in the absolute worst areas. Those would be diving in pure mud, so thick it was like swimming in pea soup. No, here they were in canals with open pools. Real water. Except that as soon as they were down, no matter how carefully they moved, mud and silt were stirred up, and he couldn't see his hand in front of his face. When the mud had first begun to darken the water, he had realized why some people panicked under these circumstances. He was blinded—and painfully aware of the predators in the water with him.

There were men up in the police boats, watching. But there were no guarantees. Just as they had seen them the other day, alligators were basking on the shore of the nearby hammocks.

Rowan listened to the sound of his breathing; it was one of the things he loved about diving. It was somehow reassuring—the only time in life he ever really thought about breathing. He adjusted his regulator in his mouth, remained still at neutral buoyancy while the mud around him settled, and then he began to move. If he was careful to keep his flippers off the ground, the water would stay far clearer.

Roots tangled beneath the surface here. Grasses grew, long and thick. As the silt settled, he could begin to see the refuse of decades embedded in the dark bottom with its tangle of primeval growth. Yes, man had been here. Beer cans littered the mud. There, strangely, shining and standing up against the gloom, was the hood ornament from a Jaguar. A license plate lay half covered in the mud.

A skull.

His heart quickened. He reached out. The mud was stirred.

His gloved hands curled over the skull, and the rampant beating that had speeded up his breathing began to slow again.

Not human.

Extra long, white, with dozens of scissorlike teeth. A gator skull.

He set it back down, feeling a strange chill. He forced himself to turn carefully, roll in the water without disturbing the silt, to look around, to assure himself he wasn't being pursued by an alligator. What if one did decide to strike? They were fast in the water. So fast and fluid. And the pressure of their jaws . . .

Steady. Steady. Steady . . .

He turned back to his task.

Ahead of him, he saw something shiny. He saw it, then lost it. Like the Jaguar hood ornament, things down here had to be seen in the sunlight filtering through the water.

There . . . again.

He looked carefully, but it was still too far distant. He moved forward, and there, once again, he saw it flashing.

Something smacked against his mask.

He jerked, stirred the earth.

A fish. Just a fish.

Jesus.

He waited, irritated with himself. Once again, he'd stirred up the silt. The world around him was black.

He waited.

The silt began to settle slowly. It felt as if it was taking forever. He tried to check his computer for his time and his air. At first, he couldn't see it. He drew it closer to his face. He'd only been down twenty minutes. He had plenty of air.

Out of the corner of his eye, he caught movement. He turned, careful now. But whatever it was, it was gone.

He watched his bubbles rise. Waited. Still.

There it was, glistening ever so slightly. A flash of brilliance, here, gone.

He moved forward again.

A large branch had fallen from a tree, he saw. A big pine? The flashing seemed to come from one of the branches.

Very slowly, very carefully, so as not to lose it again, he moved ever closer. Yes, there it was, on a narrow branch of the tree.

He reached out.

A bracelet, he saw.

It was beautiful, and delicate. Gold, with tiny diamonds here and there.

He reached out, wondering if the bracelet might have belonged to the victim they had found the day before.

He touched it.

And then he realized that . . .

Yes. There was a big tree limb down. A massive, multi-branched limb down in the water. But the bracelet wasn't snagged on a branch.

Not a branch. Not part of a tree . . .

It just looked like slim, delicate branches drifting in the water. Beckoning. Beckoning like a human hand . . .

Because it was a human hand.

What was left of one . . .

When Sam went back to her office, after a therapy session with one of her clients, she was startled to find Kevin Madigan seated in a chair in front of her desk, reading a fitness magazine. He looked up when she entered.

He wasn't in gym clothes, and he certainly hadn't been working out. He was impeccable in a charcoal-gray suit, wheat-patterned tie, and cranberry shirt. With his dark hair and good looks, he could easily have been posing for *GQ*. They had gone out together once, perhaps two years ago. He'd been pleasant, charming, and a perfect gentleman. He'd taken her hands and just brushed her lips with the barest kiss at her doorstep. He'd suggested they go out again, but she'd sputtered out something about having to travel for a while. There had just been something at the time that bothered her. She wondered now if she'd just been impossible to please, wanting someone not so perfect, someone a little more earthy, real, rugged—wanting Rowan. Or was there something about him that really was . . .

Slimy.

He was just too damn perfect. Tall, dark, and handsome, and smart. An attorney, a man going places. He had a habit of trying to unobtrusively check out his appearance. In fact, he was doing it now—looking at her and yet past her, into the mirror behind her desk. She almost smiled. Joe liked to check himself out. But he just did it. In fact, if you were in the way, he would politely ask you to move aside.

"Kevin! I thought you were going to work out."

"I'd thought about it, but I decided not to. Is that all right?"

"Sure."

"Busy place you've got going here."

"Yes, there are a lot of people in here for a Friday morning. Usually we're busiest right after five, people on their way home from work, stopping off. Saturday and Sunday mornings are busy, too."

"Well, this must be a Friday for people playing hookey." He leaned forward. "Did you see who was out there?"

"Well, I think I saw almost everyone."

He sat back. "Did you?"

She folded her hands on her desk. "Didn't I?"

He smiled, like the cat that had eaten the canary. "Phil."

"Pardon?"

"Phil, the contractor. Phil, *Marnie's* contractor."

No, she hadn't seen Phil, but then, the place was crowded. She smiled. "I thought Phil was a friend of yours. I mean, he's done work for a lot of your clients. Wasn't he working on a house for Chloe Lowenstein when she disappeared?"

"My point, exactly."

"Maybe you should mention that to the police," Sam said.

He shrugged. "I was trying to get your take on the situation. I mean, I knew Marnie. Lots of men knew Marnie. We had a relationship in which we needed one another now and then. But still, you knew her better than anyone else. You're the only one I know that Marnie honestly liked. She couldn't find anything bad to say about you except that . . ." He paused, grinning.

Okay. She had to ask.

"Except what, Kevin?"

He hesitated, but then gave her a small, rueful smile. "Except that being friends with you was like being friends with the Virgin Mary from time to time. Holier than thou, you know."

Sam shrugged, refusing to comment.

Kevin was glad to move on to another subject. "Ready for lunch?" he asked.

Rowan would be ready to throttle her, she was sure. But he had told her to stay away from the club, and she wanted to get Kevin out of here—to a place where she could ask him about his involvement in the club.

"I . . . sure. Just let me change."

She left him in her office and hurried into the women's locker room. It was empty. She opened her own large locker, found a sleeveless knit dress, and pulled it out. She shed her gym clothes standing by the locker, then froze.

She thought she heard a noise from behind her. She spun around. No one.

And yet . . .

Chills assailed her.

She felt as if she were being watched.

I can see you . . .

She could almost hear the voice again. Feel it, against her ear.

I'll be watching . . .

She slipped into her dress and sped out of the locker room, wondering how it was possible for her to feel such stark terror in broad daylight.

Chapter 19

Rowan wasn't the only one who made a discovery that day.

Teddy had come across a femur.

Al Smith, a leather-skinned old diver, had brought up another arm, and another mass of something. They recognized bone; that was about it. Like the torso and the piece of pelvis they had found, this also had bits of muscle or some tissue remaining.

Sitting in the police boat, waiting while their finds were properly bagged and tagged, Rowan felt numb. He'd been through some bad times in his life. He'd seen death. He'd known losses that ripped his soul apart.

But nothing like this.

Human life reduced to remnants. Food for primeval predators. He wasn't a believer in the body having meaning after death; nothing had ever made so much sense to him as being an organ donor. But this . . .

Perhaps it was the callousness. Maybe it was wondering if the person had been alive or dead when she had been so viciously dismembered.

Bone, muscle, tissue . . . trying to decide what body part they held. And then the remains that he had found. Hand, fingers . . . barely held together. Arm, wrist . . . delicate tendrils of remaining tissue.

And the bracelet. Something so personal and intimate

as a piece of jewelry. The bracelet bothered him. Really bothered him.

He felt that he'd seen it before. It was a gold band with diamonds set into it in a delicate, elegant pattern.

Had he seen it on Marnie?

Al Smith suddenly gave him a hearty pat on the back and handed him a thermos of coffee. He took it gratefully, looking out at their surroundings. The swamp looked so peaceful. There were alligators sunning on the embankment of the hammock to his left, but the sun had begun to go down. They were cast in shadow. The day itself seemed to be painted in colors of red, gold, crimson, mauve. A long-legged crane waded to his right. Trees dipped beneath their own weight, branches touching the water, and the water itself shimmered on the surface, touched by the colors of the setting sun.

Smith sat down beside him.

"Gotta admit, I wondered what the hell they were doing, letting a long-haired hippie rocker go down with us."

Rowan grinned, wondering just how old Smith might be. "I kind of missed the hippie stage, and this is about the longest I've ever had my hair," he told Smith.

"Well, it doesn't matter much. Seems like sometimes, when I look back, it was the long-haired hippie types who cared the most about the Everglades, who were watching out for the panthers and the manatees. Then again, you know, certain things just span all time, and all years, you know? Think of a sports dive out in the islands somewhere. You take rich people, people who just scraped up the money, young people, old people—and they're all suddenly just the best friends in the world, pointing out a moray eel to one another, pieces of shipwreck, a shark coming into view, maybe. It's like something that you either love or you just don't. Like the swamp. Years ago, we didn't know quite so much about conservation, and then again, we didn't have quite so many private interest groups, all vying for the water—sugar farmers, developers . . . It was one of those better times, you know, like they say, those easier times. There were macho guys who liked to hunt and fish, and they came. And there were peace-loving bird-watchers, and they came. And mostly, the hunters shot up their beer cans, and the bird-watchers tended to their bug bites."

"Doesn't look like it could have changed too much," Rowan said. The coffee was good. The sun was still coming through the trees. The day was hot. He was chilled. He was grateful for the coffee.

"It hasn't. Not really. It's still one hell of a place to dispose of a body," Smith said, staring moodily out across the water.

"You think she was definitely murdered?"

Smith turned to Rowan and arched a brow high. "Why, hell, what do you think? She came out here on her own and told the alligators, come get me?"

"Might have been accidental—"

"Is that what you think? Gut feeling, that's what counts. So you tell me, take one good look, and what do you think?"

Rowan grinned. "You've made your point."

"The woman was murdered, son."

Teddy came over, leaping from boat to boat. "Guess we've got about everything properly bagged and tagged, ready for the M.E.," he said. He called to the young officer at the boat's helm. "Let's head on in." He took a seat opposite Rowan and Al. "All right, old-timer," he said, shouting over the sudden sound of the motor. "Did we do all right?"

Smith leaned back, crossing his arms over his white-haired chest. "Yeah, you boys did the force proud, Detective Henley."

Teddy shivered. "Got to admit, even I felt a little green."

"You're a homicide detective," Rowan said. "You see bodies all the time. It's your job."

"Yeah, but . . . well, this sounds awful, but thank God, most of the time my bodies are fresher than this. But Al . . . Al has to go in a lot where water and decay have been working at the remains. You've been through a lot worse, huh?"

"Yeah, I've been through worse," Al said. Then he shrugged. "But this . . . this is pretty damn bad."

Teddy looked over at Rowan. "You've been through it pretty bad, too, huh? You found your wife, right?"

Rowan stared back at him. Ted Henley kept including him in everything he did. Yet it was as if he was seeking out a weakness.

"Yeah, I was with my wife. And Billy—the old drummer for my band," he explained to Al. "There was a car accident. I tried to get his keys from him. He had an extra set, a magnet under the driver's seat. I followed when I knew he had gone." He hesitated, then looked at Teddy. "That was bad. Real bad. I got his wife out of the car. Then it exploded."

"Don't let no one ever tell you any different," Al said. "Death don't ever get easy. You kind of get a numb feeling at times. 'Cause you know things should never be so horrible. You wonder how in hell there can be a God when man does to man what he does. It don't ever get easy. Ever. And don't ever let it get too easy. That's when you know you're no better than the animals out there. Hell, you can't blame the gators for something like this. They're just predators. Part of the food chain. No, when you're looking for a real savage animal, seems to me you're always looking for a human being."

They were nearly back to Big Al's.

Rich Mira, from the M.E.'s office, was waiting for them. He'd been working with the body parts brought in so far. Rolf Lunden and his team stayed outside at first, supervising as their finds were turned over to the assistant M.E.

"Did you come up with any answers yet?" Teddy asked.

"Yeah, she didn't drown, I can tell you that."

"Do you know who she is?"

"A certainty, no. But you've brought me more to work with."

"Well, what do you think?" Teddy demanded.

"Detective Henley, how many times have we worked together? You know damn well that as soon as I have something solid, I'll tell you."

"Well, work fast. I need something solid."

"Let's get a beer!" Al Smith told Rowan, leading him into Big Al's. Smith bought the beer.

"Thanks. I owe you."

"Good." Smith grinned. "You can sign a CD for my kid."

"Sure. My pleasure."

"Hey, you want a Twinkie?" Al Smith asked, his eyes brightening as he saw the display near the check out counter.

"Twinkie, no. I guess I'll pass."

No Twinkie, but the beer tasted good, just like the coffee had. He drained it, then was surprised to turn and find Al waiting with another, grinning. "Hell, son, you ain't driving."

"Thanks. Excuse me. I've got to make a phone call."

He tried Sam at work, but she had left. He tried her house and got her machine. He left a message, then hung up, wondering why he felt so disturbed.

He checked his watch. She should still have been at work. Maybe she was on her way from one place to another.

He closed his eyes tightly, regretting his carelessness

in leaving her. Even for a minute. He fought the sense of panic seizing him. It was just the body parts he'd been finding.

No. There was good reason to feel afraid.

The phone call. The threatening phone call she had received.

He tried her at work again and talked to Didi. "Didi, this is Rowan Dillon. Do you know where Sam went?"

"Where she went . . . well, I'm not sure, actually. I think Sam went to lunch. Late. I could ask Joe, except I haven't seen him for a while, either. Let's see . . . did Sam come back . . . well, honestly, it was just so busy in here today. Marnie's brother came by, looking for Sam. Everyone was anxious to talk to her, you know?"

"If you find her in the next few minutes, have her call Big Al's. After that, have her beep Teddy, okay? We'll be on our way back in soon."

"Well, of course. Don't worry about her, though, Mr. Dillon—she's probably just hiding out."

"All right, Didi. Thanks. As soon as you see her, have her call, either Big Al's or Teddy's beeper. Don't forget."

He hung up. As he did so, he saw that Rick Mira was coming into Big Al's.

Mira went straight for the coffee dispenser. He poured coffee.

"Hey! Detective Henley!" Mira called.

"Yeah, doc, what is it?" Teddy called back.

"You wanted something solid, right?"

"Yeah! You've got something on our victim?"

"Victims."

"What?"

"Solid fact, Detective. *Victims.* Unless you had one very interestingly deformed woman, you've found body parts to two people."

*   *   *

What a day, Sam thought, entering her house, walking straight to the back, plopping into a chair, and staring out at her pool and the bay beyond.

Lunch with Kevin Madigan had been bad enough. He'd been defiant about the club, insisting that his own involvement had been because of Marnie and that it was just financial, nothing more. It made big bucks for everyone involved. She'd had a headache by the time she left him.

As soon as she got back to work, she'd found Phil, the contractor, working a Nautilus machine, his teeth grating as he strained, biceps bulging, face angry. Then, of course, he'd released the weight he'd been pressing and smiled at her. "No Marnie yet, eh? The cops have been all over me. Why can't they understand that she owes me money?"

"You should go a little slower on the lift, Phil. You're not giving those biceps the full benefit of the movement," she said.

"What? Hell, honey, there's all the benefit you can imagine in these biceps."

He grinned. She smiled back pleasantly.

"With the work I do, hon, I don't really need to be in here."

"Then why are you in here?" Kevin asked, walking around Sam to stare right at Phil.

"Why?" Phil said blankly. Then he laughed. "Well, I may be the supervisor, but that still means getting down and dirty, you know. Got to keep strong. Don't want to strain anything while I'm working."

"Now, that makes sense," Kevin said. "And I was thinking that you were a member here just to meet all Sam's rich clients who might want their costly homes redone."

Phil's face darkened. "Hell, Kevin, and I thought that

you kept your membership here just to acquire her wealthy clients who might sue one another."

"All right, guys," Sam said, pulling on Kevin's arm. She smiled, afraid that at any minute they were going to start demonstrating the power they had gained from her gym. "Pay your gym bills, and your motives are entirely your own. Kevin, come on."

"Good. Thank God. Let's get out of here. The old man is on a walker."

"What?"

"Mr. Daly is in there, walking on a treadmill. Running on a treadmill. If he has a heart attack, I don't want to be around."

Kevin had been holding her arm, forcefully. She wrenched free and walked toward the room where she had been earlier. It was filled with mirrors, and had televisions in every corner. Each person could use speakers that broadcast either TV, or music. Just as Kevin had said, Mr. Daly was on a treadmill. He wasn't running, and she didn't think he was in any great danger of a heart attack. He was walking quickly. He wasn't listening to the television or to music. He looked like Phil. He was wearing an expression of anger so fierce that she couldn't help but feel uncomfortable. *What if Marnie had been kidnapped and killed? By someone she knew, someone close to her. Someone who had kidnapped and killed before.*

Someone with whom Marnie had had sex. That left such a wide array of suspects!

Joe was by the door, talking to a new client. He saw Sam's face as she headed out with Kevin.

"Careful," he warned her jokingly. "You look mad enough to kill someone." That was because she was.

Sam walked out back and stood by her pool, watching the bay for a minute. The breeze was picking up. A definite indication of a storm to come.

She turned toward Marnie's house. The lawn and shrubs showed signs of being trampled. Marnie would not be happy.

She looked back at the water, sighing softly. She thought she heard a car door slam. Walking around her yard, she checked the street. There was a cop car out in front of Rowan's house. He must have come back from his diving expedition.

Did he know that she was home? Maybe not—she'd put her car in the garage. She walked on down to the dock, looking for Mollie. The sea cow wasn't around. Maybe Teddy had come back with Rowan. Maybe Teddy knew some of the results from the search of Marnie's house.

She walked around again, but the police car was gone. With a shrug, she came back to her own yard. The wind was lessening. Maybe the storm would blow over.

Yet . . .

It was darker. Dark . . . overcast. Gray. Menacing.

She looked toward her house. She bit her lower lip, realizing she had left her back door open when she walked around to the front.

Beth Bellamy let out a sigh, pausing to mop her face with a tissue. It was a long walk from the main road to the houses at the far end of the peninsula. But she'd made that walk with the solid determination that she would manage to speak with Rowan.

Or with his neighbor. The girl he'd been sleeping with before. While still married. Oh, she knew so much about him now. Beth was very proud of herself. She'd done her homework. And she stayed right on top of things.

He was going to talk to her. And if she couldn't find him . . . well, she might just find his lover. Beth smiled. Too bad about the girl. He was a hunk. Tall, dark, and handsome. Moody. Like Heathcliff on the moors. She'd

gotten really great interviews with some of the powerful
men she'd slept with before.

Some of her colleagues abhorred her for her methods.
She thought they were foolish. She was young, attractive,
and energetic. She was going to have a sex life no matter
what. It made good solid sense to combine that sex life
with getting great stories.

She paused again, watching the houses. No cars in
sight . . . was that good or bad? Well, she would just sneak
around a bit. Wait. Wait all night if she needed to.

She'd worn the right shoes—sneakers. And she'd actually worn the right clothing—a green halter-top dress
with a swinging shirt. Cool and easy to walk in—and easy
to hide against the bushes in.

Rowan's house rose before her. She paused, then
ducked against the foliage and ran around the back.

There she was . . .

Sam.

There, so close.

Staring back at her house now. Afraid? She should be!

*He watched. The way she moved, the way she looked
out on the world.*

*He remembered. Watching her. With him. Watching the
way she moved against his body. The things that she did.
Watching another man . . . touching her. Feeling her flesh.
She wasn't pure. She pretended, just like all the rest . . .*

*She wouldn't let things go. She just wouldn't let things
alone.*

She knew!

*He felt an awful sense of panic. She was dangerous, so
dangerous . . . and still.*

He remembered.

Watching her touch . . .

Being touched . . . naked . . . there.

*   *   *

Sam started, spinning around. She thought she had heard something. *Not* from her house. From Marnie's place? Just the wind, the rustle of the bushes. And still . . . she was ever hopeful.

"Marnie?"

No answer.

"Rowan?"

And still the bushes were rustling . . .

"Damn you, whoever you are—!"

Someone was there, stalking her.

"Stop! Damn you, stop!" she cried. There was darkness now, all around her. The sound of the wind, the menace of the night . . .

There! In the bushes again. Someone, something . . .

Leaving? Hiding.

"Damn you, come out!"

To her own amazement, she charged the bushes. There was more rustling. More and more.

Whoever it was was going to get away.

"Stop!"

There was suddenly silence.

She spun around.

And screamed.

For someone was there, in the darkness. Not in front of her. Behind her.

Reaching out.

Reaching for her.

A hand came through the shadows of the night . . .

Chapter 20

Loretta was always cheerful when she worked. It was sometimes a facade, but an important one. And basically she liked people. She believed sexuality was a part of human nature and that most of the time people were just out to have a good time.

Her party began quite early—cocktail hour. She barely had time to make it there from work. It was a bachelor party for a business type, a guy in his late thirties, finally taking the plunge. First-time marriage.

She'd been procured by the best man, the groom's brother, a nice enough fellow. He was shy, turning red as he talked to her when she reached the private club on the beach where it was being held. "Bobby's never been a really wild guy," the brother explained. "But, you know, I figure he's got a few fantasies. Everybody does, right?"

Loretta wondered if that was true. She didn't think there was much left she could fantasize about. After a while, almost everything had become okay, just another part of the job. She'd been with men, with women, black, white, yellow, and in between, and in all honesty, she didn't see much left. She'd been tied, spanked, sandwiched, and she'd wielded a whip while dressed in leather.

"Yeah, everybody's got a fantasy . . ." the brother said with a sigh.

And he was right. She did have a fantasy. Just to be loved by the right kind of guy.

"Don't worry," she said impulsively, smiling. "I'll make sure he has the time of his life."

"Thanks. Hey, you're really nice. What's your name?"

"Sheila," she lied.

She never told the truth. She never wanted her secret life discovered by anyone who wasn't leading the same secret life.

"Thanks, Sheila. I felt a little strange doing this. You know, I got your boss's number from a friend who got it from a friend who got it from a friend. I felt a little weird. I mean, this guy isn't even listed as an escort service."

Loretta forced a smile. She'd never met the "boss." He was just a voice on the phone. A voice that had become scarier as time had gone by. "We don't pretend to be escorts," she told the brother sweetly.

He laughed. "Well, the stage is set up over there. The music is ready. You come out and . . . and you give him a lap dance, right?"

"Yeah, right," Loretta said, suddenly feeling tired. "The best lap dance he's ever had," she added softly.

Sure, why not?

If you were going to a job, you might as well do it well.

Rowan stepped into his shower, turning the water on hot. For long minutes he just stood there, letting the water sluice over his head, feeling the steam rise up around him. It felt good to wash away the muck. The feel of the swamp.

The scent of death.

He closed his eyes. He couldn't shut away the visions that remained. Pieces of bodies. The carnage.

The wrist with the bracelet . . .

Even with the heat beating down on him, he suddenly felt cold. He remembered exactly where he'd seen the bracelet before . . .

A scene in the swamps. The swamps where they'd

been. The water, the hammock, the birds, the beautiful sunset . . .

A woman rising from the water, walking. Her naked back visible in the painting, but not her face. A long, beautiful back, long limbs. Arms by her sides as she casually sauntered out of the water, sensual, compelling, arrogant . . .

Wearing nothing but her jewelry.

The bracelet he had seen on her wrist.

He reached out, trying to grasp the water spigot and turn off the water. He faltered. Yes, he'd seen the bracelet before.

And dear God, he knew who the woman was . . .

No. He knew who the woman had been.

"Hey! Wait! You stop, please!"

Sam's scream faded. She felt like an idiot. She was staring into the face of the reporter who had been hounding Rowan.

"What the hell are you doing, sneaking around my yard?" Sam demanded harshly.

"I was looking for you—"

"Looking for me? You scared me half to death. If you were looking for me, why didn't you ring the bell?"

"You wouldn't have let me in."

Sam was still shaking. She had been so scared—and so stupid, really. "You're damn right. You're trespassing, you know. You have no right to be here."

"I needed to talk to you."

"Look, if Rowan doesn't want to be interviewed—"

"I'm trying to help him!"

"That's between you and Rowan. I—"

"Oh, come on. Everyone knows that you were his mistress—while he was still married. I know you have influence with him—"

"No, I do not have influence with him. Apparently he

doesn't want to talk to you. And I don't want to talk to you. You need to leave. You have no right sneaking around people's houses."

Sam was so unnerved, she didn't hear Rowan when he first came around the bushes into her yard.

He was furious. Once he had her attention, it was riveted on him. She'd never seen his neck so taut, his features so twisted. "What the hell are you doing here, Beth?" he demanded angrily of the young reporter.

She instantly defended herself. "It's a free world—"

"And this is private property."

"This isn't your property. I was talking to Miss Miller."

"Well, get the hell off her property!"

Sam wasn't sure if he actually took a step toward the woman of if he leaned toward her. The reporter moved back, brushing the bushes. She finally looked frightened, as if she knew she had overstepped her bounds.

Well, Rowan was frightening right now, Sam thought. So tall, dark, and foreboding in the fading light. She saw his hands, clenching and unclenching into fists at his sides. He watched the reporter walk away. His features were so sharp and striking. Handsome.

And at the moment deadly.

He turned toward her, about to speak.

She didn't let him. "You didn't have to scare her like that."

"Sam—"

"You scared me too." She crossed her arms over her chest, amazed to realize that she was doing so in a protective gesture. Just then it occurred to her: Why had he been so eager to go out to find dead bodies in the swamp? Was it because he wanted to know what the police had found?

She was afraid.

Afraid because he might be a killer? She couldn't believe it.

Afraid because what she was feeling might not be real. She could just be one of so many people in his life . . .

"Sam, please . . ."

He took a step toward her, arms reaching out. She stood still. His arms were around her. She inhaled his scent, breathed him in. He was freshly showered, with a hint of musky aftershave. He lifted her chin, touched her lips with his own.

"No!" She jerked away, slamming a fist against his chest.

"Sam, damn you, don't push me away! You shouldn't be out here alone right now. You can't blindly trust people—"

"No, I should trust you!"

"Fine. Don't trust me."

But he took another step toward her.

"Rowan!"

He didn't take her gently; he didn't try to kiss her again. He swept her up and walked with her back to her house, faltering awkwardly as he struggled with her and the door. Her heart was thundering. Dear God, he was strong. She felt his muscles jerk and move, felt the steel-like heat of his strength, and she fought a rising fear. *He could do anything he wanted! She was strong herself, a fitness expert, and yet . . .*

She was fighting him, twisting, kicking, hitting . . . and he didn't seem to notice. He had the power to do anything he wanted. She couldn't begin to fight him.

He got her door opened and stepped inside.

"Rowan, damn you, don't you—"

He set her down, and stepped away—right outside the back door. "Don't trust me. Hate me, loathe me, throw me out of your life. But damn you, don't be an idiot!"

She walked to the door. She needed time to think all this out. Her fingers were shaking as she slammed the door.

Just as he had done to her, a lifetime ago. Right now she was just so cold. She couldn't help herself. She locked the door.

He stared at her through the glass.

"Keep it locked!" he said softly.

Then he turned and walked away.

Sam stood very still for a moment, watching him go. Her heart hammered in her chest. She wanted to call him back. Tell him that she had just been taken by surprise. She just stood where she was.

The darkness kept falling.

The moon began to rise.

And still she didn't move.

She stood there shaking. Wanting him back.

And afraid . . .

Beth stood very still in the shadows, seething, watching Rowan Dillon's house. Now on the other side of his property, she nursed her wounded pride.

She had given in far too easily. He had threatened her, what was he going to do? Beat her up on his girlfriend's property? Next to Marnie Newcastle's house? My God, what headlines. Maybe they would be worth a few bruises.

He had looked angry. Really angry, enough to strangle her. What was she willing to risk for a really good, juicy story? A broken nose, yes. Her life, no.

She smiled. So he had thrown her off the property.

She inched a little closer to the house. She could see him on the bottom level of the place, through the windows that gave him such a great bay view. He was sitting at the drums, pounding away. Venting his anger?

Or his fear that she was closing in?

He moved suddenly, restlessly, putting down his drumsticks. He stood, looking toward the windows as if he might be coming out. Although Marnie's house was to the right of his, the property to his left was vacant, the lot not deep enough for a home. She couldn't hide against the bushes there. She looked around, then decided she needed to scramble down to his dock, maybe hide in his small boat.

She backed away from the windows.

Low, stay low! she warned herself. Ah, stay low, but it seemed as if it would be all right. He went back to the drums. Picked up the sticks . . .

Hammered out a hard beat once again.

She watched, still backing away, staying very low.

She was crouching nearly to the ground when she backed into another body. She knew instantly that it was a man.

A scream rose in her throat.

A hand clamped over her mouth.

"Sh!"

In escalating panic, she tried to turn.

"No, no . . . oh, damn it!"

She twisted . . .

She saw . . .

But then an oar crashed over her head, and the shadows of the night faded to black.

Agitated, Sam stood in her kitchen, brewing tea. The phone began to ring. She stared at it, then made a dive for it.

"Hello?"

There was silence.

Then . . .

The voice. The voice she had heard before . . .

"I told you to leave it be."

"What? Who is this? What are you talking about?"

"I can see you. I can always see you. I'm watching. I watch and watch. I always watch. I see your every move. I'm watching . . .

"And I'm waiting."

* * *

Piece of cake.

Easy money.

Right, Lacey thought. Easy money, and she was literally a piece of the cake. Tonight, she was part of the pastry. There would be raunchy movies, drunkenness, and maybe a few real prostitutes had been hired as well. Not her. No matter what they said.

She was just a piece of the cake. And she would be no more.

But here she was. She would never go near the club again, and she wasn't sure she could ever do this again either. But she needed the money for her trip. Her face burned. She could have asked Rowan Dillon for it. He would have helped her. She hadn't asked him. She had been so ashamed. She'd sworn she wouldn't go back to the club.

She hadn't said anything about working a private party.

Arriving at the exclusive home in Gables Estates had been easy. She had wondered what the neighbors thought. If they bothered to think—if they cared. They were so well insulated.

Most of the houses were huge, most directly on the water. Nor were they little zero-lot-line places. These were elegant waterfront homes on fair chunks of land, some on as much as an acre, maybe even more. Some of them had massive docks—with boats bigger than her own house.

Most of them were the kind of homes that allowed you never to see your neighbors if you didn't want to. Automatic garage door openers gave people the option of entering and leaving their houses without ever having to set foot in their own yards. Faceless, anonymous, they could come and go in the privacy of their luxury vehicles with their tinted glass.

She was feeling nervous. She didn't know why. Her own hair was covered with a wild red wig. She was heavily made up. So why was she so jittery? She had danced dozens of times. Taken off her clothes dozens of times. It was just that . . . this was more personal. She was going to have to talk to people. They would be close. Without bouncers to protect her if they came too close.

She had left her car at the airport. Everything she needed for tonight and her trip was neatly packed into the duffel bag she carried. She meant to take a cab out of the place straight back to the airport. No luggage, just a quick check-in at the gate, and she'd be on her way. She instructed her cab driver as to where they were going, although it was rather like the blind leading the blind. He pulled into the massive driveway, to the side of the catering truck. The house was down along the street that passed through the main entrance of the gated enclave. Though it appeared to be an old Mediterranean villa, she thought the house was actually fairly new. It was a style that was built frequently in this area. The home looked as large as a small Italianate palace, with courtyards, archways, tiles, and fountains. Beautiful.

She exited the cab, paid the driver.

Even as she surveyed the place, a young man—beer in his hand, wearing cut-offs and a Florida State T-shirt—came hurrying up to her. He had slicked-back blond hair, cool blue eyes, and, despite his dress, a white-collar-executive look about him. A certain arrogance. By day, she thought, he was a stockbroker, a lawyer, a banker, or a rising young businessman. Still, she doubted the house belonged to him. This was a big-money place. She thought somebody's rich, well-established parents owned this place—they were just using it for the party. He was cute. He was smiling as he came toward her. She started to smile back. She would have danced with him if she'd met him out at a club.

She was conservatively dressed at the moment, in jeans and a tailored cotton shirt. But as he came toward her, he let out a lascivious whistle, his eyes roaming over her in a way that made her feel deeply uncomfortable.

"Hey, cool, you're gonna be just great. You're the stripper, right?"

"Dancer," she said.

His grin was a leer. "Hey, honey, you call yourself what you want. I hired a stripper. So you go ahead and dance, but make sure the clothes come off good, okay?"

"I know what I was hired to do," she told him icily.

He started to laugh. "I'm paying big bucks. You tell me, just what were you hired to do?"

"Dance," she said, gritting her teeth, hesitating. "And strip," she added.

"Right."

"No more than that!" she told him tartly.

"Are you trying to get more money out of me?" he asked.

Her eyes widened. "I was told—"

He might have looked cute, but he wasn't. He was young, with an executive job bought and paid for by his daddy. He had a spoiled arrogance that made him ugly and obnoxious. "Don't go getting those panties up in a wedgie already. You were told right," he said, laughing. "But if you've got any specialties—like if you want to do a little oral this or that—there can be a lot more in it for you."

Her cheeks were flaming. She'd never felt dirtier, slimier, *squirmier* on the inside. She wanted to run away, but she wanted this money. She was supposed to be flying out late tonight to meet up with Janet, Sara, and Kasey in New York City. A chance to audition for a touring company of a real show, a professional show, a dream show.

"I don't do anything but dance," she told him, eyes narrowing.

"Hey, don't get angry. You do dance naked, right? If not, sweet cakes, you are not in the right place now."

"Yeah, I dance naked," she agreed through gritted teeth. "But that's it. You got it?"

"Sure."

Tears were stinging her eyes; she wasn't sure why. She wanted to shout at the young man, tell him that her father was a cop and that if he tried any funny stuff his ass would be in a sling.

But of course she couldn't say that. She needed to work, to get her money—and head for the airport. She was going to be cutting it close.

"Where do I go?" she asked flatly, her eyes pure frost, her chin high.

"Come on in. I'll show you."

"I need the money up front—and I'm out of here at eleven. You have a cab waiting for me. That's the deal, right?"

"That's the deal, but you can stay, you know. Sweetheart, you don't begin to understand what money there can be in this. If you're any good at all—hey, these guys will be so drunk it won't matter if you're any good at all! You can make a thousand bucks a pop, you know."

"I have to leave at eleven. That was the agreement."

"You are one stuck-up little whore, aren't you?" he asked.

Any second she would start crying. Great. She'd have endured this awful, filthy feeling, and he would send her away, and she wouldn't make the audition in New York. Hey, even if she made it, it didn't mean that she'd make the cast. Dozens, maybe hundreds, of girls would be trying out for the roles. She lifted her chin. "You, sir, are one arrogant asshole. Now, either you pay me and accept my terms or—"

"I'll pay you, I'll pay you. Cash, here and now. Hell, we can call in some other girls later. You should be worth the money for what you do. You'd better be."

He led the way.

She bit her lower lip hard.

And followed.

Rowan slammed down on his cymbals with a sudden, furious, cacophonous beat, then caught the shell, stilling its movement. The sound faded.

It was frightening how vulnerable and hurt he felt. Sam still didn't trust him. He'd been so honest, never lying about Marnie, trying to protect her.

He stood up. He'd never had a chance to tell her what he'd seen, how he'd realized himself that it was Chloe in Thayer's painting. Thayer had painted Chloe in the swamp. He knew, because he'd seen that bracelet on Chloe's wrist. He'd called Teddy, but had only been able to leave a message. He'd wanted to tell Sam, but Beth's appearance had made him forget.

Should he tell her? No, let Teddy do it, after he'd had a chance to tell Teddy.

Rowan clenched his teeth again. No. She was alone. He hadn't reached Teddy. What if Thayer came over?

He exited his house by the rear. The moon glistened on the water. Something . . . was floating.

He hurried down to the dock. At first he thought it was just the sea cow. Sweet, bulky Mollie. Then he realized that the sea cow was pushing something, nosing it toward the dock . . .

Someone.

"Mollie . . ." he breathed, jumping into the water. Yes, a body, someone.

Beth Bellamy.

Blood streamed from a gash in her head, turning the water red.

Chapter 21

"Teddy! He called again!" Sam said frantically. She curled the phone cord around her fingers, trying not to feel so panicky. It seemed that it had taken her forever to reach Teddy. He hadn't answered his phone. She'd beeped him, then beeped him again, and finally he had called back.

Was the killer watching her right now?

Waiting right there. Would he appear any minute while she was alone, vulnerable?

"Sam, I'll be there as soon as I can. We'll check out the house together," Teddy said. He was in his car, she thought. She could dimly hear a police radio in the background.

"Sam, we may have found Chloe Lowenstein," he added.

"What?"

"Rowan found a hand with her bracelet."

"Oh, my God . . ."

Her doorbell suddenly rang. She almost jumped sky high.

"My doorbell!"

"Sam, it might be Laura. She was coming over to talk to you about going to a concert in the park on Sunday."

"All right, stay there on the line. I'm going to see if it's her."

Sam walked to the door, shaking. She looked through

the peephole, breathing a sigh of relief. It wasn't Laura, but it was Joe. He was all dressed up, as if he was going out. Too bad. He'd have to come in for a minute.

"Joe!" She swung the door open and dragged him in.

"Hey, kiddo, what's up? What's the matter?"

"A freaky phone call," she told him. "Joe, please come on it. I've got Teddy on the phone, but I'm feeling really spooked. Will you look around the house for me, please?"

"Sure. Go back and talk to Teddy. Tell him I'm here. I'll check out the upstairs."

She went back to the phone. "Teddy, it's Joe. He's looking around upstairs for me—" She broke off, hearing the sound of sirens. They were coming toward her house.

"Teddy, do you have your siren on?"

"Yeah, Sam, gotta go. I'm right outside now. There's been an accident at Rowan's," Teddy said.

The line went dead. She stared at it.

"Rowan?" she murmured.

Suddenly, she wasn't afraid of going out; she was afraid that something had happened to Rowan. She dropped the phone and went flying out the back. She charged through the bushes and hedges, dashed through Marnie's yard and into Rowan's.

The ambulances and police cars she had heard had arrived. Teddy was there as well. Rowan, soaking wet, was standing by an ambulance, talking to Teddy and a paramedic. It was pure pandemonium. The medics were working on a body, talking to doctors at the hospital at the same time. An I.V. was up, blankets were being handed out, hectic conversation was buzzing.

She looked at the body. It was the reporter. Beth Bellamy. Her eyes rose. Met Rowan's.

Suddenly someone was behind her. Joe. He set his hands on her shoulders. "It's all right, it's all right."

No, it wasn't all right. Her eyes were locked with Rowan's. They slipped to the body of the reporter, back to his.

What had he done?

No, no, Rowan wouldn't have . . .

Too late. Her initial thoughts must have been in her eyes. He turned away from her. Another officer had joined Teddy. They were all talking. Rowan disappeared into a group of officers. A uniformed policeman came up to Sam and Joe. "Excuse me, but you'll have to leave—"

"I'm a neighbor," Sam said.

"How close?"

She pointed.

"Fine. Thank you. I'll need your name and any other information you can give me. Where were you for the last half hour? Have you heard anything unusual, seen anything—"

"It's all right. I'll take over here." Teddy patted the policeman on the back, indicating he could move on.

Sam was shivering. "It's Beth Bellamy?"

"Yes. Rowan said that was her name. You knew her too?"

Sam shrugged. "She was a reporter. Always after Rowan."

"Did you see her tonight?"

"I—yes."

"When?"

"Well . . . not long ago. She was kind of skulking around the yards."

Teddy was quiet for a moment. "Did Rowan see her?"

"Yes."

"And?"

"He told her to go away."

"Did he threaten her?" Teddy asked.

"No, no! No, really, he just told her to—go away."

"Oh, jeez!" Teddy said softly. "He did threaten her, didn't he?"

"No!" Sam was shaking. "But what—what happened?"

"He says he came out of his house and saw her floating there."

"Floating?"

"By the shore."

"And he fished her out?"

"So he says."

"Oh, Teddy! I need to talk to him—"

"Not now. He's going down to headquarters."

"He's under arrest?" she asked incredulously.

"No, he's coming down voluntarily."

"Sam, Sam, it's all right," Joe said reassuringly.

"Listen, I need to go down and keep track of what's going on. Laura is on her way over. Joe, will you go in with them and take a good look around and then lock up the house? Sam, we'll get a tap on the phone tomorrow—don't answer it tonight. Let the machine pick up. If I really need you, I'll call you on Laura's cell phone, okay?"

She nodded jerkily. "Teddy—"

"Don't worry about Rowan. He's a big boy."

But she was worried. She could see Rowan again. He had a blanket around his shoulders now, a cup of coffee in his hand. He seemed to tower over the officers surrounding him.

Beth Bellamy was being rolled to an ambulance. Rowan's eyes met hers once again. He turned away, his sense of betrayal complete, she thought.

"Come on, Sam," Joe said gently.

"Teddy, Beth is leaving in an ambulance, not a—"

"They've gotten her heart beating again," Teddy said, "but . . ."

"Yeah?" Joe said.

"She's still in a coma. According to Rowan, she came out of the water unconscious. Hey, go on home. I'll be in touch. I promise," Teddy said.

"Come on, Sam," Joe said.

Rowan was gone. He had disappeared. Police were still milling about, but she couldn't see Rowan anymore.

"I'll be in touch," Teddy swore. "Trust me, you're going to have to give a statement. Especially if . . ."

"If she dies?" Sam asked.

"Go home."

Joe led Sam back across the yards and into her house. "We left the door open again," Joe said. "I'll start checking things out."

She just stood in the back, numbed by what had happened.

"You know," he said, trying to tease, "it has been one bitch of a day. The house can wait a minute." He strode on into the kitchen and poured her a glass of wine. He brought it back to her, forcing it into her fingers. "Now, swallow that down while I brave the dark jungles of this old barn!"

She nodded. The doorbell rang. Joe answered it. She heard her cousin's voice. Laura had come.

She came through to the back, walking straight to her, slipping her arms around her. "You poor dear, what an awful week! But it's all right. They can't really arrest Rowan. He'll be out, don't you worry. And I'll be here."

"I'll be here," Joe said sternly.

Sam gave herself a shake. She had wanted to find Marnie. She had decided before that she wasn't going to be a coward. "No, you're not staying, Joe. You're all dressed up. You were headed out."

"It doesn't matter. It's not that important—"

"Joe, have you checked out all my closets and rooms?"

He grinned, flexing his muscles. "I threatened every shadow!"

"Then go on."

He looked uncertainly at Laura.

"I'm going to be here. And the alarm works. I'm not

afraid, and I'm the world's worst coward. We'll set the alarm. We'll be fine."

"All right," Joe said at last. "I'll call and check up on you, though."

"Fine. Thank you." Laura smiled, then said, "Sam doesn't like guns, but I have an old police special with me. Once upon a time when we liked each other, Teddy taught me how to shoot it."

"Well, in that case . . ."

"Go on out and have a life," Sam said.

Joe nodded and started for the door. "Come lock me out." Laura followed him, locking the door, setting the alarm. She returned, shaking her head. "This is so awful. That stupid reporter."

"Laura, she's in a coma!"

"Sam, it's her own fault. She hounded him."

"She might die."

"Well, Rowan didn't do it."

"Do it?"

"She was struck on the head."

"Oh, God!" Sam sat down, shaking. She swallowed the wine in her glass in a gulp. Laura was there to rescue the glass. Sam threaded her fingers through her hair. "Oh, God, oh God . . ."

"He wouldn't have done it!" Laura said indignantly.

Sam looked up at her cousin. "No . . . you . . . you don't know. He was so angry! He looked like he was going to hit her. I'd never seen him like that."

"He wouldn't do it. He wouldn't!" Laura said fiercely.

Sam shook her head slowly. "Laura, he's been good to you. You want to believe the best—"

"Yes," Laura said stubbornly. She lifted her chin." He's my friend, and of course, I believe the best. You supposedly love him. No wonder he slammed a door in your face. You wanted his trust then, you didn't deserve it. You don't deserve it now!" Laura turned her back on Sam indignantly and walked away. "I'll be reading in the living room if you need me. I'm not sure I have anything more to say to you tonight."

"But—" Sam began. Her words faded. Because maybe Laura was right.

Once she had claimed that she would be there, stand by him, and stand up for him.

Believe in him . . .

She heard a phone ringing. A cellular. Laura's.

A minute later her cousin reappeared. "Sam, that was Teddy. He said that if we see Thayer Newcastle, we're not to let him in, under any circumstances."

"Why?"

"Because one of his paintings is of Chloe Lowenstein. Naked. In the swamp."

Loretta did the lap dance of the century. In fact, it was so damn good that she wondered if the no-longer-so-shy young executive would have any juice left for his own wedding. It had been a nice group. A heavy-tipping group. A lot of guys, though. High-class, big-money types. Doctors, lawyers, architects, builders, politicians! And cops, naturally. No matter how you dressed them up, she could smell out the cops every time.

Some came close and were wild, some stood in the background, in the shadows. She'd gotten down to a garter belt and a G-string, and both had been filled with money.

And still . . .

If you're going to do a job, do it well. She had done it well. The guys had been great. She just didn't feel so great herself as she dressed to leave. She'd had hands everywhere on her flesh. Not really part of the game, but the money had been there. She'd gotten just a little carried away herself. And now . . .

Time to go.

She asked the brother to call her a cab. He said he would. Then she heard a voice at her ear.

"Sheila, huh? *Sheila?*"

She spun around. Her heart flew up and crashed down. "Oh, God!"

He smiled, he touched her cheek. "Loretta . . ."

His smile was so . . .

His hand was on her arm. "Let's go."

Then she stepped outside to leave. And there was one of the guys.

Sam decided to make cookies. She was completely unnerved. Beth Bellamy was in a coma, Chloe Lowenstein was dead—and now, she couldn't get the image of Thayer Newcastle's painting out of her mind.

Was he a killer?

She didn't know why she decided to bake; it was just something to do. She was cutting out the dough when Laura came into the kitchen. "What are you doing?"

"Cookies. Heck, if I'm going to be trusting and loyal, I'm going to want to take home-cooked baked goods when I visit my man in the lockup, huh?"

"Very funny. For your information, Rowan left the police station hours ago."

"How do you know?"

"Teddy called." She made a face. "He was already out partying himself. I could hear the music blaring away in the background."

"Laura, he cares about you. You know he cares about you. And at that club the other night, well, you two were on each other like rabbits, you know."

She shrugged. "It was a nice night, but nothing more. Not now, anyway. I really don't care at the moment. I just worry about the kids."

"Why? Lacey seems to have a real opportunity this weekend."

"Yeah." Laura leaned against the counter. "I just wish I could help her more."

"You do help them. You encourage them to fulfill their dreams, and that's what everyone needs."

Laura smiled. "Well, that and an audience. I need everyone I can get for Sunday."

"I'll call everyone I can."

"And Rowan. If Rowan will just sit in for a set . . ."

"I'm sure he will." She hesitated. "If he isn't arrested."

"Teddy will be there, and lots of cops. I do give him that. He supports his kids."

"I can call some of my clients." She hesitated again. "The law firm is a damn strange place, but Kevin Madigan is being awful friendly. He can get some people to show up, too."

"And we can watch them, right? And interrogate them?"

"Laura, people in that firm own the strip club. Along with Lee Chapman."

"I know. Teddy told me."

"Don't you think it's . . ."

"Slimy? It's just business."

Sam shook her head.

"The dancers were pretty. Sexy. It's adult entertainment." She grimaced. "I certainly wound up entertained."

"But, Laura . . ."

"What?"

"I don't know. I just have to wonder where else it can lead."

"Decent people do that kind of thing for a living."

"You think Chapman is decent?"

"No, but that doesn't make all club owners, dancers, bouncers, and so on bad!"

"All right."

Laura laughed suddenly. "So if you know any dancers, strippers, bouncers, con men, be sure to invite them for Sunday, too."

"I'll invite them all."

"That will be great."

"Seriously, lots of friends will show. I know Joe will come. Harry and Ann Lacata and Gregory—they always support us."

Laura laughed. "And we can get Phil the contractor! He'll do anything for you, hoping to suck up enough to get you to redo this place with him."

"Marnie always came, and Thayer—"

"Thayer!" Laura shivered. "Oh, Sam! I didn't see the painting, but it's really scary, isn't it? Rowan told Teddy that you can very clearly see the bracelet on the woman's wrist in the painting."

"Well, I imagine it means he definitely knows Chloe Lowenstein. But, of course, he knew her. She worked with his sister."

"But he painted her *naked*. Coming out of the *swamp*."

"Where her body was found," Sam agreed, looking at Laura.

Suddenly the phone began to ring. Both women jumped. Then they stared at one another. The machine picked up.

Silence . . .

Lacey wanted to die.

To crawl under a table and die.

This was horrible. She would never, never do it again.

Yet it was finally over. And soon she'd be headed out on a big silver bird. Headed for the Big Apple. With plenty of money. But money would never matter quite so much again. This was it.

They weren't supposed to touch, but she'd been mauled and pawed. She'd yelled, she'd been angry—and then she'd been booed.

But it was over, over! And she was dressed and ready to

*go. It was early, plenty early. They really hadn't wanted
her to stick around . . .*

She stepped outside onto the beautiful grounds, breathing in the clean night air. The arrogant ass who had hired
her said that he'd called the taxi, but she had a feeling that
he would let her sit a while first. She didn't care. Never
again. Never.

"Lacey!"

Her name was said so softly. With such empathy and
sorrow.

She winced, turning, her heart beating. Who could it
be? Who had recognized her? Oh, God, he would never,
never understand . . .

"Oh!" she said miserably.

He shook his head. She felt her face flame.

"I—I needed the money. Please, don't . . . I . . . oh, my
God, it was awful, I'll never, never, never do it again,
honest, I—"

"My car is over there. Ready?"

She nodded. He directed her to his car. He seated her on
the passenger side, took the driver's seat himself. His engine revved. They left the scene of her infamy behind.

"The New York thing is real, a big break—"

"I know."

"But we're not heading for the airport."

He looked at her. "There's time," he said.

She was so ashamed. She had to keep silent.

And yet . . .

They were driving and driving. Out of the city. Out on
the Trail.

Heading toward the swamp, she thought.

Toward two o'clock Sam decided to go to bed.

The first caller hadn't spoken.

Teddy and Joe both called back to check on her.

Not a word from Rowan.

She tossed and turned restlessly, seeing horrible pictures again and again in her mind's eye.

The corpse in the water.

Or the piece of the corpse in the water . . .

Beth Bellamy, on Rowan's lawn.

The painting. Thayer Newcastle's painting of a woman, walking out of the swamp.

Despite the pictures in her mind, she slept.

Then she awakened, filled with terror. She didn't know why.

Then she did.

There was someone in her house. Laura, yes, of course, Laura. Laura was sleeping down the corridor in the guest bedroom.

No. There was someone there. In her room.

No, no, no . . .

But there was!

She could see the shadow. The shadow of a man . . .

In her doorway. He wasn't moving. He was just . . .

Watching.

Waiting.

I can see you . . .

Terror filled her. She tried not to move. Not to let him know she had awakened. She had to find a way to slip away in the darkness of the night.

How?

Oh, God, she would never . . .

Laura had a gun.

Where was Laura?

Had he already found Laura? Surprised her, hurt her. Was Laura already . . .

I can see you.

I'll be watching . . .

Waiting.

I can see you . . .

He started to move.

Too late. She had nothing. She opened her mouth and started to scream.

"No!" His voice was harsh, gruff.

He leapt across the room, landing on her before she could flee, his hand falling over her mouth.

"Sam . . ."

Chapter 22

Rowan could have killed Laura. He'd told her to wake Sam, to ask Sam if she wanted to talk to him. But no, Laura, determined to be a dedicated matchmaker, had sent him straight to Sam. And he'd knocked on her door to awaken her, to alert her . . .

But she woke up in terror anyway.

He tried to show her it was him. Tried to say her name, tried to get her to quit screaming—for God's sake, there was a plainclothesman in a car outside. Rowan was in enough difficulty without the cop rushing in, convinced that he was killing Sam.

"Sam!"

His hand was over her mouth. She was kicking, screaming, thrashing, fighting like a maniac. He was on top of her, barely stilling her.

"Sam!"

Finally she went still. Eyes very green in the shadows, going wide as she stared up at him. His fingers were tangled in her hair; he was a heavy bulk against her. Maybe she did think that he was killing her—she hadn't seemed to have much faith in him tonight.

"Please quit screaming. If you don't, I will most likely be arrested."

He eased his grip slightly.

"Get your hand off my mouth!" she snapped.

He sat back. "What the hell do you think you're do-ing?" she cried.

"Damn it, I knocked. Laura let me in—"

"So you attacked me in the bedroom?"

"I didn't attack you—"

"You sure as hell did!"

"I knocked on your bedroom door, and you started screaming bloody murder. I had to stop you."

"What are you doing here?" She tossed back her hair, eyeing him narrowly.

"Trying to talk to you!"

Her lashes fell over her cheeks. "You're definitely out of jail."

"I wasn't in jail. I went down for voluntary questioning. They'll be by to take a statement from you in the morning. Don't worry—I told the truth, the whole truth, and nothing but the truth."

"And that was . . ."

He sat back on his haunches. She was wearing some-thing soft and blue. A material that clung to her form. Very distracting. He swallowed, remembering the evening with bitterness. "Somebody attacked Beth Bellamy and left her in the water to die. She would have died—if it hadn't been for that manatee."

"Mollie?"

"She kept her from sinking, pushed her toward the dock."

"And then you . . . saved her. Pulled her out of the water."

"I don't know if I saved her or not. She's in a coma."

"But you pulled her out . . . and called nine-one-one?"

"Yes."

Sam leaned back on her pillow, staring up at him. Her eyes were wide and beautiful, her hair was like a rich fan-tasy, spread out around her head. Her breasts rose and fell against the soft blue stuff she was wearing. He heard her breath, felt her heartbeat. She was a memory come to life, one that had lived in his soul forever, or so it seemed. But he was worn. More bitter than he had ever wanted to be. He could fight forever if he had to, but he couldn't fight against her doubt, not at this point.

He leaned toward her. "I love you. I never fell out of love with you. Maybe what I did was wrong, but I did it to protect you." He frowned, rubbing his forehead. "Look, you have to start trusting me. That's the way it has to be. Take me, or leave me."

She looked at him a long time. "Did you know that your clothes are still soaking wet?" she asked.

He shrugged. "It's warm enough and the cops gave me a blanket."

"Could you, um, get up?"

He did so, watching her suspiciously. She rose as well, smiling. "I'll get you a towel. You're salty as well."

He just stared at her.

"You know where the shower is. Should I make you some coffee, or tea, something hot? I think I have chicken soup—"

"God, no, I don't want chicken soup."

Chicken soup? What the hell did that mean, what was she thinking? He'd laid his damn heart on the line, and she was suddenly turning into a nursemaid.

He went into the shower. Strange, he hadn't felt the salt on his skin until now. There was actually a piece of seaweed down his shirt. He shed his clothing, and turned the water on very hot for the second time that day. No, it was Saturday now. Dawn would be coming soon enough.

He turned off the steaming water, stepped out of the shower, and toweled himself dry. Going from the light of the bathroom to the darkness of the bedroom, he was momentarily blinded.

Then he saw her.

The soft blue thing she had been wearing was gone.

She was standing in the center of the room, waiting for him. She walked toward him, a feast for the senses, soft, warm, her hair perfumed, her flesh delicious.

She came against him, high on her toes. Kissed his lips. Whispered against them. "I love you. Forgive me."

"Forgive you . . ."

"Forgive me," she repeated. Her lips found his once again. Her tongue moved over them. Her breasts pressed softly, teasingly, against his chest.

"Why?" he asked softly.

"I didn't trust you. Believe in you enough. And trust is . . ."

"The most important thing."

"But I doubted you, too."

"You tried to protect me. From you. You succeeded too well."

He held her away from him for a minute, studying her eyes. "Thank God we've got a second chance."

She smiled. "Thank God."

"I really would die for you, you know."

"Don't say that!"

"But it's true."

Her eyes remained on his, and she told him, "I think I would die without you now."

She moved against him, a trail of kisses covering his chest. He feathered his fingers through her hair. Felt the softness, inhaled her scent. Hunger flared within him. He felt himself against her, wanting. He waited. Let it build.

What an agony. Waiting.

What an ecstasy.

Her body was silk and magic, moving against his. Her lips were sweet, fiery titillation, each kiss a peppering of molten lava against his flesh, his desire. She moved, caressed, cradled, hands and mouth upon him.

Touched.

Feathered kisses . . .

She moved down. So fluid. So sensual. Her touch, her caress . . .

He could have died happy at that very moment . . .

A sound exploded from him and she was in his arms. He was within her, and he knew he had always loved her, wanted her. Their bodies were slick with sweat, movements were urgent, everything within him was focused on one part of his own anatomy, and still, he knew . . .

He would, simply, die for her. And perhaps she was right—he would die without her.

Lacey Henley sighed softly, shaking her head as she looked at Thayer Newcastle.

She'd missed her plane, but it was all right. She'd get the crack-of-dawn flight out. She had called the girls, explained that she would be late.

She and Thayer had talked and talked, and the more they did, the more she thought they were kindred spirits. He spoke with an artist's heart. He was older and wiser, but still, that artistic wonder was him; he understood the dream. He didn't condemn what she had done. He just made her see that her talents far exceeded what she had been doing.

"I don't know how you've survived. I've heard my folks talk, my mother . . . Sam. You had a terrible childhood. And your sister can be so mean—I'm sorry, I shouldn't have said that."

"It's all right. My sister can be mean."

He was so handsome. Lean, but so strong. And his eyes . . . beautiful.

"And your father . . . well, I've heard about him, too. He could really hurt you—"

"He could, but . . ." Thayer paused, then shrugged. "He's dying. He's known for a while that his liver is eaten to shreds. They gave him a few months, tops. And do you know what he did when they told him?"

"No, what?"

"Went out and bought himself a new bottle of whiskey."

"I'm sorry."

"I don't know what I feel. He's my father, but . . ."

"I know he hurt you, but he doesn't still . . . do . . . things . . ." she finished lamely.

Thayer shook his head. He grinned at her. "Hey, I became strong at a very young age. The worst hurt is that I don't love my father. He never loved us, and I don't love him. Everyone should have love."

"Oh, Thayer," she said softly. She looked at her watch. Nearly four in the morning. "I have to get to the airport. Or I'll miss the next flight, and my cheapie airline fills up on the flights at normal hours."

"Sure," he said, looking at her. Then he reached for her, pulling her toward him.

"Thayer . . ." she protested.

But he had told her the truth. He was strong, very strong.

Rene Deeter was the nurse on duty that night when the lights began going crazy from Room 6308. She tore down the corridor. Her patient, the coma victim, Beth Bellamy, was flatlining.

"Shit!" she swore to herself and hit the code button.

Within minutes, her colleagues were rushing in.

"A coma victim, what the hell . . . ?" demanded Terry Larson, the doctor on red-eye duty. "Clear!" he snapped.

The emergency team worked frantically. Then . . . a wave in the line. She was alive. She might make it.

Dr. Larson put a hand on Rene's shoulder. "Good work, kid. Your speed might have saved her. These cases . . . well, usually, you know, if she makes it out in the next few days . . . they're so curious . . ."

"Yeah, so is this," said Connie Flannery, another nurse. Larson and Rene both looked where she was pointing.

Someone had pulled the plug on Beth Bellamy.

"I did not do that!" Rene said passionately.

"You didn't trip on a wire—"

"No! I did not."

"Maybe the LPN—"

"Sherry took her break. It's four-thirty a.m.—the hospital isn't teeming with people."

Larson stared at Rene for a long moment. She was very certain. She'd been nursing for twenty-five years. She was a good nurse, efficient, dedicated to her patients.

Dr. Larson made a decision. "Someone call the cops. Hell, this girl needs protection."

"There was no official guard, but that homicide guy, Ted Henley, was here late. He went down to the machine for coffee a while ago," Rene said.

"Call security. Get him back up here. And Rene, keep a tight eye on her yourself all night, huh?"

"Yes, Doctor. I certainly will."

Sam slept very late. She rolled over quickly to see if Rowan remained beside her, but he was gone. She rose, showered, and came downstairs. Laura was making French toast. Rowan was sipping coffee and reading the newspaper. Laura was talking; Sam wasn't sure that Rowan was listening. He frowned, staring at the paper. He had been home, she thought. He was in denim cutoffs and a green polo shirt.

"Sam, hey, you're up. A quick rundown—no change in things. Beth Bellamy remains in a coma—"

"Tell her the rest," Rowan said.

"Someone pulled a plug on her machines," Laura said.

"At four-thirty a.m."

"Well, you were here—"

He smiled at her. "You were sleeping. Are you positive I was here?"

"Yes," she said firmly. "But Beth survived the attack?"

"She's still in a coma."

"And she now has a police guard," Rowan said. "And I'm glad that you have faith in me. Trust me, the police would still question my whereabouts."

"Oh!" Laura exclaimed, "and Teddy asked Rolf Lunden to bring Thayer Newcastle in for questioning because of the painting, but no one has seen hide nor hair of him. This is getting very frightening. Rowan and Teddy and the divers found extra body parts yesterday—"

"Extra body parts?" Sam said, pouring herself coffee.

"She means parts to a second body," Rowan said, refolding the paper.

"Could the extra parts be . . ." Sam began, fear gripping her, her voice trailing off.

"Marnie? No."

"But it does seem then that someone is killing women and dumping their bodies in the swamp," Sam said. She sipped her coffee, leaning on the counter. "It was definitely Chloe Lowenstein that we found? How did everyone know so quickly?"

"They identified her by her medical history—a fracture of her hip when she was about eighteen. A riding accident," Rowan explained.

"Did you know when we found her?" she asked him.

He shook his head. "Not for certain. But when I got home, I admit, I knew. We, um, well, one of the things we found yesterday was a bracelet. I remembered seeing it on Chloe in Thayer's picture."

"I always thought the boy was a little weird," Laura said.

"You can't hang him yet," Rowan warned.

"Let's see, he painted a picture of a naked woman in

the swamp and that same woman wound up in that same swamp, dead?"

"It's his sister who is missing now," Sam reminded her.

"Yes, and doesn't he gain the world if she turns up dead?" Laura asked.

"Not while their father is alive," Rowan said.

"Yes, but that old sot could drop dead any minute. He drinks like a fish. He can't have a liver left," Laura said.

"Ah, but he may be pickled," Sam said bitterly. "Preserved for all time."

"Let's pray not. Horrors!" Laura exclaimed. She shook her head. "All right, I care about Marnie, I'm worried about Marnie, but I can't do anything about Marnie. And yes, we're in the middle of a very nerve-wracking and worrisome time, but we are living. The world is going on. Sam, I don't mean to be a pest, but will you start calling people about tomorrow?"

"Tomorrow?"

"Aidan is playing in the Grove, remember?"

"Oh, of course."

"Rowan has said that he'll sit in for a few numbers with the group."

Sam slowly arched a brow at Rowan. He grimaced in return. "I told her I'd do what I could. They may be better off without me, though."

"Why?"

He turned the paper around, showing her the local headline. PRYING REPORTER GOES TOO FAR? ACCIDENT OR FOUL PLAY IN THE CASE OF BETH BELLAMY?

She took the paper from him. The article was about Rowan. Beth would have been proud. His past was rehashed. The disappearance of his next-door neighbor was brought up. It ended: "Is there a serial killer loose in our midst? How long has he been murdering women? Who is he?" The implication, although not written, was there. *Could this killer be Rowan Dillon?*

"I'm so sorry—" Sam began.

"You shouldn't be. You should be glad to realize that you weren't the only one suspicious of me." He sounded worn and somewhat bitter. "I think I'm going home for a while—practice some for tomorrow. I haven't played anything in front of a crowd for a long time. Laura, stay here, and keep your gun handy."

He left by the back. Sam watched him go.

"Well, you deserved that," Laura said.

Sam swung around. "Laura, it's good to know you're always on my side."

"I am on your side. Don't be an idiot. Go get him."

Sam smiled, then followed Rowan out the door. She cut across Marnie's yard—around the bushes and the police tape—and came to Rowan's house. She could hear him playing his guitar, working the frets. He must be in a rare mood—he was playing a Jimi Hendrix lick.

She crossed by the pool and walked to the door of the basement level. It was open. She let herself in. He knew that she had come. He ignored her.

She walked to the drums. Her fingers felt itchy. She picked up the sticks, sat. Tested the bass, then the snare.

Then herself.

A drummer's job was to keep the beat. Any decent drummer could keep the beat. The rest was style.

She had beat. And it was amazing just how quickly touches of her old style returned.

She loved the drums. The sound, the action, the physical pounding and tapping. Her father had taught her to play. She suddenly wondered why she had ever given it up.

Had she been punishing herself?

He played; she played. Then he stopped. He set down his guitar. He walked over to her. She kept on playing.

Pulse and thunder. Passion . . .

She looked at him. His eyes were golden, his smile was rueful.

"Damn, but you can play!" he told her.

"I've missed it," she admitted softly.

"The drums more than me?"

"Nothing more than you. But I do love the drums."

"Thunder away," he told her. But he didn't mean it. He took the sticks from her hand. Pulled her to her feet. Into his arms. "I just can't resist a good beat," he told her.

"Such emotion."

"Tempest."

"Passion."

"Fire!"

He eased her down to the floor. She threaded her fingers through his hair, touched his face. They made love in a bed of towels on the floor by the drums.

Day or night. Night or day. So much darkness. Did it matter anymore?

She closed her eyes, opened them. Hot, cold. Afraid. Wondering. She'd been bitten by so many insects.

The darkness, the fear. She had gotten to where she just stayed still. No. She couldn't do that. What if he didn't come back? What then? There had to be a way out; there had to be light. She was brave, she was strong, she was who she was, she was going to make it. But she had tried before. Tugged and worried at the rope that held her until her fingers bled. So she thought. She couldn't see them in the darkness . . .

Then she heard his voice. Her heart went still. She froze.

"Hi, sweetheart!"

He could see in the awful darkness. He was right by her. He'd been watching her. Did he know what went on in her mind? That she thought constantly about escape, that there had to be a way, that she was strong, that she would figure it out . . .

He was right by her. His hand was on her head. He hunkered down, touched her chin. "Have you missed me?"

"Bas—" she began.

He hit her hard. She felt the blood in her mouth. Tears sprang to her eyes.

"Tell me you're sorry, sweetheart."

He was right next to her. Sitting by her now. She thought of some of the other ways he had hurt her. God help her. She wasn't so strong.

No, no, no, don't say it!

"I'm sorry!" she whispered. "I'm sorry."

"Did you miss me?"

"Yes, I missed you. I was afraid and alone without you."

"But I'm here now."

"You'll protect me from the darkness."

"Yes. I'll take care of you. You'll take care of me. That's the way it works. And of course, if you don't obey me as a good woman should, you know what happens, right?"

She knew.

"And you know what I want, right?"

Tears filled her eyes again. She knew. And she would do whatever he wanted. No matter how much she wanted to die, no matter how she felt, no matter how horrible . . .

She was a survivor.

Later, she heard him laughing. Felt his hands in her hair. "You are a clever girl. The most clever."

"Why are you saying that?"

"Because you will do anything to live, won't you?"

"I don't know what you mean—"

"Yes, you do. Not everyone is so clever."

"I don't know what—"

"Yes, you do. I can only keep one woman. Yet you

know there are others besides you. Move just a bit to your left . . ."

She didn't want to. She couldn't help it.

She touched flesh.

She began to scream. He pulled her back to him, laughing first, then shaking her. "You want to live, right? Let's see how clever you can be. There will be more again. But only one I can keep. We'll see, won't we? You'll keep doing as I say."

She would. God help her, she knew that she would. She wanted to live. In tears, she shook her head. He continued to touch her hair in a nauseatingly gentle way. "You'll do whatever I say, whatever I say." And he laughed again, as if he could not contain his pleasure. She wanted to die.

But not nearly so much as she wanted to live.

"I can see you. I can always see you."

"Yes."

"Touch me . . ."

And she did.

In the late afternoon, Sam went downtown to police headquarters and gave a deposition on everything that she had seen happen with Beth Bellamy the night before. She didn't lie, and she was concerned. Though Rowan had pulled Beth out of the water and called emergency, his argument with her made him look guilty. The detectives looked at Sam strangely. Why would a woman be so taken with a man that she was willing to believe in him against the odds? Angry, she went on to tell them about the strip club and the law firm and Lee Chapman. They just told her that it wasn't illegal to own a strip club with the proper permits in the state of Florida. They were, however, a little aggravated. The cops weren't happy about Lee Chapman being a free man either.

The day was disturbing to her. She felt restless, afraid

that things were beginning to unravel. And though she was glad, she was afraid that the situation would get worse before it could get better. If Beth Bellamy would come to, it would help. But Beth had nearly died two times now. The police were trying to make sure that there wasn't a third time.

She was uneasy that day but never alone. Rowan drove her to the station, and he drove her home.

Her telephone line was tapped. If the caller dialed through with another message for her, they had a chance of trapping him.

She didn't forget that life did go on. As Laura had asked her to, she put through calls to her friends and associates. Each time she talked to a man, she wondered if his voice was the one she had heard, the husky, threatening voice that had warned her to "leave it be."

She couldn't reach Loretta, but she left a message on the woman's answering machine.

"What do we do now?" she asked Rowan when they were alone together.

"Wait. Go on."

"We can't just wait. Marnie could be in danger—"

He smoothed her hair. "Sam, I'm so sorry. You know that Marnie is most probably dead."

"No. She hasn't been found. There's hope."

That evening Aidan came by with his group. They weren't disturbed about the article on Rowan. They thought it would help.

That disturbed Rowan, but he went ahead and practiced with them, and Sam even sat in on a few sets. Laura was happy. "You see, it was our grandfather—Sam's and mine—who was a really great musician. He played all over Europe. Musical talent must be genetic."

"Then what happened to you, Mom?" Aidan teased.

But Laura shrugged. "It skips people now and then," she laughed.

They barbecued on Rowan's patio, and the guys in the band stayed late. Teddy came by, listening, applauding. They had yet to identify the other bones found in the swamp. Divers were out again today, and they would go out again tomorrow.

"We're having to go back on everything, now that Chloe's disappearance is a homicide."

"Are you the lead detective now?" Laura asked him.

"No. It remains Rolf's case," Teddy said. "But I'm still allowed to assist."

"Oh?" Sam said. She realized that Rowan was looking at Teddy.

"Are they thinking of bringing me back in?"

Teddy shrugged. "Aldridge is an ass, you know."

"He wants me arrested?" Rowan asked.

"Teddy!" Laura said.

"On what charge?" Sam demanded. "They can't have any evidence—"

"Oh, there's evidence on a charge of attempted murder. Of Beth Bellamy."

"Rowan," Sam said, "maybe you should go somewhere—"

"I'm going to Coconut Grove tomorrow," he said firmly. "If they want to arrest me, hell—Sam has invited Kevin, and he is one damn good lawyer. Whatever else he may be."

The party spirit was broken. Bit by bit, the boys in the band began to leave.

Teddy and Laura left together. Sam was glad to see them together.

Rowan went back to playing the drums. He was a better drummer than she was. But then, he was a natural musician. And he was angry.

Her turn. She walked to him, and took the drumsticks from his hands. "Don't worry."

He shook his head at her. "I'm not afraid of being arrested. It's happened before. And they will have to release me. I'm innocent."

"If Beth dies . . ."

"But if she doesn't, she'll recognize the man who did this to her."

"She's got to pull through."

"I believe she will," he said, and she knew that he meant it.

"Then . . . why are you so . . . tense?"

"You."

"Me?"

"I'm worried about you."

His words sent a shiver down her spine, but she wouldn't let him see it. "Don't worry about me."

"You want to find Marnie. You ask questions. You cause things to happen. Please, listen to me now—stop asking questions. And stay near me. At all times. Do you understand?"

"Of course."

"Don't leave me—no matter how much you want to find Marnie."

"I won't." She smiled, and stroked his cheek with her palm. "I just love a good beat," she told him softly.

And he smiled at last. And rose, and took her into his arms.

The phone at Sam's house rang very late. Rowan, awakened, glanced at his watch. Three a.m.

He rose quickly, grabbing a towel to wrap around his middle. He hurried to the machine and waited, wondering if the killer was calling again.

He was surprised when he heard his own name called by Teddy. "Rowan? Rowan, if you're there, pick up. Please, pick up. Hey, Sam, if you hear this, have Rowan call me. At any time. It's important. It's—"

Rowan picked up. "Teddy, it's me."

"Is the machine off?"

"Yeah."

"I don't know if you want Sam to hear this or not . . .
I'm not even sure if I should be telling you, but . . ."

"Teddy, dammit, you called."

"Yeah, well . . . the phone companies have done some
serious traces. Since Marnie disappeared, there have
been two calls made to Sam's house—from Marnie's
cellular phone."

Ice seemed to shoot through Rowan's veins. *The killer
was after Sam. Afraid of Sam. And she was in danger.*

"Teddy, something has to break on this."

"Yeah, well, this police psychiatrist has been telling us
that a guy like this may start off slow, a woman here and
there . . . but eventually he begins to lose control. He gets
careless."

"Thank God."

Teddy hesitated. "Whoever he is—he's already gotten
careless."

"Oh?"

"Marnie's cell phone was found. Last night. One of the
cops picked it up."

"Where?"

"Your yard."

Rowan exhaled on a long breath. "So . . ."

"I wanted to warn you—I thought you should know."

"Is there a warrant out for me yet?"

"Not yet, but it may be coming. The cops will be
watching you."

"Thanks."

"Sam will eventually have to know—"

"I'll tell her first thing in the morning."

*It was the middle of the night. He sat in his small boat
in the bay. His car and hitch were south; he always kept
them south. Far away. Because he was smart.*

But it was getting out of hand. He had to be careful. This would not be good. Before, he was patient. He would wait. Choose his women. And keep them. And they would serve, until they would serve no more. And then . . .

He would keep them no more.

And now . . .

It was becoming a crowded house. A harem, he thought with humor. But it was dangerous, far too dangerous.

It didn't matter.

He wanted Sam. It was her turn. People did disappear. They disappeared for years, and eventually those around them gave up the hunt. He was smart, he was thorough, he could even frame those around him and enjoy the confusion that followed.

But then there was Sam . . .

I can see you, Samantha! I can see you.

And I want you . . .

He closed his eyes, remembering. He had watched her tonight. Watched them. They hadn't known yet. Known that he had left the phone in Rowan's yard.

Soon the police would come for him. Poor Sam. She'd be alone. His turn.

Love, or passion, had made them careless. They had been behind the drum set, but he could see them.

He could still see her . . .

Shedding her clothing.

He could see him.

Touching her. Sliding against her, down on his knees before her. The toss of her head, the arch of her back. He sat in agony. Oh, God, he could almost hear her, smell her, feel her . . .

Soon.

Soon.

I can see you, Samantha.

And soon . . .

I will have you.

It was too dangerous, no, no. Too dangerous. But the danger was part of the game.

He was moving too quickly. He couldn't be careless! Never careless.

He sat tense. In pain. Watching. Gritting his teeth.

Tomorrow. Before they arrested Rowan, before he could not be blamed for all that happened . . . and was to come.

Chapter 23

Aidan had been worried about their audience. He needn't have been. Sam had called in favors from everyone she knew, but she needn't even have done that. It was a beautiful day, food and radio sponsors were hosting the event, and the park was filled when the first, least-known band began to play.

It was funny to see Kevin Madigan in shorts and a baseball cap. He looked cute.

"I actually wanted to get Loretta to come out with me," he told Sam, standing by her side while the band members worked unloading equipment. "I couldn't get ahold of her."

"I called her once yesterday, too. Come to think of it, she didn't call me back," Sam said.

"Maybe she went away for the weekend." He looked at her. "She works side jobs, you know."

"Side jobs? You mean, at the club?"

"Yeah, well, other side jobs," he said. He was wearing a funny kind of smile as he looked at her. "She didn't tell you what kind, huh?"

"No. What kind, Kevin?"

"Parties. Private parties. Bachelor parties, birthday parties."

"Oh, God, Kevin—"

"I don't make her work, Sam. I had nothing to do with any of this. I may be rude at times, and abrasive, but . . . I have nothing to do with how Loretta chooses to make extra money. I swear it. Can I get you anything? Want a soda, a beer?"

"No," she said, and added a grudging "Thanks."

"Look. There's Lee Chapman, right behind us. Did you call him and ask him to come to this?" Kevin asked Sam.

She couldn't believe he was asking her that. She hoped that Rowan hadn't seen the man.

"You know," Kevin said, "I might have mentioned it. You said you needed all the people you could get."

"I think I used the word 'people,' " Sam murmured.

By then, though, Chapman was up with them. "Hello, there."

Sam nodded stiffly to him.

"Have you talked with Marnie's secretary, Loretta?" Kevin asked him.

"Nope. Not in the last few days. She worked Friday night, I know," Chapman said.

"Excuse me. I'll go help the guys with that big amp," Kevin said. He walked away.

Sam looked at Lee Chapman. He smiled at her. Where was Rowan?

"You don't like me, do you?" he asked her.

"No," she said honestly.

He laughed. "Fair enough. Maybe you have good reason. But I'll tell you again, I haven't had anything to do with women dying. I like women. More than one at a time, come to think of it. But with your friend, Marnie Newcastle—honey, I need Marnie Newcastle."

Sam stared at him, alarmed to feel that he was being honest. No, she didn't like him; she never would. But she somehow believed him.

He was so open about being a sleazebag.

"How do you know Loretta worked Friday night?" she asked.

He stared at her a long moment, assessing her. He still

seemed to be smiling. "Because I do have money in the strip club. And I schedule some of the talent. She told me she had a side gig."

"Oh, well, maybe it extended through the weekend—"

"No."

"How do you know?"

"Well, honey, because she's a stripper—and when she really likes what she sees, she's willing to go for a little prostitution on the side. Don't go getting any more ideas about me. I'm not a pimp. I have nothing to do with it. I just manage a totally legit club. I'm not a murderer, Miss Miller, just a capitalist. I heard back about Loretta's party on Friday night; she left after having done a damn fine job."

"Well, who does manage the side jobs?"

"Don't you know?" he asked.

"No!"

He shrugged. "I'm not at liberty to say."

"The police will make you say!"

He smiled. "Then have me arrested, Miss Miller. Too bad you aren't a bit more of a capitalist—we'd have room for you at the club. Excuse me, I'll move on."

She watched him go, gritting her teeth, making a mental note to tell Teddy everything that he'd said. Tonight. When this was over, when they were all out of here. She needed to tell Rowan as well. But not here, not today. He was already tense enough. Somehow, they just had to make it through today.

Side jobs . . .

If someone was setting up side jobs, then perhaps all the girls who had disappeared had done so because of those side jobs.

He wasn't going to tell her anything. Still smiling, mocking her, he moved on. She was still feeling chilled when Phil touched her arm. She nearly jumped. She forced a smile.

Phil, with the contractors and construction workers, was wearing a tank top that showed most of his tattoos. He was still a good-looking guy, so well muscled, with his handsome, cocky grin. He'd started drinking beer pretty early, so it seemed, and was in a cheerful mood, introducing Sam to far more men than she wanted to know.

But by the time he started his introductions, Rowan had finished helping Aidan and his friends. He was sticking to her side like glue, so she felt safe.

Thankfully, he hadn't noticed her talking with Lee Chapman.

The construction guys were big. Rowan was very tall, though, and they seemed to think he could hold his own. He most probably could.

She remembered the bodyguard at the strip joint.

Yes, he could take care of himself.

Joe had made it. He was standing with a number of their clients, working the crowd. She saw that even Mr. Daly had come. Teddy was there with a number of cops, some of them watching Rowan warily.

Sam was frightened, really frightened. Rowan had told her that morning that Teddy had called to warn him. The calls to her had definitely come from the killer.

Who had used Marnie's phone.

And now the phone had been found in Rowan's yard. The good thing was that it could so obviously be a plant. The bad was that there could have been so much commotion that, to police minds, Rowan could have simply gotten careless.

He squeezed her hand, looking around. It was a spectacular spring day. The temperature was in the seventies. The foliage surrounding the cleared areas was lush, and bougainvilleas were in bloom. From the park, they could see down to the water and the marina. The sky was crystal clear, the water glittered in the sunlight. Boats seemed to sway lightly and dance to the music.

"Aldridge is trying to convince his sergeant that I should definitely be arrested. Maybe they're waiting to pounce."

"We can leave—"

"No, we can't. But if I'm taken in, I want you to stay with Laura until bail is arranged. Do you understand?"

"Sure, but—"

"Hey!"

Harry Lacata, with Gregory and Ann at his side, was waving to them. They waved back. Gregory suddenly left his parents. He came to Rowan and hugged him. He didn't look up. He moved, hugging Sam next. She smoothed back his soft hair. She loved him so much.

"Well, thank God!" Harry said. "Sam, can he go down front with you two?"

Ann laughed, adding, "Harry and I are old fogies. Gregory loves the music, you know—"

"He'll be fine with us," Sam assured them. "Rowan is going to play some—"

"And Sam will, too."

"Sam!" Ann said, pleased.

"No, I'm not playing today. Maybe some other time." She stared at Rowan. "Hey, you know what, Aidan's up on the side of the stage. I think he's looking for you."

Rowan shielded his eyes against the sun, then slipped on glasses. "Yes, he's looking for me. Now you—"

"Gregory and I are coming right up," Sam promised him. But he wasn't listening. He was looking past the bandstand.

"What?" she whispered.

"It's—Thayer. Thayer Newcastle. I thought that he would come to this. He always seems to come when Aidan is playing. I've got to get to Teddy. No, maybe to a different cop. Tell him."

"Why not Teddy?"

Could he think that Teddy was somehow guilty?

"I—I don't see Teddy," he said. Was he lying? she wondered.

She gritted her teeth. Thayer was a distance away. He seemed relaxed. If he thought the cops might be after him, he surely didn't show it.

"Hurry," she said somewhat coolly. "You can't disappoint the group."

"There's a cop right in front of the bandstand," Rowan said, and headed that way. "I'll talk to him. You follow me!" he added sternly.

"Right," she murmured, adding in a quick whisper, "There are hundreds of people here. I'm as safe as can be."

"Sam, if we get parted, we'll find you at Borders after the concert, café area, all right?" Ann Lacata asked.

"Perfect," Sam assured Harry and Ann. By the time the music ended, it would be bedlam around the bandstand. Things would quiet down and thin out near the bookstore.

Sam took Gregory's hand, and they started through the crowd.

A young man of about eighteen, shirtless, short-haired, smiled at her, then shouted. "Lady, you may want to move back with the boy! This area might turn to mosh pit."

Right. Mosh pit. Aidan's stuff could be kind of hard. Kids loved to "mosh" one another, pass each other around. It was dangerous and she was glad it wasn't a fad when she'd been that young.

"Thanks! Gregory, we're going to move back just a hair."

Moving wasn't easy. It was packed.

She found a new position. Then she found herself staring at the young man in front of her. He was shirtless. His back was heavily tattooed. The tattoos were all the same. They were of a naked woman. She was sitting spread-legged, a dozen of her, all the way down the guy's spine. Every time he flexed a muscle, her legs spread further.

"Oh, Gregory, this isn't exactly the right place for you either," she murmured, and they started back again. She paused, looking across the crowd, holding her breath.

The police had reached Thayer Newcastle. They talked to him—he protested vigorously. She saw an officer take him by either arm.

Shaking his head, he looked across the crowd, as if for help. His eyes caught hers. He looked completely lost—wounded. Then, for a moment, it looked as if he would break free from the police and run.

She felt horrible, like an adult punishing a child. He might have killed Chloe Lowenstein, left her in the swamp, left her to the awful predators there, she reminded herself.

The painting! How could she forget the painting?

Still, something felt wrong.

She watched his shoulders slump, watched him give in to the police. For some reason she simply felt that he wasn't guilty, no matter what the evidence.

But if not him, *who*?

Rowan watched as the police escorted Thayer Newcastle out of the park. He tuned his guitar, making sure. He should have felt relieved. Thayer's painting had given him chills, it had been so lifelike, it had so definitely been Chloe. And he had been the one to find the bracelet, the bracelet that had been so obvious in the painting . . .

But he didn't feel relieved. He felt as if he was missing something. Maybe the police would feel that way, too. And they would have second thoughts. Marnie's cellular phone had been used to make the calls. And the phone had been found in his yard.

A dozen people might have taken that phone from her at lunch that day—including Thayer.

A dozen people could have taken the phone, period.
And used it during the past week to make calls to Sam.
Yes, a dozen might have taken it, but . . .
Just how many of them might have planted it in his
yard?

Whoa, it was crowded! This was really dangerous . . .

*No, it was so crowded, no one would ever see anything.
And loud! The first group finished up; Aidan's group was
going on. A radio announcer was saying that Rowan Dillon of Blackhawk fame would be joining the group, and
the crowd was going wild.*

*Dangerous, yes! And exhilarating. So exciting. The
challenge was like a high he'd never known before. The
music was great. Thundering.*

So many people.

He smiled.

Hide in plain sight. Hide in plain sight!

*There she was. With the boy! Damn the idiot boy.
He had seen. He knew, but he was an idiot . . .*

*Sam. In soft, form-hugging jeans and sneakers. Her
hair loose, beautiful. A natural woman. She was in a knit
halter top. It showed off her beautifully formed back and
flowed with her movement . . .*

*Did she want to live? Enough to be all he wanted her to
be? He was so anxious to find out. All he had to do was
lure her . . .*

*The music suddenly seemed louder. The crowd roared.
The sound was deafening . . .*

So many people, but he saw only Sam.

And the kid.

The kid suddenly looked at him. And began to scream.

*He froze, then ducked, and started through the crowd.
Now! Now was it. The kid had forced his hand, this
was it . . .*

The kid, in panic, ripped free from Sam.

And began to run.

Sam was dead still for a moment. Stunned. Then she ran after him.

His heart was pounding, yet he began to laugh. They were heading in the right direction. Down toward the boats. Out of the park, across the street. Toward the boats. He was prepared. He felt in his shirt pocket for his chloroform.

He needed split-second timing. His smile, his concern, the smile and concern she trusted so much . . .

After them, he told himself. It was now or never! And so he ran in pursuit himself. He ran and ran and ran . . .

Rowan pictured events in his mind's eye. This last Friday night. Beth had been there, they'd fought, and then she'd been in the water. He thought of the man he had seen with Sam. A man she trusted. She had leaned on him. But he had been there. With every opportunity. Every opportunity to attack Beth, and then—reappear. Concerned. Ready to help out . . . tender, caring, protective.

Oh, God. He could see over the crowd. Gregory, breaking from Sam. Running.

A killer . . .

A killer he should have known, suddenly streaking after Sam, reaching her, talking, there to help and support her once again . . .

No, Sam!

But she smiled, ready to accept the help he offered.

Rowan leapt up. He had to reach her.

"Gregory!"

She'd never seen him in such terror. He heard her voice, acknowledged it. But then he looked at her, and then past her, and he started to run again.

"Sam!"

She turned. Thank God! Help had come.

"Gregory's terrified, racing through the crowd. I don't know what happened."

Sam had long since given up saying, "Excuse me" to the people around her. She had help with her now. They plowed wildly through the crowd. Gregory somehow managed to stay ahead.

He streaked out onto the road.

She screamed herself, so afraid that he'd be hit by a car. But the road had been closed off for the day's event. Gregory kept going, running hard for the docks.

"Wait!"

She tore after him, alone. Her friend had fallen behind. Dear God, but Gregory was fast. Faster and faster and . . .

He could swim, she reminded herself. He left the road, ran over the grass. He was heading toward the boats, down the first of the public docks.

At the very end, he stopped.

Thank God. She had thought she was about to have a heart attack. She could barely breathe. She had to pause, her hands on her knees, to get her breath. She gasped in air, smoothing back her hair, staring at Gregory, then shaking her head.

"Gregory—"

He pointed.

And once again he started to scream.

Puzzled, Sam turned.

There he was, panting as well, right behind her.

"Hey!" she called. "I think we've got him cornered. I don't know why he's so afraid." Then she backed up, frowning, because he was coming at her. And Gregory was still screaming, louder and louder . . .

No one could hear.

There were thousands of people.

None of them was listening.

"Sam, there's stuff all over your face."

"What?"

"You need a handkerchief."

And he had one.

"No!"

But he was there, with his handkerchief, and she smelled it, and she realized . . .

"No!"

She broke away, staggering. She could hear something. Her name? Rowan . . . God, was that Rowan rushing toward her?

"Damn you, Sam!" her attacker said. "I don't want to hurt you. Make it easy."

She tried to focus on him. "Stop it, what are you—" she began.

He suddenly hunched over. He'd picked up an oar.

She started to scream.

The oar smacked the side of her head, and she went down, dimly aware that Gregory was still screaming . . .

Right in the middle of the number, Rowan unslung his guitar.

Aidan turned around, frowning. Rowan shouted a name to him.

He leapt off the bandstand.

"Hey! Dillon, stop!" one of the cops, guarding the bandstand area, called to him.

He couldn't stop. He didn't dare take the time to talk to a cop. The cops had Thayer, but Thayer was innocent, and they still wanted to arrest him. He looked the most guilty.

He made it through the crowd, out of the park. He looked around desperately. For a moment he couldn't find Sam. Then he saw Gregory at the far end of the dock. Screaming, pointing. He saw Sam, trying to get her breath.

He started running again.

"Hey, Dillon, wait, man, you're not going anywhere—"

"I have to. Come with me. Just give me a minute—"

"No, man. Hey, you're not running—"

It was a fellow in a uniform, pulling him back. Rowan swung around, forced to look at him. "Damn you, you may be famous, but—" the cop began.

No time.

"Sorry," Rowan apologized. He swung with his right fist. The officer went down.

Rowan started running again. "Sam!" he screamed her name. She was stumbling around on the dock, as if she were drunk. Drunk . . .

Drugged.

But not enough! She had fought it!

He saw the man. Tall and dark, taking the oar. Swinging it.

"Sam!" he screamed her name again.

She went down.

He raced across the road, over the grass, along the dock. Full speed, heading straight for the man with his back to him, now hunkering over Sam's fallen body.

"You bastard, I'll kill you!" Rowan shouted.

The man was up, with Sam in his arms. Thanks to the music, to Gregory's screams, he still seemed oblivious to Rowan. He hopped off the dock, Sam securely in his arms, down into a fair-sized motorboat with a small cabin.

Gregory continued to scream and point. Rowan kept running like hell.

Sam's attacker disappeared into the cabin.

Reappeared.

Rowan knew him. Goddam, but he knew him.

He carried a gun. He was aiming it at Gregory. "Idiot boy!"

"No!" Rowan shouted.

He had almost made it. "Run, Gregory, run!" But the

boy was just standing there, staring. God, no! Rowan couldn't reach the boy. He could reach the killer.

He took a flying leap from the dock to the boat to tackle the man. They fell together. The gun went off. Gregory's screams began to fade.

Rowan's vision began to blur.

Shit!

Then he knew.

He'd been shot.

The blackness was total. In fact, Sam wondered if she had opened her eyes at all, the darkness was so great, weighing down upon her, blinding her.

But then she tried to move, and the pain that streaked through her head brought with it a searing, bright light. Like a shaft of lightning, bursting through her skull, wreaking havoc on her mind, her nerves.

The pain was so great that she saw blackness again, slipping, fading, into nothingness.

But then the pain began to subside to a dull throb. She tried to move again. The darkness was encompassing, yes, but she wasn't blind. She could see that the world was really more gray, deep, dark gray, but it had shape and shadow and substance. She had not fallen into limbo, a black hole. Nor had she died and fallen into a black pit of hell.

No. She wasn't dead.

Not yet.

She closed her eyes, fighting the wave of nausea that seized her. She closed them tightly, gritting her teeth. The awful feeling in her stomach was good.

Even if . . .

It came with a sense of paralyzing dread.

Fear shot back into her heart and mind with the knowledge that she was still alive. Of course, she was still alive, she had to be alive to feel this kind of explosive pain. She almost groaned aloud, yet cautioned herself that she must not do so.

Carefully, carefully, she opened her eyes again. Yes, it was dark, dark as a tomb.

Bad comparison, she warned herself.

She kept her eyes open, looked around. She tried to move her limbs. With tremendous gratitude, she realized that she could do so. She was somewhere . . .

Where the killer had taken her, of course!

Yes, of course, but where was that? She had to think, to reason, to find her senses. She couldn't lie here, wallowing in fear and wonder. Because if she did, she wouldn't be alive for long.

She swallowed carefully. Her throat was dry. A wave of sickness swept through her again for a moment, and she thought, *Yes, of course, the drug. It's his way!*

She waited again for the feeling to subside, cursing herself as she did so. She'd had to know the truth, she'd had to find Marnie.

Don't think about that now. Find out where I am, so that I can escape.

She was on her stomach. She carefully rolled onto her back. It seemed that every muscle and bone in her body hurt. Why? She couldn't quite remember.

Where in God's name was she? The smell around her was strange. It was a smell of decay. It was like a hot, humid night locked in, a smell of mud, of trees, of earth, and of rot . . .

A smell like death.

Fear nearly overwhelmed her again. She closed her eyes tightly, took a deep breath, and told herself that she had to find the strength to move, to find out where she was. She had to escape. Because she knew what would happen if she didn't . . .

She began to move, cursing herself feverishly. She'd

been warned to be careful by everyone. Even the killer had called and warned her. *Leave it be.*

Would anyone come for her, would anyone help her? Oh, yes, Rowan *would come if he could.*

If he was not dead already . . .

She had heard him. Heard him calling her.

And she had heard a shot!

Oh, God, he had tried! He had warned her!

She had to live, to survive. She could not let others fall into this trap.

Gregory had known all along. Gregory had seen the face of the killer. But Gregory couldn't help.

Feverishly, she tried to move. Her ankles were tied, her wrists were tied. She brought the rope to her teeth, ripping her lips as she gnawed it, alternately cursing and praying, and working harder at the knots, reminding herself that God helped those who helped themselves.

The knot wouldn't give. Wouldn't give, oh, damn, damn, damn . . . Tears welled in her eyes.

No!

Be patient. Keep at it.

How much time did she have?

Please, God, please. She wanted to live so badly. She would never whine about petty things again, so help her. *Please.*

The knot began to give just a little. He must have tied the knots in a hurry, been distracted by all the commotion.

Slowly . . . slowly at first.

And then . . .

The rough cord bit at her lips, tearing, rasping against the tender flesh. Her throat was dryer than ever. Her tongue seemed swollen as a balloon. Every muscle in her body ached as she strained to free herself.

Then the knots gave, and the rough rope that had chafed her wrists fell away at long last. She sat up, working at the rope that tied her ankles together. Her nails were torn and split; the tips of her fingers, she was certain, were bloody.

Her ankles were free. In a panic, she kicked the rope away. She tried to stand. Dizziness swept over her until she was almost ill. She went still on her knees, praying for the blackness and the whirling to go away again.

Too soon to stand.

She began to crawl.

The floor beneath her was wood.

Old wood, covered with dirt. The dirt had a thick smell to it. Like a mud that was naturally rich with the decay of foliage.

Move slowly. Don't panic again, she warned herself.

Because it was quiet now. Quiet meant that maybe the killer wasn't around. That she could find out where she was. Get away.

She'd had to know, oh, God, she'd just had to find out the truth about Marnie.

She crawled, came to a wall, backed away, started again. And then . . .

She touched flesh.

And the fear and the terror bubbled in her throat. She fought not to scream.

She hadn't just found out the truth about Marnie. She had found Marnie.

Marnie, yes, cold, how cold? Dead, alive, so cold, where was her throat, a wrist, a pulse, any sign of life?

"Marnie!"

Marnie did not move.

Her horror was so great that at first she didn't hear. Then she did. Noise . . . from beyond the darkness.

Footsteps.

The killer was coming back.

And now he was coming for her . . .

* * *

Rowan dimly felt . . .

The rays of the sun. Weak. They were the rays of a dying sun.

And still . . .

It must mean that he was alive.

Where?

Sam! Where was she? Think, remember. Gather your strength, get it together so you can help her . . .

He remembered the boat. The shot. He had taken the shot intended for Gregory. Had to be glad for that.

He had failed Sam. No, he was still breathing, dammit, and he would find her. But where was he? What had happened? The shot. Then he had been unconscious. And then . . .

He frowned. It hurt. Hurt was good. More proof he was alive. But how hurt?

Yes, the boat. He remembered the motor. And then . . .

Then he had been dragged. A blanked had been thrown over him, and he'd been dragged and thrown. They'd reached a different marina; the boat had been taken out of the water. He'd been in the back of a truck, and the killer had stared at him, talked to him, even though he had never opened his eyes.

"You dead yet? You will be. You're bleeding like a stuck pig. That's okay, I can't keep so many. So I'll take one, and leave her there with you, like she shot you, dying herself. The story will be great."

The killer was a powerful man. Rowan had been vaguely aware again when he had been carried. But the pain had been excruciating. He'd known he was back in the boat. He'd even known how the killer had worked. He'd stalked his victims from the bay. Taken his boat out of the water at a marina south of his stalking grounds, driven to the Everglades, then gone by boat again out to the canals—and hammocks.

Just like now. From the truck bed, Rowan had been thrown back into the boat.

And now . . .

He opened his eyes. It hurt. He closed them. Tried again. Yes, the rays of the sun were pale. It was late afternoon, almost dark. And the thick, verdant foliage in the area always made it a green darkness.

There was an unmistakable scent around him. He knew that he was deep in the swamp. He heard a grunting sound. Like pigs. No . . .

Alligators.

He twisted his head. There were about five of them. Basking on a hammock maybe a hundred feet from him. He lay on the ground. In mud. Blood from his side oozed into the mud. *Bleeding like a stuck pig, yes, that was him.*

The alligators were watching him, he thought.

Waiting for movement, waiting to run, to attack?

Stay still, don't run, don't let them see that you're injured prey. *Where the hell is Sam?*

He narrowed his eyes. Damn, it was getting darker and darker. He would never find her without help, where . . .

And then, in the midst of the foliage, he saw it.

Far back. Old and rotting, it matched its surroundings perfectly. A man could stare straight at it and not see it. One of those places Teddy had talked about. A lodge for weekend warriors. Most of them torn down by government command, and yet this one so far back and so well camouflaged that no one had seen it.

No one but the killer.

They had been so near it when they were out fishing in the Everglades. So very near, and they hadn't seen it. All they had done was find the bodies . . .

But there it was . . .

Built out of wood, now painted by the wild, overgrown foliage.

Could he reach it before the alligators reached him? Or

before another shot rang out? Where the hell was the killer? Where was Sam?

Sam . . .

Oh, God, she was in there.

He had to rise, had to find her. He had promised that he would die for her.

Perhaps the time had come to do so.

Chapter 24

"Sam!"

The killer had come right to her, he had seen her in the dark. She could still barely focus. She could make out his form, but not his face.

"Sam, Sam, Sam! Leave it to you to get the ropes off." He spoke affectionately, with admiration, as he had spoken to her so many times before.

She knew him, yes, knew him so well. But she'd been busy worrying about Rowan, thinking that Thayer was a little weird. Thinking that Chapman was an evil murderer.

Well, Chapman might be a murderer.

But he hadn't killed Chloe Lowenstein.

Joe had.

Joe Taylor. Her own partner. A man she saw almost daily. Tall, dark, and very handsome. Joe, whom she had trusted to check out her own house against a killer.

Joe, who had used that very opportunity, holding her that night, to plant Marnie Newcastle's cellular phone in Rowan's yard.

"Joe," she said it aloud, sickly.

"Hi, baby. Yeah, it's me. You never liked it when I called you baby, huh? But things are different here, and now."

Yes, they were. She had never known such terror, or such a tempest of emotion. Rowan, where was Rowan?

Dead, God, no, please, but she'd heard him, heard him coming after her, and if he were alive . . .

Then there was Marnie. Alive? Dead? So near she could reach out and touch her . . .

She gritted her teeth. Fought a wave of nausea and blackness.

"Why?" she asked him. "You're going to kill me no matter what I do."

"No, no, my sweet! Honestly, you know, you're different. Different from the others."

He was suddenly kneeling down before her. She felt his palm on her face. She wanted to wrench away.

She didn't think it would be wise.

"Oh, good, honey, you are a clever girl. I really don't like to kill. Sometimes I have to. Sometimes, well, the women make me. I set them up to have some fun, to make some good money, and you know what happens? They go behind my back."

"Set them up . . ."

"Sam, you are naive. The club. The strip joint. I've got an interest in it, too. More than an interest. I've had a side thing going. Sending them out to special parties . . . but then, sometimes, they think that they can just break free. *Prostitute* themselves." The disgust in his voice had a vicious edge to it. "They learn. There are rules here. I make the rules, and even I follow the rules. You follow the rules, and you may live a long time."

She gritted her teeth, trying not to shiver. *Was that it? While he was in control of a woman, she was fine. When she stepped outside the boundaries he had created, did it trigger something inside him? Dear God, she had been working all this time with a psychopath, and she hadn't known it.*

She was different, so he had said.

Yes, then she had begun to sleep with Rowan, and perhaps it had seemed the same to him.

She heard a soft moaning, and despite her paralyzing fear, she felt a sudden, soaring elation. Marnie was alive. She was desperate to reach out to her friend. Touch her again. Find out how she was injured. Help her.

Oh, God, she had to help herself somehow!

"Joe, Marnie is hurt."

"Marnie is drugged. You see, I have to leave her often. When I go, she could hurt herself. So I drug her. It keeps her alive. Oh, she may have a few bangs and bruises. She started off fighting me. But now she knows."

"Joe, please, she could be really hurt—"

"No, no, Sam. None of that. Marnie is a bitch. We all know that. There are others like her." Sam couldn't really see Joe, but she could sense his smile. "I always told you that she was a bitch, and exactly what I thought of her. She thought she could use me. That I was a toy, not quite good enough for always, so I've taught her that she's the toy, not me. There are other women like that. Not so many now that I've taken care of a few, but . . . take Chloe. She thought that her money made her next to God. I taught her otherwise. She didn't learn well. I gave her lots of chances."

"Joe, Marnie needs help. She's learned her lessons well, I'm certain. She can still live."

"No, she can't."

"Why, what have you done to her?"

"Nothing too terrible. Yet. But you see, there are rules, though I had to break them for you. You see, I didn't really want to take you, but you just wouldn't let the thing with Marnie go. And then, well, Rowan came into town, and . . . once, I thought you were just really a good girl when you rejected me, but you're not, not at all. I watched you, you know. And then I decided that like the others, you should make it up to me."

Sam fought hard to remain calm, to stay sane. "Joe, where's Rowan?"

"He's dead."

"No . . . he can't be."

"At least, I hope—for his sake—that he's dead. I shot him, you know. I wasn't even trying to, but he got in the way of the shot meant to kill Gregory. The kid should die, Sam. He's dangerous to me. Out here, it's survival of the fittest. Gregory is not at all fit. And Rowan is wounded now, if he isn't dead. Weak and wounded. They'll find him soon. My pets. I keep strange pets. Powerful, like me. On land . . . they'll rip him apart. They'll all get into it, like a frenzy. I've taught them to enjoy human meat, you see."

She was going to throw up. She couldn't. Rowan had been shot. He was somewhere near. Maybe alive. She had to believe. And Marnie was alive. She couldn't give up, she had to fight. Play the game, until . . .

Oh, God.

"Joe, you have to listen to me. I can help you. I understand what your feeling was, but it's all over. They're going to find you out—"

"How? You told the police about Chapman and the strip club. Everyone will be looking in the wrong place."

Sam said, "Joe, you've been setting strippers up to work private parties. All the girls stripped—and worked a private party for you, right? And Gregory saw you."

"The guy who sets strippers up is nothing but a voice on the phone. A pay phone. I'm an alias with a post office box. They can't trace me. And as to Gregory . . . he's an idiot."

"No, he's not! He let us know something had happened at the house."

"Yeah, I can just see him on the witness stand."

"But they found Chloe, and . . . pieces of another girl. And Marnie is missing—and now me!"

"They'll find another victim and the remnants of your lover, and assume you're out here somewhere as well.

No, I'm still safe. It's not your concern, anyway, Sam. From now on, I'm your concern."

"What do you mean, another victim?"

"Sam, I least want it to be you."

"Joe, you can't ask . . . anything of me if you kill Marnie—"

"I may give Marnie a little more time. But you see, Loretta can be so amusing, too."

Her heart skipped a beat. "You have Loretta here?"

"Oh, Sam, she really deserves to be here. You should have seen her in action. Such a harlot! Marnie taught her everything she knew, and still . . . well, I have a soft spot for Marnie. She has learned so well."

"Joe, listen to me, you know that I'm your friend—"

"No. You rejected me, Sam. You just pretended to be my friend."

"No, Joe, no—"

"Good. You can make it up to me. You're going to make me happy, Sam."

"Joe, I am not—"

"Then I'll kill you," he said simply.

"Joe, I won't give in to you," she said, trying to be firm but hearing her voice falter with the tears that threatened to spill down her cheeks. "Don't you understand? I love Rowan. I loved him before. I was still in love with him. That's why I rejected you. You've got to understand this. If Rowan is dead, then you can't hurt me. I won't care what you do to me—"

"Oh, Sam, you think you're so noble now. But you'd care if I started cutting up Marnie, wouldn't you?" he asked pleasantly. "Come here, Sam."

She held very still, in agony.

"First lesson, Sam. Come here. I have a very big knife, can you feel it?"

She flinched. Yes, she could feel it. She hadn't seen it in the darkness. Now she felt it against her cheek.

"Come here . . . or I'll cut off Marnie's hand. She's so close. It would be so easy. I could smear you in her blood."

She had to think of something. Was Rowan dead? She didn't dare believe it. She would die herself . . .

She came to her knees. Inched toward Joe. He reached out for her, drawing her to him. She felt the huge biceps in his arms, the knotted power in his chest.

Yes, she had thought that a killer needed strength. Joe certainly had it . . .

"That's better, Sam." His fingers brushed her cheek. They smelled of blood. She was afraid that she would pass out. Was it Rowan's blood?

"You know where you are, Sam, right? Even if you were to get out . . . well, the hammock is filled with the alligators that I've, er, hand-fed. They're better than Dobermans." His fingers threaded into her hair. She felt his lips on her mouth. How many times had she kissed him on the cheek, hugged him, felt safe with him?

She was afraid she would throw up.

No. The important thing now was staying alive.

"Open your lips, Sam," he murmured against her.

She couldn't do it . . .

At her side, Marnie moaned. Alive. Still alive . . .

He started to kiss her deeply, his fingers moving through her hair. He was pressing her back to the floor. His hands were on her. She started to struggle.

"No, no . . ." he warned.

She went still.

Where was the knife? She tried to feel on the floor for it.

"Looking for this?"

He rose above her. She saw the blade, so near her own throat.

"No!" She realized that she desperately wanted to live.

"Liar. And for that . . . for that you have to pay."

"Please!" she whispered as he brought the blade against her cheek.

He was going to cut her. It was going to hurt. She was going to die a slow and horrible death out here, cut to ribbons, fed to prehistoric beasts.

"No . . ."

He straightened suddenly. Dead still, she realized that something had disturbed him. Something from outside the cabin.

"Move again, and I'll slice off your breast when I come back!" he warned.

He stood up, and left her. She saw a flash of light, and then a door slammed. He was gone.

Move again, and I'll slice off your breast . . .

But she had to move. This might be her only chance.

She turned, crawling to her friend. "Marnie! Marnie! It's Sam, we've—"

"Sam, oh, Sam!" She could hear tears in Marnie's voice. "Oh, no, he's taken you . . ."

"Marnie, we've got to get out of here. Are you tied?"

"No . . . no . . . maybe . . . I don't know anymore."

She wasn't tied. Sam moistened her lips, realizing that Marnie had grown so terrified of Joe that she did as she was ordered. She was barely clad, with nothing on but an oversized shirt. How many times had she been raped, cut, beaten? Had she seen others used up, cut up, cast away to the creatures that roamed the hammock?

"Marnie! We're going to get up. We're going to get out of here." Yes, they had to get out. But then, Loretta was there somewhere. And from what Joe had said, she was still alive. They couldn't leave without her.

If they could manage to leave.

"Loretta?" She whispered it loudly.

"She's probably dead. I heard her screaming before."

"Marnie. I have to get you up. You have to help me help you. Try to stand."

"I can't anymore. I can't . . ."

"Get up, Marnie."

She tried to drag her friend up. She almost made it.

Then the door burst open.

Shot, yes, damn it, Rowan thought bitterly, and the bullet was wedged in his side somewhere. He'd lost a lot of blood.

He'd watched the cabin long enough. There was an old shotgun leaning against the front of the weathered shack. Get up, get the shotgun. Get in the shack.

What if the gun wasn't loaded? Joe wasn't a fool. It would still make a good club.

Joe was armed.

Then Rowan would have to surprise him.

He had to get into the cabin. That was where Joe had gone. That was where he kept the women before . . .

Before he killed them.

Rowan carefully ripped up his shirttail and bound his wound. Then he waited, breathing deeply, until he could wait no more. He stood. There was a broken branch at his side. When the first alligator began to move his way, he grasped the branch. Thankfully, it was large.

The effort half killed him, but he let out a growl and threw the branch hard. He thought of a Highland game. Yeah, it was like a caber throw. It caught the first gator smack on the nose. The beast retreated.

The others . . . watched.

He looked toward the cabin, wondering if the noise had been heard. He started for the door, but realized it was about to burst open. He ducked behind a stand of pines.

Joe came out. Walked to where he had lain. Rowan prayed that he hadn't left a trail of blood. For several long minutes Joe stared at the spot, his hands on his hips. Then he looked around and shouted, "Dillon, you are dead meat. I will hunt you down. I'll hand-feed you to them, guts and all, hands and feet first." He lifted a fist in the air. "I will find you! After I have your girlfriend, Dillon. She's mine now."

Joe waited for a response. Then he swore and started back for the cabin.

Sam was in there.

Alive.

For now.

Rowan didn't dare wait.

"I thought I told you not to move," Joe snapped.

The door bursting open again had caused her to freeze.

He walked to where she stood, trying to keep Marnie on her feet. He stared at them both, then struck Sam a backhanded blow that sent her spinning. She heard Marnie fall as she plummeted to the ground herself. A second later he was on top of her. The knife was in his hands.

The knife was coming at her. She screamed.

"No, Joe, no!"

"You won't behave, Sam."

"No!"

Miraculously, even as she screamed, he was wrenched from her. Torn from atop her. He was a big man, a heavy man with his rock-hard bulk. He might have been light as a feather. He flew across the cabin.

She lay stunned, but then she knew why. Rowan was there. Light filtered in from the outside. He had burst down the door and come for her. But he was covered in blood. White as a sheet. He was staggering, about to fall to his knees. "Get Marnie and get out," he roared to her. "There's a boat."

"No!" she cried, reaching for him. "I won't leave you—"

"He's coming!" Marnie screamed hysterically.

Joe was getting up, shaking his head, finding his bal-

ance. Sam saw that Rowan hadn't fallen flat because he
was leaning on a shotgun.

"Shoot him!" Marnie screamed.

"No bullets," Rowan said, wincing. He gritted his
teeth, letting out an awful sound. He managed to rise and
spin. He caught Joe in the gut with the butt of the shotgun
just as he stumbled back toward Rowan.

And Joe went down again, howling in pain.

But Rowan was staggering. He started to fall. Sam
tried to catch him again. Oh, God, he was so heavy, too.

This was life or death, life or death . . .

She was strong. She had learned strength once to help
her mother. She spent every day trying to teach people to
keep their bodies fit.

She held Rowan. And she kicked Joe hard when he
came to his knees.

Rowan managed to straighten, meet her eyes. "Good
girl. Now get out!" He turned away from her, then fell on
Joe with all his weight, forcing him down hard. "Can't
keep him down. Get out, get help, the boat's on the water!" Rowan grated out to her.

"I'll kill you yet!" Joe bellowed. "You're just a punk—"

Rowan slugged him hard in the jaw.

"Rowan, come on!" she begged.

"Can't, he may get up again—"

"No . . . no!" Sam said. "I will not leave you!"

Joe was down, yes. Rowan had brought him down. But
she wouldn't leave Rowan. She grasped the fallen shotgun and brought it down hard on Joe's head.

"He must be out, come on! Marnie, help me, we have
to find Loretta and go!"

Rowan gritted his teeth and grasped his side. With
Sam's help, he came to his feet. "Where is Loretta? Is she
alive?"

"Back against that wall, I think," Marnie said.

With the door open, Sam could see where they were. It

was a very simple shack with some high vents. The windows had been boarded over. There was a cot and a trunk. Storage containers. Water barrels. Joe had tortured his victims, but like a good weekend warrior, he had kept the place supplied so that he could keep them alive as long as he chose to do so.

And against the far wall . . .

A tangle of flesh and blond hair. Loretta.

Rowan pushed away from Sam and went to the woman. "Is she alive?" Sam asked anxiously.

"Barely," Rowan said. Grunting, he picked her up.

"Rowan, you won't make it—" Sam began.

"Go!"

But she rushed to his side, supporting him. They started out. He turned back. "Marnie? Can you come?"

But Marnie wasn't listening. She was staring at Joe.

And she had seen the knife on the ground.

She started to scream, reaching for the knife.

She gripped it and came to life. She flew at Joe's fallen form. And she began to stab him.

Again and again. Sam heard the blade hit flesh, bone. The sound was terrible.

"Marnie!" Rowan said. He put Loretta down, easing her toward Sam. And he went back for Marnie. She was wild, and she nearly stabbed him as well. Her arms flailed. She sobbed.

"Marnie, Marnie . . ."

She fell into his arms.

"Marnie, come . . ."

Sam suddenly heard the sound of a motor.

"My God, there's help!" she breathed. Thank God. Loretta was naked, as cold as ice. Sam could only pray that she would make it.

"Help?" Marnie whispered. "Please . . ." She pushed

away from Rowan. Sam followed her quickly as she staggered out into the dying green daylight.

It was true. An airboat was arriving. Teddy, Rolf Lunden, and two other uniformed cops were on it.

And Gregory. Gregory, who saw them and began to scream and shout and point.

Sam started running to him.

"Sam, the gators!" Teddy shouted.

Too late. She had raced across the shallow water, sunk to her middle. She was moving faster than any alligator. Teddy dragged her up on the airboat, and Gregory was in her arms. She held him for a very long time. She was vaguely aware of shouting and commotion as the cops went to help pull the others aboard the vessel. Then Rowan was with her. His arms were around her. Gregory burrowed against Rowan. He was shaking. Rowan soothed him. He calmed down at last but remained with the two of them, his head bowed low against Sam's shoulder, his eyes tightly closed.

Together, she and Rowan watched as the cops retrieved Joe Taylor's body. He wasn't going to be left as food for his own beasts. Teddy was too much of a cop for that.

"How did you find us?" she asked Teddy.

"We had an idea, naturally. Rowan had shouted Joe's name to Aidan. Aidan got me . . . we came right after you, but you know the swamp, it wasn't easy. We might not have found this little twist in the canal, seen the cabin . . . if it hadn't been for the boy. He's the smartest damn idiot I've ever met."

"Idiot! Teddy, that child is a genius!"

Marnie was on the airboat then. Heedless of her cuts, bruises, bites, lack of dress, and blood-drenched hands, she reached for Gregory, pulling him into her arms. Her words had held her old confidence, her old bravado. But they faded into a gulp and then tears. Sobbing, she hugged him. "You saved my life!"

He studied her face. "Marnie," he said.

Clearly. Loudly.

He had known. He had known all along. He had fought for her all along.

They simply hadn't known how to listen.

Two nights later there was a gathering at Sam's. The bullet had been removed from Rowan's side. They had made him stay in the hospital overnight. Sam had stayed with him. She wasn't about to be parted from him for anything. Not for a very long time.

Marnie was suffering from exposure, bites, dehydration, and more. She had refused to stay in a hospital any longer than twenty-four hours. Loretta would have to remain hospitalized for another few days. She had been completely dehydrated, and several of her ribs had been broken. It seemed that Joe's psychosis was usually tripped when a girl agreed to leave a party with a man; in Loretta's case, he'd been just waiting for the right opportunity.

They had put together some of the pieces when they had all given statements to the police, and when the police, in turn, had shared their information.

Tonight, it was over.

Teddy was there with Laura. They weren't exactly back together, but they were becoming friends. For the two of them, that was the most important thing for the time being. So Laura had told Sam. But she had also told her that she had put away the past. Teddy had spent a few more nights at the house, and they had been wonderful.

Aidan was there, as well as Lacey, who had just come home. She was sitting with Thayer, who had been exonerated. His arm was around her. Lacey was euphoric, having returned to find out that everything was all right. Her own trip had been great, but her life, she said, had been turned around by Thayer. She had confessed her secret life to Sam, who had promised not to tell her parents unless the time came when she absolutely had to. Thayer had been at a party that she had worked, and his shock and disappointment—and support and unwavering friendship— had been all she needed that night to know that she was done. "He picked me up. We went for a long ride. We talked and talked and I took a later flight."

She had told Sam the truth while they sat together in the hospital, waiting for Rowan to come out of surgery.

That night, at Sam's house, she told them all, "I may have a role in the play, I may not. But I will get one someday."

Rowan's eyes met Sam's. He smiled. She had found out from Lacey how he had stood up for her, kept her secret—and threatened Chapman on her behalf.

So much for being suspicious of Thayer. He was proving to be a fine young man. He was not the least bit bitter about having been arrested.

Marnie had greeted him with tremendous affection, and he had been treating his sister like a porcelain doll.

Marnie stared at Sam as they sat, shaking her head. "I've had time to reflect on my life lately. Too much time to reflect on my life. No, maybe not enough, because I was afraid that I was going to die at any time. But Sam, you know, in all honesty, I did know I was lucky to have you as a friend."

"Sam insisted there was something wrong from the very beginning," Teddy said.

Sam grinned. "Marnie, I have to admit that your eccentric ways were part of what absolutely convinced me that something bad had happened to you. Your makeup tray was out of order."

"When Joe kidnapped me we struggled. The makeup scattered. He thought he was putting it all back right . . ."

"But he didn't," Sam said.

"And then, thanks to our young friend Gregory always staring at the house," Rowan added quietly, "we found the tiny blood drops on your bedpost."

"He thought he was so perfect!" Teddy said bitterly. "And he almost was."

"How could he have been so crazy . . . and we not know?" Sam asked for the hundredth time.

"Who would imagine? A man so virile, so handsome," Teddy said. "But that was the point in this case. He wanted perfection, and then he was only wanted for the perfection he achieved in himself. He couldn't form a real relationship."

"He needed to be adored. Worshiped," Marnie said. She leaned her head back, closing her eyes. "Chloe always said that she used him for his body. She said it to his face. I—I wasn't much better. And still . . ."

"Still, he's dead. It's over," Thayer said.

"Will I go up for murder?" Marnie asked. She seemed different. Subdued.

"You'll never go up for murder," Teddy assured her.

"And I'm alive!" she breathed happily. Then she tousled her brother's hair. "So, Thayer! They arrested you!"

"Well," he said, "I did know Chloe. And at the time I had a tremendous crush on her. She never looked my way. But that's why she was in my painting."

Marnie gripped her brother's hand. "Have you seen the house yet, Thayer?"

"Yeah, kind of—"

"It's yours."

"What?"

"I never want to stay in it again."

Thayer was quiet for a minute, then he smiled at her. "I

have never been a bum, Marnie. My path is just different from yours."

She sighed, looking at him. "No, you've never been a bum. You've looked after that bum who is our father. Forgive me, Thayer."

"I love you, Marnie."

"You, too. I still want you to have the house. I just won't be comfortable in it again. And I want to go away. I want to travel."

"To where?" Sam asked.

She made a face. "Somewhere cold. Very cold. Without swamps."

They all managed to laugh.

Epilogue

Miami, Florida

Late afternoon, temperature eighty-two degrees.

Life, Rowan reflected. It was just *life* itself. Or, perhaps, the realization of a new and very humble appreciation for life that made Rowan feel very generous toward Beth.

Maybe it was because they'd been in the same hospital after the night in the Everglades.

Then again, there had been Sam's suggestion . . .

Whatever the case, Rowan had given Beth first shot at the interview of a lifetime.

It was a beautiful day, the sky was blue, untouched by even a hint of clouds. A soft breeze moved in off the bay.

Television cameras were there, news stations, other media—but Beth was the one asking the questions today. She looked smart in a satin two-piece suit, dressy enough for a guest, business-y enough for the cameras.

Music played, flowers were everywhere, champagne flowed. Caterers in tuxedos carefully stepped around the pool to deliver up trays of delicious delicacies to the many guests at Rowan's house by the water.

"First off, Rowan," Beth said, "tell us, how do you feel today?"

"Wonderful. Better than I've felt in my entire life."

"Does the bullet wound still you give any trouble?"

"I'm breathing; it's all I need."

"You were in the hospital after the incident, however, right?"

"Yes, as was Miss Newcastle."

"She's not here today! And she was such a good friend to Samantha Miller. Why wouldn't she be here on this very special occasion?"

"Ah, well, she and Sam are still very good friends—but Miss Newcastle is attending her own wedding. She's marrying her old boss, Mr. Daly, and the two of them are setting up a new practice in Montana."

"Montana?"

"Miss Newcastle was looking for somewhere with a cooler climate to live."

"What about her beautiful home?"

"Her brother has taken it over. He's actually become engaged to a young cousin of Sam's, and I believe that, together, they'll dispel whatever ill will might linger in the house."

"Ill will . . . Well, Rowan, you've certainly done well living past the ill will that plagued your life here in Miami! I know that many people were suspicious of you . . ." She hesitated. "Especially after *I* was attacked on *your* property. I saw the attacker, but I was unconscious and couldn't help the police. How did you know to follow Samantha that day? How could anyone have imagined that a man as handsome and virile as Joe could be a psychotic killer?"

"Process of elimination. I didn't actually *know* though, until he was in the process of kidnapping her. He was always looking for perfection in himself—and in others. He was fascinated by strippers, fascinated by the body. It was when the women he watched agreed to work the private parties he himself arranged that his mind seemed to snap. Except for Sam. She became dangerous to him. And I believe that no matter what type of a front he was putting up, he was coming closer and closer to snapping all the time. We were lucky. Very lucky," Rowan said, and he suddenly turned slightly from Beth, aware that Sam was approaching.

She had just changed from her wedding dress into the smart black pantsuit for their flight. His heart quickened; his wife was beautiful. *His wife.* They'd made it; they'd endured. The past had been riddled and torn by suspicion and tragedy, but the future was theirs. And he had never felt so positive about anything in his life. Her gaze touched his. Her lips curved. There were so many things they shared now without ever a word being said. There was so much warmth in her. Passion and courage—and the kind of commitment to those she loved that was totally unique.

Wonderful. He felt wonderful. Better than he had in his whole life.

Sam reached him. He slipped his arm around her. She smiled at Beth. Sam had actually been the one to suggest that he lay *all* his demons to rest by giving this opportunity to the reporter.

"Sam, how does it feel to be Mrs. Dillon at last?"

Sam grinned up at Rowan. "Wonderful."

He grinned.

"And you've shared this happiness with family and friends. Your parents are here?"

"My mother and my stepfather are over there. And that's Rowan's dad, the very handsome gentleman standing with Lilly Vincent, the artist."

"Perhaps there's more romance in the future?"

"They do seem to be hitting it off," Rowan said.

"And the band is wonderful!"

"Some old friends—and some new ones. Aidan Henley and his group—and Gregory Lacata on drums."

"Gregory! A very special boy. What about children? Do you plan to have your own family? How many children?"

"Three—" Sam had begun.

"Four," Rowan said.

They laughed.

"Three and a half?" Sam asked, with a shrug. "It doesn't matter—time will tell. We certainly both love them and want them."

"Tomorrow, don't you think?" Rowan suggested.

"Certainly."

"Then perhaps you'd better get going. Where will the honeymoon take place?"

"We're not telling exactly where. . ."

"But there's snow there," Sam said, smiling up at Rowan.

"So are you two looking for somewhere cold to move as well?" Beth queried. "What a loss it would be to our community."

Rowan grimaced at Sam. She answered for him. "Oh, no, we're coming back. We both love the water and the sun and boats—Mollie in the bay at the docks . . . and even the Everglades. I'm not terribly fond of alligators anymore, but . . ."

"We love the area. We wouldn't dream of leaving it for good," Rowan finished. "And now, if you'll excuse us . . ."

The Swiss Alps.

Dusk.

Temperature thirty-two degrees.

It was a beautiful evening. Snow covered the distant lodge on the hill, and the rolling landscape in front of their small ski lodge. The world was white, delicately shaded in pastels by the dying sun. Outside, it was cold. Inside, a fire raged. Champagne cooled in a bucket, there was a hot and inviting Jacuzzi, and the mammoth bed in the center of the room was piled with pillows and down comforters.

He heard Sam come out of the shower. Felt her slip her arms around him and study the snow, as he was doing.

"Beautiful," she said softly.

He turned her in his arms. Her robe was loose. He felt her naked flesh, breasts against his chest, belly . . . legs.

"Beautiful," he agreed.

He kissed her. Long, deep, lingering . . . longer, deeper, more lingeringly.

Then his lips broke from hers. "I never knew it was possible to be this happy, this . . . secure. My God, we came so close to losing it all . . . losing everything, life . . ."

"But we didn't. You rescued me, remember?"

"Well, you kind of rescued me, too. I was dumb enough to get myself shot."

"Not dumb. You saved Gregory's life," she reminded him.

"The kid was well worth it."

"And so are you!" she teased.

"And there's the future. We still have so much ahead, so much to decide. Sam, what do you want out of the future?"

"Only to wake beside you every single morning," she told him.

"What if I were to go on tour, what if we have children, what if—"

"*Almost* every single day of my life!" she said, laughing.

"No, every single day. I'd never tour without you— you're the best drummer I know. And when you have those three and a half kids, I'll be in the hospital beside you."

She shook her head, looking up at him. "Don't you see, Rowan, you are always with me. And I'm always with you. Even if we're not together!"

And he smiled. And kissed her again. And he felt the

pressure of his arousal against her and the sweet warmth of the fire and the taste of her . . .

And he knew they had talked enough. The future would wait.

He swept her into his arms.

The fire crackled in the hearth.

The ice melted in the bucket.

Their future was beginning.